Paul Doherty was born in Middlesbrough. He studied History at Liverpool and Oxford Universities and obtained a doctorate for his thesis on Edward II and Queen Isabella. Paul is now ‌eadmaster of a school in north-east London, and has been ‌warded an OBE for his services to education. He lives with ‌‌ family in Essex. Paul's first novel, THE DEATH OF A KING, was published in 1985. Since then he has gone on to write over one hundred books, covering a wealth of historical periods from Ancient Egypt to the Middle Ages and beyond.

To find out more, visit www.paulcdoherty.com.

Praise for Paul Doherty's historical novels:

'Teems with colour, energy and spills' *Time Out*

'Deliciously suspenseful, gorgeously written and atmos-‌‌eric' *Historical Novels Review*

‌premely evocative, scrupulously researched' *Publishers Weekly*

‌ opulent banquet to satisfy the most murderous appe-‌‌' *Northern Echo*

‌tensive and penetrating research coupled with a strong ‌ and bold characterisation. Loads of adventure and a ‌zling evocation of the past' *Herald Sun*, Melbourne

‌ell-written historical novel with a fast-paced, action-‌‌ plot. Highly recommended' www.historicalnovelsociety.org

DEVIL'S WOLF

PAUL DOHERTY

HEADLINE

First published in 2017 by
HEADLINE PUBLISHING GROUP

First published in paperback in 2018 by
HEADLINE PUBLISHING GROUP

1

Cataloguing in Publication Data is available from the British Library

ISBN 978 1 4722 3374 5

Typeset in Sabon LT SDT by Palimpsest Book Production Limited,
Falkirk, Stirlingshire

Printed and bound in Great Britain by
Clays Ltd, St Ives, plc

HEADLINE PUBLISHING GROUP
An Hachette UK Company
Carmelite House
50 Victoria Embankment
London EC4Y 0DZ

www.headline.co.uk
www.hachette.co.uk

In memory of my beloved wife Carla.

CHARACTER LIST

Edward I	The old king of England
Edward II	King of England
Peter Gaveston	Royal favourite
Thomas	Earl of Lancaster
Margaret de Clare	Wife of Peter Gaveston
Robert the Bruce	Scottish war leader
Lord Henry Percy	Owner of Alnwick Castle
Lady Eleanor Percy	Wife of Henry
John 'Red' Comyn	Lord of Badenoch
Sir Hugh Corbett	The Keeper of the Secret Seal
Ap Ythel	Welsh master bowman
Ranulf-atte-Newgate	Principal clerk in the Chancery of the Green Wax
Chanson	Sir Hugh Corbett's clerk of the stables
Alexander Seton	Scottish hostage
John Sterling	Scottish hostage
Richard Mallet	Squire to Alexander Seton
Malachy Roskell	Squire to John Sterling

Anthony Bek	Bishop of Durham
Brother Adrian Ogilvie	A Benedictine monk
Richard Twyen	Prior of Tynemouth Priory
Robert Wishart	Bishop of Glasgow
Brother Ailward	A monk at Tynemouth Priory
Brother Oswald	A monk at Tynemouth Priory, a former smith and smelter
Brother Julian	Sub-cellarer at Tynemouth Priory
Brother Sebastian	A monk at Tynemouth Priory
Brother John	Librarian at Tynemouth Priory
Edmund Darel	A northern knight
Geoffrey Cacoignes	Court fop
Walter Thurston	Constable of Alnwick
Kathryn	Sister of Walter Thurston
Hockley	Cousin to Edmund Darel
Richolda	Darel's witch woman
Ravinac	A Gascon captain
Matthew Dunedin	A Scottish clerk
Bavasour	A captain of hobelars
Andrew Harclay	Keeper of the Western March
Sherwin Ap Vynar	'The Houndsman'
Douglas and Randolph	Henchmen of Robert the Bruce
Rachaela	A recluse at Tynemouth Priory
Lady Hilda	Aunt to Edmund Darel
Ralph Wodeforde	Master of *The Golden Dove*
Marissa	A member of the Black Chesters

HISTORICAL NOTE

A savage and cruel war broke out during the 1290s as Edward I of England, then his successor Edward II, battled to bring Scotland under the English Crown. A deep darkness settled over both kingdoms, a time of bloodshed and betrayal, and as the war clouds gathered, so did the monsters.

HISTORICAL NOTE

PROLOGUE

'Then the Lord King set out for Scotland and came
first to Berwick.'   *Life of Edward II*

The Rogation Days, March 1296

Berwick was burning! The most valuable port on Scotland's east coast, just across the border from England, was no longer the Jewel of the North. The Scots had risen once more against their oppressor, the devastator of their lands, Edward I of England, whose influence now swirled like a black cloud over the northern kingdom. A mist of murder had engulfed its valleys, glens, towns and churches from Coldstream to the Northern Isles. The Scots, provoked beyond measure, had risen against the English tyrant; a sudden, savage eruption of popular discontent and resentment at Edward's constant interference in Scottish affairs. They knew he would not rest until he made himself king and master of their realm.

Berwick had protested and paid the price. The once bustling port now reeked of death, stinking and smouldering, with blood snaking down its narrow wynds like wine from cracked vats. The English had unleashed horror upon horror against its citizens. Edward was determined to make an example of the town and so terrify into subjection anyone foolish enough to rebel against him. On land he had brought up his great war machines: trebuchets, catapults and battering rams with names that reflected the devastating damage they inflicted. Most terrible of them all was the Wolf, a massive catapult that hurled faggots of flaming wood and straw bound by chains, followed by smouldering beams soaked in pitch and tar, to smash against Berwick's makeshift defences. At sea Edward's ships had suffered badly, which only provoked the English king to greater fury. Even worse, just before the final assault on the port, one of the king's kinsmen had lifted his visor to cool his face and a Scottish defender had loosed a crossbow bolt to shatter the Englishman's skull. Edward, enraged beyond measure, had unfurled his standard and issued the order: 'No quarter, no mercy, no prisoners.' There were to be no exceptions.

Berwick became nothing more than a slaughterhouse; its citizens, penned like hogs in the narrow streets and lanes, were cut down by hack and thrust so that the very air crimsoned with a bloody mist. Armed knights moved like black storm clouds through the town, slashing with axe, mace and sword until the cobbles ran red, whilst the knights' horses, frantic with fear or fury, slipped on the hot wet stones and greasy slivers of human flesh. Horrible cries and screams echoed like a constant hymn as skulls were smashed and bellies ripped open. Men, women and children were sacrificed to Edward of England's blood-fed vision of taking Scotland under the English Crown. No one was spared; even the Flemish merchants who sheltered in their own enclave, the Red Hall, were shown no quarter when they resisted. Edward's troops, beaten off in their frantic assault, simply brought up catapults and sacks of oil. They drenched the hall and a volley of fire arrows turned it into a raging inferno in which all thirty of its defenders gruesomely perished.

By the second day of the sack the pillaging was completely out of control. Edward set up his standards outside Berwick's stately Guildhall: this would become his throne room, ringed by hobelars, archers and Knights of the Body. The royal banners, glorious and gorgeous, billowed and snapped in the smoke-drenched wind, proclaiming the snarling golden leopards of England; the red lion rampant of Scotland and the dragon displayed as a blood-red nightmare against a snow-white background. In Edward's own words, 'The dragon had been unfurled and the dragon displayed' to herald a season of bloodshed in which no compassion would be shown or mercy given.

The destroyer of Berwick had commandeered the once comfortable solar at the Guildhall. All of its treasures – the resplendent tapestries with their precious brilliantly coloured thread; the triptychs painted so skilfully in an array of eye-catching hues by artists of Hainault and Flanders; the richly carved furnishings, the ornate crucifixes and soft Turkey rugs – had been seized and piled into the war carts drawn up in the cobbled bailey outside. The English were determined to strip Scotland of its treasures, sacred relics and royal regalia.

On that particular Rogation Day Edward, the self-styled 'Hammer of the Scots', slouched in the solar's high chair, the table before him strewn with manuscripts: muster rolls; lists of supplies as well as goods seized; above all, the names of those rebels killed, captured or in flight. He scratched his grizzled cheek, then one spotted, vein-streaked hand clawed at his iron-grey hair, tugging at the sweaty knots, whilst the other combed his tangled beard and moustache. Perspiring and wearied, he stared down at the royal armour on the floor beside him, his gaze caught by the richly woven royal tabard stained with gore. Outside, the hellish hymn of conflict, screams, yells, cries and battle chants, echoed constantly. Edward, his throat bone dry, gulped from a goblet and glared at Anthony Bek, Bishop of Durham, who had led the second column of the English army across the Tweed. The king beat a hand against the arm of his chair.

'They burnt my ships,' he roared, 'they slaughtered my crews. They have renounced their allegiance. They are deserving of death. I will break these rebels. I will burn this land and sack its cities. I will turn it into a wilderness until I have my way.' His furrowed face suffused with rage. 'I do not trust any of them,' he spat out. 'Not even those like Bruce who plant their banners next to mine.' He clenched and unclenched his fist. 'I will take his head, I'll gut his insides. Has he forgotten

Wallace being cut up at Smithfield? His belly opened, his genitals hacked off . . .'

Edward paused as the door opened and a girl of no more than twelve summers slipped like a ghost into the solar and walked slowly towards him. She was dressed in a dark-green smock, drenched in blood, which also stained her hands and wrists. She paused before the king, her eyes dark rings in a face as white as snow, mouth opening and shutting like that of someone being strangled, fighting for breath. 'St Oswine,' she murmured. 'St Oswine, pray for me!'

'What is it, child?' The king recognised the daughter of the Guildhall bailiff, whose life, along with those of his family, had been spared provided he disclosed the whereabouts of the Guildhall treasures. For a brief moment the girl reminded Edward of his own beloved daughter Eleanor.

She shook her head and held up her badly scorched wrist for the king to see. Edward was about to speak again when a knock on the door made him look up. He smiled as Hugh Corbett, the youngest yet most able clerk in the Chancery of the Secret Seal, came into the chamber with his escort, the Welsh master bowman Ap Ythel.

'Hugh.' The king forgot the girl. He rose, walked across the solar and threw his arms around the clerk to exchange the kiss of peace before holding him at arm's length. 'It is so good to see you. You've brought messages from the Chancellor?' He turned to Ap Ythel and winked. 'A good, safe journey, there and back?'

'We came by sea. The roads north are dangerous.'

Edward broke free of Corbett and clasped hands with the Welshman, who had proved to be the most loyal and skilled of bodyguards. Then the king stepped back. He'd caught a look in Ap Ythel's eyes. The archer seemed agitated, dark eyes questioning, bearded face pale, mouth slightly open as if surprised. Edward noticed the stains of vomit on his jerkin. The king glanced at Corbett. The clerk seemed equally tense. His raven-black hair was tied in a queue at the back, his olive-hued face taut, the skin stretched tight over the high cheekbones, whilst his deep-set eyes brimmed with tears. Corbett clawed at the neck of his dark-russet leather jerkin. He undid the cord, rubbing a finger beneath the collar of his cambric shirt, scratching at his sweat-soaked skin.

A hideous scream echoed from outside, followed by the neigh of a horse and the clatter of hooves. Someone, somewhere was sharpening a sword, a harsh jarring sound to set the teeth on edge. Edward breathed in. He caught the stench of smoke and the salty iron tang of blood. He studied these two men whom he trusted with his life.

'Hugh? Ap Ythel? What is the matter? Have you been attacked?'

'Your Grace.' Anthony Bek had been standing in one of the window embrasures. He now came forward and pointed at the young girl, who had crumpled to the floor. Ap Ythel and Corbett hastened to assist her. The king crouched down to face Corbett, who stroked the girl's face, brushing her hair back. She was still praying to

St Oswine and nursing her blackened wrist. Corbett took a goblet of wine from the bishop and tried to force it between her lips.

'Hugh?' the king demanded. 'In heaven's name what is the matter?'

'Sire, she saw what we did as we entered the Guildhall bailey. Berwick has become a flesher's yard. There's more blood outside than in the slaughterhouses of Newgate and the Shambles on Lammas Day. As we came in through the gates, so much blood was swilling about it wetted the fetlocks of our horses. Body parts litter the ground, great hunks of steaming flesh. Corpses being nosed and gnawed by dogs. The broken bodies of children, girls and boys with sightless eyes . . .'

'They are rebels, Hugh. They are all rebels.'

Corbett gazed coolly back and pointed at the girl. 'Is *she* a rebel, sire? Is her little brother who is crouching outside a traitor?'

'Hugh, you have been in battle.'

'God forgive me, sire, I have, but not like this, not like what I have just seen.'

'What did you see?'

'Your Grace, we came upon it too late. There was nothing we could do.'

'Tell me what you saw.'

'A pregnant woman giving birth, and as she did, one of your mercenaries stabbed both her and the child.'

Edward groaned and turned away, putting his face in his hands.

'In the name of God, sire,' Corbett whispered, 'this

is not war but mortal sin. I understand it's been going on for two days. I have spoken before and I will speak again. You are sowing a dreadful seed; what is being done here is truly evil. I beg you . . .'

Edward dropped his hands, rose and gestured at Bek. 'Bishop, issue the order. All the hostilities, the killing must end.'

PART ONE

'However, a great and potent son of Satan, a henchman of the Devil, approached.' *Life of Edward II*

Northumberland, September 1311

Sir Hugh Corbett, Keeper of the Secret Seal and personal envoy of King Edward II of England, quietly conceded to himself that he was in a land of deep shadow. He had journeyed north into Northumbria, his mind crammed with the secret instructions of his king and a whole sea of problems to resolve. He and his cohort had now entered the upper moorlands of the kingdom's most northern shire; they were following the ancient route to Lord Henry Percy's stronghold of Alnwick, a rugged castle built on the south side of the River Aln only thirty miles south of Coldstream and the city of Berwick.

Corbett paused in the fringe of trees and closed his eyes. Berwick! The very name brought back those dire, dreadful memories: nightmare images of hacked flesh, snouting dogs, blood swilling in the streets, black clouds of smoke drifting from the houses, lamentable cries and heart-rending screams. He recalled that when the slaughter had finished and the corpses were gathered, the mounds of dead reached at least two yards high: men, women and children, even babies at the breast. Corbett had issued a prophecy that day, how the old king had sowed a dreadful seed, and now the harvest was no better. Scotland was in full revolt and their leader, Robert the Bruce, was on the verge of a great victory.

Corbett opened his eyes and went deeper into the copse of ancient trees, which formed an almost perfect ring around his encampment. He was glad they had found it. He stared up at the sky. The September sun was setting; a glorious evening, even though the breeze had turned sharp and cool. In a while, darkness would fall, cloaking off everything, shrouding the land, the bustle of the day giving way to the eerie sounds of the deepest night. His gaze was caught by a sight that had been fairly constant over the last few days. Across the wild sea of gorse, the land rose to the brow of a low hill, where three trees stood black against the fading light. From each of these dangled a corpse, a macabre black shape, a chilling message to all who travelled across this desolate landscape. Brother Adrian Ogilvie, the Benedictine monk who'd accompanied them north from London, had explained how they were now in the devil's domain. They were crossing the estates of the robber baron Edmund Darel, a northern knight who had exploited the chaos in the kingdom to carve out and defend an enclave, a fief in the north where the king's peace and the royal writ were largely ignored. Corbett crossed himself. He knew Darel of old, and what he had recently learnt about that warrior warlock was not very pleasant.

He narrowed his eyes as he recalled today's date: Lady's Day, 8 September, the Year of Our Lord 1311. It had been some fifteen years ago, at the end of March 1296, that he had entered the sacked, pillaged town of Berwick and witnessed the birth of a lasting horror. The old king's poisonous legacy to his own son, which over the years had turned into a real and living nightmare. Edward I had truly sown a tempest, and his son and heir, Edward of Caernarvon, Edward II as he was regally styled, was reaping the most savage whirlwind. England's war in Scotland had slipped from bad to worse. Horror piled upon horror had not prevented the emergence and rise of a new Scottish war leader, Robert the Bruce.

Worse, at home Edward II was fighting his great barons, led by his own cousin Thomas, Earl of Lancaster. King and noble had clashed bitterly over the question of Edward's darling favourite, his 'true sworn brother', the Gascon Peter Gaveston. In the eyes of the great English seigneurs, Gaveston was a mere commoner, yet Edward had created the parvenu Earl of Cornwall and given him in marriage his royal kinswoman Margaret de Clare. Honour after honour had been heaped on the king's favourite until Lancaster and the other great lords rebelled. Calling themselves 'the Lords Ordainers', they had seized control of the Royal Council and issued the most dire threats against Gaveston if he did not leave the kingdom immediately.

Corbett loosened his war belt. His stomach was upset

and he blamed what he'd eaten earlier in the day. Ranulf and Chanson, his two henchmen, had complained of similar discomfort. He gave a deep sigh. The day was dying fast and the midnight mist was creeping over the moonlit moors. Somewhere a dog howled at the darkening sky, and Corbett felt an immediate chill. The howling was abruptly cut short, yet his suspicions were pricked. Were they near a village or a farm? His scouts hadn't reported that; they'd talked of a sea of grass as far as they could ride. The howling was not the raucous yapping of some farm dog; more like the baying of a war mastiff. But why should some peasant keep such a great hound? Or was it just his imagination, now prey to all forms of sinister thoughts at the end of a day when he felt tired and agitated, not to mention the effect of crossing this bleakly beautiful landscape?

The party had followed the 'eagle roads' laid out, according to local legend, by the ancient Romans. They had crossed Caesar's great wall to the south and entered this haunted home of the badger and the curlew, trundling along trackways that were really nothing more than drovers' paths or sheepwalks. Their guide, Brother Adrian, had proved most useful. A student of nature, he was quick to point out a shrike, or the difference between the osprey and the fork-tailed kite, and had thoroughly enjoyed teasing Corbett as he described the different types of crow, be it the hooded or the common. Corbett accepted the play on his own name, which originated from *le corbeil*, a derivative of the Norman French for 'crow', as well as the name of a town in Normandy. The crow, its black wings extended, was his main heraldic device, displayed on both banner and pennant.

As they rode deeper into this wild countryside, Corbett, his unease growing by the day, had decided to let everyone know who he was and where he came from. He had unfurled both his war banner and the royal pennant displaying the king's coat of arms in the rich Plantagenet colours of red, blue and gold. Such a display should warn off any threat, yet Corbett was not convinced. The austere beauty of these moorlands was deceptive, the very ground treacherous. Brother Adrian had pointed out the deep-brown peat banks as well as the dangerous mosses, puddled soft ground spiked with clumps of marsh grass and dotted with willow scrum, which concealed a cloying black mud, a truly deadly trap for both man and beast. Corbett just thanked God the weather had held and they could negotiate such marshes and manage the steep, slithering hillsides. Yet these were not the only dangers . . .

He turned at a sound behind him. Ranulf-atte-Newgate, principal clerk in the Chancery of the Green Wax, together with Chanson, Corbett's clerk of the stables, came out of the gathering dark, forcing their way through the gorse, bramble and briar that formed a natural wall, a line of defence between the ancient stunted trees of the copse. Both men were dressed like their master in dark quilted jerkins over linen shirts, hose of the same colour pushed into riding boots.

Corbett pointed over their shoulders back at the camp. 'All well?' he asked.

'Horses settled,' Chanson replied. 'Pottage pot bubbling merrily. You can smell it, master.'

Corbett sniffed the air, catching the reek of woodsmoke and simmering oatmeal. He patted his stomach. 'A fast will do me more good.' He clapped Chanson on the shoulder. 'I know what you want to do; go back to your beloved horses, my friend.'

'And don't sing,' Ranulf added, stepping back to avoid Chanson's playful blow. 'Or touch any weaponry.' Not only did the clerk of the stables have no ear for music, but when he wielded a weapon of any sort, it posed more danger to himself than to anyone else.

Chanson, muttering under his breath, stamped off. Ranulf's smile faded.

'He's worried,' he told Corbett. 'He may know nothing about singing or armour, but he knows everything about horses. He's picked up tracks, the hoof marks of those garrons the reivers of this desolate place ride, small but sure-footed mounts. Chanson believes there is a screed of enemy scouts around us.'

'I agree.' Corbett answered tersely, staring into the dark, his gaze caught by the corpses swinging from their twisted trees, so stark against the fading light. 'See those, Ranulf? God knows what the poor souls did, but their cadavers are being used to threaten, warn and frighten us. But by whom, why and against what?'

'Whoever it is, are they out there?' Ranulf asked.

'Oh yes!'

Corbett stared at his henchman. Ranulf's pale face had grown ascetic, like that of a fasting monk. Before they had left London, the Clerk of the Green Wax had cropped his fiery red hair to a mere stubble and shaved his face close so he could wear his chain-mail coif and helmet more comfortably.

'The monsters are out there,' Ranulf murmured. 'Whoever those monsters are. I hate these places! Brooding, silent grasslands with concealed marsh and bog, treacherous paths that lead nowhere. Dark copses of trees that are nothing more than lurk-holes where a legion of wolfsheads could gather.'

Corbett laughed, but Ranulf's slanted green eyes did not crinkle in merriment nor his bloodless lips part in a mischievous grin.

'Sir Hugh, I am a city riffler, a street fighter. I prefer the sewers, alleys and runnels of London to this great yawning expanse, so beautiful at first glance yet it can hide all kinds of horror. I remember when I was a boy, my mother took me to Epping Forest to the north of the city. I have been in battle, the most bloody street fights. I have trapped professional assassins and been hunted by the same, but I will never forget that vision of twisted, tangled trees, the trackways nothing more than holes through the forest, with branches blocking out the sun and the sky. Dark wings floating. Mysterious sounds echoing from the undergrowth.'

Corbett clapped his companion on the shoulder. 'Ranulf, what has brought this on? You have grown worse since we left Pontefract. You sit on your horse all wary, vigilant like some hard-bitten moss-trooper.'

'That's because I am one, Sir Hugh. I have fought

here like you have. When you retired for a while to Leighton Manor, to the Lady Maeve, your children, your beehives and your manor choir.'

Corbett caught the strong tinge of envy in his companion's voice and wondered what bitterness had seeped into Ranulf's soul.

'I envy you, Sir Hugh.' Ranulf's face relaxed now, almost into a smile. 'I really do. Anyway, I fought here with the old king. His soul had turned to iron; he didn't know the meaning of the word compassion, and showed no mercy to friend or foe alike. So yes, this journey north has summoned up all kinds of ghosts, opened the door to demons and foul memories. You know, Sir Hugh, there were days when I was in the king's army when I prayed for a day without killing. I believe those times have returned. We have entered a land of deep shadow and its monsters cluster all around us.' He pointed across the grassland now swaying under the strengthening evening breeze. 'And before you say it, I am not imagining things. Listen.' He paused.

Corbett strained his hearing. 'Nothing,' he whispered, 'and yet . . .'

'Precisely.' Ranulf walked forward, staring out into the gathering murk. 'No bird call, no rustling or scrabbling in the undergrowth.'

Corbett followed the clerk's gaze. A spasm of fear, a sudden chilling of stomach and heart, swept through him. Ranulf was right. The silence was unnatural. Out there on the heathland, some malignant mischief was gathering.

'Why?' Ranulf demanded, turning back. 'Master, why are we really here?'

Corbett was making to reply when a roar of laughter rose from the encampment.

'The food is being served,' Ranulf murmured, 'and the wine casks broached. Master, my question: why are we here?'

Corbett steadied his nerve. He tried to ignore the brooding, gathering dark, the imminence of nightfall, the threats that might lurk deep in the shadows, ready to lunge out of the murk. He gestured at his henchman to follow him back into the trees. He suspected Ranulf's unease sprang from uncertainty. Corbett would have to resolve that, but he couldn't do so right now. He would not divulge the secrets the king had sworn him to before he left Westminster, information that others would pay a royal ransom to obtain.

He squatted on a fallen log, indicating that Ranulf sit next to him, and smiled at his companion through the darkness. 'We are here because we are royal clerks, Ranulf. We do the bidding of our masters as far as conscience will allow. So first, Edward, the present king's father, plunged his kingdom into total war against the Scots. He stole their coronation stone as well as their royal regalia and he tried to impose rule from Westminster. The Scots, under their self-proclaimed king Robert the Bruce, have resisted with all their force and might. Second, the old king is now four years dead and his heir, God bless him, has inherited this bloody war, which he is going to lose. Bruce has the upper hand; he will never give up.

'Third, Edward, our present king, has failed disastrously at home. The Royal Council has been taken over by the Ordainers, a coven of great lords who now control both the Exchequer and Chancery, the very reins of power. Thomas of Lancaster leads them and he now dictates terms to both Crown and Council. He has insisted that the king release Scottish prisoners: two hostages, Alexander Seton and John Sterling, together with their squires Richard Mallet and Malachy Roskell, who were imprisoned in the Tower. Lancaster demanded their release so they can be exchanged for English prisoners held by Bruce. Fourth, Lancaster has insisted that I, the Chancery's most senior clerk, personally escort these hostages to Alnwick, where an exchange of prisoners might take place. I suppose my presence lends some importance to the occasion.'

Corbett paused. Ranulf was correct. Night had fallen. Noises echoed from the camp, yet the silence around them remained unbroken. The very stillness was eerie and threatening. No night bird soared or chattered. No yip or shriek from the hunter or the hunted. Corbett stared up at the sky: clouds were gathering and the stars did not hang so low, whilst the sliver of moon seemed wan and weakly.

'But there are other matters, aren't there, Sir Hugh? Secret business?'

'Secret business,' Corbett agreed. 'I wish I could share it all with you, but I am under oath not to speak or to reveal anything until the appropriate time. My friend, you mustn't think our king is just jumping because

Lancaster has kicked him. He is using my presence in the north for his own secret purposes. Some of these matters are of the present; others have been lurking in the past.' He pointed out over the heathland. 'Even now, here I am waiting for someone: Geoffrey Cacoignes.'

'Cacoignes!' Ranulf exclaimed. 'The court fop? He was a member of Edward's household before the young king was crowned. I thought he had been killed in Scotland, spliced by the rebels and dangled from a peel tower some five years ago.'

'Well, Ranulf, he is either a new Lazarus or he didn't hang. According to the evidence, he was captured, imprisoned and then escaped. He hoped to cross the marshes, reach Alnwick and await further instructions; that was four months ago. He never appeared. We then heard he had joined the retinue of one of the north's great robber barons, Edmund Darel. Just before we left Pontefract, a chapman brought me a cryptic message telling me how Cacoignes promised to join us when we least expected it. I would say a place and time like this would fit such a description. Moreover,' Corbett added, 'according to Brother Adrian, our self-proclaimed expert on all matters north of the Tees, the wolves who are shadowing us probably come from Darel's lair at Blanchlands. Oh yes, Cacoignes could very well join us on a night like this.'

'And Seton and company?'

'Another reason for our journey north. As I said, the king may have been forced by Lancaster over the question of the hostages, but he also wants to use our chevauchée for other business, which I will share with you eventually but not now. Not now,' he repeated as if to himself.

'But you can tell me why Alnwick is so important?'

'Oh yes, it's obvious. Alnwick is a formidable fortress that dominates all roads through the north-east into Scotland. The castle once belonged to the de Vescy family. Two years ago Henry Percy bought both the castle and its estates. The king wants to discover what he is doing with it. Is he turning Alnwick into one of this kingdom's great fortresses? And if he is, for what purpose?'

'And there's more?'

'Naturally.' Corbett tapped the hilt of his dagger. He wondered if Cacoignes would really come on a night like this. After all, they would soon be in Alnwick. He glanced to his right and left. Ap Ythel had set up a guard, though the real defence of their camp was the rough undergrowth, the snarl of briar, bramble and hard grass that stretched like a wall between the trees. Horsemen would find this as difficult to penetrate as they would a phalanx of spearmen, whilst those on foot would become hopelessly entangled in the coarse vegetation. If Cacoignes did approach the camp, he would have to be very prudent, careful not to be mistaken for an enemy.

'Sir Hugh?'

'Red Comyn.' Corbett shifted on the log. 'Red Comyn, or to give him his proper name and title, John Comyn, Lord of Badenoch. As you may know, Comyn was one of Scotland's great barons, a war leader and a rival to

Bruce. He also had a claim to the Scottish throne. When Alexander III died leaving no heir, Edward, the old king, set himself up as Lord Paramount with the right to decide who, if anyone, succeeded to the Scottish throne. He seized all the Scottish regalia: the crown, orb, sceptre and sword of state. He had the Stone of Scone, the Scots' coronation chair, moved to lie beneath his own throne at Westminster. Such arrogant meddling was deeply resented, but Edward thrived on the rivalry between the claimants, Bruce and Comyn in particular. Some five years ago, in February 1306, Comyn and Bruce met in the Franciscan church at Dumfries to resolve their differences. Daggers were drawn. Bruce, allegedly assisted by his retinue, stabbed Comyn before the high altar and fled. A truly sacrilegious act, a blasphemy that cost him a great deal of support. The Comyns say their leader was the innocent victim of a most heinous act. Bruce and his coven argue that Comyn was the aggressor and Bruce was merely defending himself against a murderous attack.'

'And was he?'

Corbett got to his feet and stood listening to the chatter and noise of the camp, a stark contrast to the stillness stretching out across the moorland. 'To answer your question, Ranulf, I don't know. But matters have been given a twist. I have not seen the actual document, but according to the king and Lord Gaveston, the Chancery received a sealed letter, written anonymously, claiming that its author had been in that church when the incident took place and was prepared to go on oath that Bruce was as guilty as Herod. According to Gaveston, the letter was extremely well written in Norman French, the parchment was of the best quality whilst the document mentioned certain details that only someone present could have known about. The writer said that if His Grace sent me, Sir Hugh Corbett, Keeper of the Secret Seal, north to Alnwick, he would reveal himself and make a statement about what he had seen.'

'When did this letter arrive?'

'On the eve of the feast of St Benedict, the eleventh of July. Naturally His Grace and Gaveston were deeply interested. If it could be proved beyond doubt that Bruce killed an innocent man who had agreed to meet him under a pledge of safety before the high altar of a church, then Comyn's death is that of a martyr, in many ways similar to Thomas a Becket's murder in Canterbury Cathedral. The Pope would have no choice but to issue a bull of excommunication, cutting Bruce and all his followers off from both the Church and the community.' Corbett waved a hand. 'If that happened, anyone who assisted Bruce in any way, be it within or without – even a powerful king such as Philip of France – would suffer the same severe sanction.'

'Sir Hugh, why didn't they show you the letter? After all, you are the Keeper of the Secret Seal.'

'Do you know, Ranulf, I cannot answer that. I certainly put the same question to them. They maintain the letter contained something I should not see, but I don't know. To be perfectly honest, I am deeply suspicious about that anonymous letter, as I am about the

Scottish hostages and the details about possible meetings with Bruce. All I have been told is that I am supposed to wait at Alnwick, and when the Scots approach me – heaven knows how or when – I must respond. I've listened to Seton and Sterling when I can. What do *you* think is suspicious about them, Ranulf?'

'They are surly, they keep to themselves.'

'And that's what makes me wary. They are warriors going home to hearth, kith and kin, yet you would think they are being taken out for execution. On a few occasions I have tried to discuss Bruce with them. Oh, they answer my questions but they seem to have little love for their leader. All I know is that the king and Gaveston are playing sophisticated games. Edward needs to protect his favourite, whilst he would love to extricate himself from the Scottish war. And that's why we are here, or at least in part, and no, Ranulf, like you, I do not like it. I have spent years campaigning along the Welsh march, where your wits are honed to sense danger, an ambush, that something is wrong.'

'And you feel that now?'

'Yes, I certainly do, both now and about what the future might hold.'

'So the fate of Red Comyn is one reason why we are here, but not the sole one?'

'I will answer all your questions in due course. But to go back to the hostages, God knows what will happen to them. Lancaster and the Ordainers have insisted they be returned. Edward and Gaveston suspect that Lancaster and his coven hope to arrange a truce with

Bruce, but on their terms. Lancaster would also like to separate Edward from the likes of myself, members of his household, his own chamber; hence he is only too pleased to see the back of me. To be honest, I feel as if we are riding into a tournament without knowing who is waiting for us in the lists.' Corbett sighed. 'But that is the way of the world and the plotting of princes. So for the time being, we will let matters rest and rejoin the others.'

They returned to camp to find the cooking fires burning. The captain of archers, Ap Ythel, had built up the central fire and a large bowl of pottage was bubbling noisily over the leaping flames. Corbett and Ranulf joined those sitting around. Both clerks refused a bowl, helping themselves instead to strips of dried meat and coarse, hard bread laid out on a common platter, along with a cup of watered wine. The conversation was desultory. Corbett sensed the company had all caught that sense of unease that seemed to pervade the camp.

The clerk stared around. The captain of archers was also not eating; he sat cradling his pewter goblet, staring gloomily into the flames. Like Ranulf and the rest, the Welshman had shaved his head and rugged face to ease the constant wearing of coif and helmet. The two hostages, Alexander Seton and John Sterling, along with their squires, Richard Mallet and Malachy Roskell, sat huddled in their own group. All four men were fluent enough in Norman French but they insisted on speaking in the Gaelic tongue, so Corbett and the others had little idea what they were talking about. The Scots had been held hostage for at least six years, captured and imprisoned by the old king. They showed the effects of their long confinement: their cloaks, quilted jerkins, hose and boots were scuffed and patched, their hair and beards tangled and untended. Corbett had offered all four a barber and better clothes, but they had morosely refused. They were taciturn, bitter men with wind-burnt faces that emphasised their sharp, glittering eyes. They seemed impatient and short-tempered; all four reminded Corbett of attack dogs waiting to be unleashed.

Ap Ythel's voice with its sing-song intonation rang out above the murmuring whispers. 'Brother Adrian,' the Welsh captain's face creased into what he regarded as a smile, 'this land reminds me of the Welsh march, yet I will be glad to be out of it. When do you think we will reach Alnwick?'

Adrian Ogilvie, a lean-faced young monk, his black hair cropped to show his tonsure, brushed crumbs from his robe and turned to the two people sitting next to him, Walter Thurston, Constable of Alnwick, and his sister Kathryn. 'Walter?' Ogilvie smiled. 'Our companions want the safety of Alnwick.'

'We should be there the day after next.' The constable put his hand on his sister's arm. 'We too look forward to being safe and secure.'

'Against Darel.' Kathryn Thurston almost spat the words out. 'A robber and a rebel. If our new king was like his great father or had the virtues of St Oswine . . .' She fell silent as her brother clutched her hand and changed the conversation to cover her indiscretion, quickly describing what was left of their journey.

Corbett studied the three members of Lord Henry Percy's household. The Benedictine was chaplain at Alnwick and highly valued by Lord Henry. A young man with an old head on his shoulders, Ogilvie had studiously ignored the Scottish hostages and, when he could, indulged in the sharpest diatribe against Bruce and his coven. Corbett reckoned he was well past his twenty-fifth summer: severe-faced, with hooded eyes, a strong mouth and chin and a bell-like voice that undoubtedly made him a redoubtable preacher. He had been a member of the Benedictine communities of Rievaulx and then Tynemouth, and made it very clear that he was now loyally committed to the Percy family. He and the Thurstons had been dispatched to London as a courtesy to greet Corbett on behalf of their master, as well as to assist him on his journey north. Once the party had left Pontefract, the three had acted as scouts, eager to advise Corbett and his retinue of twenty-five Welsh archers that the sooner they were at Alnwick, the better.

Walter Thurston too was a young man, but auburn-haired and soft-featured, with ever-blinking eyes and a slight stutter; dressed in a long murrey-coloured cotehardie, he also wore the Percy colours, a blue tabard with a white lion rampant. He constantly deferred to his sister, a comely faced woman a few years his senior. Kathryn wore a tight, old-fashioned veil and wimple and hid her 'shapely form', as Ranulf had described it, beneath a Lincoln-green riding robe. She insisted on wearing thick, heavy dresses with cuffs that almost covered her hands. A quick-tempered, sharp-eyed woman, she had robustly rejected the attempts by various members of the comitatus to win her attention. Even Ranulf, although she warmed to him with a smile, was kept at arm's length.

Corbett leaned closer, moving slightly to one side to obtain a better look at her. Kathryn abruptly raised her head and glared at him, as she often did. Corbett forced a smile, bowed and glanced away. He wanted to go back to the edge of the camp, yet he had to make sure all was well here. The company was settling quickly. He noticed how many of the Welsh archers had simply stretched out on the ground, wrapping their blankets around them, not even bothering to clean their bowls and pewter spoons in the water of a nearby burn. Some of those around the main campfire were struggling to their feet, declaring how tired they were. Corbett felt the threat of danger sharpening, even though all seemed well enough. At the far end of the clearing the horse lines were orderly and quiet; their mounts, sure-footed garrons, were placid, with feed bags fitted over their muzzles. The four huge war carts that carried their supplies had been carefully covered with leather cloths; the dray horses, hobbled nearby, munched the sparse grass.

Corbett rose to his feet, gesturing at Ranulf to join him. He collected a small lanternhorn, lit the tallow candle within and walked back to the edge of the clearing.

Ignoring his companion's warnings, he strode out onto the heathland, pushing through the gorse and long grass milling like waves under the strengthening wind until he came to an outcrop of rock. He placed the lantern on top and made his way back through the dark.

'An old trick I learnt in Wales, Ranulf. Place a glowing lantern in the dark; watch, the glow spreads. An enemy will avoid the flame, so keep your gaze to the left and the right of it. A friend who wishes to be identified but is fearful of being taken as a foe in the dark will seek the light. I do believe someone is out there, very close and about to manifest himself.'

'Sir Hugh,' Ranulf grasped Corbett's shoulder, 'listen.'

'Nothing.'

'Exactly. The camp has fallen silent. I have never seen so many men tired and sleepy.'

Corbett, his gaze riveted on the lanternhorn, was about to look away when he saw a shape flit behind the light, a swift, darting shadow.

'Walk forward,' he called. 'Show yourself to be friend or enemy.' He drew sword and dagger from their sheaths on his war belt; Ranulf likewise.

'In all things boldness,' the stranger replied, quoting one of Edward of Caernarvon's favourite sayings.

'Very well,' Corbett shouted back. 'Pick up the lantern with both hands, and I mean both hands, then walk slowly forward, and make sure you don't stumble.'

'I can't see you.'

'That's not important,' Corbett replied. 'We can see you.'

The stranger, no more than a shifting shape in the glow of the tallow candle, lifted the lantern and walked forward. Ranulf laughed softly as he watched the lanternhorn rise and dip, and heard the stranger's curses as he forced his way through the gorse and over the broken ground. Corbett repeated his warning about keeping both hands on the lantern. He also wondered why the guards deployed to the left and right of this line of trees had made no move to discover what was happening. At last the stranger was before them.

'Who are you?' Ranulf demanded.

'Geoffrey Cacoignes, once a squire in the household of the Prince of Wales, recently a prisoner of Robert the Bruce till I escaped and became a reiver under a different name in the retinue of that child of hell Edmund Darel.'

Corbett grasped the lantern, lifted it and exclaimed in surprise.

'Oh yes, Sir Hugh. I recognise you. Now you look on a man who has greatly changed.'

Corbett was shocked. Cacoignes had been one of Prince Edward's coven, a coterie of beautiful young gallants resplendent in their puffed, quilted doublets of damascene silk or cloth of gold, tight multicoloured hose and fantastical pointed shoes; their hair constantly crimped and coiffed, their smooth-shaven faces slightly painted, dark kohl rings under their eyes, lips a cherry red. Now, though, in the light of that lanternhorn, he looked as rough and coarse as any border outlaw, his dark hair, moustache and beard uncombed and greasy with dirt, the high cheekbones burnt raw by cold winds and sharp rain. He was garbed in a filthy doublet that fell to his knees over a thick green jerkin and hose of the same colour. He was, however, firmly booted and well armed, a dagger belt across his shoulder and chest, a broad war belt around his waist with a longbow slung on his back and a narrow quiver of arrows looped over the hilt of his sword. He tapped the lantern with his fingernails.

'Well, Sir Hugh, what are you going to do, kiss me or kill me?'

Corbett laughed, put the lanternhorn down and stretched out his hand. Cacoignes grasped it, then greeted Ranulf too.

'Sir Hugh,' he spoke urgently, 'the night is passing. Danger approaches even faster. You and yours will face a bloody onslaught. We can chatter later if we are still alive to do so.' He pointed over his shoulder. 'Sir Edmund Darel comes on swiftly. I know. I was with him until I seized the opportunity to desert. I have been waiting for you, but so is Darel. He intends to attack just before sunrise, and he is bringing his war dogs with him.'

'Sweet angels of heaven,' Ranulf breathed.

Corbett recalled the howling he had heard earlier. 'They are very close, aren't they?' he said.

'Closer than you think. I also believe your company houses a traitor. Darel and his henchmen seem to know a great deal about you.'

Corbett hid his unease. Cacoignes' sudden appearance out of the dark was unnerving. Nevertheless, it had a logic all of its own. Something he would have to reflect on later, if God gave him life and health.

'Come, come.' He gestured at Cacoignes. 'Ranulf, I am concerned about our guards.'

They'd hardly entered the camp when Ap Ythel came hastening across.

'Sir Hugh, look around!' Corbett did so. Apart from a few individuals preparing to settle for the night, including the Thurstons, everyone was asleep. The guards as well. Ap Ythel moved across to one of his bowmen, crouched and roughly shook him. 'Owain, wake up! Owain!' He kicked the archer in the leg, but the man simply groaned and rolled over.

'They are drugged,' Cacoignes murmured. 'Some potion, some powder.'

'You are correct, stranger, whoever you are.' Ap Ythel leaned down to shake another archer; he too just moaned and shifted away.

Corbett introduced Cacoignes and gave Ap Ythel the news as he looked around. The Thurstons, now alarmed, came hurrying across. Ranulf briefly explained what was happening as Corbett, Cacoignes and Ap Ythel discussed what could be done. Ap Ythel agreed with Corbett: some malefactor, spy and traitor had mixed a sleeping powder with the pottage. Only those who had not partaken had escaped its malignant effect. Corbett whispered a brief prayer of thanksgiving that he had not been drugged. Debate about who could have perpetrated such an act was ignored in the face of more pressing danger.

Corbett organised those now conscious to fetch buckets of icy-cold water from the nearby burn to douse

37

the sleeping men. For at least an hour there was chaos. Those who were thus roused rolled, groaned, cursed and fought back, kicking and punching until they were awake. Kathryn Thurston brought them to warm themselves by the fire that her brother had built up, at the same time advising them about what had happened. The archers, sleepy and evil-tempered at such a rude awakening, soon realised the danger confronting them. At last the heavy sleepers, Brother Adrian amongst them, had all staggered awake. The Benedictine, who had fallen asleep on the far edge of the camp, cursed so colourfully that Ranulf whistled in deep appreciation.

The effects of the potion were soon dissipated as the men drank cold water and spooned hot oatmeal freshly cooked in a carefully scrubbed cauldron supervised by Kathryn Thurston and her brother. Corbett stared around the clearing as the men gathered about the fire. It seemed an age since they'd set up camp here the previous afternoon; now it was to become a battle ground. He, Cacoignes, Ranulf and Ap Ythel swiftly conferred. Cacoignes informed them that at least a dozen war dogs would be released, followed by enemy foot, whilst horsemen would ensure that no one escaped.

'The war dogs,' Ap Ythel explained, 'are those massive man-hunting mastiffs with jaws stronger and sharper than any wolf. Darel knows what he's doing.' He pointed to the ring of trees and the heavy gorse. 'The mastiffs will be starved; they will smell the horse flesh and make short work of the brambles, briars and whatever else the undergrowth holds. They will break through to deal out wounds and death to men and horses alike. Eventually their keepers will sweep in to finish the gruesome task. A massacre, brutal, sudden and savage. So what shall we do?'

Corbett pointed at the four great war wagons. 'Empty those and form them into a square, then everyone – and I mean everyone – is to climb in, about eight to each cart; that square will be our castle and we will be able to fight on every flank. We will also be protected. The sides of the carts are far too high for the dogs and we will be able to pour arrows on anything that approaches. I also want fire pots prepared; flaming arrows will discourage the dogs.'

'And the horses, if the dogs break through?' Ranulf asked.

'They mustn't. Keep all our mounts hobbled and position two archers amongst them. Don't forget, Darel and his coven will not expect what we have prepared for them.'

The camp settled down. Some of those affected by the sleeping potion were sick and had to relieve themselves urgently amongst the trees. Others had recovered more swiftly. Ap Ythel, at Corbett's insistence, dispatched scouts to snake through the long grass and wait for any sign of the enemy. The darkness was thinning when these scouts hurried back to report how they had glimpsed figures moving, whilst the early-morning breeze carried the stench of the kennels. Corbett ordered the four groups into the carts, leaving two archers amongst the horse lines. Then he crossed himself and breathed a prayer. He thought momentarily of Maeve's sweet face, and of his two children, Edward and Eleanor. He quietly commended them to God, then winched back the arbalest he carried and inserted the bolt.

The silence became oppressive. The darkness turned into a murky grey light. Tendrils of mist threaded through the trees, stretching out like the ghostly fingers of some earth-bound wraith desperate for human warmth and company.

'Notch!' Ap Ythel's soft yet harsh order rang through the clearing. The Welsh archers readied their powerful war bows, one yard-long shaft strung, another at the ready. Ranulf, standing beside Corbett, brought up his own arbalest, his keen eyes sharp on the edge of the clearing.

'Here they come, master.' His words were followed by a soul-harrowing howling. Dark shapes, bellies close to the ground, burst like demons into the clearing. Long-bodied, with massive heads and gaping jaws, their glossy short-haired coats glinting in the light. Several of them threw themselves against the carts, while others, eager for soft, sweet flesh, lunged towards the horse lines.

'Loose!' Ap Ythel roared.

Corbett released the lever of his arbalest and watched the bolt smash into the skull of a leaping mastiff. There was no time to insert another bolt. He grabbed one of the spears pushed through the slats of the cart, thrusting its blade deep into the flank of another mastiff already grievously wounded by a crossbow bolt. The real damage, however, was inflicted by the Welsh archers, who could loose their goose-quilled shafts in a matter of a heartbeat. The arrow storm swept through the war dogs, killing some outright, crippling others. Fire arrows followed. At such close range the archers could not miss. One mastiff did reach the horse lines, only to be badly kicked by one of the dray horses and finished off by one of the archers hiding there.

The attack was sudden, short and brutal and ended just as swiftly with mastiffs stretched in spreading pools of blood, their bodies pierced by clusters of arrows. A few, sorely wounded, were given the mercy cut by the archers, who clambered back into the carts as a second wave of assailants broke into the clearing. For a moment, the sight of the war carts filled with archers, bows bent, arrows at the ready, and the sprawling corpses of the mastiffs startled the attackers. They faltered in their assault even as Ap Ythel screamed at his men to loose.

Another hail of arrows whirled through the air like a swarm of angry hornets. The shafts struck face and chest. Some of Darel's men wore mailed jerkins and conical helmets; others were dressed in nothing but hardened leather jerkins and armed only with round bucklers and swords, clubs or daggers. They had no real protection against the piercing barbed arrows and would have turned and fled immediately, but mailed horsemen in war helms carrying oval shields threaded their way through the trees, forcing them back towards the carts. Nevertheless, the battle was over. The sight of the dead mastiffs and the crumpled corpses of so many foot soldiers, as well as the constant hail of sharpened arrows, proved too much. As the horsemen faltered, the rest of the attackers broke and fled.

'We should pursue them!' Ranulf shouted.

Ap Ythel agreed and Corbett saw the logic of it. The enemy must not be allowed to regroup and plan fresh assaults on their column. He issued the order. When he turned to the horse lines, he noticed that one of the milling mounts was already geared and buckled, but the archers on guard could not say who had done this, so Corbett dismissed it.

The rest of the horses were quickly saddled and harnessed and the pursuit began, Corbett leading his cavalcade out of the camp. The sun was now rising, giving them a clear view, whilst their horses were fresh, fed and watered. They spread out across the heathland and were soon amongst the enemy stragglers. Sword and axe rose and fell; no quarter was asked and none was given. Corbett glanced around. Most of Ap Ythel's archers were there, along with Thurston and Ranulf. The constable seemed to know the terrain, and followed the overgrown trackways, the same paths the enemy had used to break free of the tangling gorse, shouting and pointing ahead with his sword.

As they breasted a hill, Corbett reined in and stared down at the hamlet nestling in its lea. Wary of an ambush, he led his comitatus cautiously down the drover's path and into the village. The houses here were squared-off dwellings with oak pillars, the willow withers packed between them covered with dried clay, their roofs made of thick, hard turf. These dwellings stood silent, their doors and shutters flung open. Their occupants had apparently fled. The cavalcade passed empty hog and cow pens, the beasts driven away into the protection of the nearby treeline. Corbett noticed fresh horse and dog dung, as well as the smoking embers of spent fires.

'They camped here last night,' he declared. 'The hill shielded the lights of their camp. The dogs were kennelled in the piggery, the horses stabled in the cow pen.' He stared at the thick line of forest to the west of the village.

'We've slaughtered their dogs and foot soldiers,' Brother Adrian declared, reins in one hand, a war club in the other. He pushed his mount alongside Corbett's.

'A warrior?' Ranulf teased. 'I thought priests were forbidden to fight.'

'No, canon law forbids us to use swords, hence . . .' The Benedictine lifted his club splattered with hair, blood and fragments of bone. He pointed this towards the line of distant trees. 'The horsemen have followed the villagers into the woods. We will never catch them now. Wouldn't you agree, Walter?' He turned to where Thurston had reined in behind them.

'It would be like chasing will-o'-the-wisps,' the constable agreed. 'But we left the camp so swiftly; what about the Scottish hostages?'

'Manacled,' Ap Ythel replied. 'Firmly clasped to a cart wheel and guarded by four of my lovely lads.'

Corbett turned his horse, staring round the deserted

village. The sun had now risen, yet he felt cold and tired and wished he could be gone from here. He noticed three of the archers dismounting outside what looked like the village tithe barn.

'There will be little to plunder here,' he observed. 'The peasants are canny enough—'

He broke off at shouts and cries from the barn.

'Owain Glenith!' Ap Ythel exclaimed. 'He has the hearing of a hunting cat.' The door to the barn was flung open and the three archers re-emerged, pulling and pushing a man and a woman. The prisoners struggled violently until Ap Ythel, who had swung himself down from his own horse, drew his sword and pressed its tip against the soft whiteness of the woman's neck, shouting at both of them to be quiet.

Corbett studied the prisoners. The man was youngish, with the narrow face of a questing rat: pointed nose, receding chin and slit-sharp eyes. He was clean-shaven, his wispy hair coated with nard. Dressed in a quilted jerkin of dark leather with matching hose, he stood quivering, trying to hide the fear bubbling within him. The woman was startlingly different; truly beautiful, but with the hardness of a diamond: large, lustrous dark eyes in a snow-white face framed by long black hair. She conveyed a fierce resolution yet was strangely voluptuous, her full lips slightly parted, one hand almost clawing the air. She stood glaring at Corbett even as she tugged her gold-spangled blue robe more tightly about her.

Thurston got down from his horse and pointed at

the woman. 'You are Richolda, Darel's witch woman. And you are Hockley, her guardian and bodyguard, Darel's first cousin.' He turned back to Corbett. 'They must have been sheltering here. They expected Darel's attack to be successful, but now their comrades have fled, taking their horses with them.' He pointed to a tree. 'We should hang them immediately.'

Richolda, her face now all sweet and alluring, replied in Norman French, though Corbett caught the slight trace of a northern accent. 'Sir Edmund Darel will pay any ransom for our release.' She smiled dazzlingly at Corbett, who heard Ranulf's swift intake of breath.

'Lady Richolda is correct.' Hockley too spoke in Norman French, with a strong rustic burr. 'Sir Edmund will pay our ransom.' He spread his hands. 'It is unfortunate that you captured us. If you detain us, we will be more of a problem than any profit.'

'Bind their hands,' Corbett ordered. 'Mount them on horses and let's get out of here.'

They returned the way they had come, passing the straggling line of corpses killed during their pursuit. The camp was no different, littered with dead, both dog and man. Corbett ordered the corpses of the mastiffs to be heaped in a pile and left to rot, while Ap Ythel organised burial parties for the dead attackers. The archers hacked the wet earth, cleared shallow graves and rolled the corpses in, fashioning makeshift crosses to mark the burial places. Brother Adrian recited a swift, pithy office of the dead. Once he had administered the last blessing, the Welsh archers sang one of their battle hymns. Corbett was only too pleased to join them. Afterwards the wine cask was broached, every man being given a stoup to drink and a small loaf of rye bread to break his fast.

Corbett, followed by Ranulf, approached the two prisoners, who squatted on the ground, their hands tied to the wheel of a cart.

'You should set us free,' Hockley taunted, his rat-like face twisted into a smirk. 'Release us or my lord Darel—'

Ranulf punched him in the face. 'Do not threaten the king's envoy,' he snarled. He punched Hockley again, so that the bruise beneath Hockley's left eye blossomed into a bluish red.

'You should be more prudent and careful,' Richolda murmured.

'And why is that?' Corbett turned to face her squarely, marvelling at how truly beautiful she was, with her ivory-skinned face, large expressive eyes, midnight-black hair and swan-like neck. He noticed the pentagram on a silver chain around her throat and leaned forward and yanked it off. She startled, her eyes blazing with anger.

'You treat a lady like this?'

'No lady,' Corbett retorted, 'but a witch, a traitor, a wolfshead and one who would have rejoiced to see me and mine slaughtered by ravenous mastiffs. You came with the war band to gloat over our death throes.'

'I ride with my lord on all his chevauchées.'

'Raids,' Corbett corrected her. 'Your paramour murders, rapes and pillages to his wicked heart's content. Anyway, why should I be careful and prudent? Strange advice from a woman who lacks so much prudence she was captured.'

'We knew you were coming.' Richolda ignored Hockley's restraining hand. 'We knew your strength, your disposition and the treasure you carry.'

'What treasure?'

Richolda just blinked and glanced away.

'And you would have killed us all,' Ranulf accused.

'Who betrayed us?' Corbett demanded. 'Who?'

'If I knew, I would tell you.' Richolda widened her eyes flirtatiously. 'But if you return me safely to my lord Darel, he—'

'Sir Hugh, Sir Hugh!' Ap Ythel hurried across. 'It's Roskell! You'd best see for yourself.'

The two clerks followed the Welshman across the camp into the trees and down the slight incline to the burn, an underground rivulet that surfaced just within the clearing, washing over the pebbled sandy soil. Roskell, who had been freed on their return to the camp, sprawled slightly to one side near the water. The squire's face was hideously blotched, eyes popping in the strain of death, half-open mouth secreting a thick white mucus.

Brother Adrian came hurrying across. Pushing his way through, he knelt and turned the corpse over on its back. He quickly murmured the last rites before moving aside to allow Corbett to crouch next to him. The clerk pulled up Roskell's jerkin and the threadbare linen shirt beneath. The dead man's hairy white stomach was much swollen, dark red spots blotching the soft flesh. Corbett moved the man's head and pushed a gloved finger between the yellowing teeth, searching around before withdrawing his hand.

'Nothing,' he declared, examining his glove. 'He's been poisoned, but how, with what and by whom?' He shrugged and got to his feet, leaving the corpse to the Benedictine.

'So it begins,' Corbett murmured to himself. 'Murder and treachery, those demon twins have followed us here.'

'Sir Hugh,' a voice whispered hoarsely behind him. Corbett turned and stared at the one-eyed archer, his hood pulled up to frame a rough scarred face half hidden by a thick moustache and beard. The archer raised a gauntleted hand to scratch at a bead of sweat beneath his eye patch.

'I saw you when I returned,' Corbett murmured. 'I am glad you are safe. You must be prudent during these escapades.'

'So we have murder here. We should meet, talk . . .'

Corbett drew closer. 'Not here, my friend. We have a traitor and an assassin amongst us. We must be careful. We shall meet at Alnwick. Now,' he raised his voice, 'see to the unharnessing of my horse. Tell Captain Ap Ythel we will bury Roskell's corpse with the rest before we leave for Alnwick.'

Corbett stared around the spacious but stark chamber he had been allotted on the second floor of the rounded Abbot's Tower built into the soaring curtain wall of Alnwick Castle. He and his party had arrived at the great fortress after a further day's journey. Stewards of Lord Henry Percy had immediately ushered them to their sleeping quarters. Corbett felt well rested. He had slept soundly on the feather-filled mattress stretched out over the four-poster bed, elegantly shrouded by thick woollen curtains dyed a deep green and edged with silver thread. The chamber also boasted a scribe's chair, a chancery desk, a chest and a coffer. The window was a lancet, yet broad enough to provide good light, whilst the stewards had also brought in a number of candle spigots along with two small wheeled braziers and thick Turkey rugs for the floor. Once settled, Corbett had supervised the placing of his Secret Chancery chests in the great arca in Lord Henry's fortified chamber beneath his dining hall. The clerk now lounged at the chancery desk and tried to organise his teeming thoughts into some form of orderly schedule.

Item: they had successfully completed their three-hundred-mile journey from London with the Thurstons, Brother Adrian and the four Scottish hostages. They had travelled north through Pontefract, following the Roman roads into Northumbria. The weather had proved fine and they had encountered no difficulties until Darel's savage assault the night before last.

Item: they had been warned about this attack by Cacoignes, but could he be fully trusted? Worse, someone in their company had certainly mixed a sleeping powder or potion into the evening meal the night before the attack. Only God's good grace and the tender stomachs of Corbett and a few others had saved them.

Item: there was certainly a traitor in their company. The witch Richolda, now lying with her guardian Hockley in the dungeons deep beneath one of the towers, had confessed as much. Was this traitor also the assassin? Was the same person who'd informed Darel responsible for mixing the sleeping potion and killing Roskell? Yet how and why? Roskell was of little significance: a hostage, a former Scottish squire held captive for at least six years. A very quiet, taciturn man. Corbett had noticed him constantly threading Ave beads through his fingers. The other hostages kept to themselves. Roskell had been a virtual recluse, more interested in pattering his Aves than talking with his comrades. Moreover, he had been given the same food as the others. None of the other hostages could recall the victim eating or drinking by himself. Indeed, for most of the morning Roskell had been manacled and guarded; his keepers, Ap Ythel's archers, could report nothing out of the ordinary.

Item: if the traitor and the assassin were one and the same person, why had they plotted the ruthless massacre of Corbett's party? Did this person also know about Corbett's more secret instructions?

Item: the Scottish hostages. Corbett was to arrange some form of meeting with Bruce's coven and hand them over. Did these same hostages plan to begin negotiations about a possible truce between England and Scotland? Had Edward and Gaveston also secretly charged them with this duty? Both the English Crown and its great lords desperately wanted an honourable end to the conflict in Scotland.

Item: the murder of Red Comyn in the friary church of Dumfries in February 1306. The English Crown had been offered an eyewitness account of what had truly happened. This eyewitness had also insisted that such testimony would only be handed over at Alnwick. When? How? And by whom?

Item: Alnwick Castle itself. Corbett had walked the fortress, now turned into a sprawling building site. The northern baron and his family seemed intent on displaying and enforcing their power along the Scottish march. Percy and his wife Eleanor had met Corbett on his arrival. Lord Henry, one of the king's great killers, was a tall, burly man with the dangling arms of a swordsman. He was red-faced, balding and bulbous-eyed, with a wide mouth above a strong stubbled chin. Corbett had met him on a number of occasions and regarded him as a grim, stern-hearted man who took to war as a hawk to flying. Eleanor, his wife, was equally hard-souled. She was hatchet-faced, gimlet-eyed, a long, sharp nose above thin, bloodless lips; as Ranulf had whispered, there was no prettiness or delicacy about the Lady Eleanor. She dressed as soberly as any nun, her dark hair tightly twisted into long plaits that hung down to her shoulders. This noble pair had insisted on taking Corbett around their new domain.

Alnwick Castle had been originally built by the de Vescy family on a promontory overlooking the south bank of the River Aln, which served as the first line of

defence around the castle. Alnwick's soaring battlemented curtain wall also included strategically placed
towers or donjons such as the one Corbett was lodged
in. A majestic barbican controlled the fortified main
gateway, which was shielded not only by a moat fed
by the Aln but also by a reinforced drawbridge and a
heavy porticullis with murder-holes. This barbican led
into an outer bailey, where the stables, mews, granaries,
smithies and a whole range of storerooms were located.
A second fortified and stoutly defended barbican
guarded entrance into the inner bailey and the most
originally constructed keep. Instead of one soaring
donjon, as seen in most castles, the inner bailey at
Alnwick consisted of a ring of half-rounded towers and
other buildings overlooking a great cobbled yard. This
truly was, Corbett concluded, a place built for war. A
massive, formidable fortress that could become the kingdom's premier defence of its northern border. However,
it could also be used to threaten the Crown, with Lord
Henry becoming 'Cock of the North' and the arbiter
of English policy along the Scottish march.

Ostensibly, Lord Henry Percy was loyal to the king,
but he had ties with Lancaster and the Lords Ordainers.
A noble who kept to the shadows, quite happy to hunt
with the hounds and run with the hare. A dour, hard
man, Lord Henry was already winning a reputation for
ruthlessness. Alnwick might be impregnable, but it was
also a grim place, with harrowing displays of Lord
Henry's power of axe and tumbril. Corbett and Ranulf
had already seen the corpses dangling by their necks

from the castle walls, whilst cages hanging on either side of the barbican contained malefactors condemned to be exposed to the elements until they were dead. The stench from these executions was truly offensive. Constable Thurston, refusing to meet Corbett's eye, muttered how Lord Henry kept those condemned to the cages confined until their very flesh rotted.

Corbett got to his feet and walked to the lancet window. He peered through and glimpsed Percy's retainers bustling about in the bailey below. The various noises of the castle drifted up: the cries of children mingled with the clatter of wheels, the creaking of ropes and the neigh of horses. Once again he reflected on that camp in the clearing: Cacoignes slipping out of the darkness even as members of Corbett's escort succumbed to the sleeping potion. Who had done that, and how? He had questioned Ap Ythel and the others closely, but they had pointed out how the pottage had been stirred and ladled by many. As for Roskell's poisoning, on their approach to Alnwick Corbett had interrogated the other hostages and their guards. He was firmly convinced that they had told him the truth. Nobody could explain how Roskell, who only ate and drank what the others did, could have been fed such a noxious potion.

A knock on the door made him turn. Ranulf ushered Cacoignes into the room, gesturing that he should sit on the stool close to the scribe's chair. Corbett clasped the man's hand and studied him closely. The castle barber had shaved Cacoignes' head and face, and Corbett could glimpse traces of that courtly softness so common amongst the coterie of beautiful young men surrounding the king.

'You've broken your fast, Master Cacoignes?'

'Spiced oatmeal, light ale and some fresh bread. I feel—'

'Tell me what happened,' Corbett broke in brusquely. 'I mean over the last five years. Master Cacoignes, time is short. I do not really know who you are or – forgive me – if you can be trusted.'

Cacoignes pulled a face. 'Very well.' He rubbed his hands together and glanced quickly over his shoulder at Ranulf sitting on the edge of the bed behind him. 'Five years ago, during the old king's reign, after his victory against the Scottish rebels at Methven Bridge, I, along with others of the royal retinue, was ordered to seize the Scottish royal regalia from the abbey of Scone, the Scottish royal chapel and sacred enthronement place, and take it south to Westminster. Our group was charged with one item, the precious Lily Crown of Scotland, fashioned out of the pure golden rose that Pope Lucius III sent to William the Lion in 1182. The old king was being cunning; he wanted different items taken by different groups. I don't think he fully trusted the honesty of everyone, and of course it confused the Scots.' Cacoignes pointed at Corbett. 'I understand you had retired from the royal service at the time?'

'I heard about what Edward did. I wrote to the old king and urged him to be more conciliatory. He not only seized the royal regalia of Scotland but placed some of Bruce's womenfolk, including his wife, in cages at various castles. I believed then, and still do, that those actions were both cruel and very, very stupid. But continue . . .'

'Each of the groups was under a captain. Ours was a Gascon, Ravinac. You may know him, Sir Hugh, a man loyal to the old king. We seized the Lily Crown from Scone and rode like the very furies for the border, only to be attacked by a Scottish war band. We resisted stoutly, but only Ravinac and myself escaped. We fled across the border to Tynemouth Priory on its rocky promontory overlooking the sea.'

'And Prior Richard welcomed you?'

'Yes, he did, a very astute, cheerful soul. He gave us good food and comfortable quarters.'

'You delayed there?'

'We were exhausted, wounded after the fight and our flight, our horses blown. Then Ravinac fell ill of some illness of the belly.'

'And the Lily Crown?'

'Sir Hugh, I swear by all that is holy, after we arrived at the priory, Ravinac and I quarrelled about the treasure, who should look after it and whether we should take it by ship or by land to London.'

'Who did look after it?'

'Ravinac did. I left the priory to search for a way south. By the time I returned, Ravinac's fever had grown worse. He had also hidden the Lily Crown. He was too delirious or too obstinate to divulge its whereabouts. He died at Tynemouth and is buried there, and the secret with him.' Cacoignes wetted his lips. 'I left the priory again, going down to one of the coastal villages.

I was there when it was suddenly attacked by Scottish pirates. I was captured and taken to a hideous peel castle north of the Forth. Last Yuletide, when my guards were drinking heavily, I escaped. I made my way south and crossed the border. I visited Tynemouth, but Prior Richard could not help me. I learnt about the old king's death, the accesion of Edward of Caernarvon and the exaltation of Gaveston. However, by then I was posing as a mercenary under a different name, a swordsman waiting to be hired. I blundered into one of Darel's war parties foraging out of his fortress, the great coastal castle of Blanchlands. I had to continue the pretence, which was easy enough: I am a skilled swordsman and archer. I looked and acted what I claimed to be. I sealed indentures to wear Darel's livery and became his man in peace and war, against all enemies both within and without. Believe me,' Cacoignes wiped his mouth on the back of his hand, 'you do not alienate Darel lightly. He and his henchmen are brutal and ruthless.'

'Blanchlands?' Corbett queried. 'What is it really like?'

'A fortress like this. Darel's own patrimony. He has fortified and enlarged it. There is a formidable curtain wall with watchtowers; this, along with a deep moat and battlemented barbican, is its first line of defence. The inner keep is cordoned off by equally daunting strongholds. Only Darel and his henchmen are allowed to enter there.' Cacoignes blew his cheeks out. 'In many ways Blanchlands is similar to Alnwick.'

'And Darel's power?'

'Sir Hugh, you have witnessed what is happening in

the north. The Scots raid with impunity. The Sheriff of Northumberland is a laughing stock. Outlaws and other wolfsheads plague the forest and wasteland. Darel at least offers safety and protection to the peasant farmers, traders, tinkers and travelling merchants. He levies tolls and exacts his dues, but God help anyone who infringes his peace.'

'And his relationship with Lord Henry?'

'Wolves very rarely turn on each other. Rumour has it that Percy sees himself as king of the north. He is building up his strength at Alnwick so that one day he can attack Darel and utterly annihilate him.'

'So why did Darel attack us, a royal party?'

'He received information . . .' Cacoignes lifted a hand. 'Sir Hugh, how or from whom I cannot say. However, whispers claimed that you were bringing the Lily Crown back to Scotland as a bribe to open a peace dialogue with Bruce.'

'The Lily Crown!' Corbett shook his head in disbelief. 'In God's holy name, why did Darel think I was carrying that?'

'Why else would the English king's most senior clerk be travelling north with war carts and a comitatus of Welsh archers?' Cacoignes retorted. 'And why else would Darel attack you unless the enticement was very great? I mean, no self-respecting outlaw or wolfshead would go anywhere near a war party displaying the royal standards.'

'Yes, yes,' Corbett whispered. 'I can see how he was lured into attacking us. Well, he failed, and he must be furious: his war dogs slaughtered, foot soldiers killed, his kinsman Hockley captured along with his witch woman Richolda.'

'Is she a witch?' Ranulf demanded.

'To misquote the prophet Jeremiah,' Cacoignes replied, 'there are three gateways to hell: the first is in the desert, the second in the ocean and the third is through Blanchlands. As I have said, we were not allowed into the inner keep, but there was rumour aplenty about how Richolda is the leader of a coven devoted to demons and the blasphemous rites of midnight. They call themselves the Black Chesters, after a local village where the ancient religion is still venerated.' He ignored Ranulf's sharp burst of sarcastic laughter and leaned forward, hands clasped together. 'Trust me, Sir Hugh, Darel is obsessed with Richolda. They claim she has all sorts of powers, like being seen in two different places at the same time, conjuring up demons and invoking the dead to come to her.'

Corbett nodded. He walked across to the window and stared moodily down. What Cacoignes had told was true of so many places in the kingdom. Witchcraft and the worship of demons had a vigorous life of its own. Wandering warlocks claimed to possess magical powers. Corbett didn't know what to believe, though he had found two constants in his study of those who practised the midnight rites. First, there was more trickery in them than truth, and secondly, it was the use of powders and potions that created trances and dreams, visions and nightmares, rather than any real skill in summoning up the powers of hell. As Ranulf had once remarked, anyone could call Satan up from the deepest pit; the real question was, would he come?

Noises from the bailey below distracted him. Brother Adrian was busy with his parishioners, children of the castle seated around him. The monk had changed his black robe for working clothes and was talking to them about Christ; he was holding up a wooden crucifix and asking the children to come forward and kiss it in veneration. However, when they did, he made a subtle sleight of hand, and the crucifix would mysteriously disappear to be replaced with an egg; or a sweetmeat would mysteriously be discovered in a child's pocket, or behind an ear, or even nesting in someone's hair. The children loved this and shrieked with delight.

A sharp clatter of wheels and the cries of soldiers claimed the monk's attention, and his audience also turned to watch whatever was happening across the bailey. A bell began to toll. Corbett decided to go down and see for himself.

'Sir Hugh!'

He turned.

'I would like to join your retinue.'

'Master Cacoignes, that would be fine. I think we are going to need every swordsman we can get.'

Cacoignes thanked Corbett and left. Ranulf closed the door behind him and leaned against it.

'Master, you were retired when the old king won his victory at Methven. Afterwards the Chancery became very busy issuing letters, writs, licences and indentures regarding the Scottish regalia. I certainly remember the king's fury over Cacoignes.'

'Pardon?'

'Yes, Sir Hugh.' Ranulf pushed himself away from the door. 'When we heard about the attack on Ravinac and Cacoignes, the old king organised a thorough search of the northern march. I had the distinct impression that Cacoignes wasn't trusted, but that's just a suspicion. Perhaps we should ask Ap Ythel; he was a member of the comitatus sent to find out what happened.'

'Ap Ythel?'

'That's what I recall.'

Corbett made a face. 'I certainly will. But come . . .'

They left the tower to find the outer bailey very busy. Two catapults had been pulled out of their storage place and were being hauled close to the entrance through the barbican. Lord Henry's siege men were busy positioning these clumsy machines of war, placing blocks beneath their wheels to keep them stationary and steady before they began pulling at the ropes to bring the deep-bowled cups at the end of the throwing poles back in taut suspension. Close by, two huge braziers had been lit, the flames leaping hungrily as the fire was fed by sweat-soaked spit boys, who heaped on tinder and bundles of dry wood. Some distance away, others were stacking squares of dry straw from the castle barns, along with bulging oilskins.

'What is the matter?' Corbett asked Brother Adrian, who came hurrying across. 'Are we to be attacked, besieged?'

The monk scratched his shaven face, eyes narrowed as he peered up at the parapet spanning the barbican. Corbett followed his gaze. Lord Henry, Lady Eleanor, Thurston and his sister were standing there staring out over the walls. Corbett glanced behind him. Seton, Sterling and the squire Richard Mallet huddled close together, deep in conversation. All three hostages had been given their freedom to wander the castle after they had taken solemn oaths over the pyx in the castle chapel not to escape 'or do anything malign, be it by word or deed, to harm Lord Henry, Alnwick Castle and all who dwell there'.

'Sir Hugh, Sir Hugh!' Thurston came hurrying down. 'Lord Henry asks you and yours to join him on the parapet walk. Your captain of archers is bringing the prisoners up.'

'Why?' Corbett demanded. 'And why now?'

'Outriders have returned. Lord Henry dispatched them before dawn. They've brought news of Darel and a cohort of his mercenaries making their way towards Alnwick. They apparently approach with banners furled, so they wish to negotiate.'

'About the prisoners?'

'Of course.' Thurston spat his answer. 'But we have to be careful with that viper.'

'You do not trust him?'

'Would you?'

Corbett smiled and shrugged. 'You hate him?'

'I hate him and his kind, Sir Hugh. I was born and raised in these parts. My family are from Berwick; we were there when it was sacked. Darel was one of the king's captains. For days Berwick was given over to be pillaged and burnt. Darel, I understand, was foremost in the slaughter.'

'I was there too,' Corbett replied. 'Ap Ythel and I arrived just before the king ordered an end to the massacre.' He shook his head. 'I know Darel of old: a mailed clerk, a true blood-drinker, a killer to the very marrow of his being. But Master Constable, you say you were raised here?'

'My sister and I were orphans. We entered the household of Anthony Bek, Bishop of Durham. When he sold Alnwick to Lord Henry, he secured the position of constable for me—'

A piercing scream shrilled across the bailey. Ap Ythel and his archers were leading Hockley and Richolda out through the inner barbican. Both prisoners were heavily manacled. Hockley was sullen and uncooperative and had to be pushed and shoved by his escort. Richolda was fighting and continued to do so until one of the guards drew his dagger and pressed the point against her throat.

'Lord Henry is waiting,' Thurston murmured.

Corbett and Ranulf followed the constable up the outside steps and onto the parapet walk that spanned the top of the majestic barbican. A strong breeze whipped their hair and faces. Corbett steadied himself against the crenellations and stared out over the heathland that lay either side of the trackway leading up to the moat. The water in that deep ditch glittered in the early-morning sun, reeking strongly of the filth floating on its surface. He heard the clank of chains as the broad drawbridge was pulled up and the porticullis lowered. Lord Henry and Lady Eleanor stood staring out over the moorland, men-at-arms ranged either side, helmeted and buckled for war. They carried long oval shields, which they would use to protect both themselves and their lord and lady. Corbett turned and stared down into the bailey. Hockley and Richolda were still struggling against their guards. Brother Adrian, together with Kathryn Thurston and Cacoignes, were trying to calm them.

'Master,' hissed Ranulf, 'look either side of the gateway.'

Corbett stepped up onto the narrow fighting platform and glanced over the wall. Just below him hung a cage fashioned out of blackened wooden lattice and reinforced with iron strips. The cage, two yards high and about the same across, was bolted to the wall. On the top was a door that could be hooked back to allow the prisoner to be lowered inside.

'There's another on the other side of the gateway,' Lord Henry declared, acknowledging Corbett for the first time. 'The cages are held fast, the door on top is padlocked. Food and water, if I agree to it, can be thrust down for the prisoner. Not the most comfortable of quarters, but at least they have been hosed down after their most recent use. Master Thurston,' he bellowed, 'fetch the prisoners.'

Hockley and Richolda were pushed up the steps. Hockley was pale-faced. Richolda, now realising that her shouts and protests meant nothing to this northern lord, was weeping in terror, begging for mercy. Lord Henry blithely ignored her, his only response being to hawk and spit in her direction. Castle guards, skilled and experienced in what they were doing, now took over from Ap Ythel. One soldier used his spear to hook back the lid of the cage; his comrades lifted the screaming woman and lowered her into the gap to collapse on the floor. Hockley was then pushed along the parapet, Lord Henry and the others stepping aside to let him past. The guards hoisted the prisoner onto the fighting platform. The door of the second cage was pulled back and Hockley was lowered inside, then a guard gingerly climbed over and drew across the three heavy bolts, thrusting them deep into their clasps. The prisoner had no chance of stretching up to reach these cleverly placed locks. Once he was satisfied that the cage was secure, the guard pushed through the lattice opening a small waterskin and a loaf of coarse rye bread, the same being given to Richolda.

'My lord,' Thurston exclaimed, pointing to the dust rising further down the trackway.

'Oh good!' Lord Henry exclaimed. 'Welcome to the feast,' he added sarcastically.

'They have wasted no time,' Corbett declared.

'Those we drove off yesterday probably met Darel coming to find them,' Thurston replied. 'But we shall see.'

Corbett waited until Ap Ythel came up the steps;

then, plucking at the Welshman's sleeve, he led him away from the rest.

'Sir Hugh?'

'You did not tell me that you led a comitatus north five years ago to search for Cacoignes.'

'No, Sir Hugh, I did not. I also haven't told you that there are men in this castle who have served alongside me, whilst the same could be said of those approaching under Darel's banner. For God's sake, Sir Hugh,' Ap Ythel's voice became sing-song, 'we live in a state of constant war. Yes, I was sent north. I discovered very little. Yes, I visited Tynemouth, and for a number of weeks whilst we searched for Cacoignes, I sheltered here in Alnwick Castle when Bishop Bek was its lord. Believe me, Sir Hugh, it was a grim and very boring watch. Things change. Today's friend is tomorrow's foe.'

'Why were you sent?'

'The old king did not fully accept the news that trickled south. He entertained doubts about the accepted story and he suspected mischief. He asked questions: why was Cacoignes' group attacked? How did he and Ravinac escape? Where was the Lily Crown? Sir Hugh, Cacoignes was a fop. He had a reputation and not a very pleasant one. Rumour had it that he came from these parts, so how could he blunder around and be captured?' Ap Ythel heaved a sigh. 'But there again, many of the Prince of Wales's handsome young men were the subject of lurid tales, including my lord Gaveston. Wasn't his mother allegedly burnt as a witch?'

Corbett stared at the rough-faced, taciturn Welshman,

a skilled master bowman and a loyal member of the royal retinue. 'Did you discover anything about the attack on Ravinac's party?' he asked.

Ap Ythel laughed sharply, as if to himself. 'We gleaned the scantiest of details. Local peasants talked of a furious attack by black-garbed reivers.'

'Black-garbed?'

'Yes. I too was surprised. The Scots do not usually don the robes of the black monks, the Benedictines, the likes of Brother Adrian. Anyway, we then journeyed on to Tynemouth. On our travels we captured a Scottish clerk.' Ap Ythel's smile turned genuinely sad. 'Matthew Dunedin. A clever, merry, very learned young man. He was a member of Bruce's household. He was carrying valuable documents, an important figure in Bruce's coven; his capture was some consolation for our fruitless mission. We kept him at Tynemouth, then took him south. He was imprisoned with Seton and Sterling.'

'And he died?'

Ap Ythel looked away as if hiding his face. 'They claim he fell down steps in the White Tower and sustained savage injuries to his head and neck.'

'Was foul play suspected?' asked Corbett.

The Welshman now looked at him squarely. 'Yes. People blamed the other prisoners; some claimed it was an accident. You know how it is.'

'And at Tynemouth?'

'Well, Prior Richard certainly remembered both Cacoignes and Ravinac; the latter died there.'

'Poisoned, murdered?'

'No, no,' Ap Ythel declared. 'Ravinac died of some belly ailment. There's no proof of foul play. According to Prior Richard, there had been a heated disagreement between Ravinac and Cacoignes over the custody of the Lily Crown. Ravinac refused to give it up. Cacoignes left for a while, and by the time he returned, Ravinac was dying or dead. Apparently the good prior had heard Ravinac's confession and promised he would send a message south to Edward of Caernarvon.'

'And this was some months after Cacoignes and Ravinac were attacked?'

'Oh yes, in the spring of the following year. The old king was failing. Ravinac had been in his grave for months and Cacoignes had disappeared from the face of the earth. Sir Hugh, you had retired then. Everything was in confusion. I didn't like returning empty-handed, so we came here to Alnwick. We must have spent the winter here, two or three months; a godforsaken experience. The castle was more like a mausoleum. The de Vescy family had gone, Anthony Bek, the Bishop of Durham, wished to sell the place as swiftly as possible—'

'Horsemen!' a sentry yelled. 'Look, horsemen!'

Corbett hastened back to Lord Henry, who was pressed against the parapet wall, staring out at the fast-approaching cloud of dust. Trumpets and horns brayed. Corbett looked back down into the bailey. The two catapults were now primed, the throwing cups winched back, the iron tubs burning fiercely. Alnwick was on a war footing. Men-at-arms, archers and spearmen hurried up the steps onto the fighting platforms along the curtain wall to the left and right of the barbican. Lord Henry brought up and displayed his standards and pennants proclaiming the Percy insignia: a white lion rampant against a blue background. The beauty and calm of the autumn morning was shattered by the clatter of armour, the clash of weaponry and the rank smell of burning from the tubs and braziers.

The cloud of dust drew closer. Horsemen appeared carrying Darel's standards displaying six black martlets against a silver background. Richolda clawed with her hands at the cage and screamed, a truly heart-chilling sound. The horsemen reined in just out of bowshot, though Ap Ythel murmured how his archers could probably find their mark. Lord Henry lifted a gauntleted hand and shook his head. Down below, a rider holding a stark black crucifix, a white cloth tied to the pole beneath it, urged his horse forward to the edge of the moat. He was dressed in a mail hauberk covered with a tabard displaying Darel's insignia; his face was almost hidden by his coif and conical helmet with its broad nose-guard.

'Lord Henry?'

'I am he.'

'My lord and master Sir Edmund Darel demands the immediate release of his kinsman Hockley and his ward the woman Richolda. They are to be freed immediately along with compensation for their capture and ill treatment in your cages. For each, five hundred pounds sterling to be paid by Michaelmas. Until then, we demand hostages.'

Corbett stepped up onto the fighting platform. 'I am Sir Hugh Corbett, Keeper of the Secret Seal.'

The herald peered up at him.

'I carry the king's mandate and ride under his colours. You attacked me. That is treason.'

The herald gathered the reins in his hands, his horse skittering backwards on the trackway. Another rider spurred forward. In a magnificent display of horsemanship, he swerved just before the moat, turning his mount even as he hurled a lance into the raised drawbridge. Both herald and lance-thrower left in a clatter of hooves and clouds of dust.

'Two bowshots!' Lord Henry screamed at the siege men around the catapults. Winches creaked, ropes tightened, levers were released; the wheels of the catapult grated backwards and forwards as the throwing cups were hastily filled with cloth, straw and kindling drenched in oil. The death-bearing bundles were torched and the ropes released, the throwing beams shooting forward with a screech; the fiery missiles hurtled through the air, crashing very close to the group of horsemen, who hastily retreated. The flaming bundles were followed by a hail of shafts, a veritable blizzard of arrows. The horsemen turned and thundered off, dust rising like a protective mist behind them. Thurston shouted for calm.

'For the moment,' Lord Henry declared, turning to Corbett, 'all is peaceful.'

'But they will return.'

'Oh yes, Sir Hugh, and they will bring their full power. Darel wants the return of his woman.' Lord

Henry spat over the wall in the direction of the cage. 'Until then, she can rot. Darel will pay handsomely.'

The castle garrison now broke off from all hostilities. Bows were unstrung, swords sheathed, helmets taken off, the soldiers streaming down the steps to greet their women and children, who had hastily retreated across the bailey. Slowly the castle returned to its normal routine. The porticullis was raised, the drawbridge lowered; riders went out and swiftly returned to report how Darel's comitatus had fled the area. Richolda screamed her defiance, to be answered with a torrent of abuse from the hard-bitten guards, some of whom undid the points on their hose and urinated over the cages. Corbett shouted at them to stop, but the men just laughed and turned away.

PART TWO

'Robert Bruce declared he did not care much for the King of England's peace.' *Life of Edward II*

Corbett followed Ranulf down into the bailey. They sat on a bench enjoying the sun. Corbett kept an eye on the soldiers manning the fighting platform. He did not wish further abuse of the prisoners. Moreover, he knew Darel. If the situation abruptly changed and fickle Fortune give her wheel a spin, the northern knight would inflict hideous punishment for such treatment. Brother Adrian came bustling over saying how he hadn't been able to join them on the parapet walk as he greatly feared heights.

'Where are you from, Brother?' Ranulf squinted up at the friar. 'You are English?'

'I was born and raised on a farm between Hexham and Corbridge sacked by the Earl of Buchan in the spring of 1296.'

'Ah,' Corbett intervened, 'the notorious Massacre of the Little Clerks, as it was known. The Scottish rebels under Buchan are supposed to have seized a group of young boys, locked them in their school house, set fire to the building and burnt them to death. They say the old king's sack of Berwick later that same year was in retaliation for that outrage.'

'Yes, yes, they do.' The Benedictine squatted down on the ground before them. 'I escaped but my family perished during Buchan's hideous campaign to kill all those living between Hexham and Corbridge. I was taken in by the Benedictines and . . .' he shrugged, 'here I am near my birthplace and close to Lord Henry, a man who hates Bruce and his ilk as much as I do.'

'Brother Adrian, our journey here. When we came to that clearing the night before the attack, and supper was being prepared?'

'Sir Hugh,' the monk fingered the cross on a cord around his neck, 'let me make it very clear, I saw nothing untoward. I agree, someone mixed a potion or powder into the meal, but that pot of pottage had been bubbling over the flames for some time. I suggest that anyone in that camp – and don't forget that early in the afternoon we were visited by chapmen and tinkers – could have slipped the sleeping potion in. Anything is possible.' He grinned. 'I ate some of the pottage and paid the price. I fell asleep under a bush on the edge of the camp. When I was roused, I realised what had happened; I did some service as infirmarian at the abbey of Rievaulx in Yorkshire. I had all the symptoms of a sleeping draught: heavy eye, dry mouth,' he waved a hand, 'and so on. Thank God it wasn't the poison Roskell ate, and again, Sir Hugh, God knows who approached him and gave him – what? A noxious drink, tainted food? We all know he only ate and drank what the others did. Sir Hugh, I swear on my priesthood, I saw nothing untoward.'

'And now?' Ranulf leaned forward. 'You know Darel, or at least of him?'

'I am afraid I know very little and I prefer to keep it that way. Darel has a reputation as a ruthless killer. His patronage of the Black Chesters is a mystery, but his obsession with Richolda is well known. He will certainly try to get his witch back, trust me.' The monk rose and walked towards one of the castle men, who, to divert the children, had cooked some sweetmeats and laid them out on a tray to cool. The young boys and girls scrabbled to get these, putting them into pockets and pouches and laughing as Brother Adrian threatened to eat them all.

'Sir Hugh,' Ranulf broke into Corbett's reflections, 'what now?'

'Ah yes, Ranulf, what now? We should really deal with the hostages, though I don't know how and when the exchange will take place.'

They made their way back to the Abbot's Tower, where Corbett had his chamber, with Ranulf's on the stairwell above. Ap Ythel was waiting for them, looking ill at ease. Corbett noticed he was eating a piece of pure white cheese, a delicacy made from ewe's milk with a unique sweetness all of its own. The captain of archers had confessed that whenever he felt agitated, the very taste of such a comfit calmed him.

'Ap Ythel?'

'Sir Hugh, Darel will return all embattled for war. I am concerned. My archers are the best, but we are a small comitatus. Are we going to be caught up in a bitter war between northern lords?'

'No, my friend, we certainly are not, but there is something else?'

'Lords Seton and Sterling, together with Mallet their squire, have adjourned to the castle chapel; they want words with you.'

'Do they now? Then let's not keep our Scottish lords waiting.'

They crossed the outer bailey and through the inner barbican; its drawbridge had been recently lowered, the cruel, sharp-toothed porticullis raised and held secure with chains and winches. Nevertheless, Alnwick was still prepared for war. Armoured men-at-arms, dressed in battle harness, patrolled the barbican's yawning entrance, ready to seal off entry to Lord Henry's inner sanctum. The bailey inside, its close-set semicircular towers now being refurbished and strengthened, only enhanced the dark military menace of the castle and the warlike tendencies of its lord.

Corbett peered up. The guards on each tower overlooked not only the countryside but the castle as a whole. St Chad's chapel, a low, long, barn-like structure, was wedged between two of these towers. Corbett pulled back the half-open door and entered, followed by Ap Ythel and Ranulf. Inside, the nave was cloaked in darkness. Pools of light were created by candles and tapers burning before the lady altar and either side of the

Percy insignia, carved and picked out with paint on the drum-like pillars close to the baptismal font just within the entrance. Lancet windows high in the wall allowed in shafts of light, but these only made the chapel even more like a haunt of ghosts, a hall of shifting shadows.

'Close the door, Sir Hugh.' Seton, sitting on the steps leading to the rood screen, rose to his feet. Sterling and Mallet, praying in the lady chapel before a statue of the Virgin, came out to join him. Corbett went back and closed the door, whispering to Ranulf and Ap Ythel to accompany him.

'On their way north,' he murmured, 'they could hardly exchange a pleasant word with me. Now they summon me as if they are my lord. My friends, I think we are going to learn something.'

Corbett and his two companions walked down the nave and followed the Scottish lords up the steps into the sanctuary, where Seton had set out two benches. Corbett, Ranulf and Ap Ythel sat down on one of these, Seton and his two comrades on the other. The sanctuary was a stark, bleak house of prayer, its altar nothing more than a heavy black oaken table covered with a dark-red cloth, with candlesticks at either end. Above this hung the pyx box on a thick brass chain, next to the sanctuary lamp, which glowed in a red glass vase. Corbett stared around this gloomy, shadow-filled place, fingers tapping the hilt of his dagger.

'We are alone, Sir Hugh.' Seton pointed across to the sacristy door. 'That is locked. There is no outside entrance, whilst Mallet,' he indicated with his head, 'will guard the entrance.' The squire rose, sketched a bow and left, hurrying down the nave to stand close to the main door. Corbett watched him go.

'You want words with me?' He turned back. 'I suspect you've summoned me here to tell me something I do not know.'

'Red Comyn was our master.' Seton laughed at Corbett's surprise. 'Red Comyn,' he repeated. 'Sir Hugh, your king gave you instructions to take me, Sterling and our squires – God rest poor Roskell – to Alnwick and arrange a transfer of hostages with the usurper Bruce.'

'Yes, I believe communication with Bruce will be set up. We are to wait here for his henchmen to bring four English prisoners across the march and, under a cross of truce guaranteeing safe conduct, hand them over to me in return for you. I do wonder,' Corbett added wryly, 'how the death of Roskell will effect such negotiations.'

'No need, no need.' Sterling spoke up. Corbett noticed how the Scottish accents of both lords had diminished greatly, whilst their grasp of Norman French was as good as his. 'There will be no exchange of hostages and never mind the oaths taken here,' Sterling continued, 'for we shall, at the appropriate time, slip out of Alnwick across the march and into Scotland.'

'Will you now!' Corbett made to rise but sat down as Seton held up a hand.

'We shall enter Scotland. We will proclaim what we know and we will kill Bruce.'

'You are assassins!' Corbett exclaimed. Seton slid his hand into his loose-fitting boot and drew from a secret pocket a thin scroll of parchment, which he handed to Corbett.

'Your king, Sir Hugh, asked me to give you this here in the chapel of St Chad at Alnwick.'

Corbett broke the seal and unrolled the scroll. Its message was brief and succinct. 'To our well-beloved clerk Sir Hugh Corbett, greetings. We ask you to listen most carefully to Lord Seton in the chapel of St Chad at Alnwick. You are, under your allegiance to the Crown, to provide him and his with every support and sustenance to enter Scotland secretly.' Corbett hid his smile at the concluding sentence. 'Another, whom you know well, will explain and confirm the reasons for this. Given at Westminster under our personal seal . . .'

Seton stretched out his hand; Corbett shook his head.

'Not for you, sir.' He folded the parchment and put it into his own belt wallet.

'The letter promises us help and sustenance, surely?' Sterling queried, his raw-boned face all severe.

'It does, and I shall do what I am ordered. Nevertheless, let me have your tale from beginning to end. We are no longer in the safety of the Tower or the comfort of Westminster. We truly are in a land of deep shadow. Outside this castle lurk our enemies and those of the king, whilst within we have to decide who is our real friend and who our secret foe. I must make judgements, sound judgements. So first, why all the subterfuge?'

'Your king and his . . .' Seton smiled wolfishly.

'The lord Gaveston,' Ap Ythel interrupted warningly.

'You trust him?' Seton pointed at the Welshman.

'With my life,' Corbett retorted, 'as does His Grace the king; and, Lord Seton, you may very well have to do the same in the days ahead. Now I am listening. I want to know why our king's open instructions to me have been so radically changed. Oh, by the way, why did you ask if I trusted Ap Ythel? Why not Ranulf?'

'The Welshman was one of our gaolers,' Sterling replied. 'Weren't you, sir?'

Ap Ythel smiled thinly.

'Did he treat you well?' Ranulf asked.

'Severe but fair, I would say,' Seton replied. 'He seemed very upset by the death of Matthew Dunedin.'

'Dunedin was my prisoner,' Ap Ythel said slowly, staring hard at Seton. 'He was my responsibility. I captured him.'

'He was held for ransom,' Sterling taunted. 'And of course you get nothing for a dead man.'

'It was more than that,' Ap Ythel declared. 'I liked Dunedin; he was a merry soul and you know that. He was homesick. I will be honest, there were times when I wished he could just leave and rejoin his beloveds in Scotland.'

'He slipped, didn't he?' Sterling asked. 'He stumbled on those steep steps in the White Tower and died of his injuries.' He pointed at Ap Ythel. 'Are you one of those who claim he was pushed? If so, by whom, and why? Where is the evidence for such an allegation?'

Corbett stared at the Welsh captain of archers, who glanced swiftly at him, winked and looked away.

'And you?' Corbett decided to return to the business

in hand. 'Dunedin is dead and so is Roskell. What do you three hope to do?'

'Scotland fights England,' Seton declared, 'but Scotland is divided. Your old king and his captains may have been bloodthirsty and ruthless but Robert the Bruce and his coven are no different. Let me give you an example. You have heard about Douglas's larder? In March 1306 James Douglas attacked an English force whilst they were in St Bride's church for the Palm Sunday celebrations. Douglas appeared in disguise as a common thresher, garbed in a threadbare shirt with a flail over his shoulders. He was joined by members of his cohort and attacked the English in a furious, bloody affray. They killed twenty men and took ten prisoners. Afterwards Douglas feasted, eating and drinking to his heart's content. Then he collected what plunder he could, piling up the wheat, malt and flour seized from the bins and broaching the heavy wine casks, soaking everything. Finally he took the ten prisoners and beheaded them over the pile of food, creating what is now called Douglas's larder.'

'That's the Scotland we now wish to enter.' Sterling spoke up, staring down the nave to ensure Mallet still guarded the door. 'Yes, we were taken prisoner by the old king's troops. However, we are not Bruce's men but the faithful and loyal retainers of Sir John Comyn, Lord of Badenoch, foully slain by Bruce before the high altar in the friary church at Dumfries on the tenth of February 1306—'

'Others say different,' Corbett interrupted.

'Others weren't there; we were,' Seton rasped.

'What?'

'Oh yes.' Seton wiped his mouth with his fingers. 'I'm sure you have heard Bruce's version, but the truth is very different. When Red Comyn met Bruce before the high altar of that friary church in Dumfries, Bruce demanded from our lord complete support for his claim to the Scottish throne. Comyn refused to even consider it.'

'He had a claim himself, didn't he?' Corbett asked.

'He certainly did. Comyn was one of those who pleaded with the old king to confirm his right to succeed to the Crown. Now our lord had come unarmed to that meeting. Bruce, however, was secretly buckled for battle, as were his retainers, hidden deep in the shadows of that ancient church.'

'Where were you?' Ap Ythel demanded.

'Our master had left us in the sacristy. There was a grille on the door that gave us a view onto the sanctuary. Bruce learnt about this and turned the key on the outside. We could only hammer on the door as Bruce, aided by his henchmen, stabbed our master to death. Afterwards they fled. Eventually we escaped, but there was nothing we could do so we went into hiding. However, after Comyn's death, the old king's troops flooded the locality. They controlled every road, trackway and highland pass. We were captured, and despite our pleas that Bruce was our blood enemy, we were dispatched south to the Tower.'

'We pleaded our cause.' Sterling took up the story. 'We begged for an opportunity to put our case before the old king. However, the self-proclaimed Hammer of the Scots would not listen, and neither would his son and heir until my lord of Gaveston heard our plea. We reached a compact, a secret understanding that we would be taken north as hostages but allowed to escape and make our own way across the border. Anything else would be too dangerous.'

'Of course,' Ranulf broke in, 'Bruce would love to seize followers of Red Comyn, especially men who knew the truth about their master's murder.'

'I swear before the Blessed Sacrament here in Alnwick's chapel that what we have just said is God's own truth. If we were handed over to Bruce we would hardly survive a day. We need only your help to be free of this place, to be well supplied with purveyance, weapons, coin and horses. We intend to go to a Scottish church and proclaim the truth on the Gospels before witnesses, then invoke the blood feud against Bruce and kill him in just vindication of our master's brutal murder.'

'You are sure of that?' Ap Ythel asked. 'Others argue a different story about Red Comyn's death. How your lord plotted Bruce's murder and that Bruce only escaped due to his own quick wits and the loyalty and courage of his entourage.'

'Do they now?' Seton taunted. 'And what do you, a Welshman, know about Scottish affairs?'

'Very little apparently,' Ap Ythel replied casually. 'Except that other stories have also taken root about your lord's death. How Comyn persecuted Bruce and brought him into disrepute with the old king, who began to turn on him, so much so that Bruce became deeply fearful for his life. Bruce's followers maintain that their lord had no choice but to kill Comyn, assert his claim and move into full rebellion.'

'You asked a question, Welshman,' Seton declared. 'Are we sure of our case. Yes, we certainly are. Sir Hugh, your king and my lord Gaveston wanted to inform you about all this,' he shrugged, 'but we begged that the matter remain secret until we reached here.'

Corbett nodded, staring across at these two men locked in their own world of blood and vengeance. 'I see why you wanted it kept secret,' he murmured. 'You needed to create and sustain the impression that you were nothing more than prisoners being transported to the Scottish march. We were to show you no concession, no flicker of friendship, not a crumb of compassion, and you are certainly facing danger. After all, your comrade Roskell was poisoned.'

'Bruce has his spies everywhere. It's possible there is one in your company, Sir Hugh. That is the world we live in.'

'And that other mysterious death?' Ap Ythel demanded.

'Dunedin's?' Seton replied.

'Yes, Matthew Dunedin,' Corbett agreed. 'I understand he was one of Bruce's clerks.'

'Matthew was a scribe,' Seton replied. 'A man of the Chancery, buckled for war but not a real soldier. He was a captive who just wanted to go home. We tried to draw him into conversation, but he kept to himself. If we attempted to discuss Bruce, or indeed anyone else, he became taciturn, pining for the manor he owned in a glen close to Loch Lomond. The only person he really spoke to was Roskell; both were very pious men who believed they were living in the Last of Days. In their eyes, the war in Scotland was the precursor of the Day of the Great Slaughter foretold by the prophet Daniel and repeated in other apocalyptic writings. They truly believed that the heavens would soon dissolve in fire and Christ would come again. They loved to search the texts to justify their view. Dunedin would often go into the chapel of St John in the White Tower to read the scriptures or borrow a psalter.'

'How did he die?' Corbett demanded.

Seton rubbed his weather-beaten face. 'Matthew did like his wine. He had a passion, a weakness for the richest and heaviest of Bordeaux. Sir Hugh, you know the White Tower? It soars to the sky and the steps inside are very steep. Matthew slipped.' He shrugged. 'That's all I can say.'

'Could it have been murder?'

'For heaven's sake, why?' Sterling snarled. 'Matthew was nothing more than a homesick Scottish clerk who had been unfortunate enough to be captured. He drank too much wine and fell.'

Corbett was not fully convinced but he decided to let the matter go.

'And Roskell?'

'Sir Hugh, we know nothing of his death: the how, the who or the why. Roskell was a quiet, placid man.' Seton crossed himself. 'He was deeply religious, fearful of death, always talking about preparing his soul. He has now gone to God, and we must go to Scotland.'

'I suppose that anonymous memorandum, the one about learning the truth concerning Red Comyn's death,' Corbett smiled, 'must have been the invention of my lord Gaveston.'

'I suspect it was,' Seton replied. 'Sir Hugh, will you help us?'

'We shall certainly do our best,' Corbett replied. 'It's a relief to know we are not going to meet and negotiate with the Scots. Indeed, the less they and anyone else know, the better. We will supply you with weapons, clothing, some food and a few silver coins. We will also have to wait for the best opportunity to arrange your escape. Once we have done that, we will have achieved everything our royal master requires.'

'In which case . . .' Seton and Sterling rose, clasped hands with Corbett and his two companions, then left, hurrying down the nave. Mallet opened the door and they were gone.

'Well, well.' Corbett paused as the door reopened and a figure, robe flapping, hurried into the church. Brother Adrian almost ran up the nave, blundering into the sanctuary.

'What is happening?' The monk paused, gasping for breath. 'I saw the Scottish rebels leave. Is everything well here?'

'All is well.' Corbett rose and clasped him on the shoulder. 'By the way, Brother Adrian, how long have you served here?'

'I joined Lord Henry's household two years ago, when he bought Alnwick from the Bishop of Durham.'

'And before that?'

'I was at Tynemouth Priory. I am happy at Alnwick. I will support Lord Henry against the usurper, the assassin King Hob.'

'You mean Bruce?'

'Naturally. I will have nothing to do with that man.' Brother Adrian became quite animated as they left the sanctuary.

A sound made Corbett pause. He was sure the main door had opened and closed just as quickly. He strained his eyes. The entrance porch was shadow-filled; one of these seemed to move.

'Justice!' a voice called. Corbett could not decide whether it was man or woman. Was it some joke, a trick?

'Justice and retribution!' the voice repeated.

'Down!' Corbett screamed, cursing his own inaction. 'Down now!' He half turned, gesturing at Ranulf and Ap Ythel, who dropped to their knees. He grabbed a startled Adrian and pulled him down. A crossbow bolt whirled above their heads to clatter in the sanctuary beyond. Corbett drew his dagger. Brother Adrian tried to crawl forward. Corbett, dropping the knife, forced the monk to lie down and stay still. Another barbed bolt cut through the air, to crack and splinter against the coarse wooden rood screen behind them. Somewhere a bell began to toll, its pealing growing more strident as it declared that some other danger was fast emerging.

'Stay!' Corbett urged his companions. He peered down the nave and saw the main door open and close. He crawled towards the entrance porch, where he felt the cold breeze seeping beneath the door. He glimpsed a small hand-held crossbow and a squat leather quiver lying on the floor; their attacker had apparently left these and fled. He could tell at first glance that they were probably from the castle armoury, one of those weapons commonly left in guardrooms or tower stair-wells. He lifted his head. The tocsin was now constant in its pealing.

'Our attacker has fled,' he called out, getting to his feet.

'In God's name!' Brother Adrian exclaimed. 'Who was that? Why such an attack? And the bells, is the castle under assault?'

Corbett gestured at the others to follow as he hurriedly left. People were streaming across the bailey towards the outer barbican. He realised how easy it would be for their assailant to mingle amongst these or slip down one of the many narrow runnels that cut between the buildings. A man-at-arms explained that the alarm had been raised because something had happened to the prisoners in the wall cages. The bell kept clanging. Corbett, Ranulf and Ap Ythel, Brother Adrian hurrying before them, joined the crowd gathering at the foot of the steps leading up to the parapet that spanned the main barbican. The autumn sun was beginning to set, the first tinges of a cold darkness making themselves felt. Corbett suppressed a shiver as he watched two corpses being carried down in sheets from the parapet walk. He glimpsed their discoloured, twisted faces, the popping eyes, the creamy scum around the liverish lips. He turned to Brother Adrian and Cacoignes, who had pushed their way through.

'Take the corpses to the chapel,' he ordered before climbing the steps to join Lord Henry and Constable Thurston.

'Sir Hugh,' Percy gestured down at the corpses, 'you have seen them? Murdered, poisoned! God knows this will bring a torrent of troubles upon us.'

'We need to inspect the cages,' Corbett said. 'Secure whatever food and drink they were given.'

Lord Henry grunted his agreement, shouting at his men-at-arms along the parapet to assist. Corbett dug into his purse and gave two volunteers each a coin. The soldiers climbed onto the fighting platform and eased themselves over the crenellations, slipping down into the cages. Corbett urged them to search most carefully and bring out any food or drink. Both soldiers eventually emerged clutching the small waterskins given to each prisoner as well as the remains of the coarse rye loaves.

Corbett summoned Ap Ythel and instructed him to mix the bread and water into a bowl. A rat was to be trapped and caged, its appetite whetted before it was let loose on the bowl and its contents. He then had words with Lord Henry, asking him to convene a meeting as soon as possible. Percy agreed. Corbett whispered to Ranulf to learn as much as he could from the chatter and gossip around the castle, adding that he would return to his chamber in the Abbot's Tower.

Once there, he locked and bolted the door, pulled the shutters over the window and laid out his chancery materials. For a while he sat listening to the sounds outside the tower. The clatter of armour was now constant; Lord Henry was determined to prepare Alnwick for an imminent assault. Once Darel learnt about the violent deaths of Richolda and Hockley, the robber baron would undoubtedly unleash his fury against the castle and all who sheltered there. Corbett was tempted to go down and view the corpses immediately, but he felt it best to let matters settle before he began any inquisition. There was no hurry. They would be safe in the castle chapel. The church had only one entrance; Ranulf would seal this with the royal insignia whilst Ap Ythel would set up a guard to keep careful watch.

Corbett dipped his quill pen in the bluish-green ink and began to list what he regarded as pertinent and relevant. Item: the king was correct: Lord Henry intended to make Alnwick a mighty fortress that would eventually dominate the Scottish march. The building work within the castle proved that, especially the inner bailey, which was being turned into a fortress in its own right. The Percys would undoubtedly stamp their authority on the northern shires, so much so that there was a real danger that the Lord of Alnwick might become king of the north. Moreover, Lord Henry had sided with those powerful barons who opposed the king and now controlled the Royal Council through their ordinances. Thankfully the northern lord was still on the fringe of such mischief. Perhaps he could be bribed, cajoled or threatened to withdraw his support of the other great nobles and become a stalwart adherent of the king's party.

Item: Edward the king faced a veritable storm of troubles. The barons had demanded that Gaveston be exiled. Edward had been forced to agree, and his favourite was to depart the kingdom for Ireland or any sanctuary he could find, protected from those who hated him. But how could he leave unharmed? Both the king and Gaveston were deeply fearful that he might be ambushed and caught before he reached safety. All the ports were watched, the captains of ships could be bribed, and of course war cogs could be dispatched in pursuit of the fleeing favourite. One thing was regarded as a truth. If Gaveston was captured, the great lords would show no mercy but immediately carry out summary execution. They claimed that the favourite had been tried and found guilty: it was either exile or death. Corbett had been charged on his solemn oath to make sure Gaveston passed safely from the kingdom to foreign parts, but how, when and where had yet to be decided. 'A most dangerous enterprise,' he murmured to himself. 'And why do I busy myself with it?'

He leaned back in the chair. The answer, in truth, as he had confessed to the Lady Maeve, was that he felt sorry for Edward and Gaveston. Despite their arrogant stupidity, Corbett liked both men. The king had proved to be a most loving and loyal husband to his young French queen Isabella, but that was Edward! If he was your friend, he would always stand by you. In this he was quite different from his redoubtable father, a great and terrible king who would sacrifice anyone, kith or kin, on the altar of expediency, as Corbett had found to his own cost. In addition, Corbett had taken the most solemn oath some years ago that he would watch, protect and assist the old king's heir. He could recall many occasions when Edward had grasped him by hand, arm or shoulder and reminded him of his promises, his vows.

For his part Corbett had tried to influence the king, begging him not to alienate his flamboyant heir, but the last years of Edward's reign had been fraught with deepening tension between royal father and son. Time and again from his manor at Leighton Corbett had written to the king advising him to seek peace with both his son and Scotland; that he was embarking on a long, dark path from which there would be no return.

He shook his head, clearing his mind of memories. Now was not the time to go down the dust-filled gallery of the years. He picked up his quill pen and continued writing.

Item: despite Corbett's total support, Edward and Gaveston had not been as forthright and honest as they should have been. Alexander Seton and his party were not hostages but prisoners of the old king's Scottish wars. According to the evidence, they were in fact bitterly opposed to Bruce, and had invoked the blood feud because of Red Comyn's brutal murder in that Dumfries church some five years ago. Corbett had been publicly instructed to take the prisoners north and await an approach from Bruce through intermediaries. Of course that would never happen. His orders had now been radically changed. Seton and his companions were to be released so that they could carry out their planned assassination of the Scottish war leader. They were to be provided with money, food, weapons and horses. How Corbett was to arrange that was yet to be decided.

He paused. 'Why?' He lifted his head and spoke to the empty room. 'Why didn't the king and Gaveston tell me the truth?' Corbett had been retired, living at Leighton in the depths of Epping Forest, when Seton and his companions had been captured by the old king's troops. He had only recently realised how deeply ran the divisions amongst the Scottish rebels. 'I am certainly learning now,' he murmured. Of course by not telling him, Edward and Gaveston were protecting Seton and his companions as well as the real reason for why they were being taken north. However, Corbett also suspected that the two men knew that he, as Keeper of the Secret Seal and the king's most senior Chancery clerk, would not be too happy assisting self-proclaimed professional assassins. The murder of Bruce sat uncomfortably with Corbett whatever arguments were deployed to justify it. 'I will let you go,' he decided, 'provisioned, armed and mounted, but I will do no more.'

Item: Edmund Darel, a knight whose family hailed from this locality, a man who had cleverly exploited the growing unrest both in England and along the Scottish march. Corbett had conceded nothing to anyone on this, but he knew Darel of old. The northern baron had been a mailed clerk in the Chancery, a comrade of Corbett's until their ways parted. Even as a clerk he had been highly disrespectful of authority, impetuous, and a born meddler in the black arts. Corbett recalled a famous occasion when Darel had returned from some midnight sacrifice in a disused church north of the old city wall. He had been quite subdued, confessing to Corbett how a witch had prophesied that he would die high on a scaffold. He had eventually returned to Northumbria, whilst Corbett had continued in the royal service. Over the years, letters and memoranda came in from the sheriff and other royal officials in the north describing Darel's emergence as a robber baron. 'Charming, ruthless and treacherous,' Corbett whispered. 'Edmund Darel, you take to mischief and mayhem as a hawk to hunting.'

Item: who had informed Darel about their approach and strength? Richolda had admitted that someone in Corbett's group had played the traitor. According to Cacoignes, Darel had been informed that Corbett carried the precious Lily Crown of Scotland. That was preposterous! Corbett did carry gold for the secret business the king had entrusted to him, but only he was aware of that.

Item: Geoffrey Cacoignes, former court squire. He had been sent with Ravinac and others to take the Lily Crown south to Westminster. They were ambushed by black-garbed riders – who were these? Ravinac and Cacoignes had somehow escaped the trap but the rest had been slaughtered. The two survivors reached Tynemouth, where they were given comfort and sustenance by Prior Richard. Ravinac had fallen ill – some sickness of the belly – and Cacoignes had left to reconnoitre the countryside. By the time he returned, Ravinac was delirious and later died. Ravinac was the one who carried the Lily Crown, and according to the meagre evidence, he must have hidden it somewhere around Tynemouth. He certainly did not share his secret with Cacoignes. Why? Because he didn't trust him?

After Ravinac's death, Cacoignes had again gone out to search for a way through the war-torn territories of the north. He had arrived in a coastal village that was attacked by Scottish pirates and had been captured and taken north as a prisoner. Last Yuletide he had managed to escape across the border, only to encounter the power of Edmund Darel. Posing as a wandering swordsman, he had joined the robber baron's mercenaries under a different name. When he heard of Corbett's approach, he decided to flee and brought Corbett valuable information about Darel's plan of attack. He had also petitioned Corbett to join the royal clerk's retinue, determined on going south with him to Westminster. This was logical. Cacoignes was formerly a member of the English court, whilst Corbett could vouch for his good faith. Nevertheless, was he what he claimed to be? Had he spoken the truth?

Item: Darel's assault on their camp quite clearly

demonstrated that there was a spy, a traitor in Corbett's company. But who was this? Was this traitor-spy also a murderer? Roskell's death had been no accident; the Scottish prisoner had eaten and drunk only what the others had. Seton described his dead comrade as quiet and devout, a man immersed in the study of the last things: death, judgement, heaven and hell. Was there a reason why Roskell had been singled out? How had he been poisoned? And how did the murder of such a squire benefit anyone?

Item: the attack on Corbett himself and the others in the chapel of St Chad here at Alnwick Castle. Why? What did the assassin mean by shouting 'Justice and retribution'? The voice could have been man or woman, clear and ringing. It would be very difficult to place it, as like all cries, it would sound different from someone's usual tone of voice. Two bolts had been released, but at whom? Himself, or one of the others? Ranulf? Ap Ythel? Even the Benedictine, Brother Adrian?

Item: the two most recent murders . . .

Corbett paused at the knock at the door.

'Sir Hugh?' Ranulf called. 'I think Lord Henry will soon want us to meet him in the great hall. We need to inspect the corpses.'

Corbett hurriedly strapped on his war belt, grabbed his cloak and joined Ranulf. The day was darkening. Sombre clouds were gathering over the castle, the evening breeze turning cold with a hint of rain. The news of the deaths of the two prisoners had made itself felt both within the castle and beyond. Darel's reputation spoke for itself. He would exact a terrible vengeance on anyone or anything associated with Lord Henry Percy and Alnwick Castle. Peasants from the outlying farms, villages and hamlets were now seeking sanctuary. Carts trundled across the great drawbridge. Bothies and make-shift shelters were being erected in the outer bailey. Catapults, mangonels and ballistas were being prepared, their canvas sheets removed, ropes tested, winches turned, wheels oiled. Rows of glowing braziers and fire bins now ranged across the great yard. Sentries buckled for war patrolled the parapets. Mounted hobelars, the hooves of their horses sparking on the cobbles, prepared to leave; they would spread out across the rough, lonely countryside, searching for any sign of Darel's approach.

'Most people,' Ranulf observed, 'believe Darel will not let those deaths go unavenged. He will be calling up his mercenaries and retainers. I have spoken to Cacoignes. Blanchlands is well furnished with engines of war. Darel will attack.'

Corbett agreed. Darel had lost both his woman and a kinsman. He would have to do something.

They crossed the drawbridge and walked through the inner barbican into the enclosed bailey. Ap Ythel and his archers were on guard before the chapel entrance. The Welsh captain had seized the key, which he produced to open the door. The long, dark chamber of clustering shadows was made all the more macabre by the two corpses lying on sheets, with candles burning around them. Corbett insisted that more be lit. Brother Adrian, who had been waiting patiently outside, also joined them. The monk quietly pattered the office of the dead as he swiftly anointed both corpses; he whispered the words of absolution and bestowed his final benediction.

'Much good it will do,' he murmured.

'I beg your pardon?' Corbett asked.

'Richolda was a member of a coven,' the monk replied. 'Hockley worked for a lord who supported her. One thing magicians and warlocks cannot stand is the Church and its sacraments.' He laughed sharply. 'It's a wonder both corpses don't rise in protest. As they were in life, so in death: their souls will enter the state they have chosen. They are well beyond us now, Sir Hugh. All I can do is commend them to God's mercy, which they will undoubtedly need.'

'Don't we all,' Corbett murmured. He crouched down to inspect the corpses. Ap Ythel beside him whispered how they had fed the remains of the bread and water to a rat caught in the dungeons. The rodent had suffered no ill effects.

'And there was nothing else to eat and drink?'

'Sir Hugh, I have looked at the corpses myself, as well as the cages: nothing!'

Corbett shook his head in wonderment and continued his scrutiny of the cadavers. Both had undoubtedly been poisoned by the same deadly potion fed to Roskell. The faces of the deceased were contorted in agony and liverish in colour; the popping eyes, swollen lips and thickened tongues were testimony to some noxious substance being administered to them.

'But how?' he murmured, getting to his feet. 'A man and a woman, each in a cage hanging over a castle wall, with no tainted food or drink, and it's almost impossible for anyone to get close to them. I've studied some strange deaths, but this . . .'

The door opened and Constable Thurston entered the chapel accompanied by his sister Kathryn.

'Lord Henry wants them buried outside the castle,' the constable slurred, his voice thick from the ale he'd drunk. He shrugged off his sister's warning hand. 'Brother Adrian, you will sing the requiem. Oh, by the way, I was in here earlier,' he continued, 'before Corbett had the chapel sealed. Brother Adrian, you were picking up crossbow bolts; one splintered the rood screen. Was there an attack?'

'A true mystery,' the Benedictine replied tactfully. 'Some soldier perhaps, much the worse for drink,' he added warningly.

'Lord Henry wants to see you now,' Kathryn intervened. 'He needs to discuss what is happening and what the future might hold. We must take careful counsel.'

A short while later, Corbett, Ranulf and Ap Ythel joined Lord Henry around the high table on the dais in the great hall. A long, barn-like structure, with a hammer-beam ceiling, its whitewashed walls decorated with gaily coloured drapes, heavy embroidered arras and clusters of weapons. A majestic mantled hearth had been built into the outside wall with a heavy smoke stack rising up through the roof. Fire boys were busy laying logs in the grate. At Thurston's bawled instruction, the boys, faces and hands black with soot, scampered away like imps out of hell.

The long table on the dais had been covered by a white samite cloth boasting the arms of the Percys picked out in eye-catching colours. Similar insignia displaying the white lion rampant decorated the wall behind Lord Henry's throne-like chair. Corbett and Ranulf were invited to sit on Lord Henry's left, his wife Eleanor to his right. The others invited included Constable Thurston, Lady Kathryn, Brother Adrian, Ap Ythel and Cacoignes, who, Lord Henry declared, waving him to a seat further down the table, knew something about Darel and his wickedness. Brother Adrian intoned grace, blessing both the company and the table.

Once they had taken their seats, food was served. Corbett found it surprisingly delicious: chicken cooked in mushrooms, white wine and herbs, fresh bread from the castle bakery and a large common dish of vegetables chopped, diced and heavily soaked in a spiced sauce. Jugs of wine, both red and white, as well as pots of local ale were placed on the table. People ate and drank, helping themselves, horn spoons busy, knives cutting at the soft white chicken meat. The conversation was desultory as servants busied themselves around. The fire boys were summoned back and the great hearth blazed with flame. The captains of the various watches came and went, reporting to Lord Henry how everything was secure against sudden and stealthy attack.

Once the meal was over, Lord Henry, who had sat morose and taciturn throughout, invited the company to stools and benches before the great hearth. The hall was turning cold and the warmth was welcome.

'How in heaven's name was that done?' Lord Henry began harshly, his hard, craggy face lit by the dancing flames of the fire. 'How were two prisoners, kept in cages hanging over my castle walls either side of the barbican, poisoned with the same potion? Now I understand they ate and drank nothing noxious before they were imprisoned. Yes?' He did not wait for an answer. 'They were given no other sustenance except a waterskin and a small loaf of rye bread. What was left of that, I understand,' he pointed at Ap Ythel, 'was given to a caged rat hungry to eat and nothing happened. Is that correct?'

'It is, my lord,' Ap Ythel replied.

'Constable Thurston,' Corbett demanded, 'did the guards feed the prisoners?'

'No,' he slurred. 'They did not. True, castle folk came to look at them, but they were not friendly. They came to curse the prisoners and hurl abuse at them.'

'So what actually happened?'

'We don't know,' Thurston replied. 'Prisoners in the cages moan, they shake the bars. It's very difficult to see what is happening even if you climb onto the fighting platform. In fact, what eventually provoked the interest of the guards was the complete silence from both cages.' He breathed out noisily. 'The rest you know.'

Corbett stared around. The castle hall had grown darker. Rain pattered against the shutters, which rattled as the gusts of wind grew stronger. The fire was now roaring, the flames leaping up around the logs as if they had a life of their own. Nevertheless, he suppressed a shiver. He felt that something sinister and dangerous was slithering through this fortress. The rest of the company also seemed to sense an unease.

'There is a killer, an assassin loose in our castle,' Brother Adrian abruptly declared, and before Corbett could intervene, the Benedictine described the attack in the chapel.

'What does that prove?' Lady Eleanor snapped. 'We know there is an assassin here, but this trouble did not begin until you arrived, Sir Hugh. You brought Hockley and that witch into Alnwick. Richolda was a true daughter of hell; where she went, chaos always followed.'

'No, my lady,' Ranulf retorted, 'the trouble did not begin with us. It began when Edmund Darel attacked the king's special envoy, dispatched under the great seal to this fortress of Alnwick. Sir Hugh is the Crown's most senior clerk, travelling here under the royal standard. We resisted and defeated Darel's treacherous attack. We captured two prisoners, who should have been kept more safely in some cell or dungeon rather than in cages hoisted over the castle walls.'

'Be that as it may,' Corbett tactfully intervened, warning Ranulf with his eyes not to say too much, 'the die is cast, the cup spilt, the wine wasted and the goblet cracked. Richolda and Hockley are foully slain. Why, how and by whom, we do not know. Master Cacoignes,' he turned to the former courtier, 'what will Darel do now?'

'Sir Hugh, I suspect you know the answer. He will attack. He has to. Darel protected Richolda and her coven, the Black Chesters. Richolda was undoubtedly his lover, his doxy, his paramour.' Cacoignes sipped at his wine. 'Darel was very much under her influence, though remember, I was never allowed into his place of secrets, Blanchlands' inner bailey. Of course,' he put his goblet down and spread his hands towards the flames, 'Hockley was also his kinsman. Darel will have to demonstrate to the other wolves that he is fierce and will let no insult or injury pass.'

'There's more, isn't there?' Corbett turned to Lord Henry. 'Darel will wish to test your defences here. You, my lord, have taken over Alnwick. You are busy fortifying this castle. You are set to become the most powerful presence this side of the Scottish march. So yes,' he sipped from his goblet, 'Darel will attack and we must prepare a proper defence.' Corbett took a further sip. 'One thing does concern me. We have remarked on how you are strengthening Alnwick. His Grace the king watches developments, Darel too; but Robert the Bruce must also be aware of what you are doing.'

'And?'

'Bruce is aided by a number of redoubtable captains led by the likes of Randolph and Douglas—'

'Sweet lord,' Cacoignes intervened, 'I know what you are going to say, Sir Hugh.'

'Reflect on Bruce's history,' Corbett insisted. 'Time and again he and his captains have captured castles the length and breadth of Scotland by stealth and sheer cunning. Alnwick may be a mighty fortress, but I do urge you to take the most careful precautions.'

The following morning Lord Henry dispatched more mounted hobelars to scour the countryside around Alnwick. Corbett kept revising and reviewing what he had written whilst keeping a sharp eye on what was happening in this bleak, formidable place. He quietly admitted to himself that he was becoming increasingly uneasy, deeply uncomfortable. He certainly missed Maeve and the children, the green softness of the woods, fields and meadowlands of his manor at Leighton. The world he now lived in was different. Alnwick was truly grim, a house of war set in desolate countryside, wild open moorland where already the very first hints of winter were making themselves felt.

His discomfort deepened as he walked around the castle, a coldness that touched his soul and set his nerves on edge. Alnwick was preparing for war. Soldiers scurried here and there; carts and braziers and all the impedimenta of battle were being readied. The prospect of an imminent and ferociously bloody assault darkened Corbett's mood. Yet there was more. He also believed he was being watched, followed, even hunted by a malevolent presence. Ap Ythel felt the same. Accordingly, when Corbett decided to broach the next item of secret business, he decided to ride out as if helping Lord Henry and his garrison in their vigilance against attack. He, Ap Ythel, Ranulf and the one-eyed bearded archer thundered out through the main barbican and onto the wind-tossed moorland. Corbett led his party along a trackway going deeper into the heathland until they reached an outcrop of ancient rock, battered by storms but still displaying archaic signs and insignia carved by tribes long gone.

'We can watch any approach from here,' he declared, dismounting and telling the others to do the same. They hobbled their horses and Corbett gathered some bracken. In the shadow of one of the rocks he lit a fire, feeding it with twigs until it burnt merrily. They shared out a linen parcel of food – bread, dried salted bacon and some of the delicious ewe's cheese – whilst passing round a wineskin of what Ranulf called 'Lord Henry's best'. For a while they ate and drank in silence.

'Ranulf!'

'Sir Hugh?'

Corbett pointed at the one-eyed archer, his beard and moustache all tangled, his shabby hood pulled across his close-cropped head. 'Peter,' he declared. 'Remove your hood.'

The archer, mittened fingers all dirty, nails ragged and broken, did so.

'Look at him, Ranulf. What do you see?'

The Clerk of the Green Wax stared hard. The archer grinned, took off the eye patch and rubbed at his blackened teeth with his forefinger. Ranulf peered closer and gasped.

'St Michael and all his angels!' he breathed. 'My lord Gaveston! Peter Gaveston, close friend of the king, Earl of Cornwall.'

'And now an honest archer.' Gaveston grinned.

'Ranulf, if I could deceive you,' his voice changed from lilting Welsh to the harsh Norman French of the court, 'then I can deceive anyone.'

'Of course, of course,' Ranulf breathed. 'You have a great gift for mimicry, my lord, which is one of the reasons—'

'The other great lords hate me.' Gaveston finished the sentence. He leaned forward, picking at his now whitening teeth. 'I not only beat them at the tournament, Ranulf, but mimic and mock their mannerisms, which is why,' he immediately changed to a nasal twang, imitating the voice of Thomas, Earl of Lancaster, so accurately that Corbett laughed, 'they have persecuted me to the death.'

'Sir Hugh,' Ranulf glanced at Corbett and Ap Ythel, 'why didn't you tell me?'

'Truthfulness and honesty,' Corbett replied caustically, 'do seem to be in very short measure and, I confess, I am party to some of it.' He gestured at Gaveston. 'On that issue I have talked to Seton and Sterling. They have revealed their true purpose.'

'Hugh, Hugh.' Gaveston leaned forward and gripped Corbett's shoulder, shaking it gently before letting his hand fall away. 'Hugh, His Grace and I know your conscience is much more delicate than ours. All we are doing is releasing the dead Red Comyn's retainers to pursue their own justifiable blood feud as well as weaken this kingdom's greatest enemy, the usurper Robert the Bruce.'

'And this!' Ranulf exclaimed. 'Why wasn't I—'

'Lest we made a mistake,' Corbett replied, 'like I nearly did on so many occasions. Think, Ranulf. Because you didn't know, I couldn't discuss the truth with you, sure protection against any spy or assassin – and it would seem,' he added bitterly, 'there are enough of those around us.'

'I was party to the secret,' Ap Ythel declared. 'I had to be if my lord was to join my lovely lads.'

'We thought it best,' Corbett added. 'Who would look for the elegant Peter Gaveston, Earl of Cornwall, amongst a cohort of Welsh archers?'

'No one would ever guess,' Ap Ythel agreed. 'My lord Gaveston joined us as a distant kinsman in search of employment after a hunting accident in the king's forest of Caerphilly. I advised my lord to have his head completely shaved, grow a veritable bush of a dirty beard and become used to an eye patch. My lord can mimic like any mummer, but I advised him to talk little. He knows some of the Welsh tongue and he has certainly acted the part. No one has even commented on his presence.'

'However, I am not yet out of the thicket.' Gaveston rubbed his eyes. 'The other great lords want me exiled. If they seized me, they would impose a more permanent solution: swift and sudden death. Their spies and scru-tineers are as thick as fleas on a mangy dog along the London quaysides, as well as those of the Cinque Ports such as Dover and Sandwich and all other harbours to both the east and the west. The main highways in and out of London are the haunt of Judas men who hope to earn the bounty Lancaster has posted on my head. The royal palaces of Windsor, King's Langley, even as far west as Gloucester and Bristol, have their own cohort of silent watchers.'

'My lord Gaveston is easily recognisable,' Corbett declared. 'So,' he drew a deep breath, 'we decided on this. My lord becomes a common archer. We remove him from the dangers of London and bring him north. We have one true ally here: Prior Richard at Tynemouth. The priory owns a cog, *The Golden Dove*, a two-hundred-ton merchantman that does good trade with the northern kingdoms. If we are successful and reach Tynemouth, we shall shelter there. My lord Gaveston will board *The Golden Dove* and be safe. What we have to do is to sustain the pretence. If Lord Henry or Darel knew the truth, they would seize my lord, hold him hostage and probably sell him to Lancaster.'

Corbett paused. Somewhere out in the moorland, a fox yipped and there was a scream as if some creature was caught in its death throes. He looked up. A curlew screeched noisily above them, rising and falling on the buffeting breeze.

'Of course, we have other business in Tynemouth.' He turned back to his companions. 'Ravinac and Cacoignes were entrusted with the Lily Crown of Scotland. Ravinac apparently did not trust Cacoignes, a matter we will have to return to. Anyway, to cut to the chase, we believe the Lily Crown is hidden some-where in or around Tynemouth Priory. If we reach there, we must question the prior closely. Our king would love to seize such a sacred relic.' He wiped his face with his hand. 'I thought it was safest to tell you all this out here in the wilderness. My lord Gaveston, we will meet occasionally at Alnwick. You must continue to act the part of Ap Ythel's bodyguard or stableman . . .'

Corbett broke off and rose to his feet. He climbed up onto the rocks and stared around. 'Nothing,' he declared, gazing out over the heathland. 'Nothing but desolation on every side,' he smiled, 'in more ways than one.'

He climbed down again. 'The challenges we face are great,' he continued. 'We must maintain the pretence that we are here to negotiate over the hostages, but that is a deception that might soon wear thin. Once it does, speculation will grow about the real reason for our long and arduous journey north. Already someone has misinformed Darel that we hold the Lily Crown. We do carry gold, but the story about the crown is pure fable. Even so, such a possibility may well attract the attention of every marauder and wolfshead along the Scottish march. We must be vigilant, watch and plot. So, let us return . . .'

Once back in Alnwick, Corbett became even more wary and suspicious and ordered Ranulf and Chanson to be on their guard. The clerk of the stables promised he would mix with the other grooms and ostlers and report anything untoward. Corbett impressed upon him the importance of this and warned him not to become too absorbed in his love for horses. Corbett himself kept to his chamber in the Abbot's Tower. Now and again he would invite Ranulf to join him in the castle buttery or kitchens for something to eat and drink.

On the second day after his return from the moorland, Corbett decided to write a letter to Maeve in the hope that he could ask some journeyman or one of Percy's messengers to take the letter either directly to Leighton or at least leave it in the Secret Chancery offices at Westminster. He remained distracted. He knew he had heard or seen something here at Alnwick that sparked memories of the past, yet as he confessed to Ranulf, he could not for the life of him recollect what it was. He continued to feel uneasy. The prospect of attack was imminent. Lord Henry had changed his mind: the corpses of Richolda and Hockley would not be given swift burial but crudely embalmed and used as possible tokens of negotiation with Darel. They had been sealed in chests in the death house, each crammed with herbs and spices to offset the effects of putrefaction and corruption.

Corbett was also growing concerned that on two occasions he had heard someone moving in the stairwell outside, yet when he unlocked the door and drew back the bolts, there was nothing but dust whirled up by the breeze. He eventually decided not to lock and bolt the door, but to keep it closed with a primed arbalest next to him and his war belt within easy reach.

On that particular afternoon, he was about to read the office of the day. Once again he heard the sound, a scuffling as if something was being pressed between the bottom of the door and the cracked paving stones. Curious, he rose and walked slowly forwards. As he stared down, he noticed that the stem-like tube of an oilskin had been pushed under the door, the liquid pouring out of it clear and rather thick; a lighted taper was then thrust through, followed by another. Corbett hurriedly stepped back as the floor between himself and the door erupted in a seething sheet of flame. He had been half asleep, his wits dulled, but now he was alert to the danger facing him. Another oilskin was forced through and a second sheet of angry flame flared greedily, licking at the ancient door as well as the dry carpet of tightly woven cordage. The window behind him was too narrow to climb through, and the heat was growing intense as the fire assumed a life of its own.

Corbett shouted the usual cry for help, '*Aux secours! Aux secours!*' He heard shouts outside, but the smoke was now billowing around him. He hurried across to the bed and pulled off the mattress, slitting it and shaking the bone-dry sawdust within onto the fire, which undoubtedly weakened its force. He grabbed his cloak, war belt and chancery satchel, which were thankfully close, then snatched up a blanket and, taking the jug of cold water from the lavarium, drenched the heavy fabric and wrapped it around him. He stared at the leaping wall of flame between himself and the door.

'Master?' Ranulf was now outside.

'No, don't open the door!' Corbett shouted. 'It will fan the fire.'

He grasped his chancery satchel tighter, took a deep breath and, head down, lunged through the flames towards the door. The heat scorched his skin, and he could feel his hair frizzling under the sparks, but, using the edge of the water-soaked blanket, he grasped the latch, pushed it down and pulled the door open. Coughing and gasping, clothing and hair singed, he staggered out into the stairwell, where Ranulf and Chanson tended to him with cloths soaked in icy water. Corbett slumped onto a window ledge. Other servants now appeared with buckets of sand and tubs of water.

Ranulf grasped Corbett's arm and almost pushed him up to his own chamber, where they had stored their saddle bags and panniers. Corbett stripped and washed himself at the lavarium. Lord Henry and Arnulf, the castle leech, came up. The latter was so drunk, Lord Henry dismissed him and sent for the constable and his sister. Kathryn Thurston, as Corbett later declared, proved more skilled and knowledgeable than any physician. She brought salves and ointments, tending gently to Corbett's injuries, though she avoided his gaze as she chattered about the dangers of fire. Corbett didn't explain, assuring her and Lord Henry that the conflagration was an accident. Kathryn Thurston appeared to accept this and continued her ministrations, though Corbett could see that Lord Henry remained highly suspicious. Once they had gone, Constable Thurston arrived to assure Corbett that the fire was now doused and that the royal clerk could move to fresh chambers above the great hall.

'No accident,' Corbett declared once their visitors had left.

'No accident, Sir Hugh,' Ranulf agreed. 'I saw the smoke. I heard your shouts and found the two oilskins forced under the door. Both must have been bulging. The assassin simply unstoppered them, pushed the necks under the door and pressed on the full sacks, squirting oil into the chamber. A lighted taper then followed, and . . .' Ranulf pulled a face, 'the rest you know. I pulled out the empty sacks, or what's left of them; you'll find them in the corner of the stairwell. Master, your assailant could have been anyone, and it was so swiftly done. I was asleep when the alarm was raised, and of course, once it was, people came milling around so it was hard to distinguish anyone acting suspiciously. Anyway, master, are you hurt?'

'My dignity more than anything else,' Corbett replied ruefully. He stretched out both hands, turning the wrists, before dabbing at the soreness on his cheekbones and touching his singed eyebrows and hair. 'Kathryn Thurston's salve will keep them clean. I will heal soon enough.' He got to his feet.

'Did you lose much?'

'Thank God our panniers are here. My Secret Chancery coffers are sealed and held in Lord Henry's arca in the secure chamber beneath the great hall: so, there's no lasting damage.'

He left the room and stood outside in the stairwell. Once Ranulf followed him out, Corbett closed the door and imagined how the assassin must have struck at him in his chamber below. He would have crept up the stairs with the two oilskins carefully concealed before pushing them swiftly under the door. Corbett glanced over his shoulder at the squat tallow candle burning in its socket fastened to the wall. A similar light flared outside his own chamber. The assassin would have lit the tapers, pushed them under the door and slipped away. It would not have taken long. Moreover, he might have hoped that Corbett had locked and bolted the door, making it even more difficult for him to break through the flames and out of that fiery chamber.

'Even more so,' Corbett spoke aloud, 'if I had been in a deep sleep.' He clasped Ranulf by the shoulder. 'Thank God, and thank you, my friend, but who is my mysterious assailant?'

'The same person who murdered Richolda, Hockley and Roskell?'

Corbett reopened the chamber door, gesturing at his companion to follow. 'I do not think so,' he declared, closing the door behind them. 'Our assailant here in this tower and in the chapel deals in weapons: crossbow bolts and burning oil. The slayer of Roskell, Richolda and Hockley is a most venomous poisoner.' He scratched his chin. 'I do wonder if we have two assassins lurking in Alnwick, each with their own murderous mission.'

There was a knock on the door and Ap Ythel came in, followed by Gaveston acting the one-eyed shuffling archer.

'Ap Ythel, what is it?' Corbett asked, sensing the man's ill ease.

'Sir Hugh, I heard what happened in your chamber. Castle people say it was an accident.'

'Castle people do not know what they are talking about,' Ranulf snapped. 'It was attempted murder, a sin that did not reach its full foul flowering. Ap Ythel, what is the matter?'

'Show him,' Gaveston murmured. 'Show him what was waiting for you in your chamber.'

Ap Ythel lifted the bag he was carrying and emptied the caltrops onto the floor: small metal balls with a profusion of razor-sharp spikes at least two inches long. Anyone who stepped on these murderous miniature traps would shred their feet, stumble and stagger onto others. Caltrops were often deployed against horsemen, strewn along some trackway or deep in long grass. The device could also be used against the unwary stumbling into a darkened chamber or one where the floor was covered in straw. The wounds inflicted would be deadly; the shock alone might kill, whilst any injury would last for life.

Ap Ythel dropped the sack. 'I left my door unlocked, but who has a grievance against a poor archer?' He was clearly upset. 'Sir Hugh, remember I came with you on the day Berwick was sacked some fifteen years ago. You were correct: Berwick was a hideous sin.'

'My friend,' Corbett clapped the Welshman on the shoulder, 'what is the matter?'

'Sometimes I think that anyone involved in Berwick's destruction must pay for it, or make reparation. The old king sowed dragon seeds in Scotland and the harvest is harrowing. If I had my way, I would collect our horses and ride south. Ah well.' Ap Ythel slumped down on a stool, his usually nut-brown face pallid. 'I don't like Alnwick, Sir Hugh. Too close to Berwick and its ghosts. I am uneasy. Anyway, I always place a linen string across the threshold of any room when anxiety nags my soul. After the attack in the chapel, I was even more cautious than usual.'

'And the string had been broken?'

'Yes, Sir Hugh, it certainly had. So why?' Ap Ythel demanded. 'Why this, why now, why here?' He took a deep breath. 'I am going to keep an eye on Cacoignes; I think he is a harbinger of ill fortune, wouldn't you agree?'

As if in answer to Ap Ythel's question, the tocsin bell began its sombre pealing. At first slow, then much swifter as other bells took up the warning. They hurried down into the cold, greying afternoon. Constable Thurston, now dressed in half-armour, hastened across, his sister trailing behind deep in conversation with Cacoignes. Thurston pointed to the crowd gathering at the foot of the steps to one of the towers.

'Sterling and the squire Richard Mallet,' he gasped. 'They have a chamber on the stairwell of the Falconer's Tower. My task is to keep a sharp eye on the hostages.' Clearly agitated, he turned and hurried towards the tower. Corbett hastened after him.

'For heaven's sake, Thurston, what has happened?'

'I can't find him,' the constable replied.

'Can't find who?' Corbett demanded.

'Seton, Lord Alexander Seton.'

'But this is your castle; you should know every nook and cranny.'

'It's Lord Henry's castle,' Thurston retorted. 'I was looking for Seton just to check on him. I couldn't find him so I went to his chamber, but it's locked and bolted from the inside. Perhaps all three of them are there, but no one has seen them.'

The constable drew his sword, forcing his way through the castle folk staring at the hobelars who'd gathered in the main stairwell armed with a hand-held battering ram. Thurston ordered them up the steps to break down the door of the chamber that the Scots shared. Corbett immediately intervened, warning the soldiers not to enter the room until he had inspected it carefully. Lord Henry and Lady Eleanor also swept across to join the group, Percy's sour-faced wife muttering how the royal clerks had brought only chaos and trouble to their castle. Corbett ignored the insult. He and his two companions went into the stairwell and stood listening as the pounding on the door above began, the soldiers finding it difficult to wield the battering ram in such a narrow, cramped space. Corbett was relieved that Gaveston had silently and prudently slipped away once Thurston had appeared. He prayed that the pretence surrounding the royal favourite would remain a secret and that his disguise would hold until he was safely aboard *The Golden Dove*.

'They are dead, aren't they?' Ranulf whispered. 'Whoever is in that chamber, master, they're dead.'

'Yes, Ranulf,' Corbett replied. 'I suspect we will find corpses, God have mercy on them. The storm is truly gathering. Our assassin is moving swiftly, like a famished fox in a hen coop. He swerves, twists and kills whenever he can.'

The pounding was now intense, the crashing echoing through the tower like the roll of war drums. Corbett looked up the steps and noticed piles of dust and shards of timber and stone. He turned and asked Lord Henry what was happening further up the tower, receiving the surly answer that the stairwells above were being repaired: the brickwork had to be pointed and better guard rails fastened for the stair ropes.

A loud crash followed by a cheer brought Corbett back inside. Beckoning to Ap Ythel and Ranulf, he hastened up the stairs and through the press of sweat-soaked soldiers. The door to the chamber had cracked off on both sides, its leather hinges shattered, the lock and bolt clearly ruptured. The chamber beyond was dark and smelly. Corbett walked carefully forward. One of the soldiers offered a cresset torch. Corbett told him to wait. He first unbarred and opened the window shutters, the greying light poured through to illuminate the two corpses. Sterling lay close to the bed; Mallet slumped from a stool.

Corbett told the soldier to bring in the torch whilst Ranulf and Ap Ythel moved to guard the doorway. He crouched down to inspect the corpses. The flesh was cold, the limbs hardening; the faces of the two dead hostages reflected the same gruesome horror as Roskell and the other victims of poison. Corbett noticed the liverish skin, the shock-filled, startled eyes, the discoloured lips and thickening tongue and that filthy cream-like mucus that had dribbled down their chins.

'Sir Hugh?' Lord Henry pushed his way into the chamber.

'Poison, my lord, just like the rest. I would be grateful if one of your guards could bring up a caged rat. No one should come into this chamber until I am finished.' Corbett held a hand up. 'Lord Henry, I can see you are going to object, but we are hunting an assassin. Alnwick is your fief, but I carry the king's commission. Three hostages released into my care have been foully murdered. As for the fourth, Seton, God knows where he is, just as God only knows who is responsible for all of this. I need to examine this chamber most scrupulously.'

'The corpses should be anointed and blessed.' Brother Adrian now stood in the doorway.

'Do your business!' Lord Henry snapped, and stomped off.

Corbett asked everyone except Ranulf and Ap Ythel to leave, repeating his request for the caged rat to be brought up immediately. He then rose, gesturing at Brother Adrian to administer extreme unction. He went and sat on the edge of the bed, moodily watching the monk quickly anoint and bless both corpses. A soldier came up with a cage. Inside it was a large brown rodent with a humped back, long tail, scrabbling claws and constantly twitching nose, its ugly head going back as it beat its sharp teeth against the mesh of the cage, squealing in protest at being held captive. The man-at-arms also informed Corbett that Lord Henry had ordered a thorough search of the castle for the missing hostage Seton.

'Perhaps he is dead as well, murdered like his comrades,' Brother Adrian declared, putting the sacred oils back into the panniers he carried. He gestured at both corpses. 'Poor men, to die in exile. I heard Roskell's confession on our journey north. I shrived him, gave absolution for his petty offences. I felt so sorry for the poor soul. Sir Hugh, Roskell was homesick, tired of fighting. He talked wistfully of a lovely auburn-haired wife. These two were probably no different. They were murdered, yes?'

'Poisoned, certainly,' Corbett agreed. 'But of course the potion could be anything.'

'Lord Henry does not have a library,' Brother Adrian murmured. 'At our house at Tynemouth Priory we have a shelf of Palladius's works, including a full copy of his *Treatise Concerning the Virtues of Herbs*, but there's nothing here.'

'Tell me,' Corbett demanded, getting to his feet, 'would the castle leech hold such noxious philtres, potions and powders?'

'Possibly, though Master Arnulf is always conspicuous by his absence. He's a rare sight indeed!'

'Yes, I wondered why Lord Henry didn't summon him,' said Ranulf.

'That's because Arnulf is a born toper,' Brother Adrian replied. 'At times he's so drunk, he can hardly stand. I suppose you could question him when he is sober, which is about as rare as a warm January day. But there's no one amongst your company, Sir Hugh, skilled in physic?'

'On our journey north,' Ap Ythel declared, 'I tended to injuries both human and horse. My real skill is with animals and I apply that to the cuts, bruises and injuries of my comrades. Sir Hugh, we do have a medicine chest, but Master Arnulf should have a better store.'

'Ask him when you see him,' Brother Adrian declared. 'Sir Hugh, I must go. I give you my blessing.' He sketched a cross in their direction and promptly left.

Corbett immediately asked Ranulf and Ap Ythel to scour the chamber for any food, be it a morsel or a crumb. He collected the cups, water and wine jugs and emptied their contents into a bowl. Ranulf and Ap Ythel brought what scraps of food they'd found on a platter. Corbett scraped these into the bowl too, mixing them with his dagger before emptying the entire contents through the broad gaps in the mesh of the rat cage, ladling the scraps out with the tip of his knife. The rodent squealed and snouted at the morsels before swiftly nibbling at them. Corbett watched fascinated. The rat was apparently famished and made short work of the bread and meat soaked in water and wine. Occasionally it would pause to wash itself before returning to what it must regard as a banquet. Eventually it lay sated, half asleep, fat belly quivering.

Corbett decided to search the chamber, looking for anything suspicious, yet the two Scottish prisoners had been held hostage for years and their possessions were meagre in the extreme. He also inspected the window and door; both had been firmly closed and locked, and he could not discover anything suspicious or untoward. Time passed. Corbett gently kicked the cage and the rat moved sluggishly, though it showed no ill effects. In fact, now roused, its hunger satisfied, it became more determined than ever to escape. Corbett asked Ap Ythel to take it out and release it.

'It has done good service,' he declared. 'It can take its chances with the castle cats.'

Once Ap Ythel returned, Corbett asked the guard in the stairwell to leave as he swiftly summarised what had happened.

'Our assassin, the traitor, if he is one and the same person, acted with impunity. He deals out judgement and death as if he is the Lord High Satan. I was nearly burnt alive in my chamber. Ap Ythel here narrowly escaped hideous injury. Crossbow bolts have been loosed against us. We eluded death. Sterling and Mallet were not so fortunate.'

'Sir Hugh, Sir Hugh!' A man-at-arms came hurrying up the steps. 'Sir Hugh,' he repeated, 'Arnulf the leech has come to collect the corpses for the death house.'

'And their burial?'

The soldier took off his conical helmet and wiped the sweat from his bewhiskered face. 'Lord Henry has yet to decide what to do with the corpses of the witch Richolda and her familiar Hockley. Brother Adrian is to celebrate the requiem for the dead Scots tomorrow just after the Jesus Mass. As for burial, there is a cemetery beyond the castle walls.'

Corbett opened his purse and took out a coin, pushing it into the soldier's hand. 'You were on guard in this tower?'

'Oh yes. I know all its ways and what happens here. Lord Henry likes that. So yes, I was on guard here, I watched the Scotsmen.'

Corbett listened intently; he sometimes found the northern burr too clipped and swift to follow.

'Did you talk to the hostages?'

'Oh no, I just guarded this tower. I watched them come and go. I didn't talk to them; I don't think they wanted to talk to me. In the brief time they were with us, they kept to themselves.' He shrugged. 'They were soldiers, very little different from those I serve with.'

'Did anyone visit them? I mean,' Corbett amended, 'anyone of significance? Lord Henry? Brother Adrian? Constable Thurston or any of those who accompanied us here?'

'Sir Hugh, I have been on guard since daybreak. The only people who entered the tower were masons and labourers. The two hostages only left their chamber to use the garderobe, which is on the stairwell above; it has also been used by myself and others with no ill effect. Ah, here he is.'

Corbett and the guard stepped back as Arnulf the leech, nose red, bleary eyes blinking, lurched up the steps followed by four men carrying stretchers. Corbett nodded at the leech, slipped a further coin into the guard's hand then gestured at Ranulf and Ap Ythel to join him. They left the tower and hurried across the bailey through the inner barbican and up to Corbett's spacious chamber above the dining hall; a well-furnished room with a broad bed, aumbries, chests and coffers, table and desk, stools and a chair. The walls were covered in coloured cloths; dark-green cord matting rather than rushes covered the floor. The chamber was warm, heated by braziers as well as by the chimney stack that ran up from the great hearth in the hall below.

'Lord Henry is making amends,' Corbett murmured, taking off his cloak, war belt and boots before indicating that his two companions should join him around the brazier.

Corbett crossed to a table. He smelt the wine jug, tasted its contents carefully and filled three goblets. Once comfortable, he silently toasted the stark black crucifix nailed against the far wall. 'May Sterling and Mallet be allowed into the peace of Christ,' he murmured. 'But how in God's name were they sent there?'

'This is beyond me,' Ap Ythel grated. 'I see the problem. Two healthy men, soldiers, fairly young and vigorous, locked and bolted themselves in their chamber. They had food and drink, but that's not tainted. Apparently they only left to visit the garderobe on the stairwell above. They can hardly have taken poison there. Both used the jakes at different times and the same garderobe was visited by others.' The Welshman smiled bleakly. 'Hardly the place to eat or drink, be it tainted or not.'

'And according to the guard – and I am sure he spoke the truth – the only people who went into the tower were labourers. So,' Corbett continued slowly, 'how did the assassin break into that chamber and persuade, force or deceive those two Scots to imbibe a most noxious poison, men who were already rendered vigilant and careful by the murder of their comrade Roskell?'

Corbett sipped at his wine as Ranulf rose to answer a knock on the door. He opened it and Gaveston, patch over his eye, hood pulled across his head, his face grimy with dirt, shuffled into the room. Only when Ranulf locked and bolted the door did the royal favourite show his true self; he removed the patch, kicked off the scuffed boots, pulled back the hood and loosened the shabby war belts around his waist and across his chest.

'My lord?'

'Sir Hugh, they have searched high and low for Seton but there is not even a trace. Stranger still, no horse is missing from the stables, whilst every gate is closely guarded because of Darel. Lord Henry has also dispatched riders to scour the countryside, but Seton appears to have vanished like mist on a sunny morning.' Gaveston stretched his hands towards the brazier. 'Cacoignes, Geoffrey Cacoignes. I think it's time you shared more secrets with our two friends here.'

'Is he a danger?' Ranulf demanded. 'Does he recognise you, my lord?'

'No, thank God. Cacoignes was a squire in the prince's household but one I had very few dealings with. Moreover, life moves swiftly. I did not recognise him when he joined our party, whilst I doubt very much whether he would recognise me as the king's own brother.' Gaveston's voice had turned bitter. 'However, he is a danger, a man who cannot be trusted. A squire sent north on king's business, which floundered and disappeared in a mist of mystery. Cacoignes has joined us but there are questions he must answer, even though it's going to be difficult to bring him to judgement.' Gaveston rubbed his face. 'It will be good to shave, to wash, to be myself again. Sir Hugh, tell them what we know.'

Corbett sat listening to the sounds of the castle. 'Something is going to happen,' he murmured. 'I can sense it. I will be glad when we leave here.'

'For Tynemouth?'

'Yes, Ranulf, Tynemouth.' He paused. 'We do not know what truly happened to the Lily Crown. We can only conjecture on the little we have been told: that Ravinac may have hid the treasure somewhere in or around Tynemouth Priory before he fell ill of a violent fever.'

'Poison?'

'Perhaps. He was definitely delirious, or became so, but he still had his wits about him. He deliberately misled Cacoignes, informing him how he had hidden the Lily Crown in some caves in the cliffs close to Tynemouth. However, Cacoignes was captured by pirates and taken prisoner into Scotland. He eventually escaped and decided that the best way to survive was to join Darel's comitatus under a different name. I can only speculate on how he would have been received, returning empty-handed to London. I am not sure whether he would even have been recognised, his appearance has changed so much.'

'He would also have stayed in the north,' Gaveston intervened, 'to be close to Tynemouth; he hoped to return to the priory and discover the true whereabouts of the Lily Crown.'

'So why did he betray Darel and join us?' Ranulf demanded.

'First,' Corbett replied, 'Darel probably still doesn't know the full extent of Cacoignes' betrayal. Second, Cacoignes does not want to be associated with an attack on a royal envoy. Third, he is an opportunist, a cunning one who now waits to see what will happen. He is safer with us than he is with Darel. Remember, in theory Cacoignes has done no wrong; his quarrel with Ravinac has no witnesses, whilst he has acted loyally in warning us about Darel's intended attack.'

'So if the worst comes to the worst,' Ranulf said slowly, 'he can join the English court and portray himself as a hero worthy of commendation.' He grinned. 'He certainly is an opportunist. But Ravinac and the Lily Crown?'

'Ravinac died of a fever at Tynemouth. Prior Richard tended to him, administering extreme unction. Ravinac apparently told him that he had hidden the Lily Crown between heaven and earth, in God's own graveyard. The good prior considered him to be delirious but passed that message on to us.'

'Which is another reason,' Ranulf laughed sharply, 'why we are going to Tynemouth.'

'Yes,' Corbett agreed. 'We will search the priory for the Lily Crown. Our king would use that sacred treasure in any negotiation with Bruce and his coven.' He leaned over and gently clapped Ranulf on the shoulder. 'My friend, we came north for so many reasons. Some of them were told to me, some of them were not. I decided to let things develop. The less people know – and that includes you – the better it is. We cannot afford to make a mistake. It is imperative that no one discovers that my Lord Gaveston is one of our party.'

'So when do we leave?' Gaveston demanded.

'My lord,' Corbett gestured around, 'we are trapped here in Alnwick. True, we could ride fast to the coast and shelter behind the priory walls. As you know, Tynemouth is strongly fortified, a place of refuge. The problem is,' he added wearily, 'if we leave, God knows who would pursue us. Lord Henry? Darel? The Scots? Let us wait for a while. In the meantime, we must remain vigilant against the assassin who hunts us, who lurks deep in the shadows waiting for his opportunity.'

PART THREE

'In this way the whole of Scotland is now lost and the land of Northumbria lies waste.'

Life of Edward II

D arkness had fallen when once again the tocsin bell tolled high on the walls, summoning the garrison to arms. Corbett and his companions joined Lord Henry on the parapet above the gatehouse. Corbett stared in amazement at the ghostly apparition on the broad trackway sweeping down to Alnwick's main entrance. Six black-cloaked, cowled figures, their faces visored, stood around a handcart, now sloped and rested so watchers along the walls could clearly see the corpse sprawled there. Each of the macabre figures held a fiery cresset torch, the flames whipped to a fury by the strong night breeze. Similar torches had been fastened to the sides of the handcart so the face of the corpse could be seen in all its horror.

The wind shifted. Corbett gagged on the fetid, rank stench of corruption. Ap Ythel, sharp of eye, murmured how he was sure the corpse was that of the Scotsman Roskell whom they'd buried beneath a makeshift cross in the glade where they had been attacked. He asked if he and his bowmen could loose, though he added that the sinister visitors might just be beyond the range of their war bows.

Any talk of attack was silenced as midnight figures swarmed out of the darkness, two of them carrying torches. A third held a pole with a white cloth nailed to it – the conventional way of arranging a truce, though Corbett noticed that the usual cross or crucifix was missing. The three dark-dwellers approached the edge of the moat opposite the drawbridge. The torchbearers clustered close to the pole-carrying figure in the centre, bathing her in pools of light so that when the woman pulled back her hood, cries and exclamations echoed from the walls.

'Richolda!' Lord Henry exclaimed. 'Richolda the witch. But I have her corpse in my death house!'

Corbett watched intently. The woman lifted her face and the clerk suppressed a shiver. It was indeed Richolda come again. The witch-woman pointed back at the gruesome, grisly corpse clearly illuminated by the dancing torchlight.

'As he is,' she cried, 'so shall ye be! You are warned.'

'She has been brought here to shock, to frighten and to terrify,' Ranulf murmured, 'and,' he pointed further along the wall, 'she truly has.'

Corbett noticed how some of the watchers were so frightened they hurried back down the steps into the bailey. Someone loosed a crossbow bolt, which fell into the moat. Lord Henry shouted that no violence was to be offered. Corbett was tempted to ask Ap Ythel to order a blizzard of arrow shafts, but this would be a very grave violation of the customs of war: if the tide turned against them, the garrison would not be shown any mercy. Instead, Brother Adrian now arrived, with a dripping aspergillum. The monk had changed his black robes for working clothes, a common practice when confined to the castle; he had cheerfully confessed to Corbett that it helped preserve his rather costly woollen church garb. He cast holy water at the malevolent apparitions whilst loudly intoning the prayer to St Michael the Archangel for help against the armies of darkness. Others, encouraged by this, began to hurl abuse at the macabre group until the woman raised her arms and Lord Henry roared for silence.

'The Black Chesters,' Corbett murmured, 'I am sure it's them. The witches' coven patronised by Sir Edmund Darel. He houses, feeds and protects them. Believe me, Ranulf, Darel is a man who loves counterfeit, mummery. He sees his own life as one long mystery play.'

'You know him well, Sir Hugh?'

'Not bosom comrades. Edmund Darel was a mailed clerk at the old king's court. His father and elder brother died, so Edmund became the sole heir to Blanchlands and all its estates. I have met him on a few occasions since he left London, as I have Lord Henry and others we might encounter here along the Scottish march. Darel is a mummer, a murderous one; he is responsible for this bloody masque.'

'It's not Richolda, surely?' Ranulf's question was tinged with fear.

'Ranulf, only Christ the Lord rose from the dead.

Darel takes to trickery as a fish to water. Let's just wait and see.'

The eerie silence deepened. The cart with its gruesome cargo stood stark and sinister on the edge of the moat. The three dark-dwellers continued to stare up. The woman in the centre, her hood now fully pulled back, stood arms extended as if summoning up all the powers of hell. Corbett gazed quickly to left and right; he sensed that the long line of watchers either side of him were becoming increasingly frightened.

'Wench!' he shouted. 'For that's what you are. I am cold, I am hungry and I would love a goblet of wine. You are proving tedious and wearisome. In God's name say what you have to and be gone, or Master Ap Ythel here will show you greater wonders than you have shown us.'

He was pleased with the ripple of laughter this provoked. Others, including Lord Henry, also caught his mood and began to shout how it was time for bed and would she like to join them?

'I shall return at the end of the fourth watch.' The woman's voice was powerful and carrying. 'Do you understand me? At the end of the fourth watch I shall demand your surrender before my lord comes against you, banners unfurled.' She pulled her hood dramatically back over her face, turned on her heel and walked back to join the rest of her coven grouped around the hand-cart. She took a torch from one of these and threw it onto the corpse, which, soaked in oil, erupted in sudden sheets of flame, tongues of fire leaping up into the darkness to shroud the swift departure of the Black Chesters.

Corbett stood watching the fire rage. The reek of corruption was now replaced by the stench of burning flesh. Eyes straining into the darkness, he wondered about the possibilities. A hand touched his arm; he turned to find Kathryn Thurston staring at him. Ranulf had turned away to discuss the question of witchcraft with Brother Adrian, who, still armed with the aspergillum, seemed to want to bless the entire wall. The monk broke off from talking to Ranulf and went to lean against the battlements, shouting that whatever hour of darkness the demons returned, he would be waiting for them. Thurston now joined his sister.

'Kathryn, you've told him?'

'No,' she replied. 'Brother Adrian distracted me.'

'Sir Hugh,' the constable declared, 'Lord Henry wishes to meet with us. Brother Adrian,' he called out, 'you are to join us.'

They gathered around the yawning hearth with its carved wodewoses, satyr heads and grinning monkey faces of babewyns and gargoyles. Lady Eleanor almost snapped her fingers at the royal clerk. 'What is this all about, Sir Hugh? You saw those grotesques taunting us. Have you met their like before?'

Corbett stared into the flames without speaking.

'And the murders?' Kathryn Thurston demanded.

'Those poor, poor men,' Brother Adrian murmured. 'Could the witch queen who has just cursed us be responsible?'

Corbett continued to stare into the fire. Ranulf glanced at Ap Ythel and winked. Old Master Long Face, as Ranulf often called Sir Hugh, was lost in one of his deep reveries, his mind teeming with what he had just seen, heard and felt.

'Sir Hugh,' Lord Henry rubbed his hands together, 'what do you think? What shall we do? My wife mentioned those grotesques, and they certainly are, but there must be a purpose behind such malicious mummery. They were sent by Darel for a reason, not just to frighten.'

'Has Seton been found?' Ranulf asked to distract attention from his master. 'Do you think he's escaped? Is he in hiding? How can a Scotsman with no weapons survive concealed in a castle like this, or worse, out there on the heathland?'

'You haven't found him, have you?' Corbett lifted his head. 'You cannot discover Seton's whereabouts; he has disappeared completely, yes?'

'Very true,' Lord Henry agreed.

'I suspect he is dead,' Corbett declared slowly. He shook his head at the protests of disbelief. 'No man,' he continued, 'can hide so successfully or escape from this castle unobserved. I repeat, Seton has been murdered. God knows where his corpse lies. That is the only logical conclusion I can draw. His fate is shrouded in mystery, as are the murders of his two comrades, Sterling and Mallet. It's obvious they were poisoned with some noxious powder. I am not an apothecary, but from the little I know, I suspect it was some deadly plant such as nightshade.'

He paused as a thought occurred, something nebulous, an occurrence outside the ordinary logic of life around him.

'Sterling and Mallet,' he continued, 'bolted and barred themselves in that chamber. Nothing poisonous was discovered there. They did not leave the room except to use the garderobe. Nobody visited them. No one entered or left that tower except labourers, masons or carpenters working on the repairs.'

He paused again. He couldn't forget that witch on the edge of the moat cursing them, threatening to return at the end of the fourth watch. That was the thought, a possibility that intrigued him. He did not wish to share it, though, not here with the shadows closing in, sitting with people some of whom he did not trust.

He patted Ranulf on the arm. 'I agree with my learned colleague here. The charade outside was intended to frighten us. Now, what do we know about Richolda; I mean, when she was alive?'

'She had the reputation of being a powerful witch,' Brother Adrian replied, 'the leader of a coven called the Black Chesters, who used to meet for their midnight rites out on the heathland until they won the protection of Lord Darel. Richolda boasted that she possessed powers given to her by the ancient spirits who haunt these parts. But as you know, Sir Hugh, claims to such nonsense can be easily dismissed.' He drew a deep breath. 'Except perhaps for what we saw tonight, though I've heard rumours of Darel's lust for two sisters . . .'

'I assure you, Brother,' Corbett crossed himself, 'you're

correct: it's all nonsense. Witches do not rise from the dead. Richolda's corpse lies sheeted in the castle death house. I suspect the woman who acted as Darel's herald is simply someone who looks like her – a sister, possibly a twin.' His words created a pool of silence. 'She was sent to frighten us, to cower our souls, chill our hearts and sap our courage, but something else too. Lord Henry, if I could have a word with you alone?' He ignored the sharp intake of breath and gasps from Lady Eleanor and the rest. 'King's business,' he added soothingly, 'and now would be as good a time as any.'

Lord Henry reluctantly agreed. 'Leave us,' he ordered, 'everyone.'

The company broke up and, led by a petulant Lady Eleanor, swept out of the great hall. Ranulf was the last to leave, closing the door quietly behind him. Lord Henry rose, filled his goblet and offered the jug to Corbett, who shook his head.

'Is this truly necessary, Sir Hugh?'

'Lord Henry, on my journey here I was attacked. I have been assailed twice here in Alnwick since I arrived. There is a traitor, a spy, a murderer trying to inflict hideous damage. I have little doubt that Alnwick will be attacked again, just before dawn – that's when the fourth watch ends, isn't it?' Lord Henry's expression grew sharper. 'The macabre masque outside,' Corbett continued, 'was an attempt to terrify us but also to prepare for that assault. That witch was telling her confederates here in Alnwick that the onslaught will begin at that greying time that separates night and day, the murky gap between sleep and watchfulness. Now,' he pulled his stool closer, 'Lord Henry, you cannot afford for such an attempt to be successful; it would be a serious blow to your family name and to your ambitions in the north. Darel would make a mockery of you.'

'What are you saying, Corbett?'

'Think, Lord Henry: how many castles has Bruce taken by stealth?'

'Bruce!' Lord Henry exclaimed. 'But this is Darel.'

'No, Lord Henry, I suspect this is Darel with help from Bruce and his coven. Oh, I am sure there will be an assault, but if this castle falls it will be through treachery. Alnwick is a fortress mighty and strong. Darel could lay siege to it, but he's no fool. That would take time; much easier to seize it through stealth. Now there definitely lurks a traitor within the walls of Alnwick, but there are also labourers, masons working on the repair of this castle. Where are they now?'

'Some have left, others shelter in our outhouses.' Lord Henry shrugged. 'Storerooms, dungeons, empty chambers. In the main they are local men, many from my estates.'

'But some are strangers, landless men who move from one place to another selling their skills. You cannot vouch for all of them.'

'Of course not.'

'You have been here for, what, two years?' Corbett declared. 'And you know of no secret entrance into Alnwick?'

'Sir Hugh, you've seen my castle. I cannot say I know

every nook and cranny. There are postern gates here, sally-ports, small openings onto the moat. You talk of treachery within; one of these might be opened. What do you advise, that I sound the tocsin and summon all to arms?'

'No, no,' Corbett murmured. He rose and walked towards the high table on the dais, where candles glowed on spigots, their light shimmering in the great silver salt cellar, the nef at the centre of the table. He peered closely at this, admiring how the craftsman had carved it so accurately in the shape of a war cog. He wondered idly if he would get Gaveston safely on board *The Golden Dove*, as well as how he and Ranulf would fare once the royal favourite was gone. What route south should they take?

'Sir Hugh, what do you think Darel will do?'

'I tell you this,' Corbett spoke over his shoulder, 'I know Darel of old, a mailed clerk with bounding ambition who now sees himself as one of the great barons of the north. He would like nothing better than to seize and hold this fortress. I also believe he is probably in negotiation with Bruce, like many northern lords are.'

He paused, letting Lord Henry reflect on his words. He had voiced such suspicions to the king. If the likes of Edmund Darel wondered about the future, other noble families such as the Percys would be more than tempted to negotiate an accommodation with the redoubtable Scottish war leader. He walked back and sat down, hands extended towards the fire.

'Lord Henry, some of the labourers here are undoubtedly Scots. They may be innocent workers, but I suspect a few could be Bruce's men; they could open a postern gate.'

'And so what—'

'I urge you to have a cohort of men-at-arms, all buckled for war, armed with kite shield and spear. They should gather here as quietly as possible along with Ap Ythel's archers. They are to remain hidden under my command.'

'For a sortie?'

'We shall see.' Corbett was not going to share everything with this northern lord. He got to his feet. 'Lord Henry, the hours are passing. It's time to prepare.'

The knight agreed. Corbett went out and found Ranulf and Ap Ythel, bringing the two men into his confidence. Within the hour, the cohort of Welsh archers slipped like ghosts into the great hall, buckled and armoured for battle with war bows strung and their deep quivers crammed with feathered shafts, each barbed and ready to be loosed. Two of Lord Henry's household knights together with twenty shield men eventually joined them. Corbett made it very clear that they were not to leave the great hall except to use the garderobe in the passageway outside. He then had the dais cleared and, using various objects left on the high table to illustrate his plan, instructed the company on what they must do once the attack began.

Afterwards, they broke up to eat, drink and sleep as best they could until the booming alarm bell and the strident wailing of battle horns roused them. Corbett ordered the entire company to stay and wait whilst he hurried out. The cold darkness was beginning to thin, the stars receding as the very first streaks of light appeared against the eastern skies. The castle was now awake. The clatter of weapons, shouts and cries, the wailing of children and the howling of dogs shattered the silence. Trumpets blared, horns brayed and the pealing of bells carried shrill and sharp.

Corbett hurried through the inner barbican to the main gatehouse, where Lord Henry, Constable Thurston and the castle's master of arms were standing on the fighting platform staring at the threat slowly emerging out of the morning mist. The crackle and rattle of huge wheels heralded the ominous approach of a belfry, a soaring siege tower, undoubtedly seized from some English-held castle along the Scottish march. This monster of war moved slowly forward, pulled by a team of oxen. Once it was in range, the animals would be unhitched and the belfry pushed from behind towards the edge of the moat. The attackers would swiftly fill part of this ditch with bundles of wood over which they would lay down a makeshift bridge so the belfry could be thrust up against the main gateway. Torches, flames leaping against the darkness, were fixed along its top storey. On either side of the siege tower trundled two trebuchets or catapults. The attackers themselves stayed hidden behind their engines of war, wraith-like shapes only betrayed by the light glinting on blade and armour. The entire line moved towards the barbican. Corbett reckoned the attackers would try and force the drawbridge, even though he was deeply suspicious that this was only a feint.

'Well,' Lord Henry snarled, beating his fists against the wall, 'what will shield men and archers do against that?'

Corbett raised a hand for silence, ears straining. The clatter and clash of attack increased. A few fire arrows blazed against the darkness. One of the trebuchets stopped, its crew hastening around, winching back the throwing arm. Horns and trumpets brayed. Archers left the protection of these machines of battle to race forward and loose arrows, but these fell short.

'Well?' Lord Henry shouted. Corbett was about to reply when he heard screams and a clatter of arms from the bailey below.

'It's happened!' he exclaimed. 'Lord Henry, forget what you see! Ignore the enemy without; it's the enemy within.'

He hastened down the steps into the outer bailey, where that part of the Alnwick garrison not manning the ramparts had become savagely involved in a life-and-death struggle against a horde of assailants who had abruptly appeared as if out of nowhere and were fighting to reach the gatehouse. The attackers were garbed in rough, homespun clothing, though many wore helmets and seemed well armed with sword, axe, club and rounded shield. Fierce-faced, long-haired and wild-eyed, in the strengthening light they looked truly ferocious as they pressed the defenders back, desperate to reach the gateway. More were joining them; some of these looked like the labourers who had been working in the castle, now using their mallets, hammers, chisels and poles to deadly effect.

Corbett broke free of the press of defenders, running to outflank the conflict. He realised that the stream of attackers were pouring out of the Abbot's Tower, killing those they encountered and only stopped in their violent rush to the main gateway by the vigilance and courage of the garrison. The crash and scrape of weapons, the stench of death and the horrid cries of men in their final agonies had turned the outer bailey into a living hell. He hastened across to the inner barbican. A dark shape moved to his right; he turned, sword out against the attacker, who came swirling in, axe swinging, shield jutting out. Corbett darted swiftly to one side, but his assailant staggered, axe and shield dropping, eyes rolling back in his head as if he was trying to see the yard-long shaft that had pierced his skull.

Ranulf and the household knights were stationed outside the inner barbican, spearmen in the front row, a gap between each of them for an archer, war bow taut, arrow notched.

'Loose!' Ap Ythel roared.

Bow strings twanged their ominous song. Volley after volley rained down on the column of attackers streaming from the Abbot's Tower, an overwhelming assault on the enemy's exposed flank. The spearmen shuffled forward, shields raised, yet it was the cohort of archers who were causing the most dreadful devastation. Corbett hastened to join them, standing with Ranulf,

Ap Ythel and a group of household knights who formed the third line of the phalanx. He had seen before the effect of massed master bowmen who could loose shaft after shaft, and it was truly destructive. The constant hail of yard-long arrows, goose-quilled and cruelly barbed, could not be avoided.

The attackers now realised the real danger, but it was too late. They turned to confront the advancing phalanx, only to be cut down, whilst those who survived the arrow storm were impaled on the massed spear points. A few tried to outflank the cohort, but the bowmen simply turned and loosed with deadly accuracy to counter this threat. Horns brayed and the attackers broke, no longer striving to force their way through to the main gate but desperate to retreat to the tower and the secret entrance they had undoubtedly used. Constable Thurston and Brother Adrian, breathless with excitement, hurried up with the news that the attackers outside were swiftly withdrawing. The trebuchets together with the fearsome belfry were all retreating in a clatter of wheels and whining cordage.

The phalanx was now pushing more swiftly towards the Abbot's Tower. The defeat had turned into a rout and was descending into a massacre. The attackers, frantic to escape, fled back to the tower and its narrow stairwell, but the press was too great. They had to turn to confront the constant rain of arrow shafts and the pressing blades of the spearmen.

Corbett withdrew and sat down by the well, his back against the wall. He gratefully accepted the beaker of water a castle woman thrust into his hands. The sounds of battle were now fading, though heart-rending screams and soul-chilling cries continued. The air reeked of spilt blood, the stink of bellies ripped open and the acrid smoke from fires. Soldiers hurried down from the walls to hunt those attackers trapped within the bailey. Some of these tried to hide, only to be dragged out and decapitated, their heads sent bouncing across the cobbles, their upright torsos spouting a rich red fountain until they toppled over and the blood continued to flow in streams across the cobbles.

The massacre in and around the Abbot's Tower came to an abrupt end. Lord Henry bawled that he wanted prisoners, and about thirty of these were roughly assembled: fierce-looking fighters garbed in rags with scraps of armour protecting their backs, chests and groins. A few wore Darel's livery; the rest were Scots dispatched, so one of them loudly confessed in a rough, grating accent, to bring Alnwick to its knees.

'You were correct,' Lord Henry declared, patting Corbett on the shoulder. 'Darel had dealings with Bruce and these unfortunates will pay the price. Very well.' He raised his voice. 'Brother Adrian, shrive them. Constable Thurston!' He turned and yelled at the pale-faced constable. 'Take the prisoners up onto the walls.'

'The cages, my lord?'

'The cages be damned. Put a noose around the bastards' necks and toss them over.'

'Lord Henry,' Corbett murmured, grasping Percy's gauntleted wrist, 'that would be stupid and wasteful. It is not necessary. There has been enough killing for one day and dawn has just broken.' He stared up at the sombre clouds once again gathering over Alnwick. 'We can use these men as bargaining counters, and there is one prisoner in particular who may be useful.'

Lord Henry looked as though he was about to refuse. His craggy face was splashed with dried blood, his chain-mail gauntlets had pieces of human flesh caught in their mesh. Corbett glanced around. The defenders were now moving amongst the fallen. Friends were being helped towards the inner barbican and the chapel beyond, where Arnulf had set up a makeshift infirmary. Any enemy injured had their throats cut, their bodies and clothes searched for valuables. One wounded Scot was trying to crawl away, but he was closely followed by a man-at-arms who kept prodding him with his mace, teasing and taunting, till he tired of the game and smashed his victim's head with one blow of his war club.

The ground was littered with the debris of battle and widening puddles of blood. Bellies, bowels and skulls had been opened and gutted to exude a gruesome stench. Castle women who found their men dead or wounded began to keen, singing their shrill lamentations in high-pitched voices. Corbett closed his eyes. He just wanted to be away from all of this. He wanted to be back in his bedchamber at Leighton Manor. Maeve would be sleeping next to him, her head on his chest, his hand threading her thick glossy hair . . .

Sunlight pierced the oriel window on the far wall; the painted glass caught the rays and shimmered beautifully, catching the eye. Through an open window he could hear the bees buzzing over the flower boxes on the sills, whilst a thrush's song echoed lucid and liquid. He should get up now. At the noonday Mass he and the manor choir would sing a three-voiced hymn. Afterwards he would go and tend to his beehives. In the meantime, he could revel in the fragrances in the air: perfume, polish, red wine and the savoury smells drifting in from the kitchens . . .

'Sir Hugh?'

Corbett opened his eyes. Lord Henry pushed his face close.

'Do you feel faint?'

'No, Lord Henry, I feel sick. Now, I carry the king's warrant. I wear his ring. No more killing. Issue the order.'

Percy grimaced but called to Thurston and rasped at the constable how quarter was to be shown except for those enemy wounded beyond human help.

'Now,' Corbett pointed at the Abbot's Tower, 'let us see where the attackers came in. Brother Adrian, those lying in the tower might also need anointing.'

The Benedictine was having a heated discussion with Ap Ythel about the tactics used to achieve 'the miracle of Alnwick'.

'It *was* a miracle,' Lord Henry conceded roughly, clapping Corbett on the shoulder. 'My apologies, clerk, I thought you were soft, but your advice probably saved my castle. We would have manned the parapet against the belfry and the trebuchets, but that was merely a show of force, bustling and noisy, a powerful distraction.

We would only have become aware of the dire fight in the bailey below when it was too late. If those attackers had seized the gatehouse, raised the porticullis and lowered the drawbridge, the castle would have been lost. So yes, I am very grateful and I shall not forget it.'

They reached the tower. The dead sprawled all around the entrance, twisted and contorted by the agonies of their fatal wounds. Lord Henry's men-at-arms had already moved amongst them, giving the mercy cut to any wounded and removing injured defenders. They were now busy combing that place of slaughter for anything valuable, be it weapons, coins or personal trinkets. Lord Henry, Corbett and the rest waited until the corpses were removed before going down into the dark, dank, blood-reeking cellar; a filthy room with cobwebs spread like nets on the rafters and in the corners. The wall plaster was peeling. Cracked casks and barrels lay about. It had once been used as a storage room, and a wooden floor had been laid out across the beaten earth to protect against the damp seeping through.

In the corner, where a barrel had been pulled away, was a cleverly contrived trapdoor, now lifted. A square yard of wood that would be difficult to detect when in place, whilst the barrel had provided even more conceal-ment. Corbett could see the rough-hewn steps leading down into the darkness below. Lord Henry sent a torch-bearer before him; he, Corbett and the rest followed. At the foot of the steps stretched a long passageway hollowed out of the rock on which the castle was built. Corbett noticed the damp against the ceiling and walls.

'It must run beneath the moat,' he murmured.

Another torchbearer squeezed by them and they continued on into the darkness. Corbett reckoned they must have walked half a mile before they saw shafts of lights ahead of them and a set of steps hewn out of the rock. They climbed up one at a time through a square gap at the top into a box-like stone chamber, once a dwelling place but now open to the elements; its thatched roof, window shutters and door had long gone. Outside there was a small courtyard now greatly overgrown and closely ringed by trees, which shrouded and darkened this sombre, lonely place.

Corbett, trying to shake off his unease, walked back inside and stared down at the hole in the floor they had just climbed through. The floor was of beaten earth; bushes, gorse and shrubs had broken through to conceal the entrance. There was no sign of the enemy. Only a few had reached that secret tunnel and would now be fleeing as fast as they could back to Blanchlands.

'I know what this place is,' Lord Henry declared. 'It's the old hermitage shown on plans and charts of the castle.'

'The real question,' Corbett declared, 'is who knew that a hidden tunnel connected this place and the castle?' He glanced at Brother Adrian, but the Benedictine, his face a mask of surprise, just shook his head.

'I assure you,' Lord Henry declared, 'neither I nor any member of my household knew about this tunnel. In God's name, Sir Hugh, if we had, we would have taken care of it, as I assuredly will now.'

Corbett walked back into the courtyard and stared up at the crows, black as night, floating above the trees. 'This murderous mystery is deepening,' he whispered to himself. 'The assassin is a true cunning son of Cain, and I, God willing, must trap him.'

Lord Henry ordered a search of the trees and undergrowth beyond the dwelling. Corbett drew his sword and joined the line of men who moved into the surrounding copse. They entered the eerie green darkness created by a tangle of ancient trees that clustered so close their branches interlaced, the leaves forming a thick matting to block out the light and deaden sound, turning the copse into a place of sombre mystery. He was about to go back when he heard a shout to his right. He hurriedly pushed his way through the tangled undergrowth and almost stumbled into the small clearing and the horror displayed there.

A man's torso, stripped naked, lay sprawled on the ground. Next to it, a pole had been driven into the soil, on which the cadaver's severed head had been thrust. The blood from the torso was sparse and congealed, the face of the impaled head almost masked by gore-matted hair. Corbett peered closer and immediately recognised the dead features of Lord Alexander Seton.

Others joined him in the clearing. Corbett gently prised loose the severed head, trying to ignore the gruesome sucking sound, and placed it on the ground. Brother Adrian came and knelt, Ave beads out as he blessed the pathetic remains. Corbett inspected the jagged neck and dried blood. He plucked aside the hair and stared into the contorted, twisted face, a nightmare sight with its gagging mouth, thickened tongue and swollen lips. He heard the rest gather behind him, their curses and exclamations contrasting sharply with Brother Adrian's whispered words.

Once the monk had finished, Corbett squatted down by the corpse, completely stripped even of its undergarments. A raven flew out of the trees, a black shadow floating across the glade. Another followed, as if these carrion birds were eager to continue poking at the cadaver with sharp claws and razor beaks. The cawing of other birds eager to feast echoed across that haunted glade. The morning mist was thinning, but here it still swirled as if a company of ghosts stood amongst the trees watching the affairs of men.

'Sir Hugh?'

'Lord Henry.' Corbett pointed to the head. 'A real mystery. Seton was long dead when his head was severed. The flesh is cold and bone hard, the blood from the sliced neck meagre and congealed. A living head, once hacked off, creates a vigorous fountain of blood. That did not happen here. Seton, God assoil him, had already been killed when his head was removed.'

'How? By whom? Why?'

'His face has been pecked by the carrion crows.' Corbett knelt and gently turned the head over; one of the eyes, loosened by a crow, slid out. 'Predators always gnaw at the softest parts first. I reckon Seton has been dead for two days. Lord Percy, you ask by whom. Of course I don't know. As for how,' he pointed to the head again, 'notice that his face is the same liverish colour as the other victims.'

'Poisoned?'

'Poisoned,' Corbett agreed. 'And so the mystery deepens. Seton was a Scottish prisoner. He wanted to escape. He must have been alarmed by the death of Roskell. I would wager he was gone by the time Sterling and Mallet were murdered. This is only conjecture, but I suspect the assassin, the traitor, the spy in the castle, approached Seton and offered him this secret way out. Seton accepts. He leaves Alnwick, only to be poisoned here in this godforsaken glade and die in agony. Darel launches his attack; his marauders approach the old hermitage and a party of them come across Seton's corpse. They believe he is an enemy, someone trying to flee Alnwick and somehow killed. They don't really care; their blood is up, so they dishonour the corpse. They strip it, sever the head and pole it.' He shrugged. 'More than that, I cannot say. Lord Henry, you will give Seton's remains honourable burial?'

'Along with the rest, Sir Hugh, but now, we should return.'

They threaded their way back through the tunnel to the tower and into the castle. The outer bailey was still a hive of activity. Castle servants were removing all traces of the conflict, whilst Lord Henry's household knights guarded the prisoners, a long line of squatting men, some nursing wounds, chafing at the chains that secured both hand and foot. Corbett glimpsed Cacoignes, that cunning man, as Ranulf now believed him to be. He looked safe and untouched by the attack and lounged on the steps of the Falconer's Tower watching what was happening. Corbett whispered to Ap Ythel, using the agreed secret cipher. The master bowman hurried away and returned with the welcome news that Gaveston was safe, hale and hearty, breaking his fast in the garrison buttery.

'Eating and drinking as if there is no tomorrow,' the Welshman murmured. 'We must now journey on to Tynemouth.'

'Across that countryside?' Corbett countered. 'We would never reach the priory. Darel's men – and God knows who else – will be prowling the roads and trackways. No, we have no choice but to tarry here for a while, to watch and wait and at the same time keep busy. Ap Ythel, Ranulf, let us inspect the prisoners.'

Corbett and his two companions walked the line of manacled men. The clerk ignored the hostile glances and muttered curses. He stopped before one of prisoners and squatted down, staring into the man's face, noting the narrow eyes, the well-kept beard and moustache, the scar along the forehead, the right ear badly clipped, the squat nose broken and twisted.

'I'd recognise that ugly face anywhere. You are Bavasour?' Corbett edged even closer as the prisoner grinned and nodded his head. 'Once a captain of hobelars in the old king's levy till you stole a pyx from a church and deserted the royal army. Well, Master Bavasour, I am sure you have seen the days and are ready to meet God. Do you want to hang?'

'If you would join me, yes.' Bavasour lifted his manacled hands and scratched his face with a stubby forefinger. 'What is it, Sir Hugh? I remember you as well; you are not the type of clerk to bait a man destined for the gallows.'

'How would you like to walk free?' Corbett smiled at Bavasour's swift change of expression. 'Provided you tell me everything, I think you can. Well, do you want to tell me?'

'Sir Hugh, is the Holy Father a Catholic?'

A short while later, Corbett, Ranulf and Ap Ythel, with Chanson guarding the door, grouped around Bavasour sitting on a stool before them in Corbett's chamber. The mercenary put the empty wine goblet down on the well-cleared platter and rubbed his wrists where the manacles had been.

'You have been well fed and watered, so let us begin.' Corbett brought across a stool to sit opposite Bavasour. 'You were a captain of hobelars under Edmund Darel?'

'One amongst many. By the way, I noticed an old comrade, Cacoignes he now calls himself, skulking around the bailey outside.'

'Yes, we shall return to him, but the attack that failed, the secret passageway? Bavasour, you were a captain. You must have sat high on Darel's council when he described what was being plotted. Somebody must have told him about the passageway that runs from the derelict hermitage to the Abbot's Tower. That somebody also betrayed us on our journey north. So, what can you tell us?'

'As regards the journey north, Sir Hugh, all we knew was your strength, your destination and reports that you carried the precious Lily Crown. Darel maintained that the ambuscade he had contrived would be successful and we would literally seize a king's ransom.'

'How did he know that? You must have questioned him.'

'We did. Darel replied that it was his business and that he had it on good authority. When he described the ambuscade, we all approved. However,' Bavasour laughed drily, 'we know what happened there. You were waiting for us. Afterwards, I advised Darel to be more careful. Sir Hugh, Ap Ythel, false flattery aside, you both fought alongside the old king and his generals in Wales, Gascony and Scotland. You are not a group of humble pilgrims wanting to visit some shrine.'

'I thank you for the compliment.'

'It's a fact.' Bavasour picked up his goblet and Ap Ythel refilled it.

'And the attack on Alnwick?'

'The Black Chesters insisted on that, as did Hockley's kin. They wanted revenge.'

'What do you know of the Black Chesters?'

'They get their name from a local village. They are a powerful coven. Sir Hugh, the Black Chesters are not old beldams chomping on their gums or frail, ancient wise-women brewing potions in a cauldron. They truly are a midnight coven, men and women who practise the black arts and perform macabre rites. Rumour has it that their sacrifices are not cockerels or some other bird or animal. No, it's whispered that local peasants have disappeared and the Black Chesters are responsible.'

'And Darel believes in them?'

'They have promised him their full support. They certainly instil fear, and of course,' Bavasour added sharply, 'there's Richolda and her twin sister. Oh yes,' he held up a hand, 'the two are almost identical, fair of face and form but wicked to the bone. Apparently they grew up in Berwick and witnessed all the horrors when the old king sacked that town. Gossips maintain they both entertained Darel, how he was like wax in their hands. He tried to satisfy their every whim. From the little I know, they swept into Blanchlands and turned the inner bailey of that castle into their own fief or kingdom.' He fell silent.

'What's the matter, man?' Corbett demanded.

'Sir Hugh, I wonder if the Black Chesters can hear me now.'

'Don't be ridiculous.'

'They have spies everywhere, they pride themselves on that.'

'But not in this chamber.'

'Sir Hugh, I have wandered the face of God's earth and rubbed shoulders with all kinds of wickedness, every type of evil that crawls under the heavens.' Bavasour sipped from his goblet. 'Forest folk, satyrs, gargoyles, babeywns and the wild men of the woods don't frighten me, but the Black Chesters certainly do. Beautiful women or not, I kept my distance, and so did the others. I remember one night at Blanchlands being entertained by one of those wandering minstrels, a troubadour full of tattling tales about what he had seen and learnt here, there and everywhere. He talked about warlocks and witches; the powers they claimed and the cruel deaths they experienced.'

He paused. Corbett suppressed his own clammy fears as Bavasour's words provoked memories of his own childhood and the execution of a warlock in a nearby village. His parents had kept him at home, but for days people talked about the burning, the stench, the dreadful sight and hideous screams.

'Sir Hugh?'

Corbett just shook his head.

'You know,' Bavasour continued, 'that the Black Chesters are only one coven amongst many.'

'What?'

'Oh yes, according to our troubadour, such covens form a web like that of a giant spider, a net of wickedness that extends all over Scotland into England and beyond. He claimed that Richolda and Leonora, those two daughters of Satan, were mere peasants in the hierarchy of evil. Apparently they are led by a great earl of the underworld who styles himself Paracelsus, a truly sinister soul who journeys the kingdoms of earth on Satan's business.' Bavasour drank greedily from his goblet. 'Believe me, Sir Hugh, this Paracelsus, from the little I have learnt, wields tremendous power; he is feared as if he is the Great Cham of Tartary, his word life or death.'

'But you have never seen his shape or form or witnessed the power he wields?'

'No, but the claims made for him are truly fabulous.

How he has read a secret manuscript called *The Key of Solomon* and discovered the secret of how to shut up in a bottle of black glass a million Satanic spirits together with seventy-two of their kings. He can draw the circle of hell and pollute the air with the sooty stench of Satan. According to the minstrel, who later disappeared and was never seen again, Paracelsus has a demon as a familiar, a slave from hell to do his bidding. But,' Bavasour shrugged, 'these could be just hearthside tales.'

'Has Paracelsus ever been seen entering Blanchlands?'

'Not that I recall.'

'So how does he meet his followers?'

'Oh, you mean those daughters of darkness Richolda and Leonora? Well, we have seen them leave with an escort of mailed men. They return, but who they've met and where they have been, I don't know.'

'But surely the local priest, the castle chaplain must have intervened?'

'Sir Hugh anybody who objects to the Black Chesters, be he priest or peasant, simply disappears. I am nothing but a hired sword. I fight here, I travel there. I leave the likes of the Black Chesters well alone.'

'And the attack on Alnwick?'

'The Black Chesters were hot for it. I know that from the discussions in the great hall. The attack was well planned. Darel sent messages across the march asking the Scots for help, Douglas and Randolph, Bruce's closest henchmen, responded. They sent fighting men south as well as carts loaded with the engines of war together with carpenters skilled in putting them together.'

'That was swift. I mean, given the time between our arrival here and the attack.'

'Sir Hugh, Darel and the Scots have been planning such an assault for some time. Bruce's array is not far from the border; they are making good progress. Those engines of war Darel used have all been seized from castles that have fallen to Bruce. Now the Scottish war leader and his council greatly fear what Lord Henry is doing at Alnwick, building a mighty fortress so close to the border. It is said that Bruce intends to carry the war into England. He wants to launch forays, swift-moving chevauchées across England's northern shires.'

'Of course,' Corbett agreed. 'Alnwick will act as a great defence of the north. Bruce can't afford to go around it. Lord Henry would pose a powerful threat to the flank and rear of any invading army.'

'If Bruce fears Alnwick, so does Darel,' Bavasour declared. 'Alnwick might become a rival to Blanchlands. Like Lord Henry, Darel dreams dreams of becoming the lord of the north, carving a great fief out for himself.'

'So the attack itself?'

'We were reluctant, but Darel assembled his captains. He argued that we should assault Alnwick to divert the defenders from the real attack. Of course that surprised us. Even more so when Darel declared that he had discovered a secret passageway into Alnwick so the fortress could be taken by stealth.'

'And how did he know this?'

'Sir Hugh, we asked him the same question. Darel claimed he had a spy in Alnwick.'

'Who?'

'We pressed him on that.' The mercenary paused, eyes closed, lips moving. 'We demanded a name, and Darel gave some clever scholar's answer. How the spy claimed to be the Alpha and the Omega – yes, that's it. I kept repeating it to myself.'

'The Alpha and the Omega.' Corbett half smiled. 'It's Greek and it's from the Book of Revelation, which deals with the confrontation between God and the Antichrist. The actual phrase is "I am the Alpha and Omega of all things, the Beginning and the End."'

'That's all he would tell us.'

'But the precise time and place?'

'Ever since Richolda's capture, Darel had been sending his scouts close to the castle. Apparently they received a crudely scrawled message that whoever delivered Darel's defiance to Alnwick must also provide the time of the attack; proclaim it without allowing the defenders to understand.'

'The end of the fourth watch,' Ranulf murmured.

'Correct,' Bavasour agreed. 'You would think that that was when the herald would return to demand your surrender, but it was, in fact, the time that Darel intended to attack. In the end it turned out to be very simple. We went to the old hermitage and sent scouts along the tunnel; they returned safely saying all was well.' He paused to drink. 'The rest you know. Darel launched his assault, myself and the other captains gathered with our men in the tunnel and cellar beneath the Abbot's Tower. We broke out.' He pulled a face.

'We did not expect you to be waiting for us.'

'On your way to the old hermitage,' Corbett asked, 'did you come across a corpse, a poor unfortunate who had been poisoned?'

'Yes, we did. He was all buckled and prepared for battle, cloaked, booted and wearing a sword belt. He was dead; we could tell he'd been poisoned. We could not understand it. However, some of the Scottish swordsmen believed they recognised him as an enemy and insisted on stripping him. One of the Scots severed his head and placed it on a pole. I gave it little thought, being more concerned about our own attack.'

'And Cacoignes?' Corbett asked. 'Geoffrey Cacoignes? He joined Darel's retinue.'

'And betrayed it,' Bavasour snapped. 'He must have done. A mercenary in every sense of the word. I gave him little thought. Only after Darel's attack on your camp failed did we realise that he was gone and that he must have betrayed us. Before that,' he spread his hands, 'he was nothing special, one swordsman amongst many. After he joined you, however, a story began to emerge that he had been one of the old king's men, that he'd been sent north to seize the Lily Crown from the abbey of Scone and take it south to Westminster. How he and his comitatus had been attacked and he, along with another, had escaped unscathed and made his way south to Tynemouth Priory.'

'Somebody here at Alnwick must have told Darel who Cacoignes really was,' Ranulf declared. 'When he was with you, he went under a different name?'

'Of course.' Bavasour laughed. 'Don't we all!'

'Darel may have been informed,' Ap Ythel spoke up, 'but there again, since he arrived in Alnwick, Cacoignes has made no attempt to hide himself, his name or his past.'

'The Lily Crown?' Corbett asked. 'Do people still believe it's at Tynemouth?'

'Or here at Alnwick.'

'What?'

'That's what rumour says.' Bavasour preened himself at revealing something that had surprised the clerk. 'There is a certain logic to it, Sir Hugh. Some of Darel's men recognised Cacoignes' name. You know he is related to the de Vescy family, who once owned Alnwick. Indeed, they say he spent some of his youth here at the castle; that he knows it well and the surrounding countryside too.'

Corbett glanced at Ranulf; the Clerk of the Green Wax just shook his head slightly. Corbett leaned over and grasped the mercenary's arm. 'You have nothing more to tell me, nothing else to say? Think, man. I am going to give you your life and freedom. Soon you will be gone from all of this. You have no knowledge of who the traitor might be here at Alnwick?'

Bavasour shook his head. Corbett watched him intently. A man's face always betrayed a lie, and he had to ensure that this mercenary was trying to be as helpful as he could.

'Sir Hugh,' Bavasour chose his words carefully, 'Blanchlands was rife with rumour, especially about

Richolda and her kind. Somebody said that the inner coven of the Black Chesters was only twelve in number.'

'Of course,' Corbett breathed, 'and if they are a coven, there must be thirteen . . .'

'Was it someone else at Blanchlands?' Ranulf demanded.

'No, no.' Bavasour grinned. 'Believe it or not, rumour had it that the thirteenth lurks here at Alnwick.'

Satisfied that their guest, as Ranulf described Bavasour, could tell them no more, Corbett took the mercenary down into the shadow of the main barbican and told him to remain with Ranulf in the waiting chamber, a dark, murky room where visitors were detained until they received Lord Henry's permission to enter his castle. Corbett himself hurried away. He collected clothing, weapons and a stout pair of boots, as well as a linen parcel of food and a small wineskin from the buttery, and returned to Bavasour telling him to get ready to leave as swiftly as possible.

Constable Thurston, summoned at Corbett's insistence, agreed to give Bavasour a horse from the castle stables. The garron Chanson chose was the ugliest mount Corbett had ever seen. But Chanson, ignoring Bavasour's mocking laughter, assured his master that the horse, despite its strange, almost yellowish colouring, shorn tail and clipped ear, was swift and sure-footed and would not be quickly winded. Harness and saddlery were provided and the horse was prepared for its journey.

Corbett insisted on leading Bavasour out under the porticullis and across the drawbridge. Once he was beyond hearing by any of the castle folk, he plucked at Bavasour's sleeve, drawing him close.

'Ride,' he urged, pressing a silver coin along with a sealed parchment scroll into the mercenary's calloused hand, 'ride as fast as you can due west. Keep to the trackways, draw little attention to yourself. Once you reach Carlisle, you must seek an urgent meeting with my lord Andrew Harclay, Keeper of the Western March.' Corbett passed Bavasour a copy of the Secret Seal. 'Show him that, and give him my letter. Tell him to bring all his strength as swiftly as possible to Alnwick. If I am no longer here, he must press on to Tynemouth Priory. Tell my lord Harclay to do so under his allegiance to the king.

'As for you, my friend,' Corbett was standing so close he could smell Bavasour's sweat, 'do this and you will be rewarded: a full pardon and a charter appointing you a captain in the royal levy north of the Trent. Betray me,' he shrugged, 'and I will demand that you be hunted down as a wolfshead. Your task is urgent and important. What we are involved in here is vital to the Crown and its servants. Do you understand?'

Bavasour slipped coin, seal and scroll into his belt pouch, then offered his hand, which Corbett clasped. 'You have my word, Sir Hugh, and if I fail, it will be because I lost my life trying not to.'

He mounted his horse. Corbett stood and watched him go before rejoining Ranulf in the castle bailey. He then returned to his own chamber, where Ap Ythel was waiting with Gaveston acting as his servant. Corbett locked and bolted the door after ensuring that Chanson was on guard in the gallery outside to shield against any eavesdropper, then sat down in the scribe's chair.

'The attack has failed,' he murmured. 'Bavasour told us a great deal. What concerns me is why Cacoignes, equally sharp-witted, could not have told us more.' He gestured at the door. 'Ranulf, tell Chanson to bring Cacoignes here. My lord Gaveston, I would be grateful if you could act the part of archer and stand outside. We have to be careful; despite your disguise, Cacoignes might well recognise you.'

A short while later, Cacoignes sat on a stool in Corbett's chamber, cradling the goblet of Bordeaux Ranulf had poured for him.

'You fared well during the attack, Master Cacoignes?'

'Sir Hugh, I was deployed on the Falconer's Tower; the fighting did not reach us.' He toasted Ap Ythel with his goblet. 'Thank God for your archers. They inflicted hideous damage on the attackers.'

'I am glad you single out my comrade,' Corbett declared. 'Some five years ago, Ap Ythel was sent north to find you, isn't that so?' He turned to the Welshman, who now drew up a stool to sit alongside the wary Cacoignes.

'We searched for you,' Ap Ythel declared. 'We tried to find out where you had been attacked and by whom, but it was a complete mystery.'

'I have told the tale a number of times,' Cacoignes retorted. 'I survived. I don't have the crown, because Ravinac hid it. Prior Richard will be able to help. He would have little to do with me.'

'Just who are you, Master Cacoignes?' Corbett leaned closer. 'Where do you come from? What do you really want? I'll be honest, there is an air of mystery about you.'

Cacoignes coloured visibly and breathed in noisily, patting his jerkin as if the heat was too much.

'Do you know Alnwick?' Corbett asked.

'Look, look,' Cacoignes spread his hands, 'my mother was of de Vescy blood. Yes, I know Alnwick. I visited here as a boy. I played in the castle as children do. Afterwards, my parents placed me in this household or that. Eventually I was appointed to be a squire in Prince Edward's retinue. I became versed in arms, nothing singular until I was chosen to ride along with Ravinac and others and the old king ordered us to seize the Lily Crown. We did so and were attacked.'

'By whom?'

'A Scottish war party, it must have been. Cowled and visored, dark-robed.'

'Tell us the details,' Corbett insisted. 'Was it morning, noon or night?'

'Very similar to what happened to you, Sir Hugh, on your journey north. We left Scone. Ravinac had the crown in a leather sack tied around his waist. He wouldn't allow anyone to go near either him or the crown. On our first night out, we camped in the lea of a hill with bushes and gorse to protect us. We could light fires there without their glow being seen. We had guards, and I went out to ensure that all was well, and as far as I could see, all was. Darkness fell. A clear night with a good hunter's moon.' He paused. 'I tell you this, the dark riders were in before we even knew about it, two score of them or thereabouts.'

'So they must have been following you during the day. I mean, yours was a small party.' Ap Ythel's voice was challenging.

'Yes, yes, they must have followed us. God knows how or why they chose our party. There were other groups taking Scottish regalia south; that was the old king's strategy: small, fast-riding groups, each on their own.' Cacoignes pulled a face. 'We thought all would be well, but it ended in sword and dagger play, a wild melee of falling blades, rearing horses, all the noise and dust of battle. Ravinac and I broke free and fled for our lives.'

He paused, and Corbett watched him closely. Sometimes he could detect when a person was lying. Cacoignes was different. Corbett sensed that he was telling some of the truth but not all; there was a deep, dark shadow hovering over him and the eerie occurrence he was describing.

'As I have said before,' Cacoignes tried to hide his exasperation, 'we reached Tynemouth. Prior Richard gave us shelter. Ravinac was not well; he fell ill and died. As far as I am concerned, the whereabouts of the Lily Crown died with him. I left, I was captured, I bided my time. Five years later, I escaped and joined Darel's retinue under another name. I did this to protect myself. Moreover – and I freely admit to this – I remained in the north in the hope that one day I could return to

Tynemouth and find the Lily Crown.' He sipped from his wine, warming the cup between his hands. 'The rest you know. I heard of your chevauchée north, as did Darel. He made his choices; so did I.'

'And the Lily Crown, you heard no more of it?'

'No, Sir Hugh, but let me tell you, when Ravinac and I reached Tynemouth, we were not alone. Lord Henry and Lady Eleanor, together with the Thurstons and Brother Adrian, were also there. The Percys were in negotiations with the Bishop of Durham over the purchase of Alnwick. I decided there was company enough. I left to explore the surrounding countryside. I returned. The crown was hidden. Ravinac was dying. Lord Henry and the others had left. Eventually I followed suit. As I've said time and again, I do not know where he hid the crown. Perhaps he confided in Prior Richard.'

'I find this strange.' Corbett tapped his foot. 'You go to Tynemouth, you leave, you return to Tynemouth, you leave. Why didn't you just stay there, unless, of course, you believe Ravinac hid the crown somewhere else?'

'That is a possibility, but remember what was happening in the north five years ago. The rot had begun, the collapse of law and order. Tynemouth is a well-fortified citadel, but the countryside around it was certainly not in the king's peace. War bands, mercenaries, wolfsheads and peasants driven out of their farms prowled the roads. I had to find my way home. I had very little, no money, and a horse that was winded and blown. I even considered escape by sea. I was in one of the coastal villages when I was captured by Scottish pirates and taken into the wastelands north of the Forth.'

Cacoignes spread his hands. 'When I escaped, I had to join Darel's comitatus under a false name. I was given little choice. After all, even if I had reached London, would I have been welcome? I was a squire entrusted with the Lily Crown of Scotland, and I lost it; the sole survivor of that company who left Scone. Sir Hugh, you are proof enough. Ever since I joined you, it has been one question after another.' He pointed at Ap Ythel. 'I can see you don't trust me, and I don't blame you. All I can say in my defence is that when I was given the opportunity, I fled Darel's retinue. I warned you about his approach and that wasn't a sudden decision. I sent you a message saying we would meet.'

'Yes, yes, you did,' Corbett agreed.

'I have proved my good faith.' Cacoignes made to rise.

'That's very true,' Ranulf replied, forcing the man back onto his stool, 'and you have been rewarded. You are now a member of Sir Hugh's retinue under the protection of the Crown. I am sure my master will vouch for you at Westminster—'

'Fire! Fire!'

The cry of alarm was taken up by the clanging of bells and the wailing of horns.

'In sweet heaven's name!' Corbett exclaimed.

They all hurried down into the bailey. The stench of burning was strong. Wisps of smoke drifted along the alleyways either side of the chapel of St Chad. Castle folk, under the direction of Constable Thurston, men, women and children, had already formed a line to pass a chain of water buckets.

'It's the death house behind the church,' Brother Adrian shouted as he pushed his way past the carriers, gesturing to Corbett and his companions to follow him down the runnel.

Corbett flinched at the sudden gust of heat that brushed his face, whilst he caught the stench of flaming oil and the horrid reek of burning flesh. The smoke billowed and cleared to reveal the death house, a large storeroom of plaster and timber on a red-brick base built against the wall of the inner bailey. Tongues of flame licked through the thick thatched roof and danced at the square windows where the shutters had crumbled under the heat, as had the door, buckling on its hinges.

'What corpses?' asked Corbett, grasping the monk by the shoulder.

'Hockley and Richolda. I was to bury them tomorrow morning, but not now.' Brother Adrian led them back down the alleyway into the bailey and bade them farewell. The fire was now under control and Constable Thurston had rightly decided that as the death house stood alone, it was best to let the blaze burn itself out.

'That's no accident,' Ap Ythel declared. 'I'm sure it's arson. The stench of burning oil is everywhere.'

'I agree.' Ranulf pulled down the wet cloth he had grabbed from a washerwoman and tied across the bottom half of his face.

'Strange,' Corbett mused. 'The death house is being

burnt from cellar to roof. I am sure the fire was started deliberately. Now there is no threat to anyone living so I ask myself, why burn a death house? What profit is there in turning two corpses to cinder and ash? There is nothing on their persons, no value for such cadavers. No, no.' He turned and walked back to the entrance to the main hall. 'In fact, I believe Brother Adrian is the reason for the fire.'

'Sir Hugh?' Ranulf demanded.

'Richolda was a member of a Satanic coven. Whether you accept their twisted teaching is a matter for you. What is important is that they certainly believe in it. To cut to the chase: they would not want a priest to celebrate Richolda's requiem, so someone in this castle set fire to the death house and gave Richolda her own peculiar pagan death rites. No priest, no requiem Mass, no book and taper, bell or candle, incense or holy water; her soul has gone into the dark and so has her body.'

'So there must be a comrade of hers here in Alnwick?' Ranulf declared. 'Bavasour referred to that.'

Corbett agreed absent-mindedly; he was distracted by the noise and the smoke. He glanced up as drops of rain spattered down. 'Good,' he murmured. 'The rain will help douse the fire. Now, let us wait until matters become more peaceful. We shall meet in my chamber again soon. Ranulf, find Chanson, check on our horses' harness and saddlery.' He chewed on the corner of his lip. He needed time to reflect.

'Should we ask Cacoignes to rejoin us?' Ranulf asked. Corbett led his henchmen out of the hearing of any castle folk. 'Forget Cacoignes for the moment,' he murmured. 'We are surrounded by murderous mystery and we still have challenges to face. We must reach Tynemouth in safety, deliver a certain person, search for something precious and find our way unscathed out of the north. Now leave me for the moment.'

He watched them go before wandering back into the main hall and down into the cellars beneath. A man-at-arms wearing the Percy livery guarded the fortified chamber where Lord Henry kept his treasures in the great arca, the massive triple-locked, iron-bound chest that also contained Corbett's small Secret Chancery coffers. At Corbett's insistence, the guard unlocked the door and allowed the Keeper of the Secret Seal to enter. Corbett swiftly ensured that the arca was safe, secure and free of any attempt to prise it open by force or trickery.

He left the chamber and went back upstairs into the bailey, pulling his hood up over his head against the strengthening rain. He left the inner precinct and walked across to the Abbot's Tower. The entrance door was off the latch. Corbett pushed it open and climbed up to his former chamber just off the first stairwell. The place still stank of fire and smoke, though repairs had begun. Carpenters had removed the door and servants had started to clear the debris caused by the fire. The place was now deserted due to the conflagration at the death house. Once again Corbett wondered if one person was responsible for all that was happening in Alnwick: the destruction of Richolda and Hockley; the poisoning of the Scottish hostages; the attack on him and his companions in St Chad's chapel; the murder of Seton and the treacherous opening of that hidden tunnel beneath the Abbot's Tower.

He broke from his reflection as he heard a sound below. He glanced through the lancet window. The sky hung grey and forbidding, the breeze was turning sharper whilst the rain pattered harshly against the cobbles outside. Again that sound. Corbett hurried down the stairs, but only a door creaked in the strengthening breeze. He glimpsed the steps leading to the cellar and its secret passageway. The workmen and guards had left. He recalled how Lord Henry had apparently ordered the tunnel to be sealed by bringing down part of the ceiling. Intrigued, he decided to investigate. He entered the cellar, lit by torches burning fiercely in their cressets, and went down into the tunnel. Flaring firebrands pushed into wall niches turned the air hot now that the other end of the tunnel had been sealed off.

'A path into the night,' Corbett murmured, walking down it. Who would have known of it before Darel's attack? Who wanted to see this great fortress sacked and the power of Lord Henry shattered? He reached where the tunnel was sealed, then turned and made his way back. He took out his Ave beads, threading them through his fingers, and tried to pray, but his mind was distracted by other thoughts and memories. He stumbled, looked down and kicked away a kite-shaped shield. He stumbled again. There was an ominous click further up the tunnel, followed by the whirring of a crossbow bolt, which sliced through the air above his head. Corbett cursed and crouched down. Another bolt shattered against the tunnel wall. He realised his would-be assassin was moving backwards and forwards across the passageway.

Abruptly one of the wall torches, followed by another, was flung in Corbett's direction. The clerk moved back and grasped the shield. He crouched behind it and waited. Another click. This time the barbed bolt shattered against the shield. Corbett drew his dagger and yelled, moving forward, shield in one hand, knife in the other. Another bolt, but this one was not aimed correctly and smacked against the tunnel roof.

Corbett paused. He heard a crash, followed by the sound of running footsteps. He peered over the rim of the shield and stared into the silent emptiness stretching out before him. There was nothing, only the cressets spluttering and dancing in the breeze. He walked forward at a half-crouch. He did not know if the would-be assassin was one person or more, or whether his attacker had simply retreated to a better vantage point. He left the shield and sheathed his dagger as he glimpsed the crossbow his assailant had dropped: a small hand-held arbalest for use at close quarters. He picked it up, weighing it carefully: a light weapon, easily hidden but deadly enough. He placed it on a ledge near the stairs leading up into the cellar.

'Sir Hugh, Sir Hugh?' Ranulf appeared at the top of the steps.

'Did you see anyone?' Corbett demanded. 'Someone running away?'

'No, no, but the rain is falling and a host of castle folk, cloaked and hooded, are hurrying around.'

'How did you know I was here?' Corbett asked, coming up the steps.

'You may not know it, Sir Hugh, but I watch you. I realised you were coming here; I could tell that by the direction you took. Anyway, I went up to your chamber to ensure all was well and then decided to join you.' Ranulf peered at him closely. 'Something has happened?'

Corbett told him. Ranulf cursed, fingers tapping the hilt of his dagger. 'Leave it, leave it,' Corbett murmured. 'There is nothing much we can do for the moment. Ranulf, summon Ap Ythel and Chanson to my chamber, along with our mysterious archer. I want to try and make some sense of what is happening.'

'Well,' Corbett looked around at his companions, 'let us begin.'

He stretched out his hands towards the brazier, then grabbed one of the poker rods pushed through the narrow iron slats and prodded the charcoal, watching the red-hot cinders break in a blaze of flame and heat. The day was dying, darkness was falling. The rain had persisted, cold and almost sleet-like, drenching the bailey outside and rattling against the shuttered window. Castle retainers had laid out platters of freshly roasted chicken, slices of honey-coated pork, manchet loaves and a jug of hot mulled wine heavily laced with spices. Chanson, half dozing on a stool, was on guard outside. The clerk of the stables conceded that he was heavy-eyed but said he would be vigilant enough.

'Let us reflect most carefully on the tangled maze we have entered,' continued Corbett. 'First, we have five Scottish prisoners taken by the old king and imprisoned in the Tower of London.'

'One of them was captured by me,' Ap Ythel broke in. 'Matthew Dunedin was not of Seton's ilk.'

Corbett stared at the Welshman and smiled at the forcefulness of his voice. 'True, true,' he agreed. 'I must remember that. Anyway, four of these prisoners, although Scottish, were not adherents of Bruce but sworn followers of the murdered Red Comyn. They claim that their master was the innocent victim of Bruce's murderous hate and that they were witnesses to this. They placed their case before the old king, but he ignored them. However,' he pointed at Gaveston, who had now pulled back his hood and removed his eye patch, 'they convinced you.'

'Like streams flowing together,' Gaveston's voice was lilting, 'it served our purpose to send assassins into Scotland and ourselves into exile.' He laughed sharply. 'Lancaster believed our story. He insisted that you, Sir Hugh, as the Crown's most senior clerk, lead the delegation north. In truth, he just wanted you out of the way. Another faithful, loyal and skilled servant of the Crown dispatched as far from the king as possible.'

'Lancaster will certainly wonder what has happened,' Ranulf declared.

'Let him,' Corbett retorted. 'It's not his business. Let

us return to the matter in hand. The Scottish prisoners. Originally there were five, but Dunedin died in mysterious circumstances. An accident? Murder?' He pulled a face. 'We have no evidence for either, no proof of foul play. True, Dunedin was different from the other four, a self-proclaimed adherent of Robert Bruce, though apparently he was just a prisoner who wanted to go home. He seems to have befriended one of the other hostages, Malachy Roskell. They were both religious, much taken up in the contemplation of the Four Last Things and apocalyptic literature. I am not too sure whether Roskell was of the same mind as his three colleagues, but they seemed determined on Bruce's death.'

Corbett paused and drank from his wine cup. 'We were also joined by three of Lord Henry's household: Constable Thurston, his sister Lady Kathryn, and Brother Adrian, a Benedictine monk who is chaplain here at Alnwick. All three were sent south as a mark of respect, a courtesy, as well as to act as guides and advise us on our journey here. After we left for the north, someone in our party alerted Darel to our strength, gilding the story with the fable about us carrying the Lily Crown. Now why we should be doing that, I don't know, except that the Lily Crown has disappeared and could be anywhere. Darel could not resist the prospect of seizing it, so he planned to attack us. Geoffrey Cacoignes also emerged from the murk. He sent me a garbled message that he wished to join us. We've heard Cacoignes' story about being attacked, taken prisoner, escaping and joining Darel's retinue

under another name. We've also learnt about his involvement with the Lily Crown. We have to accept his
declaration that he does not know where it is because
his companion and comrade, now dead, allegedly hid
it in or around Tynemouth Priory. Cacoignes evidently
doesn't know that Ravinac confided in Prior Richard
how the Lily Crown now hangs between heaven and
earth in God's own graveyard.'

'And we don't know what that riddle means.'

'No, Ranulf,' Corbett replied absent-mindedly, 'we
don't. That will have to wait until we reach Tynemouth.
However, to return to our journey north. Who is the
spy, the traitor who informed Darel?' He pointed at Ap
Ythel. 'Your archers served as a screed of scouts around
us. Nothing suspicious was reported either in the countryside or in the villages we passed through?'

'Nothing, Sir Hugh. As I suspected at the time, we
were being followed, shadowed, but that is not unusual.
I must admit I never thought Darel would mount such
a ferocious assault.'

'Which Cacoignes saved us from,' Gaveston reminded
him.

'Yes, he did. And now we come to the murders.
Roskell was the first, poisoned near that stream. Even
more mysterious, Sterling and Mallet were killed in
their own chamber, which was locked and bolted. We
detected no sign of violence or trace of poison in that
room, be it drink, food or anything else. As for Seton,
who showed him through that secret entrance? Who
knew about it? Why did he go so willingly with the

murderous soul who secretly poisoned him – and he certainly did. A thick, tangled mystery, twisted even further by the assassin who loosed crossbow bolts at me, tried to burn me in my chamber and placed caltrops in Ap Ythel's room.'

'And beyond the walls,' Ranulf declared, 'lurks Darel and his power along with the Black Chesters. They watch and wait. Further north, the Scots also have a deep interest in us.'

'The Black Chesters are truly dangerous.' Ap Ythel spoke up. 'Sir Hugh, was Bavasour correct? Is there an adherent of that witches' coven here in Alnwick? After all, someone set fire to the death house so the witch Richolda would not be buried according to the rites of Holy Mother Church.'

'Possibly,' Corbett murmured.

'And there's greater danger facing us,' Gaveston declared. 'Sooner or later we have to leave Alnwick to reach Tynemouth. We need protection, but we cannot have Lord Henry and his retinue too close. If he discovers who I am, he will seize me and use me as a hostage against Edward, my brother. We also have to cross open countryside plagued by Darel and his devil-worshippers. Sir Hugh, I thought you were going to prepare for this?'

'I have, I have,' Corbett insisted. 'You remember Bavasour? I have sent him west to Carlisle. He is to beg Lord Harclay to bring his comitatus to Alnwick and, if necessary, on to Tynemouth.'

'What if Bavasour just flees for his life?' Ranulf demanded.

'Then, my friend, we have a further problem, and one I will have to resolve.'

Corbett held a hand up at the loud knock at the door. He rose, opened it slightly and peered out at Chanson, who indicated with his head that someone was in the gallery behind him.

'Brother Adrian, Sir Hugh. Lord Henry has sent him. He wishes to see you and yours immediately.'

Corbett collected his cloak and went out into the gallery, shouting at Ranulf and Ap Ythel to join him as he clattered down the stairs and into the great hall. Lord Henry was warming his backside against the fire whilst lecturing those seated on stools around the majestically carved hearth: Lady Eleanor, the Thurstons, Cacoignes and, just to the side, a grey-haired, grey-faced, grey-cloaked woman, one hand resting on a stout walking stick whilst the other played with the small painted cross of San Damiano on a chain around her scrawny throat. She rose as Corbett joined the group, extending a vein-streaked hand for him to kiss whilst Lord Henry introduced her as the anchorite Lady Hilda of Whitby.

'A saintly woman, Sir Hugh, who moved from the abbey on the coast to establish a community of anchorites at Clairbaux.'

'Which is where?'

'A few miles to the south-east,' the anchorite replied, her voice as cultured and refined as any court lady. She smiled at Corbett with her eyes as if to soothe his unease. The clerk could detect that this old woman must have been a great beauty in her prime.

'And what is Clairbaux?' Corbett demanded as he took the proffered seat.

'Once a great Celtic monastery,' Lady Hilda replied, sitting down. Corbett nodded, then swiftly introduced his companions, relieved that Gaveston had resumed his pretended role and promptly disappeared.

'Lady Hilda is here,' Lord Henry declared, 'at the behest of her beloved nephew, Edmund Darel.'

The anchorite laughed behind her fingers at Corbett's startled expression. 'Let me explain.' She leaned across and gently touched the back of Corbett's hand. 'Look around, Sir Hugh.' He did so. 'See the fire burns merrily? Yet it also forms shadows and sends them dancing. The Darels are like that, light and dark. My youngest sister married Darel's father, a true wolf of a man who, with sword and shield, hacked his way to wealth and served as one of the old king's bodyguards. He seized Blanchlands and held it against all comers. He became a lord of the north, a true bane to the Scots. Edmund, his sole surviving son, was educated in the halls and schools of Oxford. He later entered the chancery, becoming a mailed clerk, where he met you, Sir Hugh.' She smiled. 'Edmund trusts you. In fact, he wishes to meet with you to . . .' she paused, 'resolve all differences.'

'Never!' Ranulf retorted.

'Never?' she queried and sat up straight, head slightly to one side. 'Ranulf-atte-Newgate,' she murmured, 'Sir Hugh Corbett's faithful henchman.'

'Which is why my master will not be meeting the robber Darel, who has already committed high treason . . .' Ranulf paused as Corbett gently pressed his arm.

'You know that.' Corbett pointed at Lady Hilda. 'And so does your beloved nephew. He attacked a royal envoy travelling under the king's own standard. He later attacked us here.'

'A mistake, a dreadful mistake.' Lady Hilda raised her eyes heavenwards as if openly conceding that her reply was the best she could make in the circumstances. Corbett warmed towards her. After all, this old lady was trying to help, and he would need some form of protection if they left Alnwick.

He glanced swiftly at Lord Henry and then looked away as if fascinated by the fire. Darel was one thing, Lord Henry was another. The Percys were a bustling, ambitious and aggressive family. They claimed that their line went back into the mists of antiquity; that Percy's ancestors had fought with the Conqueror at Hastings. A Yorkshire landowner, Lord Henry had moved to Alnwick determined to create his own fief. If Darel could be placated, why not Lord Henry as well? Yet there was the rub. If Corbett went on oath, he would have to admit that he did not trust either of these lords, whatever promises they made. He, Ranulf and the others were only a small fighting group riding out across bleak, savage countryside. It would be so easy for a comitatus like theirs to be attacked, butchered and their corpses hidden. He recalled the stories he'd heard. Wasn't there a legend how, in ancient times, an entire Roman legion had mysteriously disappeared in this northern wilderness?

'Sir Hugh?'

Corbett turned back to the anchorite. 'Lady Hilda, tell us more about yourself. Why do you live at Clairbaux, and, above all, what do you hope for from this meeting?'

'I am, as I said, the elder sister of Edmund's mother, now thankfully gone to God from this vale of tears.' Lady Hilda folded back the cuffs of her grey robe. 'I also married, but my husband died during the old king's wars in Gascony. They say he was killed by an archer near the bastide of Saint-Sardos. I heard that he may have been knifed by a pimp during a quarrel over the services of a couple of whores.' She laughed drily. 'Be that as it may, I had had enough of the world of men; marriage was definitely no longer my calling. I entered the convent at Whitby.

'About five years ago, I came to the conclusion that God wanted me to follow a more ascetic life. I negotiated with Edmund and he granted me Clairbaux, a sprawl of monastic buildings once owned by Celtic monks. The hermitage there, as I now call it, is based on the Carthusian rule, which in turn is closely linked to the Celtic tradition. Every one of our members has a small brick-built cottage holding a hearth, kitchen, buttery and chancery chamber, which also serves,' she smiled at her own mockery, 'as the solar, great hall and banqueting chamber. We sleep in a bedloft, which is comfortable enough. Outside we tend our own gardens, divided into herb and kitchen plots. There's a rose garden in the cloister garth, which is nothing more than a square grassy bed around which the cottages and the church are built. We observe the hours of the day in the ancient church of St Cuthbert. Brother Adrian often celebrates Mass for us as well as providing other sacramental occasions.'

'And how many are the community there?'

'Including some servants, possibly no more than fifty souls both male and female.' Lady Hilda raised a hand. 'Gentlemen, please do not speculate about the propriety and rectitude of our house. We are not interested in matters of the flesh but in the life of the spirit. We consider ourselves a house of prayer set in a wilderness of violence.' She paused and gratefully accepted the cup of wine Kathryn Thurston proffered, sipping quietly as she waited for the others to have their goblets refilled with the hot spiced posset. 'I have watched my nephew Edmund build his new world,' she continued. 'Time and again, as Lord Henry will attest, I have intervened to give Edmund good counsel. On a number of occasions I have arbitrated between him and Lord Henry. I am doing the same today, trying to mediate with the king's own envoy to these parts whom my nephew had the temerity and stupidity to attack.'

'Where?' Ranulf demanded. 'Where will this meeting take place?'

'Darel will certainly not approach Alnwick.' Lord Henry laughed sharply. 'Whilst Sir Hugh must not enter Blanchlands.'

'Edmund suggests the hermitage at Clairbaux,' Lady Hilda murmured. 'He will come accompanied by one person. He respectfully asks that Sir Hugh do the same. At the same time, he insists that Lord Henry keep all his men confined to Alnwick. My nephew will ensure that his retinue stays at Blanchlands. As you know, Edmund's wife died some years ago, but she left him two children, a boy and a girl. As tokens of his good-will, he will send both these children as hostages to Alnwick until his meeting with Sir Hugh is completed.' She sniffed. 'For what it is worth, he will also take an oath over a crucifix and this will be done in my presence. He will swear that he will offer Sir Hugh and his companion no hurt or injury, be it of the body or the spirit.' The anchorite sighed noisily. 'My nephew wishes to make amends, to sue for peace.' Her voice turned more pleading. 'He desperately wishes to escape the dire consequences of his recent foolish actions. He freely admits he can do little to appease Lord Henry, but he has no desire to obstruct you, Sir Hugh, any further.'

'And Holy Mother Church?' Brother Adrian's voice echoed around the hall. The Benedictine's face was severe. 'Lady Hilda,' he continued, 'I recognise you as a pious anchorite, a woman dedicated to God, but your kinsman Darel has more on his conscience than opposition to a royal envoy or his most recent, unprovoked attack on this castle. He favours and fosters a Satanic coven dedicated to hellish practices, the Black Chesters. They plague this countryside, a thick mist of malice that moves with a will of its own . . .'

Brother Adrian broke off as if he realised the intensity of his outburst, a passionate cry of protest that silenced all noise in the great hall so it seemed even the shifting shadows stood stock still to eavesdrop. Corbett felt an icy tingle of fear claw his back and stomach. He stared around at the others, wondering if an adherent of the Black Chesters, a member of that Satanic coven, was here in the great hall. Lady Hilda certainly looked startled, even frightened. She swiftly drew a set of Ave beads from a purse on a cord about her waist, while her other hand continued to finger the Tau cross around her neck.

'The Black Chesters,' the anchorite crossed herself, 'what can I say? Sir Hugh, you know Edmund of old. He was always singular, with a nose for mischief and an aptitude to match. He has a penchant for the occult, for that secret world of warlocks and witches. God knows where the Black Chesters originate. Some people whisper that they have been in Scotland for decades, even centuries. How they arrived from southern France and over the years have extended their malign influence.'

'They are many?' Ranulf demanded.

'Oh yes,' the anchorite replied. 'According to rumour, there is more than one coven. Sometimes they all gather for important feasts of the dark; festivals such as the Night of the Deep Harrowing. Coventicles from all over Scotland and beyond assemble in some wild, desolate place. Ancient stones are used as their altar and sacrifices are made—'

'Sacrifices? Night of the Deep Harrowing?' Ranulf intervened. 'Do these things really happen?'

'I have learnt of such things from Edmund, scraps

of conversation, as well as the whispers and rumours that people bring to the hermitage. I fear for Edmund's soul because of these gruesome ceremonies. I understand the Night of the Deep Harrowing is when the earth is cut with a furrow, which is then filled with blood; whether this be human or not, I shudder to think. Of course,' she added with a shrug, as if dismissing what she had just said as mere fable, 'all kinds of tittle-tattle surrounds my nephew. Some portray him as a robber baron; others go much further and depict him as a devil incarnate.'

She paused, rocking herself backwards and forwards. Corbett tried to shrug off a real sense of fear, as if something was gathering in the darkness of this hall.

'Edmund's wife died three years ago. A year later, the Black Chesters swept into Blanchlands. Anyway,' Lady Hilda's voice turned brisk, 'Sir Hugh, will you meet with my nephew? It may take a few days to arrange . . .'

Corbett sat at his chancery desk and stared through the unshuttered window. He'd spent the previous day resting and reflecting, though he'd conceded to Ranulf that he had made very little progress in resolving the vexing problems facing them. The meeting with Lady Hilda, however, had ended most amicably: Corbett had agreed to meet Darel in the ancient church of St Cuthbert at Clairbaux. Each would swear an oath in the presence of a witness – Lady Hilda in Darel's case; Brother Adrian in Corbett's – that they would 'treat honourably and peaceably' and attend the meeting escorted by one person only. It was also agreed that Darel's men would be recalled to Blanchlands and Lord Henry's retainers confined to Alnwick. Darel's son and daughter, together with their nurse Ursula, would be handed over as hostages for their father's promises. Corbett had already taken his oath and made other arrangements so he could leave when the time was ready. He felt very restless.

Once Lady Hilda had left, Ranulf had also become busy. The Clerk of the Chancery of the Green Wax had absented himself for long periods of time. Ap Ythel had informed Corbett that he'd glimpsed Ranulf around the castle; 'Lurking,' the Welshman had declared, 'that's how I would describe it.' Corbett was mystified but decided to leave the matter for the time being. He also wondered about Lady Hilda. He couldn't decide who she truly was or how successful she would be in arranging a truce.

A knock at the door disturbed his thoughts. He opened it and Ranulf slipped into the chamber. He turned and spoke to Chanson outside, warning him to be vigilant, before locking and bolting the door behind him.

'Ranulf?' Corbett demanded.

'Sir Hugh, I have watched and I have waited. Brother Adrian, the Benedictine, is, when put under scrutiny, a strange man. He meets with many people in this castle.'

'He is their priest.'

'It's more the way he does it. So swiftly, a word here, a word there, then he moves on. He wanders this castle like a will-o'-the-wisp over a marsh, head down, cowl pulled over. I have spoken to the men-at-arms who guard the sally ports, postern doors and other narrow entrances to this fortress. Brother Adrian regularly passes in and out with little fuss: "a true shadow", as one guard described him. Sir Hugh, could Brother Adrian be the assassin, the spy and traitor?'

Corbett sat forward in his chair. 'Fetch Ap Ythel.'

Ranulf did so. Once he'd arrived, Corbett plucked at the captain of archers' sleeve and took him across to the window that overlooked the inner bailey. 'My friend,' he declared, aware of Ranulf standing behind him, 'if we have blundered into a trap at Alnwick, we must prepare to flee, to ride south with all speed.'

'Sir Hugh, we have our precious cargo for the *The Golden Dove*, whilst we are expected at Tynemouth, where more business awaits us.' Ap Ythel blew his cheeks out. 'But you are correct. I suspect we are going to have to fight our way out of what looks increasingly like a trap. We cannot trust Lord Henry – God knows where his allegiance lies – while Darel is totally unpredictable, and what other force is there apart from my lovely boys and our own sword arms? This is a place I'd like to leave.' He gestured at the castle folk busy in the bailey below. 'A constant chatter, Sir Hugh. They talk about Darel, but beneath that swirls a deep fear, even terror, of the Black Chesters. I have heard whispers about horrid killings and sinister disappearances. Nobody can produce evidence or proof of anything dire or heinous. There's just this atmosphere of dread, a deep, cloying fear that swirls like a mist over the wild countryside outside.'

'Then let's try and plot a way through the murk,' Corbett declared. 'Sherwin Ap Vynar? One of your kinsmen?'

'Ah, you mean the Houndsman?' Ap Ythel's face broke into a grin. 'The archer who can sniff and track, as skilful as any lurcher?'

Corbett pointed down to where Brother Adrian was deep in conversation with a group of itinerant tinkers who had visited the castle to do business and were now preparing to leave. 'I want Sherwin to keep Brother Adrian under close watch. If he leaves the castle, as I suspect he will, Sherwin must follow him.'

Bavasour the mercenary, the captain of hobelars, had left Alnwick in high spirits. He was determined to take Corbett's message to Carlisle and, perhaps, attach himself to Harclay's levy when they swept towards Alnwick and hopefully on to Tynemouth. He had travelled for a day, spending the previous night in an ancient spinney of withered trees sheltering beneath its dead or decaying branches, and had woken not so merry of soul or glad of heart. He wondered if that bleak, blighted place had darkened his mood. Aware of the grey sky lightening, he had attempted to build a small fire, but this had failed and his unease became tinged with a slight dread. In searching for kindling he had come across the mauled and mangled remnants of a pheasant, and had glimpsed the cause of such violence: a heavy-bellied, sluggish dog fox. Old Reynard, flushed from his feasting, had been startled from his deep sleep and sloped off, a dark red shadow in the early-morning light.

Bavasour decided to leave the fire. Instead he crouched down and wolfed the dried meat, soft cheese and now hardening bread he had been given at Alnwick, softening the food with mouthfuls of wine, which he hoped would soothe the pain in his rotting yellow teeth. He decided to ride as hard and swift as he could that day. The garron Corbett had provided might look ungainly, but it had more than proved its worth. Bavasour wanted to be away. The ragged remnants of the pheasant and the sloping, sly-eyed fox slinking off provoked memories of that demon hall at Blanchlands, 'the place of sacrifice' as it was known; rumour had it that it was where those sinister twin sisters performed their filthy rites.

He closed his eyes and recalled that cavernous, gloomy chamber lit by a row of cresset torches, the constantly dancing flames bringing to life the macabre scenes that decorated the walls. A long line of baleful depictions. Spoonbills cowled like monks; lizards with human heads and walking fish harnessed as if they were knights on the road to war. Goblins rode satyrs, armed with crossbows to bring down monkey demons nestling amongst the gaunt branches of dead trees. He had been allowed into the hall on one occasion only – though he had not confessed this to Corbett – and glimpsed the stuff of nightmares. He'd also heard macabre stories that he hardly admitted to himself let alone to a royal envoy. Chilling tales about the abominations that stalked the moorlands around Alnwick once the sun had set and darkness closed in. Now the nightmare memories returned to haunt him here in this truly desolate spot. Yes, it was time to go!

He hurriedly finished his preparations, ensuring that straps, girths and stirrups were secure. He then swung himself up into the saddle and urged his garron back down the hill to the ancient trackway, cursing the thick morning mist that swirled to greet him. He rode as swiftly as the nimble-footed garron would allow, doing his best to shake off the unease, his usual wariness sharpening as he also pondered the possibility that his escape from Alnwick might not have gone unnoticed.

At last the mist began to thin. Bavasour breasted a hill and sighed with relief at the small hamlet nestling below; nothing more than a few cottages with pens, stockades and outhouses either side of the beaten trackway. Yet as he rode down, his hot sweat prickled cold, his senses telling him that something was very wrong. No smoke billowed from the makeshift stacks built on the sides of the cottages. No chickens pecked at the dust; the stockades and pens were empty. He recognised the signs. The inhabitants had collected family, possessions and livestock and fled – but why? Scottish raiders? Wolfsheads? Or a comitatus sent out by some northern lord to discover what was happening along the wastelands of the Scottish march?

Bavasour rode on, leaving the narrow valley, following the trackway as it dipped and snaked between the small copses that bordered the path. As he cleared the trees, he reined in abruptly, staring at the long line of black-garbed horsemen who now blocked his path, cloaks flapping in the breeze, which also tugged at the deep hoods pulled up over their heads, the broad bands across their mouths acting as visors to conceal their faces. Bavasour's garron caught its rider's apprehension and skittered on the pebble-strewn ground, sharpened hooves clattering on the gravel. He quietened the beast, then swallowed hard and wetted his lips. His suspicions had proved correct. He had been seen leaving Alnwick and he had been followed. They had waited, they had distanced themselves from Alnwick; only here and now would he be killed. He steeled himself. These were not Darel's moss-troopers or a band of outlaws; they were the acolytes of the Black Chesters. He glanced over his shoulder to see that a similar line of horsemen had quietly debuched behind him.

'I wonder,' he murmured, turning back, 'I truly do wonder who watched me leave. Sir Hugh, God bless you. No help is at hand for you or for me.'

Bavasour made his decision. He had no intention of being taken prisoner. He'd fought the length and breadth of this kingdom and beyond. He knew what surrender would mean. Torture, long and drawn out. Fierce and brutal interrogation followed by a lingering cruel death. He whispered the words of contrition and crossed himself. One of the riders broke free and moved slowly towards him. Bavasour drew his sword.

'Friend?' the man called out. 'Bavasour, our former comrade, won't you sit down with us and break bread?'

Bavasour lifted his sword and recalled the battle cry of the old king. 'God and St George!' he roared. Better this way and go to God like a soldier. He dug his spurs in and the garron broke into a charge. The sinister line of riders moved in a ripple of cloaks. Bavasour saw them lift their arbalests, and over the clatter and noise of his horse he heard the ominous twang as bolts were released. He was still screaming his battle cry when the barbed quarrels smashed into his face and chest, flinging him from the saddle to crash to the ground.

His attackers waited until the body lay still in a fast-spreading pool of blood. The dust began to settle. The garron, skittering backwards and forwards, eventually stood still, shaking its head and blowing noisily. The leader of the black-garbed riders dismounted, drawing his sword, and approached the fallen mercenary. He turned the corpse over with the toe of his boot and stared down at the shattered face.

'Dead!' he called. 'Strip his corpse.' He gestured to his right. 'The morass we rode around, toss the body there. Take his horse and harness and let us be gone.'

PART FOUR

'Such things were spoken of openly: whether they
are true or not, God knows.' *Life of Edward II*

Corbett was surprised. He had hardly returned to his chamber that morning when there was a knock on the door and Brother Adrian, his face wreathed in a benevolent smile, slipped into the room. He asked to sit, and Ranulf vacated his stool, gesturing at the monk to take it. Brother Adrian put his leather chancery satchel on the floor, then sat, hands on his knees, staring at Corbett, who held his gaze. The Benedictine normally busied himself around, the good, caring priest almost frenetic in his activity. Now he sat calmly, watchful, and Corbett realised that he'd misjudged him. He glimpsed the humour in Brother Adrian's deep-set eyes, the cynical twist to his mouth. The monk was a soul whose waters ran very deep, Corbett concluded; he was certainly not what he pretended to be.

'Father?' Corbett gestured towards the tray of wine cups.

'Oh yes, Sir Hugh. Let's take a little wine for the stomach's sake, as St Paul so rightly says.'

Ap Ythel, who had been lying on a wall bench, got up and served the wine, pulling a face in mock surprise as he moved behind the monk. Corbett just smiled and watched the Benedictine pick up what the clerk considered to be a very costly chancery satchel fashioned out of the best North African leather, fastened and secured by intricate clasps and buckles.

'Your clerk of the stable is on guard outside.' Brother Adrian looked up and smiled. 'Whilst Ap Ythel and Ranulf, your henchmen, protect you here. We have to be safe, Sir Hugh. God knows who attacked us in that chapel. In other circumstances . . .'

'What circumstances?' Corbett demanded.

'Sir Hugh,' again the benevolent smile, 'I shall tell you. I should really ask for this chamber to be cleared except for me and thee.'

'No,' Corbett declared. 'I trust both these men with my life.'

'I thought as much. Anyway, at least that one-eyed archer is not here.'

Corbett remained impassive even as he felt a spurt of alarm. He dared not glance at Ap Ythel or Ranulf, though he trusted them not to betray any concern.

'Very good, very good.' Brother Adrian opened his chancery satchel and took out two leather containers. He removed the top from one of these, shook out the creamy scroll of parchment and gave it to Corbett, who unrolled it carefully. From the very touch he could see that the vellum was the costliest, the script in dark-red ink, elegantly written. A small illumination lightened the first two words of the document: 'Clemens Papa'. He glanced at the bottom, translating the Latin: 'Given at Avignon in the fifth year of our Pontificate . . .' The clerk bit back his exclamation as he read how Pope Clement V, exiled in Avignon, recognised Adrian Ogilvie, otherwise known as Adrian of Rievaulx, as 'Primus Mallus Maleficorum' – the First Hammer of Witches – throughout the kingdoms of England and Scotland. Adrian Ogilvie was endowed with legatine powers 'to pursue such evil and nefarious souls' with all the power of the Church and must be given the full support of every legitimate secular authority both within and without.

The monk then opened the second scroll container and shook out a similar letter signed and sealed by Robert Winchelsea, Archbishop of Canterbury, which faithfully repeated the contents of the papal missive. Corbett, with the Benedictine's permission, showed both documents to Ranulf and Ap Ythel before handing them back. He tried to hide his astonishment, Brother Adrian was not some simple parish priest or learned Benedictine monk, but a man vested with important powers. Anyone who tried to impede, block or frustrate his work could face the whole rigour of excommunication, not to mention prosecution by the Crown.

'Sir Hugh?' Brother Adrian demanded. 'You accept the documents are genuine, the script, the signature, the seals?'

'Oh yes, but why now, Brother?' Corbett asked. 'We met in London. We journeyed north. We have been in this castle some days. Now we find you are a witch hunter, a prosecutor of warlocks, demon-worshippers and all the devil's disciples. Your powers are quite extensive and extraordinary—'

'Who else knows?' Ranulf broke in. 'Lord Henry and his sour-faced wife?'

'Nobody knows,' Brother Adrian retorted, 'apart from the people in this room. And that is how it will remain until I decide otherwise. As for why now, well why not? First, you are about to enter the devil's den.'

'We are not going to Blanchlands.'

'No, Sir Hugh, but you are going to meet Darel at Clairbaux. I also understand you plan to journey on to Tynemouth, and that too is of great significance, as I shall explain. Second, I need to take you into my confidence. Sir Hugh, you may have been watching me. I certainly have been studying you and yours, including that Welsh archer – Ap Vynar, the one you sent to spy on me.' The monk grinned at Ap Ythel. 'I caught him watching me and I wondered if it was time to save you a great deal of work and tell you who I really am. Third, time is passing. Matters will soon move to a head. You are immersed in business of the Crown; I am involved in what is called Secreta Negotia Sanctae Matris Ecclesiae – the Secret Business of Holy Mother Church.'

'Which is?'

'The constant battle against the powers of hell made manifest in human affairs to the total destruction of souls.'

'And why you?'

'Why indeed? But there again, Sir Hugh, I could ask the same of you. Why Sir Hugh Corbett, the principal clerk to the king? Your answer would be circumstances, and the same is true of me. My name really is Adrian Ogilvie, born of good family here in Northumbria. I attended the monastic school of Fountains Abbey, though for most of my education as a young man I was at Rievaulx. Both abbeys, as you know, are set in the lush beauty of the Yorkshire Dales. I became a student of renown. As St Paul says, "I do not boast for the sake of boasting but for the sake of the truth." I truly excelled myself. I studied exorcism, magic, witchcraft, demonic possession; you know the litany. I read the works of Albert the Great as well as the Arabs such as Khalide and Geber. I became this kingdom's *peritus*, skilled in all matters of demonology, though not in the public sense; that is the duty of the Dominicans and the Inquisition. I tend to be more subtle, more private. I advise bishops and abbots on individual cases.

'I would have stayed at Rievaulx for the rest of my days.' He pulled a face. 'Sometimes I wish to God I had. Anyway, as you know, the Church has been dealing with Secreta Negotia for the last thirteen hundred years, from the very beginning, when the blessed apostle Peter, our first pope, crossed swords with the warlock Simon Magus. Twenty-one years ago, Pope Nicholas III clashed with the great magician Abulafic. Our present Holy Father, Pope Clement V, is now confronted with allegations of black magic against the Templars.'

'Do you believe them?'

'No, Sir Hugh, I do not. I have told our king, the archbishop and the Holy Father himself that the allegations against the Templars are a farrago of lies, the work of Philip of France and his council of demons.'

'I agree,' Corbett declared, warming to this blunt-speaking Benedictine. 'But Brother Adrian, why are you here? Why are you involved in these matters?'

'The Church must continue its confrontation of the powers of darkness. It must challenge black magic, witch-craft, the midnight rites, the devil's doings and all of Satan's subtle ways.' He paused. 'Let me be blunt. Robert Wishart, Bishop of Glasgow, believes that Scotland's present troubles are the direct work of satanic cults.'

'The same Wishart who is now a prisoner in Porchester Castle on the south coast?'

'The same. Wishart was a fervent supporter of the Scottish rebel leader William Wallace, and when Wallace was filleted like a piece of meat at Smithfield, the bishop shifted his allegiance to Bruce. Now, however, he and other churchmen passionately believe that the wide-spread devastation in Scotland was caused by demonic powers. They have argued, and continue to do so, that England should desist in its war and recognise the sovereignty of Scotland, not because they champion this prince against that; they simply believe that the present war provides the most fertile ground for all kinds of evil.'

Brother Adrian rose and stretched. He abruptly opened the door, stared out onto the gallery, then closed the door and came back. 'The royal house of Scotland,' he continued, sitting down, 'the House of Dunkeld, has sinister origins in the person of that dark prince Macbeth. Some people believe that he dabbled deeply in the black arts, that he was a murderer who consorted with witches and tried to kill his enemies through necromancy. They claim he would go out into the most desolate parts of his kingdom to seek the company of those who walked the alleyways of hell. Eventually, of course, he died, possibly murdered, and because of him the royal line became cursed. If that is true, the malignancy came to flower most foully some twenty-five years ago, perhaps even before then. Alexander III of blessed memory married Margaret of England. She died at the early age of thirty-five and was followed to the grave by all her children: Alexander, David and a daughter also called Margaret. This meant there was no heir apparent and the great lords of Scotland began to look to their swords.'

'Of course,' Corbett intervened, 'it was a real tragedy. If their children had succeeded, Scotland would have been ruled by a prince with the blood of both Dunkeld and Plantagenet in his veins. If that had happened, perhaps an eternal alliance of peace could have been arranged. I recall the old king talking about that.'

'Alexander III realised the danger,' Brother Adrian took up the story. 'No queen, no wife, no heir, so he married again: a French noblewoman, the beautiful Yolande. Alexander was hot for her, and for a son. He realised that time was passing. He was attracted to the joys of the bed, but above all, Scotland demanded an heir. On the evening of the nineteenth of March, the

Year of Our Lord 1286, Alexander left a council meeting in Edinburgh to be with his darling wife, but was thrown from his horse by the sudden onset of the most violent storm in living memory. They found his corpse the following morning.'

'And he left no heir except a granddaughter, a little girl, Margaret of Norway?'

'Correct, Sir Hugh.'

'And she, poor child, died on board ship whilst returning to Scotland.'

'Hell's teeth,' Ranulf breathed. 'Devil or not, a gambler would regard such ill fortune as exceptional. One king, his wife, their three children and a granddaughter, all gone. So sudden, so cruel.'

'When Margaret of Norway died,' Brother Adrian continued, 'the house of Dunkeld lay in ruins and the crown was in dispute.'

'And so we come to John *Balliol*,' Corbett broke in.

'True,' Brother Adrian agreed. 'He assumed the crown with permission from Edward of England, who then forced him to abdicate in humiliating disgrace. The cruel chaos intensified like one of those vicious whirlpools you glimpse swirling in the great rivers, a storm of waters that sucks everything in. Sir Hugh, look at both kingdoms as they are now compared to thirty years ago: fire, devastation, the song of the sword, the marching of troops and the savage forays of war bands are now a way of life. The countryside is blighted, the haunt of the wolfsheads. Towns and cities blaze. Famine and disease walk hand in hand like devilish twins dispatched from hell. The rottenness and decay in Scotland is spreading south, king against earl, commoner against knight.'

'And you suspect this is the devil's work?' Corbett smiled wryly. 'Well of course it is. But you believe the likes of the Black Chesters carry a heavy responsibility for all this malevolent mayhem?'

'I do, and my belief is shared by a number of leading churchmen either side of the Scottish march, as well as the Holy Father's experts in universities throughout Europe. Satan truly is a lion on the prowl. Scotland in particular has been grievously mauled: Alexander III's mysterious accident, the death of his first wife and all his heirs, the humiliation of Balliol, the brutal defeat of Wallace, and now Bruce's bloody war, but even there tragedy lurks. They claim Bruce's father is grievously stricken with leprosy. People wonder if Robert himself is also a bearer of that dreadful disease. And so the litany of lamentation goes on.'

'Tell me . . .' Ranulf, fascinated by what he was hearing, pulled out a corner stool and sat down beside Corbett.

'Tell me what?' Brother Adrian mimicked. 'I can guess, Ranulf-atte-Newgate. You want to ask the question so many people pose. How can witches and warlocks gather in some nightmare coven and create such mayhem? Now let me make it clear, human wickedness is caused by human wickedness. We all have free will. We all make decisions and must abide by the consequences, whatever they may be. However, as regards the likes of the Black Chesters, my answer is twofold. First, they pollute the world we live in. Watch a fire blaze. Notice how the smoke, the fumes, the reeking stench spreads, clogging the mouth and throat, stinging the eyes, smattering the skin with filthy ash. Covens like the Black Chesters pollute the spiritual air. They release a deadly miasma that has its effect sometimes long after the evil has been done, the devilish curse issued, the blasphemous sacrifice made. Second, on a more practical level, look how the Black Chesters wield power here along the Scottish march. They control Darel, Blanchlands and beyond.'

'For what purpose?' Ap Ythel demanded. 'Brother Adrian, I am a simple Welsh bowman. I protect the Crown and fight its enemies.'

'My friend,' Brother Adrian squinted up at the bowman, 'there is a word derived from the Greek: pandemonium. It means complete and utter chaos, devastating disruption, but the word also translates, in the literal sense, as "full of demons". The Black Chesters want pandemonium, they want chaos, the collapse of law and order; the violation of the Church's teaching, the shattering of all civic and religious harmony. They wish to create hell on earth and exercise power over this chaos like the lords of hell they are.' The Benedictine paused to wipe his mouth on the back of his hand. 'And they are succeeding; the chaos is spreading.'

'And what have you discovered here?'

'The Black Chesters are part of an evil web of covens across the length and breadth of Scotland, one of many though I suspect the most powerful and malignant. They shelter at Blanchlands, patronised by Edmund Darel, and are committed to waging war against the king's peace and creating divisions wherever they can. Percy's rivalry with Darel has been subtly exploited by them. The Black Chesters lie at the heart of the storm: English against Scot, Darel against Percy; Darel against the Crown, Percy against the Crown, or so they hope. The leaders of the coven are well known, though its ordinary members are more hidden. By day they are responsible citizens of the community but by night they practise their evil. They deal out judgement, they silence all opposition, but above all, as I shall show you, they heap horror after horror upon the innocent.'

'How?' Corbett demanded.

'People disappear, Sir Hugh, entire families, never seen again.'

'Doesn't Lord Henry intervene?'

'Sir Hugh, look around. Lord Henry is hard pressed. He has only been here two years and he must renovate and fortify Alnwick. Moreover, when he is not watching Darel, he turns to confront the Scots, who, as you know, are creeping closer to England's northern shires.' The monk put his goblet on the floor beside him. 'I have little support. You see, I cannot tell Lord Henry or those Crown officials still in their posts who I really am, what I truly do. Even if I did, what real help could they give? They have to deal with wolfsheads, the dispossessed, wandering bands of mercenaries and the rest. In the meantime I try to track, as a hunter would a wolf, the

Black Chesters and all their doings. I mentioned those who have disappeared. I strongly suspect they have been murdered, their blood used for blasphemous sacrifice. Now and again, here and there, a corpse is discovered mangled and torn, its face smashed in, the chest savagely opened, the heart plucked out.

'Now publicly I am a parish priest, I tend to my flock. I cannot admit to knowing too much about Darel, Blanchlands, the Black Chesters and all that trickery; that would provoke suspicion and place me in great danger. I just want people to accept me for what I appear to be. If your watchman Ap Vynar studied me closely over the days, he would see me constantly chattering to tinkers, traders, local farmers and peasants, gathering what news I can. Naturally I hear about births, people falling ill, people dying, the need for the sacraments, Masses to be said, but I also gather more sinister scraps of news, pieces of information. How a travelling tinker has disappeared or a child been abducted. Sometimes they talk of black-garbed riders at the dead of night. The devil hides deep, Sir Hugh, and you have to be a skilful hunter.'

He took out a set of Ave beads and began to sift these through his fingers. Corbett sat listening to the sounds echoing across the castle bailey. The squealing of pigs from the slaughter shed set his teeth on edge and deepened his unease; he felt a similar apprehension from his companions.

'You may ask what I can do, what I have done, what I shall do.' The Benedictine lifted his beads. 'To put it bluntly, I pray and I hunt the coven. If I can discover and trap any of its adherents, I will move heaven and earth to ensure they receive just punishment.'

'Did you poison Richolda and Hockley?'

'No.' Brother Adrian half smiled. 'In some ways I wish I had, but ask Lord Henry. I begged him not to surrender Richolda until I had closely questioned her. I needed to discover the true identity of her leader, a master warlock who calls himself Paracelsus.' He crossed himself and murmured a prayer. 'I have been hunting him for over two years.'

'And you don't know who he is?'

'No, Sir Hugh.'

'So what else is to be done?' Ranulf demanded.

'I moved from *Rievaulx* to Tynemouth and from there to Alnwick. Prior Richard and Lord Henry do not know my true purpose. When I have to, I shall reveal it. What I must do is unmask Paracelsus, destroy him and inflict the same fate on his followers.'

'So why now?' Ranulf persisted.

'I have already given you reasons for that,' the Benedictine retorted, 'but there is one pressing further reason. From what Master Cacoignes has told us, Darel is convinced you carry, or at least know the whereabouts of, the Lily Crown of Scotland.' He held up a hand. 'I know you don't, yet rumours are rife about that crown. Gossips say it is hidden in or around Tynemouth Priory. You intend to journey there. I am sure adherents of the Black Chesters here at Alnwick have informed their masters about your plans.'

'Why do they want the crown?' Corbett demanded. 'True, it is of pure gold and very valuable.'

'It was sent by Pope Lucius III to William the Lion,' Brother Adrian replied. 'Its gold is very precious and very ancient. It is claimed it once covered the Ark of the Covenant in Solomon's temple in Jerusalem. No,' he turned testily to Ranulf, 'do not scoff. The royal regalia of Scotland has a uniquely sacred history, which is why your king, the so-called Hammer of the Scots, seized it and sent it south to Westminster. The Stone of Scone, for example, is said to come from Ancient Egypt and is closely entwined with the story of Moses.'

'So they want the crown for their own secret purposes?'

'Yes, Sir Hugh. We may ridicule, dismiss it all as legend, but to the Black Chesters the Lily Crown is as important as the sacrament is to a holy priest. They regard it as sacred and ancient, and believe it holds a potency, a power they could harness. So when you do journey on to Tynemouth, the Black Chesters will certainly be watching.'

'And Cacoignes?' Corbett demanded. 'Do you know anything about him that we should be aware of?'

Brother Adrian pulled a face and shook his head. 'He is from the English court after all. Don't they claim he is a gambler, a man who likes hazard? Anyway,' he got to his feet, 'I would like you and your comrades to accompany me. Perhaps you can assist as well as act as witnesses to the truth of what I have said.'

Corbett agreed, and within the hour, he, Ap Ythel

and Ranulf, with Chanson trailing behind, left Alnwick in the company of Brother Adrian, following an ancient path up onto the wild heathland, galloping under grey skies. The scudding clouds seemed to shadow them as they rode deeper and deeper into what Corbett could only describe as a haunting loneliness. Occasionally they would pass through a copse or spinney of trees where moorland birds circled or swooped, their calls echoing harshly all around. Isolated cottages lay hidden in the shadow of these ancient woods, their presence only betrayed by a smudge of dark smoke against the sky or the raucous barking of a dog, which would be abruptly stilled.

They cantered across a burn, Brother Adrian's black cloak flapping in the breeze like a banner, and entered a fringe of trees, following a beaten trackway through the bramble and gorse. Corbett wondered if in the past, the entire land had been covered by a great forest, and these trees were its relics. He felt as if he was in an ancient place reeking of memories, a countryside that concealed secrets and kept dark things hidden. He missed the softness of his own shire Essex and felt a stab of homesickness.

Corbett shook himself free from his reverie as the path they followed debouched into a clearing. He reined in, quietening his horse as he tried to control his own sharp-edged apprehension. Something was very wrong here. This was not a haunted place, lonely and desolate; a real wickedness had swept through the lonely glade and blighted the inhabitants of the small cottage built out of wood, plaster and thatch on its rough-stone base. The cottage had its own garden, but the soil was thin and poor, the herbs and vegetables growing there stunted and ill formed. Behind the cottage stood a small piggery and two large hen coops, but these were empty. Both the door and shutters of the cottage were flung wide open.

Corbett slid from the saddle of his horse, handed the reins to Chanson and went inside. It was a poor man's dwelling, with a few sticks of furniture, and some pots in the buttery, which also served as a kitchen. He recalled the cauldron and spent embers he'd glimpsed outside. The cottagers probably used that for most of their cooking. He stared around but could detect no sign of violence. He walked back outside. Brother Adrian sat slumped in his saddle.

'No chickens, no pigs.' Corbett indicated with his head to behind the cottage. 'And I saw no sign of disturbance in there. You suspect something horrid has happened here?'

'Sir Hugh,' Brother Adrian leaned down, 'Ewen, Margota and their ill-witted daughter Edith lived here, or did so until about four days ago. Good people, they sold this and that and provided lodgings for travelling tinkers and tradesmen. One of these hurried into Alnwick to report what you have seen here. No Ewen, Margota or Edith, nor any sign of them. All valuables gone, livestock too, yet little trace, if any, of violence, robbery or assault.'

'Yes.' Corbett stared around. 'Quiet as a grave, which

I suspect is what it is. Outlaws, raiders, wolfsheads would not be so tidy.' He squinted up at Ap Ythel. The Welshman looked distinctly nervous; he kept staring into the trees as if an enemy lurked there.

'The Angel of Death,' Ap Ythel murmured. 'You can almost feel it, can't you, Sir Hugh? The Angel of Death has swept through here. These cottagers are not missing, they are dead.'

'I agree,' Ranulf declared, trying to quieten his horse.

'If these poor people have been harmed,' Corbett replied, 'we will seek justice for them. Ap Ythel, my friend, can you help?'

The Welshman dismounted along with Ranulf and Chanson, and the clerk of the stables led their horses away, humming a tune that seemed discordant in that grey, blighted place. Ranulf snapped at him to shut up. Ap Ythel, who knew all about Ranulf's deep fear of the open countryside, soothingly beckoned him and Corbett over, teasing the Clerk of the Green Wax that if he kept silent and observed sharply, he might learn something. The Welshman crouched down, staring at the ground.

'I suspect,' he declared, 'this place was visited by a group of horsemen. They dismounted in the trees then walked into the cottage. They wore very low-heeled boots, perhaps even sandals. The question is, where did they go from here?'

'Over there.' Corbett pointed to his right and the narrow dirt trackway snaking off into the trees.

'Sir Hugh,' Ap Ythel rose to his feet, 'I will make a Welshman of you yet.'

They followed the path, going deeper into the copse. They crossed a burn, nothing more than a narrow rivulet. Here the ground became softer, the grass and weeds more lush, the usual signs that they were close to a treacherous bog or marsh. Corbett crouched down. The ground was disturbed, but this told him very little. He suspected, especially from the fetid odours that swirled around them, that this place was also used to dump waste of every kind. The smell became more offensive as Ranulf pushed in a branch and stirred the scum-soaked greenery.

'I am correct,' Corbett murmured. 'The cottager used this as a lay stall, didn't he?' He got to his feet and asked his companions to draw daggers and fashion long poles out of tree branches. He insisted that the poles be at least two yards long, the surfaces kept rough so the stumps could act as hooks. Once ready, he, Ap Ythel and Ranulf, with Brother Adrian and Chanson helping, pushed the poles into the shifting, stinking greenery. They jabbed and prodded, and Corbett felt his pole jar against hard earth. He reckoned the morass was no more than five feet deep, yet still treacherous and the perfect place to hide a corpse.

He moved his pole and felt it strike something moving sluggishly beneath the surface. Ap Ythel shouted that he had found the same. Corbett glanced over. The Welshman had bravely stepped into the morass; he had begun to gently sink, yet he was still intent on dragging in what was hooked on his pole. Corbett and Ranulf hastened to help, pulling Ap Ythel back, helping to shift the swamp-caked corpse further and further from the sticky morass, which seemed so reluctant to give up its secrets. The stench was hideous, deeply offensive, as the incoming corpse broke up the mud and released more filthy water. Using their poles, they yanked it further in. Corbett glimpsed long hair; pale, haggard features; glassy eyes and the most savage wound to the left of the chest.

At last the cadaver lay completely free of the morass. They used water from the nearby burn to clean off some of the bloody mud, only to stand and stare in silent horror at the blasphemies perpetrated on this young woman. Her throat had been cut with a half-moon swipe from the sharpest dagger, the flesh deeply ploughed by the jagged blade. Afterwards – and Corbett quietly prayed that it *had* been afterwards – her chest had been smashed open with a mallet, hammer or war club, the bones roughly hacked aside so her heart could be plucked out.

'In God's name!' Corbett exclaimed. 'What demon did this? It must be the Black Chesters. They wanted her heart and those of her parents for their obscene rites. Brother Adrian?'

'Peasants have vanished,' the Benedictine had now dropped to his knees beside the corpse, 'but rarely has anything like this been found.' He held up a hand. 'I am sure if we visited those places where other disappearances have occurred, such horrors would lie close by.' He sketched a cross in the air. 'My parishioners talk of glimpsing the swift passage of hooded, visored horsemen. They arrive clustered together, cloaks flapping. There is no calling out, no reining in; they just gallop apparently out of nowhere and then disappear. The travelling troubadours call them the night-riders, the dark-dwellers, the minions of the mansions of midnight. Demons incarnate,' he breathed, 'and this is their handiwork, I will bless the body.'

Corbett crouched and scrutinised the cadaver even as Brother Adrian murmured how he would ask Lord Henry to send men to drag the morass for other corpses. Corbett half listened. He rose and walked away, then stopped as he glimpsed something lying on the stem of one of the spiky bushes. He plucked this up, examined it and quickly put it in his belt wallet. He had seen a similar decorated leather bracelet on Cacoignes' wrist. He stood staring into the darkness created by the interlacing branches. A bird called, a harsh, strident sound.

Corbett breathed in slowly, trying to clear his mind of the gruesome images of that ragged, violated corpse. He was frightened, he admitted that to himself. He was a royal clerk skilled in the pursuit of killers, but this was different. He was facing terror, sheer terror for the sake of it. He could only imagine what had happened here. The Black Chesters, all cloaked and cowled, guiding their horses through the trees, a group of demons hungry for human life. They would dismount, hobble their horses and set up guard. Did they come in the dead of night, first thing in the morning, or at the hour of the bat, just as daylight faded and darkness closed in? They entered that cottage and seized those poor people who could not resist. Corbett could only imagine the shock and fear of the simple peasants as they realised they had fallen into the hands of monsters.

The Black Chesters would take their prisoners out to that morass. They would be shivering, begging for their lives, pleading for mercy, but they were only lambs bleating on the way to slaughter. He could imagine a member of the coven slipping behind each of the captives, their hair grabbed, heads pulled back and throats slit from ear to ear. Afterwards their chests were broken and the hearts plucked out so the Black Chesters could carry out their macabre practices. They had done the same before and they would undoubtedly do it again. Corbett breathed deeply to control his fear and rage. He made a vow to himself. If God gave him life, health and wit, he would track these cruel killers down, try them and hang them. He would dig them out both root and branch.

He felt the bracelet he'd slipped in his wallet and wondered how Master Cacoignes could be involved in this dreadful business. He accepted Cacoignes' story of fleeing with Ravinac to Tynemouth, of trying to escape further south when he was captured. But one thing he found illogical: why had Cacoignes remained in the north and joined Edmund Darel's comitatus under a different name? To be close to the Lily Crown hidden in Tynemouth Priory? That made sense, but there again, why didn't he just go back to London, present himself at Westminster and describe exactly what had happened? Perhaps it was not just the lure of gold that kept him in the north but a real fear of going home. What could he possibly be frightened of? Was it fear that had compelled him to join Ravinac's party in the first place? Corbett understood from Gaveston that Cacoignes and all his group had been volunteers. So – he drummed his fingers on the pommel of his sword – what had frightened Cacoignes in London?

'Sir Hugh?' Ranulf strode through the undergrowth, kicking away the trailing briars and snaking brambles. 'Sir Hugh, we are finished here.'

'True, true,' Corbett called out over his shoulder. 'We are finished here but not finished with this. In fact,' he turned and came back, 'I strongly suspect we are going to go deeper and deeper into the darkness.'

'And I shall go there with you,' Brother Adrian declared. 'I am grateful for your help, Sir Hugh, but now we should return to Alnwick.'

Back at the castle, Brother Adrian hastened, as he put it, to have secret and urgent words with Lord Henry, while Corbett decided to seek out Cacoignes. He found the cunning man standing on the parapet overlooking the main gate, staring out across the open countryside. He seemed distracted, his eyes on the far horizon though his mind appeared to be elsewhere. Corbett greeted him and then passed on. He had seen what he wanted: on Cacoignes' wrist was a bracelet identical to the one Corbett had found in that hideous place of slaughter. Nevertheless, Corbett was suspicious. Once past Cacoignes, he stopped and took the bracelet out of his wallet, scrutinising it carefully. Nothing more than small beads and medals on a piece of tough twine, with no clasp or pin, it seemed designed for a certain wrist, to be squeezed on over the fingers. So how had it come off and caught on that briar bush where the blasphemy had occurred? Those who had attacked the peasant family had been cunning and careful, doing their best to remove any sign of the abominations they had carried out. So how was it that a bracelet, tightly clasped around a killer's wrist, suddenly became loose and slipped off? Moreover, Corbett had confronted assassins since his days as a young mailed clerk, and one thing he'd noticed was that they often wore gloves or gauntlets. Surely they would do so in a place such as that copse, where briar and thorn jutted out to rip exposed flesh? Gauntlets or gloves would be a true obstacle to anything slipping from wrist or finger.

Corbett put the bracelet away. He would watch and wait. Meanwhile, he chattered to his companions and kept drafting and revising all he had learnt, heard and seen. He was surprised by Brother Adrian's revelations, but on reflection, he accepted the logic of the monk's assertions. Holy Mother Church always took decisive action against the practitioners of the black arts, especially when such creatures of the dark plotted the destruction of the Crown's rights and the gross violation of the king's peace. Over the years Corbett had heard about the Sanctum Officium – the Holy Office – directly mandated by the pope to deal with Secreta Negotia. The truth of the situation was now clearly emerging. Edward I, by his brutal and bloody war here in the north, had sown dragon's teeth, and now that it was harvest time, a bitter, savage conflict raged like a fire out of control along the entire Scottish march. The violence created a deep pool of malignant malevolence for the likes of the mysterious Paracelsus and the Black Chesters to fish in.

Corbett did not believe for one moment the powers such covens claimed, either individually or as a group. He had witnessed enough human wickedness to understand that its perpetrators needed very little help, if any, from the powers of darkness. Nevertheless, he fully understood how such malignancy worked. First, their secret macabre rites drew members of a coven closer to each other. Bonds were created that bound them as tightly as any knight who took a feudal oath to his lord or a religious who swore his vows to his superior. Deeds done in the dark created a conspiracy in which every member was involved; there was no turning away or going back along that long road into eternal night. The ritual murders of Ewen and his family, the sacrificing of their hearts to the eternal shadows and the demons they sheltered, divided such people from the normal community. They lived, ate and drank in their own wicked world, a baleful way of life to which they were committed as passionately and fervently as a monk or nun to their rule and community.

Second, the odour of evil they created truly terrified everyone else. They played vicious games to freeze the will and so crush any opposition. Corbett had already witnessed this chilling pageantry when the Black Chesters had appeared before the gates of Alnwick. They'd performed their own murderous masque with hooded garb, ominous warnings, the display of a rotting corpse and the taunting possibility that their leader was a woman who had returned from the dead.

'No, no,' he whispered to the silence of his chamber. 'You, my enemies, are human enough, with all the frailty of our kind. You make mistakes. You can be detected. You can be trapped and so still hang for your abominations.'

The following afternoon, the alarm was raised. However, this was abruptly quietened as the small group of horsemen who approached the main gateway held up a pole with a broad white cloth flapping in the breeze. Messages were exchanged and the horsemen parted to allow two young children, a boy and a girl, to walk to the front, carefully shepherded by a woman, apparently their nurse. The drawbridge was lowered. Brother Adrian scurried across and crouched down before the children, clasping their hands, kissing them on each cheek before doing the same to their guardian. The Benedictine had words with her, then led all three across the drawbridge, under the portcullis to where Lord Henry, Corbett and others were waiting.

'Darel's children,' the monk explained. 'I recognised them immediately with their nurse, Ursula. Sir Hugh, Darel has agreed to meet you now at Clairbaux. He will be waiting in the church of St Cuthbert with the

Lady Hilda and one other. He stipulates that his retinue, including the four riders outside, will stay at least one mile from the walls of Clairbaux. You are to bring an escort of the same size; one of these will be allowed to accompany you inside. Sir Edmund will meet you in the church and, God willing, make his peace with you.'

'And, of course, he wants the meeting now,' Corbett murmured, 'before either Lord Henry or I can plot any trickery or an ambuscade – not that we would. Sir Edmund Darel believes that the world thinks like him. However, if it is to be done, it's best done swiftly. The days are passing quickly and it's time we were gone from here.'

'What weapons can we bring?' Ranulf demanded.

'Sword and dagger, nothing else.'

Corbett reined in and stared at Clairbaux, which was built in the lea of a gently rising hill. The entire demesne was bounded by a grey-stone curtain wall with a stout wooden double gate. Admission was gained by a bell under its stone coping. There were no guards on the wall or bailiffs patrolling outside. Ranulf pulled on the bell rope, then both he and Corbett dismounted. They heard the sound of footsteps, the jingle of keys, and a postern door in the gate swung back creating a narrow gap so that only one rider at a time could walk his mount through.

Inside the gate stretched a cobbled yard with store-rooms, sheds and workshops. The hermitage itself consisted of a square of buildings built around a grassy garth with a rose garden at its centre. One side of this cloister was bounded by an ancient church consisting of a tower built on the end of a dark-stone chapel with narrow windows and a red slate roof. The other three sides were lined by small cottages built of the same stone as the chapel. A quiet place, though in the dull light of the fading day, Corbett considered it to be sinister, the clammy, cold silence that of a cemetery or a mausoleum. He tried to ignore such nagging anxiety; after all, the day was sullen, a harbinger of autumn. Nevertheless, the raucous cawing of crows from the nearby trees set his teeth on edge. He was pleased when Lady Hilda came out of the church.

'Sir Hugh Corbett, Ranulf-atte-Newgate?' she called. 'You are most welcome. Sir Edmund awaits you within.' She smiled. 'No need to stand on ceremony.'

Corbett and Ranulf followed the grey-cowled porter who had let them in across the mist-hung cloisters to the church door, where both men exchanged the kiss of peace with Lady Hilda. She fluttered her fingers at the porter to gesture his dismissal before leading Corbett and Ranulf into the musty nave. Slivers of light pierced the lancet windows. Torches fixed in their sconces on the squat, drum-like pillars cast constantly shifting pools of flame. Corbett found this disconcerting as he peered through the murk at the two figures standing behind a table placed just before the entrance to the rood screen. Lanternhorns positioned either end of this table provided more light, though this did little to make the two figures more distinct.

'Hugh, for heaven's sake! Stop standing there like some lovelorn bridegroom.' Edmund Darel came round the table and strode down the nave, arms out ready to embrace Corbett as if the clerk was some long-lost favourite brother. Corbett took off his war belt, handed it to Ranulf and walked forward to meet his host. They embraced, then Darel, hands gripping Corbett's shoulders, stepped back, scrutinising the clerk from head to toe. 'The face is not so smooth, the hair not so raven black, but I'd recognise you immediately in a crowd, whilst this must be Ranulf-atte-Newgate.' He turned and greeted Corbett's henchman warmly, his rich, powerful voice echoing around the chapel.

Corbett studied the man he secretly described as 'a soul born to villainy'. The years had been kind to Darel: he was tall, muscular, his red-gold hair, moustache and beard skilfully clipped and fragrantly oiled. His face was slightly flushed but still exuded that golden look that, with the very light-blue eyes and generous lips, made him such a favourite amongst the ladies. He was dressed soberly in a dark-blue star-spangled cotehardie and hose of the richest and purest wool; his white shirt was of the finest Flemish linen whilst his riding boots and war belt were of costly Moroccan leather. Small jewels on the golden chain around his neck, the bracelet on his sword wrist and the rings on his left hand shimmered brilliantly as they caught the light. No, Edmund, Corbett reflected, you have not changed. You're brimming with the same nervous energy you always had; you find it almost impossible to stay still.

Darel abruptly turned from Ranulf as a woman's voice called his name. He grabbed Corbett by the wrist and pointed up the nave. 'Come, come! Leonora wishes to meet you.'

Corbett glanced over his shoulder. Lady Hilda had disappeared. Ranulf stood glowering, clearly uneasy at Darel's effusive welcome. Corbett strapped on his war belt and they walked up the dusty paved nave, the spurs on their boots jingling like little bells, the clip of their heels echoing like a drum beat. Corbett hid his smile. Darel loved the masque and the mummery, and the place he had chosen to meet was suffused with drama. This lonely chapel, which echoed to every sound, the dancing light, the shifting murk, the cracked pavestones underfoot, the cobwebbed dust piled high in corners and a mysterious woman waiting in the shadows. Corbett's fingers fell to the hilt of his dagger, and he glanced quickly at Ranulf, whose hand was not far from the pommel of his sword.

Leonora had not moved but remained behind the table. 'Welcome,' she whispered and leaned forward, right hand extended for Corbett and Ranulf to kiss.

At Darel's request they sat down in the high-backed leather chairs, Corbett facing Darel, Ranulf opposite Leonora, who was a truly beautiful woman, with the face of a Venus and a body like mortal sin. She was tall and willowy, with large, expressive cat-like eyes under arching brows, her dark hair, parted in the middle, rippling richly down to her shoulders. She wore no head-dress or veil and very little jewellery except for a ruby ring on her left hand; a golden cincture circled her narrow waist and a crystal silver gorget emphasised her smooth, swan-like throat. She had delicate hands with the longest fingers, and when she spoke during the introductions, her voice was low and throaty. Every movement, every gesture was refined and exquisitely ladylike. In many ways she looked very similar to Richolda, but with subtle differences; Leonora seemed calmer, more poised and definitely more certain of herself.

'You attacked us.' Ranulf spoke abruptly. Corbett hid his surprise at the outburst, yet he recognised that his henchman wished to break the spell of this ghostly, eerie place and the calm assurance of these two hell-creatures. 'You attacked royal envoys,' Ranulf insisted. 'You did so twice. We are Crown clerks, travelling under the royal standard; we are within the king's love and deserving of the king's peace.'

'A terrible mistake,' Leonora declared. 'We were misinformed. We did not know—'

'I wasn't talking to you, woman,' Ranulf snapped. His hand fell to the hilt of his dagger as Darel's face clouded. Leonora drew her breath in, a soft, hissing sound like that of an angry cat.

'A full pardon.' Corbett rapped the table. 'For the sake of the peace I will accept you made a dreadful mistake.' He pointed to the chancery tray on the table before them. 'Write out the conclusions we reach and both Ranulf and I, as royal envoys, will seal and sign the document. It will promise a full pardon for the attack on us and the assault on Alnwick. In return, you

will vow that such actions must cease forthwith, never
to be repeated. As a token of our goodwill I shall arrange
the release of all prisoners taken after your outrageous
assault on Lord Henry's castle.'

He sat back in the chair and stared up the ceiling
beams as if lost in his own thoughts now that he'd
stated the obvious. On their journey here, he and Ranulf
had discussed exactly what to do. They had decided
they would show no deference, make no plea or betray
any weakness. They were royal envoys; Darel's assaults
on them were heinous and treasonable.

Nevertheless, the reality was that they had underestimated the extent of the violence and criminal
depredations raging along the Scottish march. Lord
Henry Percy was not as strong or as supportive as
they'd hoped, whilst Darel had emerged not only as a
ruthless robber baron but a powerful lord with fingers
in many a pie. King Edward and his council, distracted
by the crisis caused by Gaveston, had not taken full
stock of what was truly happening in the north. Now
that Corbett and Ranulf were here, they had to reach
Tynemouth and search out, if possible, the whereabouts
of the Lily Crown. In addition, they had to ensure
Gaveston's secret and safe departure on *The Golden
Dove*, then make their own way south without further
loss. In order to do this, they would treat Darel harshly
and bring him into the king's peace, then deal with the
real threat he posed once they'd returned to Westminster.

Corbett shifted his gaze and stared across the table.
'There's very little to add to what I have said, sir.'

Darel smiled dazzlingly, as did Leonora. Corbett realised the two of them were one soul, the ties between this robber baron and his witch-queen stronger than life itself. He also acknowledged that Darel was treacherous and could not be trusted. So what did he really want?

'Hugh, Hugh.' Darel leaned across the table. 'I know you of old. We are comrades . . .'

'No we are not,' Corbett countered. 'If I had my way, Edmund, you'd hang and your witch beside you. Indeed, if you ever break the king's peace again in such a murderous assault, I shall personally build the gallows to string you up on. So, you will solemnly promise that I, Sir Hugh Corbett, together with my comitatus, will, as the king's own envoys, be allowed to travel the length and breadth of this kingdom unimpeded by you or yours either directly or indirectly. And that,' he pointed a finger at Leonora, 'includes you, mistress, and whatever coven you belong to, for as God lives, if I am given the chance and the right, I shall see you and yours hang.'

Corbett's harsh voice echoed like the bray of a trumpet around the nave. Leonora flushed, her head going back. Darel coughed, cleared his throat and closely studied one of his ring fingers. Then he abruptly glanced up.

'Hugh, you are being hard.'

'Edmund, I am being truthful. I beg you to be the same.'

Darel breathed in, trying to calm himself, though his clenched mouth and thin-stretched lips betrayed his anger, as did his restless, frenetic eyes. Corbett studied his opponent closely. He wondered if Darel was truly possessed by some murderous demon that had captured his soul and sent his humours all a-dancing. He shifted his gaze to Leonora, who looked equally flustered, still slightly flushed. He drew comfort from the fact that this meeting was, perhaps, not going the way this precious pair had planned.

'Agreed.' Darel breathed out a deep, noisy sigh, then relaxed, his face suffused by a friendly smile. 'Agreed,' he repeated, pushing back his chair. 'Hugh,' he gestured at the chancery tray, 'we shall draw up a memorandum of understanding sealed by our good selves. Perhaps your henchman Ranulf could assist me?'

Corbett just sat smiling at this most dangerous of adversaries.

'Sir Hugh?'

'Edmund, I agree.' Corbett glanced at Ranulf, who looked distinctly uncomfortable. Corbett's henchman was skilled in sword and dagger play, a sharp, caustic observer of human foibles. Corbett also recognised how Ranulf hated what they were now involved in, seated here in this lonely, desolate church at the very heart of a seemingly never-ending northern wilderness. Moreover, he had little time for those who boasted about being skilled and adept in matters mystical. Corbett leaned across and tapped him gently on the shoulder. 'Ranulf, a word?'

He turned back to Darel. 'Edmund, mistress, do excuse us.'

Ranulf followed Corbett into the shadow-thronged

transept, a gallery of darkness behind a row of stout rounded pillars. Corbett took a sconce torch and thrust it into a wall niche, bathing the transept in light. The dancing flame brought to life the slightly faded but still vigorously executed frescoes, undoubtedly a legacy of the Celtic monks who had made this place a house of deep holiness. He crouched and peered closer. There was no order to the paintings; just a series of images. One of the most striking was an insect-like demon with a human head; arrows pierced the monster's belly and wings whilst it held its arms up helplessly against the fire burning on its head. Next to this a blazing ship floated on a blood-red sea, its sails half submerged. Beside it a scroll proclaimed, 'Woe to the land and the sea for today Satan has come down with great wrath.' Corbett tapped this with his fingers, then plucked at Ranulf's sleeve and drew him closer.

'Ranulf, you can tell your children's children that on one occasion you truly did sit down and make a pact with the devil.' He paused. He could hear Darel and Leonora whispering behind them. 'Believe me,' he continued, 'we are going to do that today.'

'Do you trust them?'

'Does the sun set at night? Of course I don't! I just wonder what in God's name they really want. I am also curious as to why they have not mentioned the obvious.'

'Which is?'

'Come and listen.'

Corbett and Ranulf went back to their seats, Darel and Leonora watching them expectantly.

'So,' Corbett began, 'Lord Henry releases his prisoners. Your son and daughter are returned. You promise to desist from all attacks on me and mine so that we may proceed safely and securely under the royal standard to any part of this kingdom. You also acknowledge your grievous offence in attacking us twice. You are fully contrite and sue for a full pardon, which I have the power to grant and will do so. Good.' He tapped the chancery tray. 'We shall draw up the memorandum. Is there anything else?'

'No.' Darel smiled, rubbing his hands carefully, as if he was washing them in a bowl.

'Good, good.' Corbett glanced away to hide the suspicions seething within him. He stared around the chapel. He felt sure that the angel who had once guarded it had long left: beings of the light would never dwell in such a demon-tainted place. Hermitage or not, he felt a cold darkness, which hovered over an even more dreadful abyss, a place where demons lurked amongst the roof beams and devils bustled busily in the lengthening shadows. He recalled one of the wall paintings he'd glimpsed along that twilight transept: it depicted a bat-like monster, armed with a crossbow, doing battle with a gigantic fish through whose gaping mouth poured a horde of skeletons armed with spears and shields. This was a nightmare place; a malignancy lurked here, and Corbett truly believed that Darel and his paramour were the source of such spiritual agitation.

'Shall we begin?' Darel demanded.

'I don't think so.' Corbett moved the chancery tray

to one side. 'Edmund, let's talk about the Black Chesters, yes? A malicious coven of demon-worshippers who haunt the Scottish march and may be guilty of the most heinous crimes. It is claimed that people very close to you are part of that coven. It is also appropriate to talk about the traitor, the creature who calls himself the Alpha and the Omega. A villain who betrayed me, the king's envoy, both on my journey north and at Alnwick. A man who has tried to kill me with fire and sword.' He paused, and for a mere heartbeat he caught a look of pure surprise in Darel's eyes, as if he had just learnt something unexpected. Yes, Corbett promised himself, he must remember that. 'Then there's the question of Richolda, Leonora's twin sister, and Master Hockley. Who murdered them then set their corpses alight? We have been here some time and you have not even referred to such matters. Leonora, do you not grieve for your sister?'

'Hugh, Hugh.' Darel's voice was almost slurred. 'What have we to do with the dead? The Black Chesters?' He pulled a face. 'More fable than fact. As for the traitor in your midst who calls himself the Alpha and the Omega, I wonder who he thinks he is. The truth is much more practical. A tinker gave us news of your approach. As for who told us about the secret entrance into the Abbot's Tower,' again Darel made a face, 'the information was delivered anonymously. I am sorry to hear about the attempts to kill you, but like me, you live in a dangerous place at a very fraught time. Is that my fault?' He tapped the table with his fingers. 'Is it my fault that the king's peace has collapsed and war rages along the Scottish march? I am no different from Lord Henry Percy. He has seized Alnwick and turned it into a great fortress. I am doing the same at Blanchlands. Can you blame us? Bruce edges closer and closer to the northern shires, but our king is busy at Westminster fighting his leading barons over his favourite, Gaveston.'

Darel paused. 'Hugh,' he leaned across the table, 'like Lord Henry, I have to defend myself. I have to work out my own salvation. As for poor Richolda and her companion Hockley, they were killed, murdered in Lord Henry's care. One day soon he should, and will, answer for that. And the burning of their corpses?' He raised his eyebrows in a look of complete astonishment. 'Perhaps Lord Henry wished to be rid of them. A strange place, Alnwick, Sir Hugh.'

'With even stranger occurrences,' Leonora added slyly.

'Mistress?'

'I understand that the Scottish hostages you were escorting north have all been murdered, poisoned no less.' Corbett chose to ignore her taunting tone. 'You have made one friend through their deaths.'

'Again, mistress,' Corbett replied coolly, 'I do not know what you are talking about.'

'Alexander Seton and his three companions, Sterling, Mallet and Roskell,' Darel declared, 'were skilled assassins. Seton in particular, a member of Red Comyn's personal bodyguard and a most adept killer. I am sure that Lord Bruce is pleased he is dead. If Seton had escaped and rejoined the Comyns, he would have posed a real problem to Robert the Bruce.' He put his hands down on the table, fingers splayed, staring hard as if he was trying to recall other matters. 'Ah well.' He got to his feet. 'Hugh, lovely to see you, but time is passing.' He helped Leonora to rise. 'I believe we have an agreement. Let us draw up the memorandum of understanding and be gone.'

Corbett sat in the darkness of St Chad's chapel at Alnwick. The dawn Mass had long finished, the altar was cleared, the candles snuffed, the last trails of incense smoke fading away. The constant pattering of prayers had trailed into a deepening silence as people left the church, genuflecting and blessing themselves, touching the feet of the statues of their favourite saints or lighting tapers at the lady altar or in one of the small chantry chapels. Now they were all gone, busy on their own affairs. 'And so begins another day in paradise,' Corbett whispered to himself.

He stared at the crudely depicted wall fresco: St Christopher wading through the water with the Christ Child holding an orb resting on the saint's broad shoulder. On the far bank of the river they were crossing, a dragon surged up out of a ruined castle. Further along the bank, more terrifying images. A hunter had trapped a bear, hung it from a tree, then shot arrows into its chest. Corbett wondered about the significance of that. Perhaps it was a reference to something in St Chad's life or that of St Christopher. In the river, the ruins of a wrecked ship protruded through the water, just the mainmast on which three huge ravens rested. Corbett read the prayer on the scroll beneath the painting: 'St Christopher, many are your saving powers. May those who greet you in the morning smile in the evening.' He read the prayer again and recalled how his own mother had taught him that a morning prayer to St Christopher would ensure safety throughout the day. 'I pray for my safety and all those I care for,' he murmured. 'God save us and guide us out of this danger.'

He rose to his feet, walked around the chapel and returned to his wall bench. He decided that yesterday's business at Clairbaux would have to wait until he met Lord Henry and his full council. He recognised that he and Ranulf had exchanged promises with Darel and given assurances, but he didn't believe a word of it and Ranulf was equally cynical. Both clerks had concluded that Darel was manoeuvring, but for the moment, they couldn't perceive why, or how the robber baron hoped to promote his interests. Darel seemed very zealous to be admitted back into the king's peace. He'd purged his offence, apologised handsomely and assured Corbett that such actions would never be repeated. Of course he must have been wary of being put to the horn and publicly defined as 'outlaw' or 'wolfshead', but Corbett was sure there was more to it than that.

'I will return to it by and by,' he murmured to himself. 'When I meet Lord Henry and we decide to move.' Until then, it was best to shelter here in the dark silence of St Chad's and reflect not so much on his meeting with Darel as on what had started all this. Corbett had thought and thought again. Undoubtedly certain questions were emerging that would help resolve the mysteries confronting him. He was determined to find answers, yet he was also worried how this would end. He needed to discover and establish a safe way forward, but how?

'Let's go back to the beginning.' He spoke into the darkness. 'Let's concentrate on certain questions and approach the problem from a different perspective.' He leaned back on the bench and folded his arms, his eyes closed as he began to itemise certain matters. First, had Dunedin the Scottish clerk, a prisoner in the Tower, been murdered? On the balance of probability, yes. Dunedin had been an adherent of Bruce. He may have made friends with Roskell, who had also been killed. Second, Seton was apparently not only a fervent household retainer of Red Comyn but his personal bodyguard and a skilled assassin. There was a very strong possibility that Dunedin had been killed by Seton with the connivance of Sterling and Mallet.

Third, Seton and his companions had all been murdered too, but why? The only logical answer was that someone knew they intended to assassinate Bruce. 'And there's the problem,' Corbett murmured. Seton and his comrades were openly hostile to Bruce. If the latter had accepted them back, it would be to kill them as adherents of Red Comyn as well as self-declared witnesses to what had really happened when Bruce and Comyn met in that Dumfries friary. 'So,' Corbett whispered to the darkness, 'whoever killed those men realised the truth: that Seton and the others were going to be allowed to escape in order to inflict hideous vengeance against Bruce. Consequently they must have been murdered to protect the Scottish war leader.' He shook his head. But who would know the full story? Not even he had been given an indication of what was being plotted until he reached Alnwick. Only the king and Gaveston knew the truth about Seton and his comrades.

Fourth, Darel's attack on Corbett's camp in that copse before they reached Alnwick. The war dogs had come surging in, followed by a line of foot and then horsemen. So how had the traitor, the assassin, hoped to escape? A ferocious battle-hound was no respecter of persons, and neither were the wolfsheads who flooded the camp in the grey light of dawn. The traitor must also have made sure that he did not eat that tainted oatmeal or anything else that might have been polluted with a noxious potion. Corbett and his party had not eaten due to delicate stomachs. But the others? Who apart from the Thurstons had been able to assist Corbett and his comrades in rousing the drugged men? The clerk recalled Brother Adrian stumbling heavy-eyed out of the dark. The Scottish hostages? Cacoignes? Gaveston?

Fifth, the killings here in Alnwick. Corbett shifted on the bench, the very memory of such murders making him uneasy. He was pleased that Ranulf, Ap Ythel and Chanson were guarding all the approaches to this sombre chapel. The killings in Alnwick truly puzzled him. He could not impose any logic on them, nor on the assaults on his own person. He had been attacked three times, once by fire, twice with an arbalest. Nor must he forget the caltrops hidden away in Ap Ythel's chamber. Was the person responsible for all that also guilty of the murders of Richolda and the three Scottish hostages? Was the killer one and the same person or did two quite distinct killers prowl this castle?

'I cannot make sense of this,' Corbett muttered. 'How they were murdered, why and by whom. Oh Lord.' He put his head in his hands and prayed as fervently as he could. For a while he sat thinking about Maeve and his two children. He just hoped that all three were well. He glanced up at the gargoyle face on the top of a pillar, a wild-eyed, evil-grinning monkey in a jester's hat, and fought to calm the panic that abruptly seethed within him. That carved madcap face seemed to represent the fog of murderous anarchy that shrouded his life here in this grim castle. He just wanted to be away, to be free of this place. Perhaps he should concede that there was little more he could do and leave, hurry to Tynemouth, dispatch Gaveston to foreign parts then hire a cog and sail south to Scarborough or one of the other Yorkshire ports.

'Sir Hugh?' He glanced up. Brother Adrian was smiling down at him. 'Lord Henry and the others are now assembled in the great hall. We need—'

'We need to leave,' Corbett declared, getting up and clapping the monk gently on the shoulder.

'Be careful, Sir Hugh.' Brother Adrian drew closer.

'Be most prudent in what you say. I am sure you do not forget that this castle houses a soul totally dedicated to your destruction and that of everything you stand for.'

'I shall remember,' Corbett declared. He glanced over the Benedictine's shoulder. Ranulf was waiting at the door, watching them carefully. Corbett drew comfort from his henchman's presence; he felt his fear and panic recede. He was determined to go forward to confront whatever monsters awaited him.

The great hall of Alnwick was poorly lit. A few cresset torches illuminated the dais, and the high table was polished to a sheen, with the shimmering silver nef placed in the centre. Lord Henry sat in the place of power, Lady Eleanor to his right, the Thurstons on his left along with the captain of his bodyguard. Corbett and his three companions including Cacoignes took their seats. Lord Henry snapped his fingers and Brother Adrian gabbled a hasty grace. The servants came in, but there was some confusion as they were not used to such mid-morning gatherings. They milled about serving stoups of ale and platters of bread smeared with cheese and herbs along with pots of spicy sauce in which the guests could dip their bread. Lord Henry wolfed both food and drink, belching loudly as he glared about. Corbett tried to hide his disdain at such a lack of manners and frowned at Ranulf, who began to laugh behind his hand.

'Well, Sir Hugh,' Lord Henry turned in his throne-like chair, 'what happened at Clairbaux?'

Corbett gave a brief, pithy summary. He made it clear that Darel was not reconciled to Lord Henry, though the wolfshead had apologised unreservedly for his assaults on the royal envoy and welcomed the release of the prisoners, a matter Corbett had immediately addressed on his return to Alnwick. In return for this, Darel had sued for a royal pardon to cover all past offences and promised solemnly never to interfere with the royal envoy's progress again.

Once Corbett had finished speaking, Lord Henry began to clap slowly and loudly, the mocking sound echoing around the great hall.

'And you believe him, Sir Hugh?' Lady Eleanor gibed.

'By St Oswine,' Kathryn Thurston exclaimed, plucking angrily at the long cuffs of her gown. 'What nonsense do you peddle, clerk? Do you really trust Darel's promises? That limb of Satan, that lying degenerate of a man? He lurks like a beast, a true monster, in Blanchlands. He makes our lives here at Alnwick a living hell. He consorts with witches and warlocks. He is a man of blood steeped in blood. He attacks us out on the king's highway and here in Lord Henry's castle.' She glared at Corbett, who stared at her as if seeing her for the first time.

'You must pardon my sister,' Constable Thurston intervened swiftly, 'but we truly hate Darel. Wicked to the bone, he's the bane of our life, this castle and above all, Lord Henry.' He paused and drank greedily from his goblet. 'Edmund Darel wouldn't know the truth if it grasped him by the throat; that is why my sister dismisses his assurances as nonsense.'

'They are not nonsense.' Corbett broke from his reverie, his mind tumbling like dice in a cup. He stared closely at Lady Kathryn's wrists, but as always, the cuffs of her gown were pulled so far down they reached the palms of her hands. 'For the time being,' he murmured, 'they might be the way forward.'

'The Black Chesters,' Lady Eleanor demanded, 'what did Darel say about them? He shelters, protects and patronises them. Those two witch sisters shared his bed.'

'Sir Edmund dismissed the Black Chesters,' Corbett replied. 'He claims to know little about who they are or what they do.' He shrugged as the remark was greeted with mocking laughter, though he noticed Lord Henry, lips pursed, nodding in agreement.

Brother Adrian spoke up. 'You can hardly expect him to openly declare his support for a coven of witches and warlocks.' He rose and hurriedly brushed what looked like a piece of silver-gold thread from the pocket of his gown as he drew out a set of Ave beads and held up the crucifix at the end. 'I am sure that if we rode to Blanchlands and asked him to take an oath on this rosary, which carries a relic of the true cross, he would still swear that he knows nothing about them.'

'Be that as it may,' Corbett retorted, 'Sir Edmund and I have agreed on a way forward. His dispute with Lord Henry is certainly not concluded. However, Darel has promised us safe passage when we travel to the priory at Tynemouth. He claims to have no inclination or desire to be drawn into the question of the heinous murders committed in our company. So,' he brushed the crumbs from his mud-coloured jerkin, 'we will leave early tomorrow morning.'

'But do you trust him?' Lady Eleanor insisted. 'That he will not attack you?'

'I certainly do not. However, before I left Clairbaux, Lady Hilda asked if her community of anchorites, about fifty in number, could join us. They wish to go on pilgrimage to St Oswine's tomb at Tynemouth Priory.' Corbett paused at the exclamations around the table.

'Fifty of them!' Kathryn Thurston exclaimed. 'Of course, of course,' her severe face broke into a smile, 'they wish to make their devotion to St Oswine, my favourite saint as well as a very fine warrior.' She caught Corbett's look of puzzlement. 'A Saxon king who led his people in a most saintly way. He lies buried at Tynemouth, and soon it will be his feast day.' She turned to her brother.

'I think it's appropriate,' Lord Henry declared, 'for you, Constable Thurston and Lady Kathryn, to escort Sir Hugh to Tynemouth. There you can make your devotions before the tomb of St Oswine and give Prior Richard my kindest regards.'

'And I should go too,' Brother Adrian declared. 'Indeed, I have to. I have business with my good brothers at Tynemouth.'

Corbett nodded his agreement and sat cradling his wine cup. He suspected that Lord Henry was allowing the Thurstons, not to mention Brother Adrian, to accompany him in order to keep a sharp eye on the royal envoys. He did not mind this. The presence of members of Lord Henry's household would provide further protection for their journey to the coast. He was more interested in other matters. He had seen and heard something and he fully intended to pursue it, not dramatically, but slowly, in his own time and at a place of his choosing. In the meantime . . .

He was aware of the shadows dancing around him. Flames flickered, cresset torches crackled and candles fluttered constantly, yet there was a darkness in this hall that stretched beyond the veil separating the visible from the invisible, the physical from the spiritual. The atmosphere was baleful, with an aura of brooding watchfulness. He sensed that matters were now moving like a tide on the turn and he recalled the words of the philosopher: 'Sooner or later all things break down and hurry to their logical conclusion.'

'What do you know, Sir Hugh,' Lord Henry's voice was harsh and carrying, 'about Richard Twyen, Prior of Tynemouth?'

'An old king's man.' Corbett smiled. 'Very similar to his master: strict, ruthless. Nevertheless, in a world of constantly shifting moods, Prior Richard is stalwart in his loyalty to both king and Crown.'

'Yes, yes,' Lord Henry hurriedly agreed, catching Corbett's gentle hint that perhaps not all subjects of the Crown were as loyal to their king as Prior Richard. 'So,' he continued, 'you do not trust Darel, and of course I heartily concur with that, but to repeat Lady Eleanor's question: are you sure he poses no danger to your journey?'

'No,' Corbett declared, choosing his words most

carefully. The spy, the minion of the Black Chesters, could well be sitting here with them. 'I do not trust Sir Edmund, but naturally he is desirous of receiving a pardon, of being readmitted to the king's peace. He does not wish to shatter that security. Moreover, Lady Hilda and her companions are accompanying us, and I am sure Darel will do nothing to upset his redoubtable aunt.'

He fell silent as others joined in the discussion about Darel and the aftermath of his attack on Alnwick. Constable Thurston declared that all the prisoners had been released; given a linen parcel of food, taken across the drawbridge and dispatched on their way. He also mentioned black-garbed riders being seen more frequently out on the moorland. How tinkers and traders hid in ditches or deep in the grass as these riders pounded by, hooded heads down, black cloaks flapping. His words created a chill of fear. Corbett wondered if Bavasour had safely reached Carlisle; if he had, would Harclay move east to assist the royal envoys? But what if he didn't? What if Bavasour had fled or been captured? Corbett stared at Lord Henry as he recalled what his chancery coffers, sealed in the castle's arca, contained.

He glanced up. The Thurstons had now risen and were making to leave, pleading that they had preparations to make. Brother Adrian followed suit. Cacoignes, who had sat silent throughout, slipped away into the shadows of the hall. Corbett watched him go. He wanted to have words with that cunning man, but first he needed to think, to reflect, to plot and plan. Any confrontation would have to wait until they reached Tynemouth. He intended to leave at first light and journey south-east using the well-worn trackways and bridle paths that ran like narrow veins through this shire. Before he left, however, he needed to speak privately to Lord Henry Percy, and the sooner the better.

PART FIVE

'For at these times the enemy who lurked continually in hiding did them all the harm he could.'

Life of Edward II

Six prisoners – five men and one woman – had been condemned to be drowned as punishment for the murder of a fisherman and his son and the theft of their boat. Richard Twyen, Prior of Tynemouth, had indicted all six pirates before his court held in the priory chapter house and sentenced them to death. The prior had all the powers and jurisdiction of a feudal lord: the right of axe and tumbril, gallows and stocks. He could erect gibbets and execution platforms and use these as he thought fit.

The condemned had been taken straight from the chapter house and dragged down to the lonely, desolate beach over which the great crag of Tynemouth brooded like an eternal shadow. The priory occupied that rocky promontory as an eagle would its eyrie: a man-made structure built on what God had created. Others, including Corbett and his party, had joined Prior Richard on that barren strip of wave- and windswept sand. After three days of uneventful riding, Sir Hugh and his entourage had reached Tynemouth village the previous evening and made their way wearily up across the great drawbridge that spanned the deepest of ditches. Once across, they entered the armed enclosures of walls and towers that protected the western approaches to the great priory. The other three sides of the towering crag needed no such defence. Nature supplied the best, a dizzying sheer drop to the beach below where this macabre execution was now taking place.

Prior Richard had welcomed Corbett and his companions most warmly, assigning them comfortable quarters in the guest house, stables and other buildings. Nonetheless, he had insisted that the life of the priory must not be disrupted, and he demanded that Corbett, as a royal envoy, be present to witness the king's justice being done. Not wishing to alienate this formidable prior, Sir Hugh had graciously conceded. He just wished it was over.

He turned and winked at Ranulf, who sat all hooded and solemn on his mount next to Chanson. The clerk of the stables was busy judging the horse flesh of other riders, whilst Ap Ythel seemed fascinated by the priory rising from the majestic crag so far above them. It was a cold, windswept morning. The tide was still far out, the edge of the northern sea a shimmering mass. The daylight was strengthening and the ominous sound of the incoming tide was growing more distinct. The creeping waves would gather pace and, by the end of the day, come crashing in to snatch the lives of these wolfsheads lashed so tightly to the execution stakes.

Corbett stared around the desolate beach, which stretched either way, curving in to create the great cove of Tynemouth. He tried to ignore the muffled groans and curses of the prisoners.

Prior Richard, a tall, sinewy Benedictine with the hooked features of a falcon, had dismounted and was now blessing the condemned with an aspergillum. Corbett felt strangely comforted by his presence. A former commander in the royal levy, Prior Richard knew all about the rigours of war and the horrors of conflict, be it in Wales, Gascony or Scotland. He and Corbett had had a swift conversation the night before whilst sharing a jug of posset and a dish of fruit. Corbett found the prior well aware of events both along the border and throughout the shire. He called Darel 'a true son of Satan, a child of hell', adding that the Black Chesters were nothing more than a legion of demons who were acting with greater and greater impunity. Even watchmen on the priory walls had seen sinister black-garbed figures galloping across this very cove, and had also glimpsed both to north and south the glow of midnight fires that, Prior Richard was certain, marked the gathering of the Black Chesters for their infernal rites.

Corbett wiped the spray from his face. Another Benedictine, Brother Ailward, had joined his prior and was busy shriving the last of the prisoners, a woman who, in desperate hope of lengthening her life, now begged for the sacrament. Once absolution had been delivered, she too, like her colleagues, was gagged to stifle any further cry or protest. Gulls screeched and circled, swooping and rising over the coming banquet. Once the sea had done its work, the prisoners would, for at least three turns of the tide, remain lashed to the execution stakes so the birds and other creatures could gather to feast on their corpses.

A strange, eerie place, Corbett reflected, seemingly caught between heaven and earth. The ground underfoot was soft, yielding and clinging, the shifting sand peppered with black pebbles and shells. The distant sea growled like some monster creeping slowly but surely towards the land under a peculiar whitish-blue sky. The beach seemed to be a ghostly, alien country bereft of any real human presence; only the dead came here. Further along the sand Corbett had glimpsed the corpse of a beggar probably caught by the tide and drowned. Once the execution was over, that corpse would be collected, blessed and, after a requiem, buried in the poor man's lot of Tynemouth Priory.

Brother Ailward was now finished, and remounted his horse, joining Ranulf, Chanson, Ap Ythel, Brother Adrian and the Thurstons along with the priory man-at-arms and two burly lay brothers.

'I consign you to God,' declared Prior Richard, standing high in the stirrups and sketching one last cross in the air. 'It is indeed,' he continued, 'a terrible thing to fall into the hands of the living God. May the kind heart of Christ show you mercy. It is over.'

He turned his horse to lead his cavalcade back along the beach towards the winding, sand-strewn pathway that cut through Tynemouth village, across the draw-bridge and under the fortified barbican into the priory proper. Corbett did not spare the condemned, lashed on that long line of execution poles, a second glance. He had seen their handiwork, to which they'd openly confessed: the mangled remains of those poor fishermen, father and son, slit from craw to crutch, stretched out on the great corpse table in the priory death house. Prior Richard had apologised for having to draw Corbett into king's business. Sir Hugh, however, was pleased that at least someone in Northumberland was committed to maintaining the peace.

He had certainly seen the effects of the growing disorder as he had journeyed south. Of course the royal standard kept wolfsheads and any other troublemakers well away. In fact, Corbett had been pleased by the journey. The weather had proved good, the ground underfoot solid and firm. He was particularly gratified that the carts carrying his chancery coffers, now placed safely in Prior Richard's arca, had not been obstructed or impeded.

Lady Hilda had met him outside Alnwick with about fifty members of her community. The imperious old lady had insisted on riding side-saddle, lecturing her cowled, grey-garbed community and maintaining good order amongst them as if she were a royal marshal. On arrival at Tynemouth, she'd informed both Corbett and Prior Richard that ten more members of her fraternity would soon be joining them to make fervent prayer before the tomb of St Oswine and celebrate the saint's impending feast. Neither the prior nor Corbett dared demur, especially when Lady Hilda added that she and her community must pay their way and did not expect to be a burden on the priory. Prior Richard was relieved. He had confided to Corbett on their way down to execute the wolfsheads that Lady Hilda's arrival would not crowd the priory, as a number of his monks had sailed on *The Golden Dove* for London to visit their mother houses at St Albans and Westminster.

The priory was certainly spacious enough. Corbett had been allocated a comfortable chamber in the guest house, which overlooked the great cloisters opposite the main priory church. Once he'd locked the door behind him the previous evening, he had felt deeply relieved, unstrapping his war belt and kicking off his boots. He was pleased to be free of Alnwick and its darkly oppressive, ominous atmosphere; that sense of fearfulness, of being watched and not being really safe either within or without. Tynemouth was different. Prior Richard was a king's man to the very marrow of his being.

'Sir Hugh? You're not sleeping?' Corbett grinned at Ranulf and gathered his reins as the pace of the cavalcade quickened. They cantered through Tynemouth village, up its main street and onto the approaches to the soaring fortifications of the priory. The great drawbridge was already lowered, the porticullis raised, and they quickly clattered across, turning left past the gatehouse, the lodgings for the men-at-arms and the priory kennels and entering the great court, which stretched to the poultry yard, then on into the smaller court containing the church, chapter house, guest house and all the various lodgings of the priory community.

Here they reined in, and Prior Richard formally ordered his standard bearer, who had ridden ahead of the cavalcade, to furl the banner proclaiming the arms of the priory: three red crowns against a white background. Once this had been taken away to be stored behind the high altar of the church, they all dismounted. The prior, murmuring how such occasions sharpened his appetite, led Corbett's party through the warm, sweet-smelling refectory and into the comfortable buttery with its polished oak tables and cushioned stools. A light morning ale brewed at the priory was served along with squares of freshly toasted bread topped with cheese and a sharp herb sauce. One of the brothers blessed the food and drink and they all ate in silence, hungry after the cold ride down to the beach.

After they had finished, Prior Richard indicated that Corbett, Ranulf and Ap Ythel, along with Brother Adrian, should follow him across to the priory church. Once there, the doors were closed and bolted from the inside. The prior told Corbett and the rest to wait whilst he and Brother Adrian quickly went around the church to ensure that all other doors were closed and locked and no one else was present.

Corbett stood near the ancient baptismal font, its deep-bowled cup decorated with the most intricate Celtic designs. He was fascinated by this ancient church, which, by the scaffolding raised along the transepts, was being completely refurbished. He breathed in the fragrant air, a mixture of incense, candle smoke and polish. It was dark in here, yet majestically glorious. The windows were high in the walls and narrow, but many of them were filled with exquisitely painted glass. The effect was quite magical: the sunlight poured through the lancets in a myriad of rays to shimmer and shine on the polished oaken rood screen with its life-sized crucified Christ above the entrance. Beyond this lay the choir, with tiers of stalls on either side where the good brothers gathered to sing the Divine Office. The adjoining sanctuary was especially magnificent. The high altar was covered in precious metals, the oaken furniture had been carved by the most skilled craftsmen, whilst the gold and silver candlesticks, pyx and sanctuary lamp glittered like heaven's own treasures through the dark. The floor of the nave was paved, but the section between the choir and the sanctuary was covered in tiles boasting skilfully painted designs, be it the three crowns of Tynemouth, a fire-breathing dragon, a king on horseback, mythical beasts or golden angels.

Prior Richard and Brother Adrian were busy with some business in the sacristy, so Corbett and Ranulf crossed to an enclave built into the wall between the sanctuary and the choir. It contained a table-top tomb, a rectangle of shimmering white Purbeck marble. On top of this stretched a life-size effigy of a king in his cor-onation robes, in one hand a sceptre shaped in the form of a lily, in the other a rounded orb topped with a cross. The effigy exuded an eye-catching majestic beauty.

Corbett crouched to translate the Latin script carved on the side of the tomb. 'King Oswine,' he declared. 'The great Anglo-Saxon historian the Venerable Bede wrote how Oswine was an extremely holy and devout man. A prince deeply loved by his subjects, a king of great charity and munificence until he was murdered by those who hated his goodness.' He was aware of his voice echoing, and he startled when a woman's voice answered.

'King's man! A king's man praying before the tomb of a prince who in his life was the very mirror of justice.'

'In God's name!' Ranulf exclaimed, glaring around, hand on dagger.

Corbett stared across at the enclave against the opposite wall. It was very similar in size to the one that housed the tomb; however, it had been freshly bricked up and covered in an alabaster-white plaster that looked as if it had been recently primed to receive a wall painting. A gap squint high in the wall had been opened, whilst a small door to the right of this hung unlatched.

'An anker-hold,' Corbett breathed, walking across. He gestured at Ranulf and Ap Ythel, who had also just entered the choir, to stay back.

'Welcome, king's man.'

Corbett glimpsed the eyes peering out through the squint. 'And you are?'

'Rachaela; Rachaela the Recluse, as I have been for the last two years.'

'So you have met?' Corbett glanced over his shoulder. Prior Richard and Brother Adrian stood in the entrance to the rood screen. 'Come.' The prior beckoned. 'More about Rachaela later. You have walked our church?'

'And I am most impressed.' Corbett crossed to stand beneath the figure of the crucified Christ that dominated the entrance to the rood screen. He gazed up at the tortured life-size image, the contorted face, the head circled with sharp thorns hanging down in death, the nails through the crucified hands and feet. 'All done in a black metal,' he murmured. 'Most original.'

'Brother Oswald,' Prior Richard explained, 'was a former smith and smelter: a truly talented artist.' He pointed up. 'He produced an originally cast metal, what he called an alloy, which made it easier to paint. At first I wasn't at all happy. The mess and disturbance in the church was quite considerable, the reek of paint most offensive. I was also not too certain about the colour. Christ is always depicted in shimmering white ivory, but Oswald loved to turn everything on its head. He argued that his sculpture would make the figure of Christ more striking and compelling. Members of our community supported this, as indeed did Master Ravinac. He was sheltering here at the time and loved to come into the sanctuary and stare at King Oswine's tomb. He and Oswald became firm friends; they liked nothing better than to study the shrine and discuss the great king. But come . . .'

The prior led them into the small sacristy, which he and Brother Adrian had prepared, pulling out a table with chairs around it. Prior Richard sat at the top, gesturing at Corbett, Ranulf and Ap Ythel to sit either side of him. Brother Adrian closed the door, turning the key and drawing the bolts across before hurrying to join them.

'The most secure place in Tynemouth.' Prior Richard laughed as he swiftly crossed himself. 'So, to the business in hand.'

'The Lily Crown?'

The prior shook his head. 'Sir Hugh, I am an ageing, gnarled and sometimes bitter-tempered Benedictine. I have no need for treasures; well, at least not on earth. I prefer to have them stored in heaven. Accordingly, I have no desire to find the Lily Crown. Others may. However, believe me, out of loyalty to the king I have searched this priory from cellar to bell loft, but there's no sign of that crown.'

'So what happened?'

'Well, Sir Hugh, the story Master Cacoignes told you, and that you related to me last night on your arrival as we toasted the shadows and the dancing flames, is true. In the main, events occurred as he described them.' The prior smiled thinly. 'He had to tell you the truth, or most of it, for he must have realised that one day you or some other royal official would come here to discover what really happened.'

'Did Ravinac have the crown with him?'

'Oh yes, he certainly did. He showed it to me. But what happened afterwards,' the prior shook his head, 'I truly don't know.'

'Did Ravinac ever leave Tynemouth?'

'No, he did not. He declared that he felt safe here.

The accepted story was that a roaming Scottish war party attacked his comitatus, but Ravinac didn't believe this. He maintained that the attackers were different. They swept in all masked and hooded, garbed in black. On reflection, I concluded that these attackers were the Black Chesters, desperate to seize the Lily Crown with its much-vaunted mystical qualities.'

'But Cacoignes?'

'According to Ravinac, Cacoignes was in a drunken stupor when they were attacked, and escaped by mere chance or good luck. No wonder he can provide you with very few details: he was malmsy with drink.'

'That is true,' Corbett conceded. 'Cacoignes has actually told us very little. He repeats the story with a few additions here and further details there.' He scratched his chin. 'What was the relationship between the two, Ravinac and Cacoignes? Friends, enemies, rivals?'

'Ravinac liked Cacoignes but didn't trust him.' Prior Richard played with the cross on a chain around his neck. 'He believed Cacoignes to be a toper and, above all, a gambler. Oh yes, a true lover of hazard and the roll of the dice. Rumour had it amongst Ravinac's cohort that Cacoignes had fled from London to escape his creditors.'

'The hazard-makers?' Ranulf intervened from where he had been sitting next to Ap Ythel, who lounged heavy-eyed against the table. 'Lords of the dice; throwers who play with cogged dice and other deceits. You gamble and gamble again but you never win. If you become caught in their traps, God help you.'

'I agree,' Prior Richard declared. 'In my youth I shook the cup and rolled the dice.' He smiled thinly. 'And see where it led me. But to go back to your original question, Hugh, Ravinac never left Tynemouth. He was frightened after the attack and became even more so when I described the Black Chesters and their evil reputation.'

'You have crossed swords with that coven?'

'Time and time again.' The prior gestured around. 'This is the church, the shrine, of Oswine, king and martyr. Do you know his story?'

Corbett shook his head.

'Oswine was an Anglo-Saxon prince, a true son of the Church. He reigned in Northumbria before this shire rose to greatness. To the south stretched the kingdom of Mercia; its overlord King Penda was a fierce warrior and warlord, but he was also a pagan who hated our church and all it stood for. He surrounded himself with witches and warlocks who worshipped demons and darkness. Oswine opposed them, day and night, physically and spiritually, in every way he could, and for that, he was foully murdered.' The prior rubbed his mouth. 'I suspect, though I have no proof, that the Black Chesters and their ilk see themselves as the spiritual descendants of Penda and his court. "The children of hell", I call them. From the little I have learnt, the Black Chesters would love to seize and destroy Oswine's tomb and this church with it. They regard us as a beacon of light at a time of deepest night.'

'Are you saying,' Ranulf asked, 'that they would actually raze this priory and the tomb to the ground?'

'Undoubtedly,' Prior Richard replied. 'Wouldn't you agree, Brother Adrian?'

'This is a most holy place,' the Benedictine intoned. 'A sacred sanctuary.'

Corbett nodded, tapping the table with his fingers, allowing the silence to deepen. He had come to Tynemouth expecting to finish his business and be gone. He now quietly conceded he was wrong. Tynemouth could be the very place where these matters reached a head and were resolved by the most violent confrontation. He recalled his meeting with Darel. Something was very wrong. Darel had kept his word: the journey to Tynemouth had certainly not been dangerous or fraught with any peril. The robber baron undoubtedly wanted a pardon, but Corbett recalled those clever eyes, the mockery behind the mask, the way Darel had totally ignored the doings of his dark companions both dead and alive.

'Sir Hugh?'

'So Ravinac learnt more about the Black Chesters here?'

'Yes, Sir Hugh.'

'And he visited the tomb?'

'He was a regular visitor and struck up a warm friendship with Brother Oswald, who was working on the rood screen. Well, that was before Ravinac fell ill.'

'Was his sickness caused by human wickedness or human frailty?'

'The latter. Ravinac arrived here weakened by what he'd been through, a lack of good food and rest, the threat of danger. Isn't that true, Brother Adrian?'

'You were here at the time?' asked Corbett.

'I was, Sir Hugh. It was a busy time for our priory. Lord Henry and the Bishop of Durham met here to discuss the sale of Alnwick. I assisted in preparing the documentation, laying out charters, rolls.' Brother Adrian shrugged. 'I had very little to do with either Ravinac or Cacoignes. I only saw them from a distance, as Prior Richard will attest.'

'Is Brother Oswald still here?'

'Gone to his eternal reward, God rest him. He did wonder if Ravinac, deeply interested in St Oswine, hid the Lily Crown somewhere in or around the shrine. However, I have searched there, and short of actual desecration, I cannot find any trace of it.'

'And the Black Chesters?'

'I suspect very much that they have dispatched adherents of their filthy practices here under the guise of visitors in order to spy and to search. So far they have made no attempt to damage either the shrine or the church. According to Rachaela, a former member of the coven – oh yes, she was – they would love to do that.'

'I must meet with her.'

'Do so. You should also talk to Lady Hilda if you want to know about St Oswine. She and her community have come here because it will soon be his solemn feast day. They must have been only too pleased to travel here under the protection of the royal banner.' Prior Richard paused, straining his neck as if he was listening to the sounds of the church. 'As for any other business,' he declared, 'I believe we will have to wait until *The Golden*

Dove returns.' He glanced warningly at Corbett. They had agreed during their meeting the previous evening to make no reference to Gaveston and his planned escape.

Prior Richard asked if there was anything else. Corbett replied that there was nothing for the moment, except he would like to question the recluse. The prior led him out of the sacristy and across the sanctuary, and whispered through the eye squint. Corbett heard the recluse laugh, a merry, tinkling sound, before she pushed open the small door. He unstrapped his war belt and took off his cloak; he handed these to Ranulf and then, stooping, squeezed through into the anker-hold.

He straightened up and stared around. The cell was surprisingly large, about five yards square and of the same height, though its ceiling was cleverly sloped to incorporate a lancet window, which, when unshuttered, provided both light and air. Rachaela sat on a stool. She was dressed like a Benedictine nun in a black gown, her face framed by a white wimple and dark-blue veil. To her left was a narrow cot bed beneath a crucifix. She gestured at Corbett to take the stool opposite her. He did so, moving close so he could clearly see the anchorite's round pale face, small mouth and dimpled chin. A plain-looking woman except for the large, deep-set eyes, which seemed full of laughter, as if she looked on the world and found it a constant source of merriment. She was busy embroidering an altar cloth, and Corbett admired the fine, intricate cross-stitching. He glanced around. The cell was very homely; it smelt sweetly of the crushed herbs floating in water pots. The hard-tiled floor was clean-swept. The few remaining sticks of furniture – a lectern, prie-dieu and small corner coffer – were polished to a shine.

'What do you want, king's man?'

'You are a recluse?'

'That's obvious.' She laughed.

'Why?'

'To make reparation for my sins.'

'What sins?'

'I was an adherent, a retainer, a liveried servant to the Black Chesters. I became a child of hell. I rejected the light to attend the church of the damned, to worship the powers of darkness. I rejected the teaching of Christ and his followers. I wanted to become skilled, a witch-queen, a lady of the midnight sacrifice. I felt as if I had been called to it.'

'How so, mistress?'

'I was born in Durham. From a very early age I was skilled in needlework. I also had a deep and lasting curiosity about things of the spirit. To learn more, I became proficient in my horn book. I begged and wheedled the local priests to instruct me on all they knew. I married a wealthy man, but he died of a sickness, leaving me as his sole heir. King's man, I had a trade, I had wealth. I had my freedom and my youth. I was given a deep-bowled cup of self-indulgence few women can even dream of. I was beholden neither to parish nor to palace and I did not care for either. I visited this fair or that market. I was always fascinated by magical tricks or sleight of hand. I formed new friendships with people who shared my interest, and so it began.

'I was invited to this banquet, that festival. Slowly but surely I was singled out, or so I realise now. I was invited to ceremonies, festivals held at the dead of night on some desolate moorland: the Night of the Harrowing, or the Vespers of Midnight. I'd sit, squat or kneel amongst ancient, twisted rotting trees before stones that shimmered with blood. Memories, king's man! Images that float through your mind. Torchlight glowed. Voices chanted. Feet pounded to the constant beat of the tambour and the lilting tune of the lute.'

Rachaela fell silent. All merriment had faded from her eyes and face. 'You open certain doors, king's man, and you walk into a world of shadows. You drink rich red wine laced with all kinds of juices and potions. You swim in the air or ride the winds to the furthest edges of the dawn. Before you even realise it, you are a member of a satanic coven. You ride with the Black Chesters. You celebrate rites deep in the darkness of the forest. You drink their perfumed wine and stuff your belly with their rich food. You live for that life. You wait for the summons, a simple message whispered to you as you move amongst the market stalls. You are given the place, the date, the time. You come to love the mystery, the secrecy, the feeling that you are different. At first the sacrifices are a mockery of the Mass, with bread, wine and fruits of the earth, the blood of cockerels or other birds. Then it changes!'

She picked up the pewter beaker beside her and sipped

noisily. 'One night we gathered outside a shepherd's dwelling, down near the ancient wall. They say the Romans used magicians to build it, truly a place of deep mystery. We met there on horseback, full of our own arrogant importance . . .'

'Did you know each other, recognise anyone?' Corbett asked.

'No, very rarely. We were only given the time, date and place where we were to assemble. We were provided with horses and weapons as well as cloak, mantle, visor or cowl, but never information about each other. On that particular evening I gathered with the rest of the coven. We abducted the shepherd and his daughter, a wench of no more than fifteen summers. We bound and gagged them both and dragged them off at the heel of our horses to one of those ancient high places with its standing stones and sacrificial slabs. We plucked their hearts out and burnt them.' She paused, all poise and calm disappearing as she put her face in her hands. 'They were offered no opiate, no perfumed wine to soothe the pain.'

'They were alive when they were cut open?'

'Like those condemned for treason, they are sliced so their innards can be plucked out and burnt before them. The shepherd perished under the knife, but his daughter died a horrible death. In my sleep, king's man, I still hear her shrieking, a soul-wrenching cry that will never be stilled.'

'Why do they practise such barbarity?'

'The Black Chesters claim that the victims' cries are

offered to the demons, who hear them and come to feast on such cruelty. I shall never forget that night. The flames on the stone leaping and dancing like devils from hell, the blood streaming everywhere. The ruptured chests and stricken faces surrounded by black-garbed figures. And yes, I was one of them, but something happened. I could never forget that poor wench's face pleading for mercy; her eyes, her gaze came to haunt me. For the first time ever, I felt guilt, a deep sorrow, a desire to change. It's like when you drink too much wine: you wake and know you have done wrong. You vow to break free of the effects, change your habits and so change your life. I came to resent the Black Chesters, which soon deepened into an utter detestation of them. I had few relatives, and those I did have were not concerned about me. I went into hiding. I removed all trace and sign of myself until about eighteen months ago, when I fled here for sanctuary. At first Prior Richard did not trust me, but now he does.'

'And apart from the sacrifices, what else did the Black Chesters do?'

'Sometimes we met and feasted at a deserted farm or derelict manor house. You see, king's man, we were feared. A group of horsemen, black cloaks flapping, armed and dangerous. Who could oppose us? Men like Lord Henry Percy, locked in their own ambitions? The other lords of the march, terrified of Bruce creeping closer and closer? Oh yes, we saw ourselves as lords of the air and acted as such. We'd enjoy truly lavish banquets with the finest wine and the most succulent meats. The retainers of Paracelsus were not ill-educated peasants but merchants, knights, very much lords and ladies of the manor.'

'But you never recognised anyone or saw their faces?'

'Leonora and Richolda, Darel's doxies? Well, we knew who they were, but for the rest, we wore visors, soft face masks that moulded with bone and skin. We were cloaked and sworn to secrecy.'

'And at such banquets and feasts?'

'We would pray for the destruction of Crown and Church. Plead for a time of great chaos, of anarchy, and to strengthen our pleas to the dark ones, we made the blood sacrifice. Disgusting, disgusting . . .' Rachaela's voice trailed away as her face hardened. She glanced swiftly at the crucifix nailed above her bed, eyes blinking, lips silently mouthing some prayer. Corbett sensed the woman was both haunted and very, very frightened.

'You never leave here?'

'To relieve myself in the outside privy. But no, apart from that, I will stay here, God willing and Prior Richard assenting, until I die.'

'But you are frightened?' Corbett glimpsed the small arbalest resting against the wall next to a handbell.

'Of course, king's man. Once you are an adherent of the Black Chesters, you are committed in both this life and the world to come. I have heard stories about how those few who fled the coven were hunted down wherever they sought refuge. I have no illusions, king's man. I have not forgotten the Black Chesters and they have certainly not forgotten me.'

'And their leader, Paracelsus?'

'Paracelsus,' Rachaela hissed, staring wildly around her small cell as if the very mention of the name summoned up terrors.

'Paracelsus,' Corbett repeated. 'You have met him?'

'Only once,' she replied. 'On the eve of All Hallows, we and other covens met in the ruins of a great Roman fortress along the wall. Paracelsus appeared like a king on a dais. He wore a purple visor and had golden hair falling to his shoulders. His voice was like that of a trumpet, deep, rich and carrying. He spoke jubilantly about the growing chaos in England and the war in Scotland. His henchmen were there, his close retainers. I recall seeing Richolda and Leonora; they were notorious as witches. They could flaunt who they were and what they did because they were protected by the power of Lord Darel.'

'Could he have been Paracelsus in a different guise?'

'Most certainly!'

Corbett noticed her right hand trembling. 'You are very frightened,' he murmured. 'Surely you are safe here?'

'Sometimes at night I can hear the waves rushing in to hurl themselves against the foot of the crag. I recall a story telling how the rolling waters of the deep are ridden by the legions of the damned. I am frightened.' She pointed across the cell. 'Out there near the sanctuary stands the tomb of St Oswine. That saintly king protects me.'

'You think the Black Chesters will come and hurt you here?'

'If they can, they will. More importantly, they would love to destroy Oswine's tomb, pollute his remains and rid this region of a source of great holiness.'

'Did they discuss this?'

'Of course. Times have changed, king's man. The sheriff is powerless. Royal forces are committed to fighting the Bruce. Tynemouth stands isolated. The Black Chesters hunger to exploit the chaos, but of course the priory is also fortified and embattled, defended by a prior who is both a churchman and a stout warrior . . .'

Corbett left the anker-hold. Ranulf was waiting just within the church porch.

'Fetch Cacoignes.' Corbett patted the clerk on the shoulder. 'It's time we questioned our noble squire.'

'Sir Hugh?'

Corbett turned as Prior Richard, who must have come in through the corpse door further up the church, strode across.

'You have spoken to Rachaela?'

'Yes, yes, I did. Why?'

'The Black Chesters are fervent adherents of the dramatic. I don't know if it's because of your arrival, but they have begun to manifest themselves more blatantly. Recently watchers along our walls have, early in the morning or at dusk, just before the darkness descends, seen sinister black-garbed figures on the beach or along the edge of the moat just beyond bowshot. Anyway,' the prior rubbed his hands, 'I've broken bread with Lady Hilda. In two days' time, she and her community want to make their own special devotions to St

Oswine's shrine on the saint's great feast day. Perhaps an evening Mass of thanksgiving followed by a special vespers, after which we could all celebrate with a banquet in our refectory.' He bowed mockingly. 'Sir Hugh, I will leave you to what you have to do whilst I attend to what I must do.'

The prior had hardly left when Ranulf and Ap Ythel ushered Cacoignes into the church. Corbett welcomed him, clasping hands and leading him up into a soft-carpeted chantry chapel dedicated to St Alban, a serenely beautiful place with its oaken altar, glowing triptychs and perfumed air. He waved Cacoignes to a stool, then sat down himself in the celebrant's chair and stared at this royal squire who for the last five years had lived so dangerously on his wits.

'Geoffrey Cacoignes, king's squire, emissary, comrade of the now dead Ravinac, gambler and toper. No,' he gestured at Cacoignes to remain seated, 'I know who you are, whilst we have rehearsed a number of times why you are here and what you have done. However, you omitted one very important matter, which always puzzled me. Something you never explained to my satisfaction.'

'Which is?' Cacoignes brusquely demanded, fingers tapping the hilt of his dagger.

'Don't do that.' Ranulf, standing beside Corbett, waved a hand. 'Don't touch your dagger when you are in the presence of a royal envoy here in the holiest of places.'

Cacoignes' face creased into a forced grin and he held both hands up. '*Pax et bonum,*' he whispered. 'I know what you are going to ask, Sir Hugh. When I escaped, why didn't I immediately journey south to London?'

'Very good,' Corbett breathed. 'Yes, you claimed you had to join Darel. Perhaps you lacked the sustenance to journey south, as well as worrying about what reception you might receive at Westminster. Now you are a toper, or at least you were, but you are also the most fervent practitioner of hazard, the game of chance, the shaking of a cup and the roll of a dice. Yes? You lost, lost and lost again till you were steeped in debt, which is probably why you volunteered to journey north into the wastelands of the war-torn Scottish march. Then disaster struck, though I am not too sure of your involvement in that or what responsibility you bear.'

Cacoignes swallowed hard and glanced nervously away.

'I will move swiftly to the end of my story,' Corbett continued. 'You did not return to London because you could not. You dared not because you owed so much money to the hazard-makers, the lords of the dice, miscreants who are ruthless in pursing what is theirs. True?' Cacoignes nodded, and Corbett leaned forward. 'Master Cacoignes, you did me and mine great service alerting us to Darel's impending treachery. You should be, and you will be, rewarded and restored, but first the truth.'

Cacoignes closed his eyes, lips moving soundlessly as if he was praying.

'Come on, man,' Corbett urged. 'The hours pass, the light will fade, the darkness comes. An opportunity is here: grasp it.' Cacoignes opened his eyes. 'A full pardon,' Corbett continued, 'for all past crimes, a grant from the Exchequer to settle your debts and, in the months ahead, perhaps some lucrative chancery work that will take you far away from London.'

Cacoignes rubbed his face with his hands and again talked silently to himself before glancing up. 'It is as you say, Sir Hugh. You know the way of the world. I was a royal squire, one of those young men who hung around the court. I was given over to lechery, drunkenness. I was steeped,' he grinned sheepishly, 'in all those delicious, enjoyable sins. I was no different from the rest of the fops, the young court gallants with more than an eye to their own advantage. I hoped to join one of the old king's chevauchées into Scotland, perform some valiant deed like the paladins of old. I wanted to be noticed by the king, win my spurs, be knighted and granted manors, estates and a profitable marriage.'

'And that never happened?'

'Of course not. So I turned to hazard, the roll of a dice, to win my fortune. I lost and lost again. I sank deeper into debt to a group about whom, certainly at the time, I knew little. The Black Chesters.'

'What!'

'That's what they called themselves. A company of twelve or thirteen traders, merchants and other wealthy citizens who could loan you money as well as make sure you lost it at the gaming tables, the cock pit or the dog-fighting arena. Shadowy figures who used city rifflers as their heralds and servants.'

'So they loaned you money at exorbitant rates, then helped you lose it? Master Cacoignes, we are all sinners, but God doesn't expect us to be stupid with it.'

'Sir Hugh, a real gambler is possessed. A demon seethes inside him. Whatever you promise yourself and your guardian angel in the cold light of dawn doesn't even last the day. When the sun sets, the wine goblet beckons, the hazard cup rattles and the dice are rolling, you forget everything. Everything except the thrill of the throw, the excitement, the chance that you might roll a double six. You simply do not care, and every time it happens, the demon grows stronger within you.'

'Did these Black Chesters give any indication of being practitioners of the black arts?'

'Never. I just thought they gave themselves that name in the way that companies of mummers assume this title or that. There are scores of fraternities in London who enjoy the most spectacular names. The Black Chesters may not have been witches or warlocks at the time, but they soon proved sinister enough. They turned threatening and became even more so as my debts mounted. And then it happened.' He paused. 'One night,' he lifted his head, 'I arrived at the Key to Jerusalem.'

'I know it well,' Ranulf intervened, 'a true den of iniquity in Queenhithe ward. Everything's for sale at that tavern: human flesh, human life and human souls.'

'A mansion of mystery,' Cacoignes agreed. 'On that particular night I was halfway through the door when I was seized, hooded, hustled out and put on a horse. It was dusk, but my abductors knew the streets well enough to avoid the chains and the nightwatchmen. I sensed we were journeying north to the wasteland outside the city, beyond the great ditch. I smelt its stench as we crossed. Eventually we stopped. The hood was removed. I was in a dark, moss-covered ruin. I was pushed down into a cellar, a cavernous chamber lit by torches and a myriad of candles, but the light also served as a protection, hiding the faces of those who were waiting for me.' Cacoignes licked dry lips. 'For the first time, I was truly fearful. A terror seized me. I knew that some nameless evil lurked in that sombre place. A man stepped into the pool of light, yet he remained hidden. His face was covered by a silver mask, and golden hair fell down to his shoulders. For the rest, he was garbed in a dark robe.'

'Golden hair?' Corbett repeated, recalling what Rachaela had told him.

'Yes, golden hair that shimmered in the light. He declared that he was Paracelsus, leader of the Black Chesters and other such fraternities. He gave me a purse of silver as a guarantee and said he would cancel all my debts owing to the Black Chesters.'

'For what?'

'The Lily Crown of Scotland! Oh yes. Being born and raised in the north, I knew something about the crown. I had also heard how the old king was looking for volunteers to cross the northern march, invade the abbey of Scone and seize the Scottish regalia, a call that only the very brave or foolhardy would respond to. By then the war in Scotland had turned nasty, a fight to the death. Prisoners were shown no mercy; the Scots had even skinned alive some of the English commanders they'd captured.' Cacoignes sketched a cross on his forehead.

'I was released. Well, I was hooded, put back on the horse and returned to the Key of Jerusalem. Now at the time I did not really know who the Black Chesters were. In the past I had just fled from any unpleasant situation I found myself in. I thought I could do the same now, take the Black Chesters' silver, go into hiding and lie low like some wolf until the danger passed.' He paused to cross himself. 'That was a hideous mistake. I was on very cordial terms with Lucilla,' he smiled sadly, 'a Cheapside courtesan. She allowed me to hide in her chambers above a draper's shop in Farringdon. Then one morning she didn't return as I expected her to, nor the day after, or the day after that.'

'Oh Lord,' Ranulf whispered. 'I can imagine what is going to happen next . . .'

'One evening a street urchin shouted my name from the alley below. He claimed to have something precious for me. I hurried down but the messenger was gone, though he had left a small barrel in the doorway of the draper's shop. I lifted its lid. Lucilla's head, severed at the neck, rested inside, her dead eyes rolled back, glaring at me.' Cacoignes crossed himself again. 'I recognised the threat. I realised there was no escape, so I returned to the Key of Jerusalem to be welcomed as a long-lost brother. I was ordered to volunteer to journey north with Ravinac's comitatus. You know the rest. We left for Scotland, a swift-moving armed cohort with strict instructions from the old king.'

'And the Black Chesters? Paracelsus?'

'Sir Hugh, I was ordered to comply unless I wanted to receive the severed heads of more of my lady friends. I was told to leave messages in certain places at certain times. To cut to the chase, I informed the Black Chesters about our strength, when we were to leave London and what route we would take, and I suspect they followed us to Scone.'

'And when you left there, the same?'

'Precisely. You must remember, we were very well armed. We had mailed hauberks, weapons and even extra horses against one of our mounts being injured or killed. Our very appearance made people scatter and hide. Ravinac was single-minded, a competent commander especially appointed by the king, but the rest of us had grown careless. We also thought that because we'd seized the Lily Crown with little opposition, we had been successful, but to quote the old phrase, there's many a slip between cup and lip. We looted some wine; looking back, I wonder if we were supposed to find it. The Black Chesters' attack came as a complete surprise, swirling in like some dark, malevolent cloud.'

'Tell me,' Ranulf intervened, 'did you know at the time that it was the Black Chesters?'

'No, I had suspicions that hardened into certainty once I joined your comitatus and saw what happened at Alnwick.'

'Why didn't they wait for you to take the crown and

hand it over to them?' Corbett smiled thinly. 'Though I can guess the answer. They did not trust you, whilst once you were back in England, it would prove more and more difficult to actually seize such a treasure. Anyway, the attack?'

'They closed in swinging sword, axe and mace. I confess,' Cacoignes beat his breast, 'I was drunk. I was a toper. Ravinac, God rest him, had the crown and he also saved me. I was close to him; we crawled like children along the ground and reached the horse lines. Two mounts were saddled and so we escaped riding horses fresh after their long rest. We outpaced our pursuers and eventually came here to Tynemouth Priory. Again, you know my story. I left for a while, thinking that Ravinac might have hidden the crown elsewhere. By the time I returned, he had fallen seriously ill and there was still no sign of the Lily Crown. I began to think about my own safety. I realised it was time to escape the north. I left Tynemouth looking for a way out and was captured. After years of imprisonment I escaped. I dare not return to London. I am a professional fighting man, so Edmund Darel and Blanchlands provided some protection.'

'And the Black Chesters?'

'I suspect they realised the truth about what had happened: that Ravinac had hidden the crown somewhere in or around Tynemouth. As for me,' Cacoignes shrugged, 'the Black Chesters must have forgotten me. I disappeared for almost five years – taken prisoner by the Scots and lodged in the far north. The coven must have thought I had died or been killed. When I escaped, years later, my appearance had changed along with my name. I would wager that Darel and the Black Chesters only learnt I was alive after I entered Alnwick with you, but even then they must have deduced I was of very little value to them.'

'And you have no idea where Ravinac hid the Lily Crown?'

'Both before and during his illness, Ravinac liked nothing better than to come into this church and sit in the sanctuary staring at that tomb. I am sure he hid the crown close by. I do wonder about the shrine, though I am sure Prior Richard has conducted his own thorough search . . .' His voice trailed away.

'Master Cacoignes,' Corbett decided he would gamble with this hazard player, 'I believe you are a man of good faith. Now you don't know this, but Ravinac told Prior Richard that he had hidden the Lily Crown so it hung between heaven and earth in God's own graveyard. You knew the man; what do you think he meant?'

Cacoignes startled, fingers going to his lips as he asked Corbett to repeat the phrase time and again.

'It means something to you, doesn't it?'

'Yes, yes, it does. As we approached Tynemouth a mist swirled in. We asked directions from an old villager, who said the priory hung between heaven and earth, and you can see why. The place hangs in the air, supported only by the massive crag beneath. But there again, that is not much help.'

'And God's own graveyard?'

'Again, Sir Hugh, from the little I know, the crag on which Tynemouth is built was once a very ancient burial site, but,' Cacoignes gestured down the church, 'I still believe the crown is hidden somewhere in that tomb, which hangs between heaven and earth both physically and spiritually. It is a place where people who wish to immerse themselves in matters spiritual come to pray.'

Corbett recalled the bracelet he had found close to where the cottager Ewen and his family had been slaughtered. He pointed to Cacoignes' wrist.

'That bracelet you wear – why should one similar be found out on the heathland near an abandoned cottage some miles to the north of Alnwick?'

'I don't know,' Cacoignes retorted. 'And I don't really care. I never left Alnwick until we journeyed to Tynemouth. I fashioned a good score of these bracelets when I was imprisoned by the Scots; they were cheap, easy to make, a device to distract myself. I had a few with me and gave them to some of the children at Alnwick. Why?'

'It doesn't matter now.' Corbett smiled. 'It's as I thought.'

He rose to his feet, walked up and down, then came back.

'Master Cacoignes, if I gave you letters, a small purse of silver and a good horse, do you think you could journey south, following the coastline? You should be safe. You know something of the lie of the land?' Cacoignes nodded. 'Follow the coastal paths, move up onto the moorland when the tide surges in. You will find that the letters offer you full pardon for all offences as well as a petition to the Exchequer for monies to settle your debts. Now,' Corbett stood over his visitor, 'if you can, strike inland. Make your way to any city or town of importance. The Bishop of Durham's household may be able to assist and could send forces north either by land or sea to Tynemouth. If this is not possible, take ship to Scarborough or one of the other Yorkshire ports, where there should be a harbour bailiff in the service of the king's Admiral to the East. Again, use the seals I shall give you. Ask for help to be sent here as soon as possible.'

'You think you are in great danger, Sir Hugh?'

'No, Master Cacoignes, I *know* we are in great danger. I feel it here in my heart. Evil is gathering and its heralds already display their standards and unfurl their war banners.' Corbett stretched out his hands for Cacoignes to clasp. 'We need help, and the sooner the better, so God go with you.'

Corbett left Ranulf to look after Cacoignes whilst he walked across to the priory muniment room, which included a library and a scriptorium, three chambers leading into one other, the entire area surrounded by paved cloisters where the good brothers could sit at their sloping desks to take full advantage of the sunlight. The muniment room smelt deliciously of beeswax, polish, candle smoke, scrubbed vellum, ink and the other delightful aromas of the chancery. For a while Corbett just sat at a desk as he recalled his own secret chamber in his manor at Leighton: secure, luxurious and comfortable. A place of sweet sounds and fragrant odours, especially during spring and summer when the casement windows were open and he could enjoy the brilliance of the flower gardens and the lush greenery of the nearby woods. He wondered what it would be like now. Would Maeve be sitting in the garden listening to the cooing of the wood doves or the brilliant song of that blackbird that seemed to show no fear as it hopped its way across the close-cropped grass? He wished he was back there, but first, if he returned safe and secure, he must seek an urgent meeting with the king. The situation in the north was much more serious than the council realised.

'I am a royal envoy,' he whispered to himself, 'and yet I am not safe. I have to make treaties with the likes of Darel and dispatch my messengers stealthily.'

For a while he concentrated on what advice he should offer. King Edward needed to assemble a great array and make a public chevauchée, a royal progress through the north with banners displayed and standards fluttering. The sheriff of Northumberland needed to be replaced; perhaps the king would agree to the setting-up of a Council of the North with its own chancery and exchequer as well as the power to raise troops and levy a shield tax. Corbett stirred at the patter of sandalled feet and glanced up.

'I am Brother John, librarian and archivist.' The monk's gentle, furrowed face creased into a smile. 'Sir Hugh? It is Sir Hugh, yes? Can I help you?'

Corbett smiled back. 'Do you have a memoranda roll

or schedule of documents on Alnwick and its sale to Lord Henry some two years ago?'

'Oh yes, yes.' Brother John hurried away and brought back a leather carrying case crammed with documents. Corbett, keeping an eye on the hour candle glowing in a glass under its thick brass cap, swiftly went through the manuscripts. He could sift these easily, as each was clearly titled: 'Indenture of goods', 'Memorandum of understanding', 'Copies of royal charters'. He noticed how many of these had been scrutinised and checked by Prior Richard and Brother Adrian, who had scrawled their initials – 'RT' and 'AO' – at the bottom of each document. He continued his search until he found 'A roll of maps concerning Alnwick'. Some of these were crudely done – simple diagrams of the surrounding land. Others described the castle itself, its inner and outer baileys as well as the various sections of the wall and the individual towers. Nevertheless, they could not tell him much, as they were drenched in dark ink. According to Brother John, when Corbett summoned him over, these stains were the result of some accident.

Corbett sat poring over what he could. Bells rang. Sandalled feet echoed. There was a hum of voices and the faint sound of the choir intoning the psalms of the Divine Office: 'When the Lord delivered Sion from bondage, it seemed like a dream. Then were our hearts filled with laughter . . .' He was wondering if he should join the brothers when Ranulf came in to whisper that Cacoignes, armed and provisioned, had been given a good horse and had quietly slipped out of Tynemouth.

Ranulf had also supplied their messenger with all the documents and seals he needed. Corbett nodded and asked his henchman to fetch Lady Hilda and Lady Kathryn Thurston, as he wanted to ask them a favour. Ranulf looked askance but Corbett said he wished to address certain suspicions he'd entertained since leaving Alnwick.

'I have prepared for my meeting with the ladies.' He opened his belt wallet and took out a silver bracelet studded with precious stones, which he laid on the table before him.

Corbett watched Ranulf leave, then returned to the manuscripts. He felt cramped and stiff, so he got up and walked around the muniment room, paying particular attention to its wall paintings; the theme of all of these seemed to be the scrolls and books mentioned in the Book of Revelation: 'Worthy are you my Lord to open the scroll', or 'A court was summoned and the books were opened'. Other paintings, quotations and monograms celebrated the apocalyptic end of time. One of these caught his eye and he stopped, heart chilled as he gazed at the painting of Christ as the Alpha and the Omega of all things. 'So similar,' he whispered to himself. 'Is it possible? Is it even probable?'

He recalled his days studying the relentless force of logic in the halls and schools of Oxford. The open *disputatio* when he and others defended their theses against all comers. He recalled one of his masters developing the extraordinary thesis: 'If God is all love, why did he allow Christ to sacrifice himself on the cross?

How could a loving God watch his beloved son undergo crucifixion, one of the most horrible forms of execution known to humankind? How could he let him be brutally scourged at the pillar and crowned with sharp thorns?' He recalled the image carved by Brother Oswald in the priory church: Christ's agonised face under that sharp black crown with its razor-like barbs fastened and beaten so they would sink into the Saviour's skull. The magister in the schools had argued that God did not want that. That Christ's life and his brutal departure from this world was not what God had intended or planned but was the work of the human will. People might not like this, but, the magister had argued, finding a solution to a logical problem was like being in a dark circular cavern with doors built into its wall. Only one door was genuine, and that was the only one to be opened because it was the only one that could be. Such a logical approach must be applied here.

Corbett breathed in slowly to calm himself, even as he recalled a problem that had nagged him constantly: the poisoning of Malachy Roskell and the murder of that Scotsman's companions. Logically there was only one conclusion, and he realised that he must confront that, resolve it and apply the same solution to every other mystery facing him. He straightened up as he heard Ranulf lead the two ladies into the muniment room. He picked up the bracelet and hastened to meet them.

'Sir Hugh.' Lady Hilda extended a hand for him to kiss, Lady Kathryn Thurston likewise. 'Well?' Lady

Hilda arched her eyebrows. 'You summoned us, for what purpose?'

'To feast on your beauty,' Corbett teased, 'both that and this.' He held up the bracelet. 'I bought this for the Lady Maeve. However, I do wonder if it will fit correctly. I noticed that both of you are slender-wristed like my lady wife. Now the craftsman mentioned how the inside of the bracelet is slightly fretted to make sure it does not slip up or down or around but remains secure so the precious stones stay on display on the back of the wrist.' He glanced warningly at Ranulf to stay silent. He had in fact been given the bracelet by the king for the Lady Maeve.

'Of course.' Lady Hilda bared her left hand and arm. Corbett slipped the bracelet up over her bony fingers. 'My wrist,' she declared, 'is a little *too* slender.'

He tried it on the right wrist, murmuring that he liked the way the bracelet held, before turning to Kathryn Thurston. She seemed more reluctant and explained that she had sores on her right wrist, so she offered her left. Corbett fitted the bracelet, standing back to admire it before unclasping the catch, gently removing it and sliding it back into his belt wallet.

'It is as I thought.' He smiled. 'Ladies, I do thank you.' He was about to turn away but Lady Hilda grasped his arm.

'And you, Sir Hugh, you will join us the day after tomorrow when we pay our special devotion to St Oswine?'

'I certainly shall.' Corbett bowed, called to the

librarian to thank him, then left the muniment office with Ranulf striding beside him.

'Sir Hugh, what was that all about?'

Corbett stopped, turned and grinned. 'You will see, my friend. But for the moment, I am going back into the sanctuary. I want to study that tomb. I would be grateful if you would bring me a platter of food and a little wine. I will sit, pray, eat, reflect and even doze. When the good brothers come in, I shall join them in the choir. In the meantime, Ranulf, bring that one-eyed archer into the sanctuary.'

'Remember the recluse!'

'Oh, I certainly shall.'

Corbett made himself comfortable just inside the rood screen of the priory church. He spent some time studying the rood itself, that intricately carved crucified figure, as he recalled his earlier reflection about logic offering the only conclusion it could. He then moved the sanctuary chair so he had a clear view of Oswine's tomb. He heard the door open, and Ranulf and Gaveston swept into the church. The royal favourite was fully disguised, quite changed by the bushy moustache and beard, the leather eye patch, the filthy-mittened fingers, the slouched walk and the caustic, clipped speech. So complete was the disguise that even Corbett had to remind himself that this shuffling bowman was the exquisitely handsome, gorgeously attired favourite of the king and once lord of the realm.

Gaveston didn't speak, but waited until Corbett took him deep into the shadow of the church porch, where no one could even glimpse them, never mind eavesdrop on their conversation.

'What is it, Hugh?'

'My lord, one question. Only one! Seton and his comrades were publicly paraded as hostages being taken north to be handed over to Bruce. In truth, they were assassins who were to be dispatched across the border, buckled and armed for war, goodly provisioned and well harnessed. You and His Grace the king wanted them to draw close to Bruce and kill him. No, no, my lord,' Corbett hissed, 'I am not here to debate the whys and wherefores, what is moral and what is not, or even,' he smiled wryly, 'whether I should have been informed about what was plotted.'

'Your question, Hugh?'

'Who apart from you and His Grace the king knew the truth about Seton's secret intentions?'

'Nobody.' Gaveston stepped closer. 'I swear by all that is holy, nobody at all. Seton and the others swore a most solemn oath, hands on the Book of the Gospels, that they would only share their true purpose in returning to Scotland with God and their consciences.'

'You are certain that is what they swore?'

'Hugh, I was there.' Gaveston tapped his padded jerkin. 'And I don't think I should stay here much longer.'

Gaveston left, and Corbett returned to his vantage point in the sanctuary. When the monks filed in to sing the Divine Office, he was only too delighted to join them. Once the service was over, he continued his vigil. The following day he brought his chancery satchel with him and sat reviewing and revising, time and again, all he had seen, heard and felt. Occasionally he would stare at the tomb or kneel before the rood screen, gazing up at the crucified figure as his mind followed a long, twisting path dictated by the sheer logic of events. By the eve of the feast of St Oswine, he believed he knew the identity of both Paracelsus and the assassin who had dogged his own steps. Only then did he leave the church, asking Ap Ythel to dispatch three of his best archers back the way they'd come with urgent messages for Lord Henry.

Brother Julian, sub-cellarer at Tynemouth Priory, would never forget that particular feast day of St Oswine. Indeed, none of the brothers would, but Julian took great pride in the fact that he was the first to witness the horrors about to come. He prided himself on his sharp eyesight; as he always informed his brothers, that was why, so many lifetimes ago, he had been a master bowman in the royal array. Age, had not dimmed this gift, and accordingly, Brother Julian had been appointed leader of the night watch, which included all those monks excused from the Divine Office so as to act as watchmen, high in the belfry tower with its eagle-eye view over the countryside, Tynemouth Cove and the sea beyond.

On that particular night, Brother Julian had been joined by Sebastian, his assistant. The rule was very strict on this, decreeing that for safety's sake, no brother should be in the soaring belfry by himself. They had broken their evening fast on succulent chicken strips, fresh bread, a bowl of chopped vegetables and brimming tankards of ale. Now Julian stood on the parapet walk of the belfry, staring out into the night. All was ready. He and Sebastian had climbed the steep ladder into the belfry loft. They had checked on the four great bells: Matthew, Mark, Luke and John, named after the four Evangelists. Most importantly, they had lit the great lantern with its specially crafted massive candle, the dancing spear of flame being somehow enhanced by the precious concave glass of the gigantic lanternhorn. The light served as a beacon for passing ships, a matter of great importance, especially given that the priory's own cog, *The Golden Dove*, under its master Ralph Wodeforde, was due any day now. The beacon was a blessing to all seagoing vessels; if a storm blew up, they could use it to find their way into the protection of Tynemouth Cove. Brother Julian wondered if that might happen tonight. The wind had certainly quickened, whilst the moonlit sky was turning darker and the crashing of the waves more ominous.

'There is a storm brewing,' Sebastian declared sleepily from his straw-filled pallet. 'Though I suspect it will come just before dawn. Oh, by the way, have you heard?'

'Have I heard what?' Julian replied testily. 'Is it about the storm?' Sebastian was a former mariner, so if he said a storm was sweeping in, then it would happen.

'Oh no, not that. Brother Maurice was up in the heathland across the Tyne. There are rumours of a Scottish raiding party gathering near Coldstream.'

'God help us,' Julian murmured. 'We already have the royal envoys and the pilgrims; now we've got the Scots. Ah well, take your rest, Brother.'

A short while later, both monks were fast asleep. Julian was startled awake by the crash of thunder and the crack of jagged lightning as the storm broke. He shook himself, took a sip of ale and, rubbing his eyes, stared out to sea, noticing that the tide was coming in. More peals of thunder echoed. Fresh streaks of lightning cut the sky. The darkness was now beginning to thin, and he heaved a sigh of relief. At least no ship was battling against the storm. He could hear no creak or crack of timber, nor see any sail fluttering like a bird, and yet . . . He blinked. He was sure he'd heard the sound of horsemen galloping across the beach, but that must have been a dream, surely? What would horsemen want on a lonely, windswept beach at the dead of night?

Brother Julian crossed himself, picked up his psalter and opened it at the Office of the Day, reading the extract from St Peter's letter. He had studied this before and it always made him shiver, even more so with the wind howling and the waves crashing against the beach. The apostle's description of the end of all things – 'When the very elements will catch fire' – always fascinated the sub-cellarer. 'I just hope and pray,' he murmured to the sleeping Sebastian, 'that the elements catch fire when you and I are up here caught between heaven and earth.'

He finished his office and dozed for a while as the storm retreated further and further out to sea. When he awoke, dawn had broken. The storm had cleared the air, and the usual morning mist had not formed. A bright day was promised. His gaze was caught by the execution posts driven into the sand. Ten poles in all, one for each of the Commandments, according to Prior Richard. He shivered as he glimpsed the bundles of rags still tightly fastened, the mortal remains of the pirates, a grisly spectacle that drew gulls and other seabirds to feast on the wet, salt-soaked flesh. Then he narrowed his eyes and gasped in surprise. 'No, no, it can't be,' he whispered. He stared, blinked and counted again. Six pirates had been executed, six corpses displayed. No other judgements had been passed or enacted, yet there were seven corpses lashed to that macabre line of posts. Seven, not six! His yelp of surprise awoke the sleeping Sebastian even as Brother Julian scrambled up the ladder to ring the tocsin.

Corbett was awake when the alarm bell began to toll. He swiftly pulled on his boots, buckled his war belt, grabbed his cloak and hurried down into the inner court, where Prior Richard was deep in conversation with two of his brothers. Orders had already been given: ostlers and grooms were leading out horses to be swiftly saddled and harnessed.

'The beach!' Prior Richard declared. 'Our watchman claims a seventh corpse can be clearly seen. Someone has strapped it there without our knowledge or authority. A victim, I suspect, of some grievous assault.' The prior swiftly mounted but waited for Corbett and others to swing themselves up into the saddle. Once ready, they galloped across the lowered drawbridge and along the narrow high street, following the path as it pitched steeply onto the soft, clinging sand of the beach.

After a good night's sleep, Corbett felt refreshed. The morning was clear and dry, the ride exhilarating. The horsemen fanned out, galloping towards the shoreline and that grim row of execution posts. The wind sharpened, buffeting and stinging their faces with a thick salty spray. Corbett now rode slightly ahead of the rest, his horse's neck stretched as it threw itself into a full charge. He gripped the reins, digging his knees in as he brought his mount back into a smooth canter, wheeling it slightly so as to ride along the line of execution stakes facing the sea. He took one look and swallowed hard, then turned away, fighting the urge to retch. The six corpses had been ravaged by birds and sea creatures: eyeballs hung gruesomely from sockets, noses, lips, cheeks and other portions of soft flesh had been picked, plucked and pierced.

When he reached the seventh figure, he reined in, drew his sword and used its tip to force back the head. It was Geoffrey Cacoignes. Corbett groaned. The former royal squire had died most cruelly, his chest ripped open, the flesh spilling out where the heart had been gouged free. His stricken face was ghastly, his half-open mouth stuffed with what looked like rags. Corbett, aware of the others reining in behind him, drew closer and pulled the soggy remnants of parchment and sealing wax from the dead man's mouth.

'It is Cacoignes!' He breathed in noisily as he resheathed

his sword. 'They were waiting for him and they are sending us a warning. They captured and tortured him, plucked out his heart for sacrifice and stuffed his dead mouth with the letters and seals we furnished him with. God have mercy on poor Cacoignes and bring him to a place of light and peace. Prior Richard, if you could arrange for this unfortunate to be taken down and given Christian burial?'

'I will,' the prior replied. 'Strange,' he mused. 'Brother Julian, our watchman, was sure he heard horsemen cantering across the beach in the dead of night.' He hurriedly blessed Cacoignes' corpse. 'At least I can tell him he wasn't dreaming.'

Corbett crossed himself and turned his horse away. He felt truly sorry for Cacoignes even as he realised that this gruesome display was only the herald of a deeper malignancy closing in around them. The Black Chesters were gathering, poised and ready to strike. The devil's wolf was sloping through the dark towards them. Darel had been most cunning. He had promised to observe the law and he had sued for peace, but there again, he could afford to. The Black Chesters could carry on his war by proxy; they were not subject to any treaty or understanding.

Corbett rode back to the priory feeling restless. He had prayed, studied and reflected. He was ready to confront his adversary, but he did not yet know how to implement his strategy. He returned to the chapel, where he knelt in the entrance to the rood screen and peered up at the tortured face of Christ under its circlet of thorns. As he prayed fervently, he smiled to himself and let his mind drift. He was lost in reverie when Chanson shook him gently by the shoulder.

Corbett glanced quickly around. Lady Hilda's pilgrims were now filing into the church, coming to help prepare the nave, bedecking the pillars with flowers in anticipation for the special ceremony to be held here once darkness fell and the Compline bell had tolled. He blinked and stared at his clerk of the stables. He had never seen Chanson look so agitated.

'What is the matter?'

'Master, Ranulf and Ap Ythel are outside. You must come, you must come now! You must see this!'

Corbett followed Chanson out of the church, where Ap Ythel and Ranulf were waiting. The clerk of the stables beckoned them close.

'Sir Hugh,' he hissed, 'I think it's best if only you and I visited the stables. I beg you to act as if we are just checking our horses.' He glimpsed Corbett's incredulity. 'Sir Hugh?' he pleaded.

'Chanson,' Ranulf demanded, 'are you drunk?'

'No, but I wish to God I was. Sir Hugh, please?'

'You'd best show me. Ranulf, Ap Ythel, I will meet you later in the church.'

Corbett and Chanson went across into the yard, a busy place reeking of horse flesh, sweat, wet straw, dung and the various odours from the smithy. Chanson led the way into one of the stables and Corbett followed him past a number of stalls until he paused and tapped the half-door that closed off one particular one. Corbett glanced swiftly in and his heart skipped a beat, but he continued to act nonchalantly, following Chanson outside and stopping to look around before making his way back to Ranulf and Ap Ythel. Once there, he dispatched Chanson to fetch Prior Richard, with the urgent message that they must meet here in the dark transepts of the priory church.

PART SIX

'The King sent Gaveston away for a time to a very safe place.'   *Life of Edward II*

Corbett, Prior Richard to his right, Ranulf to his left, stood before the rood screen of the priory church. They tried to appear relaxed, smiling at the pilgrims assembling in the nave in preparation for the celebration of the feast of St Oswine. Outside, darkness had fallen. The brothers had sung their vespers and left. Corbett swallowed hard and whispered a prayer. Ap Ythel was here too, his company of archers, about fifteen in number, hidden deep in the shadows of the sanctuary behind them. Others had been dispatched for this or that. Corbett's heart sank as he realised that more pilgrims were pushing themselves into the nave.

He and Prior Richard had heatedly discussed what to do. Chanson and three of Ap Ythel's archers had been sent out into the countryside with strict instructions. For the rest, the royal clerk could only hope and wait. If their adversaries were alerted and the enemy within realised that they had been discovered, there was a real danger of hostages being taken: members of the community, townspeople and other innocents going about their God-given business. On one issue Prior Richard had been obdurate. Tempting as it would be to flee the priory and take refuge behind the fortified walls and barbican overlooking Tynemouth village, such a withdrawal would leave church and shrine vulnerable to those who wanted the utter destruction of both. In the end, they had all agreed. The priory church must be guarded, if necessary, with their lives.

Corbett had also insisted that they must accept that all the pilgrims from Clairbaux were adherents, retainers, followers of the Black Chesters. These so-called pilgrims had flooded into the priory, acting the part with their crucifixes, pilgrim staves, rosary beads and Ave chains. They might chant psalms and sing hymns but, he argued, they truly were the enemy within. Some of them pushed wheelbarrows or pulled handcarts; others carried bulky panniers or sacks. They were undoubtedly bringing in weapons. He had ordered that they be allowed to gather here within the nave of the church, where they could be contained and confronted. The rood screen was a natural barrier with its trellised woodwork and small windows; it could act as a defence, offering protection to Ap Ythel's bowmen.

Undoubtedly the Black Chesters must include some former soldiers, men who had participated in the savage, bloody conflicts along the Scottish march and who were used to the cut and thrust of hand-to-hand combat. In the main, though, they were mummers who acted out their masques, and while it was one thing to terrorise some hapless traveller like Cacoignes, an armed military cohort was another matter. Corbett also doubted that Edmund Darel would publicly participate in this venture; instead he would act the unknowing innocent. Ranulf had asked if they should bring Brother Adrian and the Thurstons into their confidence. Corbett had been adamant in his refusal: no one else was to be trusted.

'*Alea iacta*,' he whispered now. 'The die is cast.'

He stepped forward and glanced up at a window. Late in the afternoon, a mist had crept in from the sea. Now it swirled like a chorus of ghosts around the priory, seeping under doors and making its presence felt even here in the church. The pilgrims were milling about, rubbing their arms or stamping their feet. Candle flames flared before shrines, sconce torches spluttered. Corbett glanced down the nave. Those assembling still acted the part of holy pilgrims. Nevertheless, he noticed how many kept their hoods and cowls pulled forward, whilst their mantles covered their mouths as effectively as any mask. Of course, some of them he recognised: the Thurstons with Brother Adrian standing close to Lady Hilda.

'The die is cast!' Corbett repeated loudly, glancing at his companions. 'So let us begin.'

He raised his hands, aware of the danger now mustering against them. There was no turning back, no retreat, no concession. He was committed. He was back on the field of battle here in the nave of this holy church.

The Black Chesters were gathering. They had planned for this but they had made mistakes. They had undoubtedly killed Bavasour and stolen his horse. One of them had stupidly used that to join in the pilgrimage to Tynemouth; unfortunately for him, the garron, with its singular colouring and unique appearance, had caught the sharp eye of Chanson, a true clerk of the stables. For a brief moment Corbett wondered if this was Bavasour's way of speaking to the living, of warning them, of demonstrating to Corbett that he had done his best to keep faith. Now those who had murdered him were assembling here in this holy place to kill again and wreak dreadful sacrilege.

'We are waiting, clerk,' a voice called. There was a challenge in this remark, like a trumpet braying across a battlefield.

'Archers!' Corbett shouted. 'Archers, string your bows.'

Ap Ythel's bowmen, arrows notched, abruptly gathered in the entrance to the rood screen. Corbett quietly prayed that the enemy did not realise just how few they were.

'What is this?' Lady Hilda stepped forward.

'Today,' Corbett replied, 'I visited the stables. I recognised a horse quite singular: dun-coloured, with clipped ears and shorn tail. Its former owner was a mercenary, a captain of hobelars named Bavasour. I knew Bavasour of old. I met him again after Alnwick was attacked. He was captured but I arranged his release. Bavasour was a veteran soldier. You may not know this, but veterans never freely surrender their weapons or their horses. Moreover, the mount I gave Bavasour, the one I saw in the stables here, is a truly excellent beast. My old comrade would never have given up such a treasure. So tell me, who rode that horse here to Tynemouth?'

'It could be a different horse,' a voice mocked.

'Nonsense!' Corbett replied. 'I asked my clerk of the stables to scrutinise the animal. Chanson is an excellent judge of horse flesh. He chose that horse for Bavasour and he confirmed without a doubt that it is the mount Bavasour rode from Alnwick.' He repeated his question. 'Who amongst you rode that horse here? Answer me; purge yourself. Demonstrate that there is no wrong-doing.'

He waited. This was his last response, his final proclamation to settle matters. He had done the same on the battlefield before the standards were unfurled, the banners displayed, the trumpets brayed, the lances lowered and the long line of destriers pawed the ground ready to break into a charge.

'He could have reached Carlisle and sold it,' Lady Hilda called out.

Corbett stepped closer so he could see that clever face with its age-old eyes, its sly expression, the quick shift of mood as the woman realised the mistake she had made.

'Lady Hilda,' he asked softly, 'how do you know Bavasour was journeying to Carlisle? You must have taken his documents, the letters I wrote to Sir Andrew Harclay, Keeper of the Western March.'

She stared back at him, a hard, knowing look. Corbett hoped he had not moved too soon, but the devil's wolf was in the sheep fold and there was no avoiding the hunt.

'Open your cloaks,' he shouted. 'Unstrap your war belts.'

In response, the main door of the church was slammed shut and the mass of pilgrims in front of him moved threateningly, people pushing their way through. Walter Thurston, his sister Kathryn and Brother Adrian were dragged to the fore; hooded figures forced them to their knees, daggers to their throats. All three hostages looked pleadingly at Corbett, who realised that he must delay and delay again in the hope of help arriving in time. He gestured at Lady Hilda.

'Mistress, you play the hypocrite. No anchorite, no pilgrims; you are the Black Chesters. A coven of malignants, the true disciples of the devil, servile servants of Satan. All you say and do is nothing but mummery, a mask for your wanton wickedness.'

Lady Hilda, now protected by two of her male adherents, simply smiled, an arching, superior look, as if Corbett was beneath her. Here was a woman committed to what she really believed in. She had brought her followers to Tynemouth to utterly destroy the shrine and burn the church. Corbett wondered if she considered her death and that of her coven a necessary sacrifice to achieve this. He silently berated himself for miscalculating and underestimating the real wickedness of his adversary.

'Tell your men to follow your example, Sir Hugh.'
One of the figures leaning over Lady Kathryn pressed
the jagged edge of the dagger against the woman's soft
white neck. 'You must all place your weapons on the
floor, unstrap your war belts and do exactly as we say.
Prior Richard, send one of the bowmen out to tell the
monks beyond not to show hostility, offer any threat
or try to enter this church.'

'I recognise you, Leonora,' Corbett shouted back.

The figure lifted her head, pulled back her cowl and
lowered her visor over the bottom half of her face, then
dragged off her dusty-coloured wig and threw it on the
floor. All the time she kept the dagger close to Lady
Kathryn's throat.

'Good morrow, king's man.' She grinned, eyes dancing
with merriment. 'We have you trapped. Send the
messenger, one of your archers; he goes out and he stays
out. One fewer to oppose us.'

Corbett turned to Ap Ythel and nodded. The
Welshman snapped his fingers at Gaveston, hidden
amongst the other archers. Corbett sighed with relief
as Gaveston shuffled his way through and was allowed
down the nave. The main door was opened then
slammed shut, locked, bolted and the beam brought
down. Corbett gazed around that haunted nave. The
rood screen was now their protection. If need be, he
and his cohort could fall back behind that. The enemy
were at least sixty in number, swollen by recent arrivals.
They all hid behind heavy military cloaks and deep
cowls, and as they moved, Corbett could hear the clink

and clatter of weapons being loosened. He breathed a brief prayer for help.

'King's man?'

Corbett decided to gamble; he needed time, to delay matters as long as possible. He went and crouched before the kneeling Lady Kathryn and pointed accusingly at her. 'You are a member of this damnable coven, a demon-worshipper.' He steeled himself against the fear in the young woman's eyes. 'You tried to kill me, didn't you? You poured that oil into my chamber. Twice you used an arbalest to attack me. First in St Chad's chapel, and then in that tunnel under the Abbot's Tower. On both occasions the weapon was a light, hand-held crossbow, but of course that is all you can use, isn't it? You have a dreadful injury to your right wrist, severe burn marks inflicted when you were caught up in the sack of Berwick some fifteen years ago. When I asked you to try that bracelet, I realised my suspicions were correct. Little wonder that you are so expert in dressing burns with salves as you did for me, though you must have hated tending the very man you'd tried to kill. I saw the hateful glances you threw me on our journey north. You remembered me and Ap Ythel, whom you also tried to grievously hurt.'

Ap Ythel, standing in the mouth of the rood screen, came and crouched beside Corbett. 'Yes, I remember you now,' he murmured; Corbett had informed him of his suspicions as they'd waited in the church earlier in the evening. 'We first met in the Guildhall at Berwick some fifteen years ago.'

'You are that young girl,' Corbett continued. 'You were shocked by all the horrors and wandered into the king's presence. You collapsed on the floor, praying to St Oswine. You still have devotion to that saint, don't you? You openly pray to him. You can never forget that day. Your soul is still full of hurt, your mind twisted by hideous memories. You thought we were responsible for the horrors at Berwick, but we were not. Like you, we were caught up in that nightmare situation. I meant you well then, mistress, and I do now, but you tried to kill me and my comrade, didn't you?'

Lady Kathryn closed her eyes, moving her head as if in agreement.

'What is this?' Leonora demanded.

Corbett tore his gaze away from Lady Kathryn's face, feeling confused and uncertain as the dead hand of the past stretched out. For a few heartbeats he silently cursed the old king. The sack of Berwick had released all the demons from hell.

Further down the line, Constable Thurston struggled against his captors; he had evidently heard what Corbett had said. 'Sir Hugh,' he begged. 'My sister. I wondered about her. I know she hates all those she met on that day, a deep, lasting, corrosive resentment. She has never forgotten and she never will, but before God, although she may be guilty of attacks on you, we are not of the Black Chesters.'

Corbett stared at him. He was now determined to use everything to create as long a delay as possible.

'You kept your wrist covered, didn't you?' He grasped

Lady Kathryn's ice-cold hand and pushed back her sleeve to reveal healed yet still ugly scars.

'Enough,' Lady Hilda called out. 'For the last time, Corbett, tell your bowmen and your war dog Ranulf to disarm.'

Corbett glanced at Lady Kathryn.

'I am sorry,' she whispered. 'Sir Hugh, I am so sorry.'

'Leonora!' Lady Hilda shouted.

'Sweetly so,' her accomplice called back, and before Corbett could interject or intervene, she drew her dagger in a soft, slithering motion across Lady Kathryn's throat. The skin ruptured like an overripe plum bursting, the blood bubbling out even as Lady Kathryn's eyes rolled back in her head. Leonora laughed and pushed her away.

Corbett made to spring, hand going to his dagger, but stopped as the Black Chesters behind Leonora aimed their crossbows. He rose and stared in horror at Lady Kathryn sprawled on the floor, choking on her own blood. Constable Thurston had broken free of his captors and made to charge forward. An arbalest strummed and the constable stumbled towards the corpse of his sister, hands flapping, wild-eyed, his mouth trying to form words but saying nothing as the blood spurted between his lips, one hand lifting as if to remove the quarrel buried deep in the back of his head. He groaned, coughed and collapsed to the floor.

Corbett and Ap Ythel hastened back to the rood screen as the Black Chesters now prepared for battle. Swords and daggers were drawn, crossbows and axes raised, archers pushing to the front. Leonora was laughing hysterically. Lady Hilda screamed orders. Corbett's cohort gathered behind the rood screen, weapons ready, war bows and arbalests primed. Corbett sensed the deep fear of his comrades. The nave was packed with Black Chesters and their adherents. Soon they would try to force the rood screen and surge into the sanctuary to destroy St Oswine's shrine.

Abruptly, like a sudden close peal of thunder, a pounding began against the main door of the church. It rolled through the nave, quietening all other sound, and was followed by war cries and battle chants. Corbett hoped his ears weren't deceiving him.

'Lord Henry! The Percys!' One of the Black Chesters at the far end of the church stood on a bench and peered through a lancet window. 'Lord Henry!' the man screamed again. 'He has come with great force.'

The news created consternation. The Black Chesters were preparing to unleash their assault against the rood screen when a hunting horn sounded loud and clear across the sanctuary. The haunting, long-drawn-out call was repeated, followed by the shrill ringing of a hand-bell. A woman's singing carried through. Corbett glanced over his shoulder. Rachaela, dressed in her black robe, had put down the horn and bell. The recluse was now carrying what looked like a tray covered by the small square of silk used to protect the offertory cruets on their shelf in the sanctuary wall. Smiling serenely, she walked towards Corbett and his party.

'Let me pass,' she whispered.

Corbett caught the pleading look in her eyes and stood aside.

'Leonora,' she called, 'it is I.' She stepped through the door of the rood screen, processing slowly towards Leonora, who now stood slightly apart from the others.

'Well, well.' Lady Hilda's harsh voice stilled any whispers. 'Little Rachaela.' Her voice turned ugly. 'The traitor!'

'What do you want, Rachaela?' Leonora taunted. 'What is that you are carrying? Do you hope to bargain for your life? Nothing can buy you that.'

'What is it?' Lady Hilda demanded, 'What are you carrying?'

Rachaela stopped, still clutching the tray covered by that gold-fringed scarlet cloth. 'The Lily Crown,' she declared. 'I bring it to you, Leonora.' She walked briskly forward.

Her words had created a stillness that was broken by a fresh pounding against the main door. Rachaela was now very close to Leonora, who, all intrigued, stretched out her hands. Rachaela abruptly stepped back. The silk cloth slipped to the floor, as did the tray beneath, but Rachaela still gripped the hand-held arbalest, bringing it up so quickly that Leonora could only stare in horror. The recluse aimed and loosed, an ominous click as the jagged barb sped to shatter Leonora's beautiful face. There was a deathly quiet for a few heartbeats. Rachaela did not try to flee or hide but stood, arms extended, almost as if she welcomed the crossbow bolts that struck her in the chest and stomach and sent her staggering back to collapse against a pillar and slump to the ground.

Battle was now joined. Corbett's retinue, assembled behind the rood screen, blocked its entrance as they had planned with furniture – chests, coffers and anything they could drag from the sacristy or sanctuary – hastily creating a barricade strong enough to impede any attack yet also allowing Ap Ythel's archers to loose time and again, both from behind the barricade and through the slits and apertures of the screen. Corbett's earlier judgement proved correct. Many of the Black Chesters were not soldiers, and had no experience of the horror of bitter hand-to-hand fighting. They could not close with their opponents, who time and time again retaliated with deadly accuracy. Meanwhile, the pounding on the main door was having an effect. The crack of wood and the buckling of metal could be clearly heard above the cries, yells and screams and the macabre music of the bowstrings as they released their flying death.

Desperate to break through, the Black Chesters grabbed cresset torches and hurled them at the rood screen. Some of these hit the highly polished wood but did not set light to it. Ap Ythel directed two of his master bowmen to bring down anyone wielding a torch, an easy enough target in the dancing light. Corbett sensed the sheer frustration of the Black Chesters as they threw themselves against the barrier. Their screams and death cries grew more shrill as the Welsh bowmen loosed and loosed again, a constant hail of yard-long shafts, volleys of such force and sharpness that bodies were completely pierced and most of the wounds inflicted were deadly.

The stench of smoke and spilt blood smothered the usual sweet odours of the church. The struggle was now becoming a massacre as the Black Chesters fought against the closing trap. The main door was breached, while at the same time a fresh assault was launched on the corpse door to the side of the building, and Lord Henry's men, garbed in their blue and white livery, poured into the church along with members of the community and the priory's own men-at-arms. The barricade across the rood screen was pulled back. Armed with sword and dagger, Corbett and his party now joined the uneven struggle being waged up and down the nave. Tendrils of smoke curled from the thrown cressets, the flames spluttering in the blood that seemed to swirl everywhere. The dead sprawled as thickly as fallen leaves on an autumn day.

At last cries for mercy were heard. The surviving Black Chesters shouted that they wished to surrender. They threw down their weapons, raising their hands, falling to their knees in the puddles of blood seeping from the corpses of their comrades. In the heat of battle some received no quarter, only the deep thrust of a sword or the slicing cut of a dagger across their throats. The piteous screams trailed away as a knight in full armour with a surcoat boasting the white lion of the Percys banged his sword on the ground and roared for silence. Then he raised his visor, gasping for breath.

'Lord Henry.' Corbett sheathed his own sword and

extended his arms. 'In any other circumstances I'd kiss your sweat-soaked face.'

'Less of the sarcasm, Corbett.' Lord Henry indicated with his head. 'Shall we cut the bastards down? Take them out and hang them from the gables? Or we could save time and expense and throw them off the crag.'

'None of those.' Prior Richard, who had found a helmet that did not exactly fit him, came striding over, in one hand a battered shield, in the other a fearsome war club, its spikes clotted with human bone, hair and blood. 'Our church,' the prior spun round, addressing both victor and vanquished, 'has been polluted. The Bishop of Durham will purify and reconsecrate it. Until then this place remains a house of blood and slaughter, of filthy blasphemy and sordid sacrilege. I would dearly love to fling these disciples of the devil from the great crag, but we have the law. I exercise all the rights of a manor lord; I shall sit in judgement on these miscreants. Their fate is certain, their deaths approaching. They can die as they watch the tide surge in.'

Corbett kicked away fallen weapons and moved corpses with the toe of his boot as he walked into the centre of the nave, staring closely at the prisoners and their captors. The bloodlust had now cooled. The rage of battle was slipping away. He glimpsed Lady Hilda being dragged from one of the chantry chapels where she had been hiding. He smiled in satisfaction. He was about to continue when Brother Adrian crept out from behind one of the statues. He smiled weakly at Corbett and gratefully accepted the cloak Ap Ythel hurriedly threw around him. The monk bowed towards Corbett and Prior Richard and, shivering and moaning, scuttled for the protection of the archers thronging in the entrance to the rood screen. Once again Corbett glanced around. The nave was like a flesher's yard. Blood flowed across the flagstones and ran in rivulets down the pillars. The smell of death was deeply offensive. The stench of ripped bellies made him pinch his nostrils whilst the sounds of the wounded and dying carried like a dreadful hymn to the violence that had shattered this holy place.

He lifted one hand. 'I am,' he declared, 'the Crown's envoy. I am a royal justice. I have the power to hold a king's assize. I can appoint justices in eyre, and so I do: myself, Prior Richard and Lord Henry Percy.' He snapped his fingers. 'Have the prisoners bound; offer them no more violence. Prior Richard, you have dungeons?'

'Beneath the chapter house.'

'Good.' Corbett clapped his hands. 'Let them be taken there.'

'Dark drops,' Corbett declared as he washed his hands at the lavarium in his guest-house chamber, 'dark drops from the ocean of darkness, shadows that sweep through human affairs: such are the Black Chesters, and we have done something to check their evil.' He wiped his hands on a napkin and walked back to join the others squeezed around the chamber table: Prior Richard, Lord Henry, Ranulf and Ap Ythel. He sipped at his wine goblet, then toasted Lord Henry. 'Last night,' he smiled, 'was a miracle. The Black Chesters made a number of hideous mistakes. They thought that through the murders of Cacoignes and Bavasour they had cut me off from any help. Of course they didn't reckon on Lord Henry coming to our aid. Second, I suspect they knew that a goodly number of the brothers had journeyed south on the priory war cog *The Golden Dove*, visiting their mother houses at Westminster and St Alban's. They thought the community here would be weak and vulnerable, depleted of fighting monks as well as the men-at-arms who man that cog.' He grinned. 'They were truly wrong and this is linked to their third mistake. They underestimated the ruthless courage of our prior here, not to mention others. Fourth, we must not forget the fortitude and self-sacrifice of our recluse Rachaela. She will be given an honourable requiem?'

'Of course.' Prior Richard replied.

'Finally,' Corbett concluded, 'the Black Chesters were not soldiers but mummers. They thought they could frighten and terrify others as they did innocent farmers, cottagers, tinkers and traders trapped on the lonely roads of Northumberland. They were Satan's servants and shared his sin: they were arrogant. They made a dreadful mistake and became locked in a trap of their own making.'

'And Lady Kathryn Thurston?'

'As I said, Ranulf, when I confronted her in the priory church, fifteen years ago I knelt beside a young maiden who was muttering constant prayers to St Oswine and nursing nasty burns to her wrist. I met her in the Guildhall at Berwick. The old king was there, taking a respite from the dreadful slaughter he had ordered. Ap

Ythel and I brought messages from Westminster. We journeyed to that town and witnessed the house of slaughter Berwick had become. Murder and mayhem walked hand in hand. The young maiden, Kathryn Thurston, also witnessed it. I did my best to comfort and assist her.

'Time passed and I forgot her, but she had not forgotten either me or Ap Ythel. Somehow in her confused mind she believed that the two of us were responsible for that slaughter. I suspect the shock of meeting us again turned her wits. I certainly recall her glaring at me as we journeyed north. Anyway, little by little the drops of the past betrayed her. Lady Kathryn's constant recourse to St Oswine, the way she hid her wrists. Once we reached Alnwick, she decided to act. First the fire in my chamber and the caltrops left hidden in Ap Ythel's. She also tried to kill me with a crossbow bolt on two occasions: in St Chad's chapel and in that tunnel under the Abbot's Tower. On both occasions she had to flee, leaving the weapon behind: one of those small arbalests that a lady, particularly one with a weak wrist, could manage. I realised the weapons weren't chosen randomly. I doubt if she was skilled, yet she could have killed me.' Corbett paused. 'Prior Richard you will also see to her burial and that of her brother?'

'Yes, let them be buried here.' Lord Henry spoke up. 'I have no desire to take the corpses back to Alnwick.'

'What did they intend?' Prior Richard asked. 'The Black Chesters?'

'At another time, in a different place,' Corbett replied

slowly, 'I can give a more accurate account. In brief, I believe their dark design covered a number of matters. First, they would have sacked a royal priory in the shire of Northumberland, so the chaos grows and the darkness deepens whilst the Black Chesters demonstrate their power to all and sundry. Second, they wanted to destroy this holy place, particularly the tomb of St Oswine. Again, a demonstration of their power. Third, they were hoping to find the Lily Crown hidden away in the sanctuary, something they could use to bargain with when they moved into Scotland. Little wonder there are rumours of a Scottish raiding party moving south, possibly dispatched to assist the Black Chesters. Fourth, they would have plundered the treasures of this priory, more gold and silver to finance their filthy practices. Finally, they could boast that they had slaughtered a prior, a king's envoy and everyone who stood with us, including Rachaela the Recluse, whom they regarded as a traitor. Would you agree, Father?'

'Sir Hugh, I certainly do.'

'In which case, my lord prior, I would like some of your finest Bordeaux and a goblet. I would also like to meet one of our prisoners. The youngest, be it male or female, who could still repent and save his or her soul as well as their neck.'

'And the trial?' Lord Henry asked.

'Oh, don't worry, we shall meet tomorrow after the Jesus Mass.'

The meeting ended. Ranulf waited for the chamber to empty before approaching Corbett.

'Sir Hugh,' he whispered. 'Lord Henry, why did he come so valiantly to our aid?'

He paused as the bells of the priory began to toll; not the tocsin, but a joyous peal of welcome. Corbett plucked him by the sleeve and they joined the rest hastening out across the priory grounds to the eastern rim of the great crag, which provided a breathtaking view of Tynemouth Cove. An early-morning mist was gathering, but this suddenly shifted and Corbett smiled at the shouts of welcome as *The Golden Dove*, standards flapping, entered the calm waters of the bay. The great sail on its mainmast was already being reefed and Corbett could glimpse figures hurrying about climbing the rigging or busy in the prow ready to toss the anchorstone over. Abruptly a fire arrow was loosed from the deck, followed by another, arcs of fluttering flame that scored the sky before dropping into the incoming tide.

'The agreed signal.' One of the brothers answered Ranulf's exclamation of surprise. 'Two fire arrows to indicate all is well.' The monk smiled. 'And it certainly is!'

Corbett beckoned to Ranulf and led him back into the great court. 'Seek out our one-eyed friend now. Tell him to prepare. Wodeforde will soon lower the ship's boat. Our hidden one can go aboard and stay there until we sail.'

'We?'

'Yes, this may be our best opportunity to leave the north swiftly and safely. Master Wodeforde can dock at Scarborough or Hull. And as for your earlier question about Lord Henry? Well, Ranulf, one of my secret tasks was to see what was happening in the north along the Scottish march. I remember a dictum of the old king: 'every ship needs a captain, every pack a leader'. The north is slipping into chaos. Men like Darel are taking the law into their own hands and he is not the only one. Further south, the Middletons disregard the royal writ; they mock the king's messengers and ignore royal officials. Lord Henry may be the best cure for the sickness. You have seen him, Ranulf.' Corbett grinned. 'Not the sort of man to dance around the maypole with, but he has some idea of justice, and above all, he will enforce the king's peace. Anyway, before I left Alnwick, I took him into my confidence. I told him that he could no longer hunt with the hounds and run with the hare. He had to make a decision. I told him that I carried a warrant in my chancery coffer, issued under the secret seal, promising him an earldom.'

'Earl of Northumberland?'

'Precisely, Ranulf. Cock of the North, Lord God Almighty along the Scottish march. Percy is like Howard of Norfolk. He wants to carve out his own family estates. He dreams of the Percy writ running from the Scottish border across to Carlisle, down through Durham and Yorkshire and into Westmoreland and the other north-western shires.'

'A king in his own right?'

'Oh no,' Corbett whispered, staring up at the sky. 'We will let the Percy lion roar for a while, let him prowl and shake his mane and make his presence felt. And then, in due course, we will offer similar encouragement to his rivals, the Nevilles and the Beaumonts. Percy couldn't resist, particularly when I offered a second charter authorising him, when the time is right, to move resolutely against Edmund Darel and all his kin. Let's be honest, Ranulf, whatever his protestations, we know that Darel supported, provisioned and armed the Black Chesters, and provided the dwelling at Clairbaux for his evil aunt.

'But that's for the future. Before we left Alnwick, Lord Henry and I reached an understanding. Once we'd departed for Tynemouth, he would follow shortly afterwards, and thank God he did. He reported that he had heard rumours of a Scottish war party making its way south down the eastern coast. I strongly suspect they were coming to the aid of the Black Chesters here at Tynemouth. Lord Henry sent out scouts. The war party has disappeared, retreated back into Scotland, at least for the time being. I sent Chanson with some of Ap Ythel's archers to ask Lord Henry to hasten as swiftly as possible, and he did. Once we are safely back at Westminster, the king will elevate Lord Henry on the strict understanding that he holds the north for the Crown against all enemies, both foreign and domestic.

'However, Ranulf,' Corbett clapped his henchman on the shoulder, 'we have business to complete. As I said, I need a goblet and a jug of this priory's finest Bordeaux. We shall then visit certain individuals. And yes, I want that prisoner, the youngest amongst them. Bring him or her to me when I ask.'

*

The justices in eyre, as Corbett described himself, Lord Henry and Prior Richard, held their assize court in the bleak, stark priory chapter house. The main chamber had a heavy oaken high table, which dominated the dais. There were benches either side of this long, barn-like room and a leather-backed chair placed just beneath the dais facing the table. Corbett pronounced himself satisfied. The chamber's whitewashed walls, black-beamed ceiling and hard-tiled floor were devoid of any ornamentation, whilst the room was overshadowed by a large, age-worn crucifix hanging from the beams above the dais. Corbett believed this was the most suitable setting for a court with powers of oyer and terminer – 'to hear and to finish', although the outcome was never really in doubt.

The Black Chesters had been roped and pushed down to the dungeons. They had been shown little mercy or consideration. Two of Ap Ythel's archers lay grievously ill in the infirmary and the priory leech believed they would not recover from their wounds. Four members of the community had also been killed and others were housed in the infirmary until their wounds healed. The prisoners had been beaten and ill used until Corbett and Ranulf, swords drawn, went down into the dungeons and imposed order. Corbett assured everyone that the Black Chesters would be punished, but that would happen according to the law. Prior Richard had been with them and he had repeated Corbett's order. However, he also pointed out that another thirty execution posts were being erected along the beach next to the original ten. 'That will take their number to forty,' he explained. 'The number of years Israel wandered in the desert after the exodus from Egypt. Just punishment for their disobedience to God. Trust me,' he concluded, 'those forty posts will be used for the wolfsheads who tried to tear our flock apart.'

The assize was now about to begin, just after the Jesus mass. This had been held in the priory refectory because the church, now cleared and cleaned of all signs of the violent struggle that had raged there, would remain locked and barred till it was purified and reconsecrated. Master Wodeforde and his crew, who had disembarked the previous day, also attended, the ship's captain promising Corbett that they would leave Tynemouth as soon as the royal clerk gave the word. Ranulf, who would act as clerk, together with Brother John the librarian and Brother Julian the sub-cellarer, had prepared the judgement table with its Book of the Gospels, Corbett's war sword and his letters patent, which gave him the authority to act as the king's justice on whatever matter pleased him.

All was ready. Brother John rang the large handbell and Corbett, with Prior Richard on his right and Lord Henry on his left, took his seat on the throne-like chair provided. Ap Ythel with six of his archers acted as guard inside the chamber; the rest were in the dungeons below, supervising the prisoners, clasping on manacles and chains. Corbett, for his own secret reasons, had insisted that once people entered the chapter house, they would not be allowed to absent themselves for any reason. The chamber had its own lavarium and a garderobe in the corner; food and drink had also been supplied. The assize chamber would remain sealed until he directed otherwise.

Chanson was the court usher, and when Corbett directed, he brought up the prisoners one by one. Each of these, heavy with chains, was pushed to sit in the chair facing the dais and respond when directed. Justice was summary and bleak. Some of the prisoners just glared moodily either at their judges or the floor. Others snarled how they did not recognise the court's authority. A few begged for mercy. Most of the prisoners were bruised or wounded, bearing the scars of the ferocious affray in which dozens of their comrades had been killed. Ten more had died the previous day from their wounds, most of these inflicted by Ap Ythel's bowmen.

Each prisoner was ordered to plead or offer something in mitigation; none of them could give a robust response. The indictment against them was compelling. They had attacked a royal envoy in a sacred place, they had waged war on the king's subjects, the sons and daughters of Holy Mother Church, as well as perpetrating the most obscene blasphemy and sacrilege. All were sentenced to death immediately, without hope of pardon or amnesty. Prior Richard added that if they wished, Brother Adrian, who had been down in the dungeons offering spiritual consolation and who now sat on a wall bench as a principal witness, would shrive them. No one accepted his offer. Once sentence of death was announced, the prisoner was dragged away and another hustled in.

Corbett was surprised at the youth of some of the prisoners, the youngest being a girl of fifteen summers, the eldest no more than forty. They came from different trades and professions: servants, traders, tinkers, merchants and a few former soldiers. All betrayed a deep cynicism for religion and authority of any kind. They saw themselves not so much as above the law but free of it, totally alienated from the communities they came from. They could, however, even when offered a bribe, say little about Paracelsus. The few who begged for mercy, only to be refused, believed that Lady Hilda might know more about their mysterious leader.

The majority of the prisoners were members of the coven at Clairbaux, provisioned and sustained by Sir Edmund Darel. According to them, Darel was a leading henchman of Paracelsus, the two slain sisters, Leonora and Richolda, being his lovers and close helpmates. Most of those from Clairbaux were men. Some had served as mercenaries; these were hard-bitten, ruthless men. They used religion as a cloak for the dagger beneath and showed little fear of either God or man. One of them cheerfully confessed to being the leader of the party who had ambushed and killed Bavasour. He admitted to taking the dead man's horse because of the number of mounts they had lost when they first attacked Corbett's encampment. He and others freely acknowledged Lady Hilda as Darel's close accomplice. Listening closely, Corbett concluded that the Black Chesters were recruited carefully; once trusted and accepted, they were invited into the inner circle of

Clairbaux's coven or those secret, sinister chambers in the inner bailey at Blanchlands.

Corbett had decided to indict Lady Hilda last of all. If she was not fully compliant, he was quite prepared to submit her to brutal interrogation and torture. It was late afternoon before she was led into the chamber to sit before the assize. She had been stripped of her sandals, smock, gown, veil and cloak and was dressed only in a linen shift that covered her from neck to toe. Nevertheless, the witch-queen, as Corbett thought of her, seemed to exude a smug self-satisfaction, an arrogance that was almost palpable; her brazen face, framed by iron-grey hair, was twisted into a supercilious smirk, as if mocking everything and everyone.

No sooner was she seated than she dismissed Corbett and his fellow judges with a baleful look of contemptuous condescension. Laden with chains, she sat with her hands in her lap, staring coolly at a point above Corbett's head, before shifting her gaze to him and baring her lips in a forced grin. When asked how she would plead, she just stretched out her arms, chains rattling. Ranulf asked her again, warning her that if she did not reply, she would be pressed until she did. Lady Hilda simply shrugged, turned and spat on the floor. One of Ap Ythel's archers struck her on the back of the head. She turned, quick as a lunging adder, and spat at him. Corbett shouted at the archer not to hit her again, even as he glimpsed Lady Hilda's swift movement. She'd used the chaos to pull something from beneath the thick cuff of her shift and pop it into her mouth.

Corbett rose, shouting at the guard, but Lady Hilda's jaws were moving swiftly, chewing vigorously whatever she had slid so quickly through her lips. All the time she held Corbett's gaze. Finally she opened her mouth to show that she had swallowed whatever she had eaten.

'She's poisoned herself!' Corbett cried.

A deep stillness descended. Everyone stared at Lady Hilda, eyes glaring, manacled hands now raised as if she was making one last fervent prayer to the demons gathering beyond the pale. Brother Adrian got to his feet, but Corbett shouted at him to stay away. Lady Hilda half rose, face twitching, neck straining as if she was about to retch. She coughèd, her body jerking, then fell back against the chair, bare feet pattering on the ground. She was now choking, a blood-chilling sound that seemed to fill the entire chamber, her eyes still fixed on Corbett as she spluttered. She began to convulse violently, tipping off the chair to jerk and lash about on the floor. She gave one last horrid gasp, legs thrashing, and lay still. Brother Adrian hurried across.

'Stop!' Corbett shouted. 'Brother Adrian, stop there.'

Corbett came to stand over the now twisted corpse of Lady Hilda, her face all liverish, fixed in the gruesome agony of death.

'She was waiting for that,' he murmured. 'She wanted to go when we confronted her. She wanted to give us her reply and publicly dismiss these proceedings. Ah well.' He drew his breath in for the next confrontation. 'Take her corpse away, then,' he pointed at Brother Adrian, 'strip him!'

'In God's name, Sir Hugh!' Prior Richard sprang to his feet.

'Have you taken leave of your senses?' Lord Henry barked.

'Master Ap Ythel, strip him,' Corbett repeated.

The Welshman grinned and called across two of his archers. They would take no resistance. They knocked away Brother Adrian's hands and roughly pulled off his black robe and the linen tunic beneath, leaving the monk to stand in his loincloth. Corbett ignored the protests of Prior Richard and the other Benedictine witnesses, who had sprung to their feet and left the wall benches to advance threateningly on this royal clerk who seemed intent on the utter humiliation of their colleague. Ranulf shouted for order, and more of Ap Ythel's archers stepped in front of the monks.

Corbett, busying himself with Brother Adrian's robe, seemed unaware of what was happening. He picked up the garment and shook its folds free, then called to Ranulf to bring the gloves he had left on a stool behind his judgement chair. Prior Richard, who now realised that something must be seriously amiss, demanded silence.

Corbett crouched and stared at Lady Hilda's rigidly twisted face. It now had a bluish-tinged pallor, eyes popping whilst a dirty-white froth bubbled between the dry, bloodless lips. He spread out Brother Adrian's robe, then turned Lady Hilda's corpse over, ignoring the last gasps of air from the dead woman's belly. He pulled on the gloves and very gently eased back the thick cuff around Lady Hilda's wrist, drawing out fragments of a hard white substance that he suspected were the remains of ewe's cheese. He placed these on the black robe so they could be seen more clearly. He then inserted his fingers into her mouth and drew out the remains of what she had just eaten: soggy, chewed pieces caught between her yellowing teeth or in the upper regions of her gums.

Next he dug into the pocket of Brother Adrian's robe, searching around and drawing out a piece of neatly folded white linen that in any other circumstances would not warrant a second glance. Still squatting, he edged to another part of the black robe spread out across the tiled floor. As he undid the linen cloth and gently shook the white crumbs it contained onto the blackness, those gathering around gave a loud collective sigh. Corbett glanced up at Brother Adrian, who just stood, eyes blinking, mouth opening and shutting.

'What is this?' he gasped.

'Poison, I suspect, Brother Adrian.' Corbett gestured at the monk's robe. 'Would you like to eat the crumbs I have just shaken out? Those tiny remains of cheese distilled from ewe's milk? Usually such cheese is very nutritious and tasty. However, as you well know, these crumbs are the remains of a cheese deeply soaked in a most noxious potion: henbane, nightshade, belladonna or even the deadliest wolf's bane. You are acquainted with such poisons, aren't you, Brother?' Corbett rose to his feet. 'By your own admission you know all about Palladius's treatises on herbs. You have also served as an infirmarian in your order.' He snapped his fingers.

'Get him another robe. Chain and manacle him. Prior Richard, if the witch-queen's corpse could be removed, but not that robe.' He glanced down. 'That is evidence.'

For a while, the silence and solemnity of the court-room was shattered. Lay brothers were called to remove Lady Hilda's corpse and to clean up what she had choked out onto the floor. Corbett took off his gloves before going across to a side table where the kitchener had laid out jugs of ale, freshly made bread and strips of pheasant cooked in a tangy sauce. He filled a platter and returned to the judgement table, where he ate, his gaze never leaving Brother Adrian. The monk sat, wrists chained, between two of Ap Ythel's archers. He looked calm enough, eyes half closed, mouth slightly open. Corbett suspected he was trying to prepare himself for the damning indictment about to be laid against him.

Once the court resumed, Brother Adrian immediately sprang to his feet, knocking away the restraining hands of his guards. 'I am a cleric!' he shouted. 'A Benedictine monk. St Thomas a Becket lodged with our good brothers in Canterbury. He paid with his life for the sacred inviolability of the clergy. We, I, cannot be tried by a secular court. I demand—'

'Shut up!' Corbett bellowed. 'Shut up or I will have you gagged and chained to the floor.' He abruptly recalled the pathetic remains he had pulled from that morass outside Alnwick, and the horror visited on poor Cacoignes. 'Brother Adrian,' he declared, 'as I shall prove, by your own actions you have put yourself outside the Church. You are excommunicated, a child of hell. You will be cursed in this life and the next by bell, book and candle.'

Corbett rose and came round the table as the guards forced the prisoner back onto his chair. He wondered if the man's ankles should also be manacled, but to a certain extent he didn't care. He was determined to see this man die for his heinous sins and hideous crimes. 'You,' he stared at the monk, who glared back, 'were in the dungeons below. You are most adept, very skilled at sleight of hand. I watched your tricks at Alnwick when you were entertaining the castle children in your usual hypocritical guise of the caring pastor. You did the same here. You moved amongst the prisoners in the dungeons acting the role of the solicitous priest. In truth, you wanted to give Lady Hilda a piece of food soaked in poison. She could not face the prospect of torture, of bloodied, prolonged interrogation, which would undoubtedly have happened before she was cruelly executed.'

'Why should I do that, king's man?' Brother Adrian scoffed.

'Because Lady Hilda wanted to leave this life on her own terms. You also needed to remove the danger that, broken and wounded, she might confess that the Benedictine monk Brother Adrian was in fact Paracelsus, leader of the Black Chesters coven and perhaps many other demonic cohorts. I suggest she was the only person who knew that.' Corbett paused as his words created a stir in the chamber.

'You can prove all this, king's man?'

'Well, to a certain extent I already have. You have

poisoned others. I wondered if you would extend the courtesy of a swift death to your collaborator, Lady Hilda. You left the dungeons and came up here. I would not permit you or anyone else to leave. I hoped, and I was correct, that you would still carry traces of the poison on you. After all, you have done this many times before and never been caught. You act the holy monk but you are a killer and a blasphemer.' Corbett leaned closer. 'You assassins are all the same. You are a follower of Satan and have all his arrogance. You laugh behind your mask and in doing so make a mistake: the poison was found upon you.'

'All that proves is that I was carrying it.' Brother Adrian shrugged. 'I glimpsed that white linen parcel on a ledge in the dungeons.' He broke off at Ranulf's mocking laugh. 'If it is poison,' he added.

'Ap Ythel,' Corbett gestured at the robe, 'take this carefully away. Brush those crumbs and gather them up; trap a rat from the cellars and feed it whatever you have collected.'

'You will find enough of the vermin swarming there,' Prior Richard offered.

Corbett waited until the Welshman had left the chamber, then he picked up a stool and came and sat close by the prisoner. 'Adrian Ogilvie,' he began. 'A and O. From an early age you were interested in the occult, the study of the black arts. Heaven knows what strange fancies formed your soul. What your parents did to you. What insult others may have offered you. What horrors you witnessed in this war-torn land. I have met your kind before; your heart is dead and your mind closed to all pity or compassion. You rejoice in your secret knowledge and delight in your hidden power. As a child, were you cruel to anyone and anything that crossed your path? How long have you revelled in the pain of others? I suppose we all reach a crossroads in life. We decide to take a certain path and follow it wherever it goes.'

'You know nothing of me, clerk.'

'True, but I know of your decisions and the paths you followed. You were born in these parts. As a young man you proved yourself intelligent, resourceful and very curious. You are a soul deeply interested in power, with an uncontrollable desire to exercise it over others. Hence your decision to become a priest, but one with a difference: a priest who wished to harness and ride the devil's own warhorse; to go down paths strictly forbidden to you.'

'You, a king's man, you dare to talk of power and control . . .'

'Aye, for the Crown and for the common good, to make life a little better for those around me.'

Corbett paused. He had rehearsed his arguments time and time again. He felt more confident now his opponent had slipped so easily into the trap. He recalled his own days as a young scholar. How he would go and sit for hours in the great hall at Westminster where the Court of King's Bench tried capital offences, study- ing the skills needed to question and to interrogate. At the same time, he had learnt something he had not been searching for – how certain prisoners exhibited an overwhelming arrogance, a belief in their own superiority; that they were not just different from their fellow man but infinitely better in so many ways. This pride carried them through life, but it was also an obstacle and often brought them down. Brother Adrian was of that ilk. Already he had made a heinous mistake, and Corbett hoped he could goad him into making more.

'Sir Hugh,' Ranulf called quietly.

'Good, good.' Corbett tapped his foot on the floor. 'I will cut to the chase. There is a very famous picture; you must have seen it: a wolf dressed in the robes of an abbot preaching to a gaggle of geese garbed in monkish attire.' He paused at Prior Richard's harsh laughter. 'Of course, you understand what the artist really intends: beneath the mitre, behind the sanctimonious expression, lurks a killer who will soon show his true nature. You are that wolf, Brother Adrian, the devil's wolf. Oh, you flattered your superiors. You became adept in theological studies, particularly in the realm of exorcism, possession, demonology and the practice of the black arts. You emerged as a *peritus*, an adviser to the Church authorities on such matters. You would be called here and there to determine if someone was genuinely possessed. However, the cowl certainly doesn't make the monk where you are concerned. Nevertheless, until today, you were much revered by your superiors and your brothers.'

'True, true,' Prior Richard broke in.

'Brother Adrian, you were allowed to travel where you wanted, to do what you deemed needed to be done. You were Lord Henry's chaplain at Alnwick, a welcome visitor here, counsellor and confidant to the lords of the manor, including Sir Edmund Darel. All a pretence.' Corbett leaned forward, finger pointed. 'A brilliant ploy. For a while, you certainly convinced me, with your eloquent fulminations against the very powers you support. Your assurances that you were with me body and soul in our fight against Darel, the Black Chesters and the evil that swirls about them.

'You are certainly golden-tongued, Brother Adrian, but that only hides the dross within. You have God-given talents, even though you have used them for the enemy. You had the freedom and authority to go where you wanted, acting the solicitous priest, the caring chaplain. You would collect information here and there, and I suspect the only person who knew the truth was Lady Hilda. But thanks to you, she cannot say nay or yea to that. The two of you were evil souls masquerading as religious leaders. You grew stronger and more powerful. Holy Mother Church patronised your studies. You were given access to the Church's secret repositories, able to study rare manuscripts describing in great detail the practice of the black arts.'

'That is true.' Brother John the librarian spoke up. 'Adrian, you used our library. You were given permission to open the arca and take out two manuscripts on the power to raise demons and control spirits. I remember you studying them.'

'I am a scholar.' Brother Adrian didn't even bother to glance at Brother John. 'What I do is what I do. I can prove I am a scholar. I am waiting for this clerk to prove his heinous allegations against me.'

'Occasionally,' Corbett continued, 'you would manifest your true self, your inner soul, the demon within. You would lead your disciples on Satan's wild hunt, attacking some farmstead, hamlet or cottage. You would kill, plunder, burn and seize victims for your blood-soaked sacrifices to the Lords of the Night.'

'I would be recognised,' Brother Adrian mocked, as if Corbett was telling some fanciful tale rather than laying serious allegations. 'After all, clerk, I am well known.'

'Yes, of course. You are known as the dedicated pastor busy caring for his flock when in truth you are a butcher sizing up your victims for the slaughterhouse. You wear hypocrisy and practise it without a moment's doubt or hesitation. You are a Janus, two-faced, the solicitous priest gathering up all kinds of gossip, chatter and news but in the dark a devilish hunter of humankind. You went in disguise like the rest. When you did manifest yourself, you hid behind cloak, mantle, hood and a golden wig that fell to your shoulders. Indeed, when we search your coffers we shall undoubtedly find that and other items that certainly should not be owned by a Benedictine monk.'

'Golden wig!' Brother Adrian scoffed.

'Golden wig,' Corbett echoed. 'Remember that evening in the great hall of Alnwick. You hastily removed what

I thought at the time was a piece of silver-gold thread on your black gown. Certainly a mistake by you.'

'Which evening?' Brother Adrian scoffed.

'Yes, I remember it,' Lord Henry declared. 'When we discussed Corbett's meeting with Darel. I remember the shiny strand and how you hastily removed it.'

Corbett rose and stretched before sitting back down on the stool. He used the interruption to study the prisoner, who'd glanced quickly at the archer standing to his right, as if memorising something.

'Let us analyse,' Corbett continued, 'my intervention in northern affairs.' He pointed at the judgement table. 'Lord Henry, when you learnt that a royal envoy, the king's most senior clerk was journeying north to Alnwick, you decided to send your constable and his sister Lady Kathryn to Westminster. You did this as a courtesy as well as to provide a trustworthy officer who could both guide and advise us, yes?'

'I would agree.' Lord Henry's rough face broke into a grin, and he snapped his fingers. 'Sir Hugh, Sir Hugh,' he exclaimed, 'I can see which way this is wending. I didn't order Brother Adrian to join the Thurstons.' He spread his hands. 'I do not have the authority to do that. He asked to join them himself. He claimed he wished to visit his brothers at Westminster as well as meet you. He argued that he could help you on your journey, administer to your spiritual needs as well as assist Constable Thurston. I agreed.'

'And so!' Brother Adrian exclaimed. 'No crime in that!'

'You were curious, weren't you,' Corbett demanded, 'about who I was, why I was journeying to Alnwick. Above all, there was the question of the Scottish hostages. Let us not beat about the bush. You knew that Seton and his three companions were Red Comyn's men both body and soul, warriors steeped in the blood feud. One or all of them, with the exception of Roskell, certainly murdered a fifth Scottish prisoner, the squire Dunedin, because he was Bruce's man. Seton intended to cross the Scottish march, seek out Bruce and kill him in revenge for the assassination of his own lord and master Red Comyn.'

'And why should I have an interest in such matters?'

'Don't mock me, monk.' Corbett shifted on the stool. 'You have more than a hand in these matters. You feverishly plot to keep conflict in the north raging, war without respite all along the Scottish march. England against Scotland, Darel against Percy and so on. Steeped in sin, you are committed to creating anarchy with the aim of the total destruction of both Crown and Church. I have met your like before. You would love to see the world burn for the sake of it. If Bruce was killed, if the Scots lost another leader, perhaps it would weaken their will for war and some form of peace could be imposed. You and yours certainly did not want that.'

'But how was I supposed to know all this?'

'Quite simple. Roskell was the weakest of Seton's companions. Deeply religious, during his imprisonment in the Tower he began to reflect most fearfully on the Four Last Things: death, judgement, heaven and hell.

He knew why he and his companions were being dispatched back to Scotland. They were to murder, assassinate a prince many regard as God's anointed, the rightful king of Scotland.'

'But he was Red Comyn's retainer. As you say, he could invoke the blood feud.'

'For Roskell, that did not matter; it ceased to be significant. He drew very close to Dunedin, a man also absorbed in apocalyptic theology and the dissolution of all things. During that deep friendship, I suspect but cannot prove, Dunedin began to wean Roskell from his allegiance to Comyn, extolling the virtues of Bruce.'

'As you say,' the prisoner broke in, 'you have no proof of this.'

'Oh, that will come soon enough. Whatever influence Dunedin had, Roskell must have been deeply saddened by his new friend's sudden death. Perhaps he realised it was murder, the work of Seton and the other two, now bound for further bloodshed once they had crossed the Scottish march. Time passed. Roskell, a deeply religious man, became agitated and guilt-ridden about what had happened and what was intended for the future.

'Now where could such a man go for spiritual comfort and relief? What better person than an amicable Benedictine monk who could hear his confession, shrive him and give advice on what to do. And so Roskell approached you, and at some point on our journey north you heard his confession, during which he divulged everything. How you must have congratulated yourself on your decision to travel south to join us. Now Roskell had taken an oath on the Gospels that he would only share his true mission with God and his conscience. He truly believed, poor man, that he had kept his oath by only declaring it in the sacrament of confession. You admitted to me that you shrived him . . .' Corbett paused at the growing swell of protesting voices.

'Surely, Father Prior,' Brother Julian called out, 'the seal of confession is sacrosanct? Very rarely, if ever, in the history of our church has it been broken. Sir Hugh is accusing Brother Adrian of doing this?'

'He certainly is,' Prior Richard replied. 'But if Brother Adrian is a warlock, a demon-worshipper, a skilled practitioner of the black arts, then his priesthood, his vows must mean nothing to him. They were just a means to secure what he really wants. Scripture teaches us that you cannot serve two masters. You must hate the one and love the other; you cannot serve both God and the devil. Sir Hugh is arguing that Brother Adrian made his choice and clung to it with all his might.'

'Adrian Ogilvie violated his priesthood. He broke the seal of confession,' Corbett declared. 'He used what he'd learnt for his own wicked purposes. No one else apart from His Grace the king, my lord Gaveston and those four Scotsmen knew their mission. I only heard of it when we reached Alnwick, by which time Roskell had been murdered.'

'One or all of those Scottish hostages could have told someone else.'

'Who, Brother Adrian? When? Why? Who else was in that camp on the evening we were attacked? Who mixed a potion in the common pot of oatmeal and, after the enemy was beaten off, returned to poison Roskell?'

'Cacoignes?'

'Nonsense. Cacoignes appeared *after* the potion was mixed, and he joined in the pursuit. He was innocent of everything except a predilection for hazard. You knew about this. You mentioned it to me. How did you know?'

The monk just stared back.

'Lady Kathryn?' Corbett continued. 'She was in the camp. She certainly wanted me dead for her own secret purposes, but she had no grudge or grievance against Seton and his comrades.'

'I too ate the tainted oatmeal.'

'No you did not; you pretended to. Witnesses will repeat how you were apparently on the edge of the camp. You stumbled into the fire glow pretending to be another victim.'

'And when the war dogs attacked, would they know who to savage and who to lick?'

'Mockery, monk, is no defence. True, the war hounds swept in, but we were supposed to be drugged, easy prey for the mastiffs and their masters. You, of course, would slip away, and you are skilled at that, aren't you? When Darel attacked Alnwick, as well as during that ferocious affray in the priory church, you were conspicuous by your absence. So it was then: you planned to slip away just before the hounds reached the camp. You came staggering across, but in fact you were returning from the horse lines. When Darel's force was repulsed and we followed in hot pursuit, I noticed that one of our horses was already saddled and harnessed to leave. Curious, I spoke to one of the men who had been sent to guard the horse lines – the very man who is now standing on guard to your right – and asked him who had prepared the mount. He claimed that you were responsible.'

'He couldn't have done. I was—'

Brother Adrian broke off and sat back in his chair. Corbett caught the archer's puzzled look and quickly shook his head. The man shrugged, smiled and glanced away. Corbett rose, walked to the side table and poured himself a goblet of wine. Ranulf too got to his feet and, pointedly ignoring the prisoner, asked if any of the others wanted a drink, serving them quickly.

When Corbett had finished his wine, he returned to the stool in front of the prisoner.

'You have been thinking, Brother Adrian, planning your defence? Did you know we have been searching, ransacking your chamber and all you possess?' He half smiled at the prisoner's quick change of expression and leaned forward. 'We will find something if we haven't already: items taken from your victims or those you used in your nightmare forays.'

'I was thinking, clever clerk,' Brother Adrian almost gabbled. 'How would I, a poor monk, know about Darel's attack, the time, the hour, the place?'

'Yes.' Brother Julian, who still retained some loyalty for this accused brother, spoke up. 'How could he know such details?'

'Because the hour and the place of that attack were chosen by you, Brother Adrian. No, no.' Corbett waved a hand at the prisoner's snort of derision. 'I suggest that even before we left London, a member of one of your covens, some messenger you met deep in the shadows, was dispatched to Darel informing him of what was happening. During our journey north, we stopped at many places. Because you are a priest, a monk, you can slip here and there. Nobody is really curious; you are just another cleric on God's business. You can visit this church, that house, stand in the shadows of some tree. You have an ink pot, quill, a scrap of parchment. You could leave, and you certainly did, stark, simple messages describing our strength and our armaments. You enticed Darel into attacking us by insinuating that we were carrying the Lily Crown. Lady Hilda would encourage him further. One final message would stipulate the night the attack was to be launched. Darel would send in his war dogs and wolfsheads. You would ensure we were grievously weakened, deep in a drugged sleep. Most of us would have died up there on the heathland. More bloodshed, more murderous mayhem; above all, the removal in one stroke of a number of problems.'

Brother Adrian glanced up. For just a moment the mask slipped and Corbett glimpsed the hatred seething in that mad monk's eyes.

'You brim with arrogance, Alpha and Omega.' Corbett leant even closer. 'That's what you called yourself when dealing with Darel and his retinue. Alpha and Omega, the beginning and ending of all things, a quotation from the last few verses of the Book of Revelation: a tribute to your own scholarship as well as a token of your arrogance. A and O are also your initials. I noticed that when I was studying the manuscripts here. Brother John kindly brought me copies of the documents covering the sale of Alnwick to Lord Henry. You and Prior Richard helped with those documents, initialling them RT and AO. I also noticed wall paintings in the library that use the AO monogram from the Revelation as a decoration. I checked with Brother John about some of those documents, especially the Alnwick maps.'

'You deliberately stained those maps, Adrian,' Brother John accused. 'You knocked over a pot of very thick ink you were mixing. You claimed it was an accident.'

'It wasn't, was it?' Corbett demanded. 'You deliberately damaged those maps, one of which – and Brother John has now scrutinised them most carefully – showed the secret passageway running from the Abbot's Tower out under the walls of Alnwick Castle.'

'You are a felon worthy of hanging!' Lord Henry, who'd drunk deeply of the priory's Bordeaux, rose, swaying on his feet as he shook his fist at the prisoner. Corbett hid his smile. Lord Henry was just beginning to realise how this evil monk had almost brought Alnwick and the Percys to ruin.

'We should continue.' He turned back to the prisoner. He noticed the pallor of Brother Adrian's face, how his smooth brow was laced with sweat. 'Darel's attack was beaten off, so you turned to the poisoner's path. Roskell was your first victim. He was a prisoner, a hostage, not

347

well fed or nourished, chained and manacled as you are now.' Corbett rose to his feet so that everyone in the chamber could see him. He patted the pocket of his robe. 'On that bleak morning after Darel's attack was beaten off, Malachy Roskell was relieved of his chains. He wandered away, cold and hungry. He feels the pocket of his robe or jerkin,' Corbett drew a sweetmeat from his own pocket, 'and finds something like this, a tasty morsel for a hungry man. He doesn't know how it got there; he doesn't really care. Like many of us in that situation, he would think it was a mistake. He would never imagine it could have been deliberately placed there. Anyway,' Corbett sighed, 'he does what we would probably all do: he slips it into his mouth and begins to chew.' He bit into the sweetmeat.

'True, true,' Brother Julian called out. 'I have done the same on many occasions. A piece of food I am eating, then I put it away. The poor Scotsman, hungry and thirsty, just released from his chains, would regard it as manna from heaven.'

'But this was no accident,' Corbett retorted. 'Brother Adrian put it there. Darel's attack had failed, so Paracelsus – because that's who he really is – decided to take matters into his own murderous hands. He sidles up to that prisoner acting all solicitous. The sweetmeat, or whatever else it was, is slipped into the victim's pocket.' Corbett shrugged. 'It's now only a matter of time, because this delicacy is soaked in the most venomous poison.' Eyes on Brother Adrian, he spread his hands. 'Roskell was famished, so he ate, like all your victims did. He cleared his mouth and licked his lips, then the pain began. He went down to the burn thinking water would help, but of course he was dying.'

'You did the same in Alnwick!' Lord Henry accused. 'You poisoned Hockley and Richolda, my prisoners. You hypocritical canting priest! You went down to the dungeons to offer spiritual comfort, or so you said.' He belched loudly. 'You slipped a poisoned sweetmeat or some other delicacy into the pockets of their robes.'

'Of course he did,' Corbett replied. 'And when the prisoners, cold and famished, shivering in their cages, felt their pockets and found something to eat, they consumed it swiftly, not realising they were swallowing their own deaths. Naturally it never occurred to us at the time that the poison had been carried with them into their cages. And why should it? According to all the evidence, the prisoners had been kept under close watch and stripped of their possessions. Matters became even more mysterious when the remnants of food and drink given to them in the cages were found to be untainted.'

'But why?' Brother Adrian protested in a clatter of chains. 'Why should I murder Richolda and Hockley if they were adherents of the Black Chesters?'

'But they weren't, were they?' Corbett retorted. 'Not really. They were Darel's retainers. True, Richolda was a member of your coven as well. She and her sister, like the Lady Hilda, were links in the chain binding Darel to you, but they were not important or of any real significance to you. In fact they were a possible threat.

You do not care for anyone, Brother Adrian. Why have scruples about two stupid people who allowed themselves to be captured? In a word, they had become a danger to you. Heaven knows what they might have told us under bloody interrogation in an attempt to save their own lives. Moreover, their deaths were of great profit to you. The murder of Darel's kinsman and Darel's lover whilst imprisoned at Alnwick Castle would only intensify that robber baron's enmity for the Percys.'

'And the rest?' Lord Henry demanded. 'The other murders?'

'Finely done,' Corbett answered. 'You now have to kill Seton and his two companions. Of course there were distractions. You must have been mystified by the presence of another killer at Alnwick. Especially when you were caught up in the attack in St Chad's chapel. Little wonder you examined the bolts loosed at us. However, on reflection, you must have been pleased. You hoped that I would become distracted and confused. I might even conclude that the murderer of Roskell was the same person who loosed that crossbow bolt at me, and of course, you were with me at the time. It put you, or so you thought, on the side of the angels.

'Your next line of defence was to totally mystify me by portraying yourself as a monk commissioned by his superiors to hunt down the very people you led. How could such a close ally be an enemy? How could a monk dedicated to fighting the practitioners of the black arts be in fact the very leader of the coven you were hunting? Indeed, you complicated matters further. You stole that bracelet from Cacoignes and left it close to the cottage where you and yours had carried out your hideous midnight rites.' Corbett paused. 'But let's return to the other murders. Ah, on second thoughts, in a while.'

He held his hand up and turned slightly. 'Poor Bavasour! Lord Henry, I told you that I had sent our mercenary captain to Harclay at Carlisle, but you didn't know at the time, did you? If I recall events accurately, I took Bavasour across the drawbridge of Alnwick Castle and only then did I entrust him with that task. I offered him a reward for his services and dire punishment if he deliberately failed. Now Bavasour was a mercenary, a good one, a professional soldier. He took the money, delivered his solemn promise and left. At the time, no one knew except myself. I may have shared it with Ranulf and Ap Ythel, but outside my secret council, nobody else. Then I told you.' He pointed at Lord Henry.

'Yes, that was before you left Alnwick for Tynemouth, when we were in secret discussion together. You said Bavasour might be successful but you had growing doubts, given the way Darel's men and the Black Chesters roamed the heathland.' Lord Henry preened himself. 'I solemnly promised to follow you to Tynemouth.'

'That is correct,' Corbett agreed. 'The only other place I mentioned Bavasour's intended destination was in the letters I gave him. I made a mistake.' He turned back to the prisoner. 'I underestimated how closely you and yours watched me. You saw Bavasour leave, you became alarmed and, I suggest, immediately sent messages to Lady Hilda, who dispatched the Black Chesters in pursuit. They caught up with poor Bavasour and showed him no mercy. Another murder, Bavasour's corpse being tossed into some marsh or morass. Nevertheless, his ghost cries for vengeance and demands that God's justice be served.' Corbett smiled at the prisoner, hoping to provoke him. 'One of your most dreadful mistakes, Brother Adrian. The Black Chesters needed horses and harness, and one of them took Bavasour's, a mount that had its own distinctive appearance. If Chanson had not seen it in the priory stable, God knows what would have happened.

'Now, to the other murders.' He walked across to the side table and picked up the wineskin and the goblet that Ranulf had placed there. He turned and lifted both for all to see. 'Brother Julian, Brother John, Lord Henry. Last night, did I not visit you?' All three murmured their agreement.

'You know you did,' Brother John declared. 'We talked about the documents lodged here by His Grace Anthony Bek, Bishop of Durham. How we'd made copies for Lord Henry. We then discussed the Alnwick maps and how,' the librarian glared at Brother Adrian, 'the so-called accident with the ink occurred.'

'Good, good,' Corbett replied. 'And can you remember what I gave you?'

'For Gabriel's sake, Sir Hugh, you carried that wineskin and goblet. You claimed it to be a heavenly Bordeaux from the finest vineyards around Saint-

Etienne. I drank a few generous mouthfuls. I remember quoting from the psalms: "how wine gladdens the heart of men".'

'And you did the same to me,' Brother Julian called. 'The wine was delicious. I told you about how I had been on the night watch when your companion Cacoignes was lashed to that execution post on the beach. Why did you—'

'I know,' Lord Henry slurred, banging the table, 'Corbett, you cunning bastard. You visited me as well with the same wine and goblet. We discussed the attack on Alnwick and other matters. I know why.' Lord Henry pointed at the prisoner. 'That murderous monk did something similar at Alnwick. Oh yes, I can imagine him with the prisoners, but . . .'

'But what, my lord?'

'Sterling and Mallet were lodged in the Falconer's Tower. The guard there said that no one visited the Scottish hostages. Their chamber was on the first stairwell. It couldn't be seen by the guard, but he assured me that no one came down those steps except workmen. Of course,' Lord Henry clapped his hands like a child in some guessing game, 'our murdering monk often wore workmen's clothes around Alnwick. He did this to protect his woollen monk's robe as well as to appear as one with the men of the castle.'

'Lord Henry is correct,' Corbett declared. 'Can you imagine Sterling and Mallet, the two Scottish hostages, lonely, frightened by the death of Roskell and the mysterious disappearance of Seton? Although I concede that at the time they may not have known about their leader vanishing into thin air. However, they are lonely men, vulnerable souls, visited by the castle's genial chaplain. They trust Brother Adrian. He has been with them since they left London. He has shared their trials and tribulations.

'He brings a wineskin. He chats with them and establishes that both like rich blood-red Bordeaux. With all due respect, Lord Henry, the two Scots were imprisoned in a formidable northern fortress. Brother Adrian's visit must have been likened to that of an angel, though in truth he was the angel of death. Our monk pours a goblet for Sterling, another for Mallet. He then gabbles his apologies, says he must leave, time is passing and he has important tasks to attend to. The wine goblets are drained and returned. They and the wineskin go into a sack. Brother Adrian leaves, telling them to lock and bolt the door behind him. Poor unfortunates, they don't realise they have drunk their death. Holding the goblet and wineskin in a sack and garbed in workmen's clothes with his hood pulled up, Brother Adrian patters down the steps and out of the tower. The guard would not give him a second glance. Just another labourer going about his business.'

'Again, clerk,' Brother Adrian accused, 'you have no proof, no real evidence.'

'Except for the note.' Corbett turned to Lord Henry and winked as he prepared to bluff his way forward.

'Note?'

'Yes, Brother Adrian, note! Found in Sterling's

chamber, pushed into a wall crevice, the briefest of messages written in Latin. "The Benedictine has poisoned us." Sterling scrawled that during the last heartbeats of his life and pushed it into that crack before he died. After we left Alnwick, one of the workmen sent up to clean the chamber found that scrap of parchment. He did not realise its significance until the day Lord Henry left Alnwick for Tynemouth, when he handed it over. Sterling indicted you.' Corbett wagged a finger in the monk's face.

'There was no quill, no ink . . .'

'Pardon?' Corbett mocked. 'Are you saying you knew what was in that particular chamber so many days ago?' He waited, tapping his boot against the floor, watching this killer realise that for all his vaunted cunning and deceit, he was being cornered and trapped. Like a hare in the cornfield, he could run and swerve but he was unable to get out and the hounds were closing in.

Corbett allowed the silence to deepen. From outside he heard the sounds of the priory, the ringing of bells, the patter of feet, the creak of cartwheels and the constant strident call of the gulls. He had walked down to the beach; the execution posts were ready and he knew he could exercise little mercy. The Black Chesters had committed treason against the Crown and sacrilege against the Church, but he did wonder if this would be the end of that coven. He glanced quickly at the prisoner. Was he the true leader or just a high-ranking official? Soon Corbett would leave Alnwick and journey south . . .

'Ranulf,' he called over his shoulder, 'have the prisoner Marissa brought up.'

Ranulf snapped his fingers at one of the archers, who hurried out.

'Now for Seton and that secret passageway that cuts from the Abbot's Tower to those ruins.' Corbett held his hand up, three fingers splayed. 'In my view, there were only three people who could possibly know about that secret tunnel: Lord Henry, Prior Richard and yourself, Brother Adrian. Only two of those were in Alnwick at the time. I doubt very much – in fact I know it to be a certainty – that Lord Henry had any grievance with Seton. What concerns him is his family name and his great castle of Alnwick. He would hardly betray it to Darel and his ilk. You are different. You studied those maps now held here in the priory chancery. You arranged an accident so that that particular map showing the passageway became so deeply stained it was almost impossible for anybody else to decipher what was depicted there. No, only you knew the secret and you used it in your plot to lure Seton to his death and deliver Alnwick into the hands of Darel and his pack of wolfsheads.'

'Why?'

'To deepen the mystery, to confuse and confound my investigation, but most importantly, to depict the missing Seton as the secret assassin in Alnwick. After all, Seton had been with us on our journey north. He had been close to Roskell. He had also been in the castle when Hockley and Richolda were poisoned. Around the time he disappeared, Sterling and Mallet were murdered. No, you needed Seton to be killed but also to be used as your catspaw. According to the evidence, he had committed murder and fled; this would divert suspicion from anyone in Alnwick, including yourself. It was most opportune. You had removed all those you wanted to and sowed bitter conflict between Lord Henry and Darel. Who knows, if you had been truly successful and Alnwick had fallen, perhaps you could have blamed it on Seton, claiming that he had somehow known about that secret passageway.'

'Yes, but that didn't happen,' Brother Adrian countered. 'True, Seton fled Alnwick, but I didn't follow him. He was killed outside.'

'No, that's not how it happened,' Corbett declared. 'Once again you lurked in some dark corner or shadow-filled passageway, and God knows there are enough of them in Alnwick. Cowled and masked, you would lure Seton towards the trap. You would act as the benevolent stranger who wanted to help. You told him to be in the cellar of the Abbot's Tower on a certain day at a certain time. There, as a guarantee of your good faith, he would find weapons, clothing, a few coins and, most importantly, a package of food.'

'Seton would rise to the bait,' Lord Henry intervened. 'He was a Scot desperate for his homeland. He had nothing to lose and so much to gain.'

'God knows,' Corbett declared, 'perhaps the death of Roskell had made him deeply suspicious, worried about whom he could trust. After all, he must have been puzzled as to why someone should murder a hapless squire. There was always the possibility that Sterling, Mallet or both were involved in Roskell's death. Whatever truly happened, Seton decided to leave Alnwick by himself. Perhaps you also insisted on that. Anyway, he slipped down to that cellar, he found the weapons, clothes, food and money all ready. The trapdoor to the secret passageway was also revealed. He now realised that his mysterious helper was a true friend and could be trusted.

'Seton goes down into that tunnel and hurries along to emerge in the ruins of the old hermitage. Now I recall that like his companions, he was a true trencherman; he enjoyed his food and he had a long journey ahead. Before he continues his journey, he opens the parcel of food and quickly eats it. Now that was a mistake on your part. You could never have guessed that he would satisfy his hunger so swiftly. Anyway, our hostage finishes the food and continues on his journey. However, what he has eaten is deeply tainted and the poison begins to work. Seton collapses out there on the wild heathland and dies a very painful, lonely death. Within a short time, Darel's wolfsheads, together with Scottish mercenaries, slip like a ravenous wolf pack across the moorland. They are eager to reach that secret entrance and storm into Alnwick whilst its defenders are distracted and defending its walls against what is only a feint – a mock attack.'

'And all that nonsense about the fourth watch?' Lord Henry demanded.

'Oh yes,' Corbett agreed. He paused to stare at

Brother Adrian, who just lounged in his chair, listening intently. Now and again the monk would glance quickly around as if searching for a door or window, calculating his escape. Corbett drew satisfaction from the fact that the chapter house both within and without was closely guarded.

'Oh yes,' Corbett repeated. 'Paracelsus would have told Lady Hilda on what day and at what hour the secret tunnel should be used. However, as regards Seton, when the wolf pack drew near Alnwick, they discovered his corpse, stripped it of any valuables and then dishonoured it. There is a possibility that some of the Scottish mercenaries may have recognised him as Bruce's sworn enemy.'

'And you are saying that I brought these attackers into Alnwick?'

'Oh certainly. You told your helpmate Lady Hilda, who in turn passed the news to her malevolent nephew. I am sure he knows the truth about his aunt, which is why he so generously supported her. Edmund Darel is a royal squire, a knight of the king's household, at least publicly so. In private he is malignant and mischievous. He will not accept any authority, be it of God or man; in that respect he is just like you, Brother Adrian, a kindred spirit.' The monk smiled and glanced away. 'Edmund Darel would regard the situation as highly amusing. Something worthy of the world of Cokayne, that topsy-turvy land where nothing is what it seems to be and everything is turned on its head. How he must have laughed to watch his aunt act the pious Lady

Hilda, whilst the rest of the so-called religious community at Clairbaux were a true brood of vipers, as ferocious and as vicious as a pack of hungry stoats.'

'Are you saying that Sir Edmund knew who I really was?'

'Oh no, I am sure he had enough to laugh at when he wandered Clairbaux. I doubt very much if he knew the identity of Paracelsus. Lady Hilda would simply tell him that the Alpha and Omega had supplied her with the precise information.'

Corbett paused as the door opened and the archer returned with the young woman Marissa, her dark hair tumbling down either side or her white, peaked face. She was trembling with fear and hugged even closer the heavy cloak wrapped about her. Corbett indicated she sit on the stool near the door and turned back to the prisoner.

'I know who you are, Paracelsus, the leader of the Black Chesters. You pursue a secret life beneath the pretence of being a solicitous priest and a loyal monk. You are in fact a demon incarnate, the devil's own wolf. You are steeped in the practice of the black arts, which you allegedly studied to combat the powers of darkness when in fact you are the emissary of such diabolic forces. You revel in chaos and mayhem. Like Darel you are bitterly opposed to both Crown and Church. You take great pride in the chaos and bloodshed that has engulfed the royal house of Scotland for three generations. You lust for the Lily Crown, that sacred relic, hidden by Ravinac; that's the reason you came here and told Lady Hilda to join you on a purported pilgrimage. The two of you, together with the hellish covens you lead, intended to sack this holy place and destroy the great shrine of King Oswine, a prince who in his time fought the children of hell till they martyred him. You intended to set up, as the prophet Daniel says, at the very heart of this sacrosanct priory, the Abomination of the Desolation.

'You murdered those four Scottish hostages to frustrate their task, an offering by you to Robert the Bruce, who may have been marching south to help you here. You kill without a second thought. Hockley and Richolda were poisoned because they'd served their purpose and could be a danger to you, whilst all the time you worked diligently to deepen antagonisms and bitter feuds along the Scottish march.' Corbett paused, staring at the prisoner just brought in. 'You'd sacrifice everyone and everything. Like the wolf you are, you turn, twist, hide and protect yourself against the consequences of your murderous actions. You were preparing to flee that clearing. You planned to do the same at Alnwick, and I remember you crawling out from behind that statue after the violent affray in the priory church. You'd hoped to be able to depict yourself as one of the few survivors of the carnage and destruction inflicted on this priory, Lady Hilda likewise, whilst your coven, after ransacking the church, could take the Lily Crown and everything else for their own secret purposes or to use as a bargaining counter with the Bruce.

'Enough.' Corbett got to his feet and beckoned to

the young woman. Marissa, still hugging her cloak about her, stumbled to her feet and, helped by the archer, crept fearfully across. Corbett pointed at her. 'You are Marissa, a member of the Black Chesters?' She nodded.

'Answer the judge,' Ranulf shouted.

'Marissa,' Corbett asked gently, 'do you wish to die along with the others and your master here?'

'I am a member of the coven,' she replied, 'but I do not wish to die. Oh no.' Eyes rounded in fear, she shook her head. Corbett steeled himself against feeling sorry for her. She might look innocent, but she had participated in savage murder as well as torture and abuse.

'Marissa, tell the truth and I shall let you walk out of Tynemouth Priory a free woman. Now, before this trial began, I asked you to watch Lady Hilda in the dungeons below, yes?' The girl nodded. 'I also asked you to notice if the accused approached Lady Hilda and gave her something. I warned you that the action would be very swift, when no one else was looking. I promised you your life if you told the truth. Well, did the condemned approach Lady Hilda and give her something?'

'Yes,' she whispered. 'It was indeed very swift. The accused moved amongst the prisoners asking if we wished spiritual consolation, to be shriven, to be absolved. He approached Lady Hilda and handed something over, which she pushed down here,' she indicated her own wrist, 'under the cuff of her shift, then he walked away. It was in the blink of an eye. If you had not told me to watch so closely, I wouldn't have noticed it. Master, I am telling you the—'

She broke off as the door opened and one of Ap Ythel's archers brought in a cage. The rat inside sprawled dead, slightly twisted, a disgusting mucus seeping out from between its jaws.

'We gave it the food,' the archer declared. 'At first it ignored it, determined to break free, then it settled down and ate. You can see the consequences.'

'Marissa,' Corbett gestured at the girl, 'tomorrow morning you will be escorted out of Tynemouth. Where you go afterwards is your concern. However, wherever you journey, tell any remnants of your coven that Paracelsus is dead, Lady Hilda is dead, Clairbaux will be seized by the Crown, and the captured Black Chesters were fastened to stakes along the beach of Tynemouth Cove, waiting for the icy northern seas to rush in and drown them.'

'I wish to say something!' Brother Adrian rose and joined his hands in prayer. His wrists were manacled, with a long chain fastened to each. He looked supplicant. 'I wish to say something,' he repeated. 'I want to purge my guilt . . .'

Curious, Corbett walked towards him. As he did so, Brother Adrian, swift as a lunging viper, turned and with one hand pushed the archer guarding him, whilst with the other he plucked the long stabbing knife from the bowman's sheath. He then turned back, dagger hand scything the air, the point aimed directly at Corbett's face. The clerk stumbled back against the judgement table. Another archer, along with Brother Julian, tried to seize the prisoner, but, skilled as any street fighter, he lashed out with the knife and in a crash of chains rushed to confront Corbett again.

The clerk recovered, grasping the hilt of his great two-edged sword lying on the judgement table and swinging the blade around. Brother Adrian flung himself forward and Corbett swiftly brought the sword up, its point piercing the monk's belly, the blade twisting to skewer the flesh. Brother Adrian, mouth gaping, crashed to his knees. He tried to speak but blood choked his throat and bubbled through his lips.

Corbett watched the life light die in his enemy's eyes. He recalled all the evil this man had sown along the path of life, the innocents he had slaughtered and the murderous mayhem he had caused. He withdrew the blade, then, balancing carefully on the balls of his feet, he brought the sword back and swung it in a hissing, glittering arc of steel. It scythed the air and sliced deep into Brother Adrian's neck, severing the head in one deep, blood-gushing slash.

Corbett, Ranulf and Ap Ythel stood on the windswept beach of Tynemouth Cove, staring at the long line of the condemned lashed to their execution poles. Each was fastened tight, bound by thick cords around neck, chest and feet. In the end, thirty-eight were being punished according to the law. Corbett crossed himself as Prior Richard passed down the line, sprinkling the condemned with an aspergillum.

Corbett glanced up. The sky was light blue, with wispy white clouds. Gulls floated in on the seaborne breezes, which reeked of salt, fish and that peculiar odour wafting from the masses of seaweed the tide swept in to coat the rocks. A rather cold day; the season was about to turn and autumn was making itself felt. The tide was still out. Down near the shoreline, sailors from *The Golden Dove* stared in fascination at the grisly masque now being played out.

Once Prior Richard had finished, Corbett and his party would board the waiting boat and be taken out to the ship. All of their movables had already been transported safely to the hold below deck: panniers, saddles, harnesses, sacks, coffers and caskets neatly secured in the cog's arca and store chambers. Gaveston had been joined by the rest of Ap Ythel's archers. The royal favourite would remain in disguise until *The Golden Dove* docked in either Ponthieu or Bordeaux. The horses of Corbett's party would have to wait for a heavy transport cog; Chanson would stay with them till they disembarked at one of London's quaysides.

Corbett walked slowly down towards the waiting ship's boat and stared longingly out to sea. He would be pleased to be gone. He intended to visit Westminster, then petition for leave to return to his manor at Leighton. He stared at the strengthening surge, the sunlight twinkling in the swell and rush of the waves. The sailors had assured him that this was a calm sea, an excellent day for sailing. He felt his business was now completed. The assize had finished yesterday with his summary execution of Brother Adrian – or Paracelsus, as Corbett preferred to call him. The chapter house floor had been awash with the blood pumping out of the severed torso of the decapitated prisoner, the head rolling like a ball to rest against the dais. Corbett had no scruples about what he had done. Paracelsus had slaughtered innocent, hapless peasants who must have watched their loved ones being butchered before their torturers turned on them.

He stared around the cove, which stretched out then curved in to enclose the sea. The waves had left behind a myriad of shells, pebbles and other fragments caught up by the fast-moving tides. Gulls, as if aware of what was happening below, were beginning to circle in ever-increasing numbers, their calls harsh and strident. Beneath them, on this antechamber to eternity, stretched the execution poles, each with its gruesome offering to the incoming sea and, as one old monk had put it, the demons that rode the white horses of the surf.

Beyond the execution ground was a sandy enclave sweeping across to the base of the great crag that soared up to hold the priory against the sky. Corbett, shading his eyes, stared up at the battlemented walls as he recalled the events of the previous day. Prior Richard had decreed that the corpses of Lady Hilda and Brother Adrian need not be exhibited down here on the beach. Instead both of them, as befitted excommunicates, were to be shrouded in the rough hides of cattle slaughtered in the priory's fleshing yard. 'In death therefore,' he had intoned, 'they will be cursed, cut off from the sacred, soothing soil of God's Acre; their corpses can rot covered by the filthy dirt in which they lived as their souls go forward to meet the judgement and mercy of God.'

The two corpses, sewn tightly in their leather shrouds, had been given hasty burial after sunset. The priory cemetery, a ghostly place even in the full light of day, was after nightfall a true place of the dead, made even more so by the dancing flames of the cresset torches that ringed the pit where the corpses were tossed. Earlier this morning, Marissa had been released: she had been given clothing, some food and a few coins and had been dispatched through the main gate of the priory with Prior Richard's warnings about keeping to the path of righteousness ringing in her ears.

'Sir Hugh?' Ranulf gently grasped Corbett's arm and led him away from the monks clustered around Prior Richard as he chanted a psalm of mourning.

'Ranulf?'

Ranulf came as close as he could. 'The Lily Crown, where is it?'

'I don't truly know, but I have my suspicions.'

'Sir Hugh?'

'Up there, Ranulf, in Tynemouth Priory.'

'But where?'

Corbett led Ranulf further away from the monks. He smiled at this most loyal of henchmen. 'Only use this knowledge, only barter this secret, if you have to save life and limb. Promise?'

Ranulf, grasping the cross on the chain around his neck, held up his hand. 'I swear.'

'Ravinac,' Corbett began, 'was a good man who seized and held a most sacred relic. His very possession of such a holy object influenced both his mood and his will. He had taken the crown from a hallowed place, the abbey of Scone, before he and his comrades fled for the safety of the English border. Of course we know what happened. Ravinac and his comrades were attacked by the Black Chesters; only he and Cacoignes managed to escape. He may have come to believe he was saved for a reason. Eventually he reached Tynemouth Priory. He kept the crown hidden because he knew his companion also had designs on it. Ravinac was not well, his health had suffered, but whilst he was in the priory, he loved to visit the chapel and view the beautiful Purbeck marble sarcophagus that housed the mortal remains of holy King Oswine. In doing so he struck up a real friendship with Brother Oswald, the priory craftsman who was busy working on the rood screen. Now, what did Ravinac say about where the Lily Crown could be hidden?'

'Hanging between heaven and earth in God's own graveyard.'

'And that, Ranulf, is where it is. The crucifixion is God's own graveyard, where Jesus Christ, the Son of God, died. On the cross Christ hung between heaven and earth, an image, as you know, taken up by many artists. Now Ravinac, I am sure, facing death and still guilt-ridden at seizing the Lily Crown, took Brother Oswald into his confidence.'

'The crown!' Ranulf exclaimed.

'The crown,' Corbett agreed. 'Brother Oswald was preparing that life-sized figure of Christ in agony. The crucified Saviour is always portrayed as wearing a crown of thorns. I believe that Oswald and Ravinac took the Lily Crown, steeped it in black paint and refashioned it as the crucified Saviour's crown of thorns. Think of that carving, Ranulf; the sharp points on the crown are really lily stems.' He chuckled. 'A most fitting hiding place for such a holy treasure.'

'You will leave it there, Sir Hugh?'

'What better place? Let us respect both the Lily Crown and Ravinac's devotion to it. The crown can continue to hang between heaven and earth until peace blossoms, though God knows when that will happen. Let's leave it with God and return to the business of our king.'

They walked back to where Prior Richard and his monks were preparing to leave. All the condemned had been offered absolution before being committed to God's justice. The tide was now surging in, the water swirling about their feet as Corbett and his companions made their farewells of Prior Richard and his community. They clasped hands and exchanged the kiss of peace, the good brothers assuring Corbett of their thanks and prayers. The monks mounted their horses, intoning the De Profundis – 'Out of the depths did I cry to ye, oh Lord. Oh Lord, hear our cries . . .' The chanting echoed sombrely across the breeze-swept beach, the mournful words of the psalm broken up by the wind.

The tide was now running fast. The boatmen called at them to hasten. Corbett led his party down to the water and they clambered in. Once secure, the master mariner told his six-man crew to pull vigorously on their oars. The boat shuddered, rising and falling in its battle against the incoming surge. Corbett, sitting in the stern, turned for one last look at Tynemouth Priory, its crenellated walls, turrets and towers dark against the sky. The waves were now sweeping in, their clamour growing stronger. The sea broke around the long line of execution posts, but it was already rising as if hungry to devour the row of bound, gagged prisoners. 'From the horrors of the deep, Lord preserve us,' Corbett whispered before turning back to stare at *The Golden Dove* riding at anchor, impatient to break free for its voyage south.

On the soaring clifftop, a white-shingled promontory to the south of Tynemouth Priory, two horsemen also watched *The Golden Dove*, studying it closely as it turned to take full advantage of the strong northerly wind that would speed it south. The cog's great sail had been unfurled to bulge in the wind and the ship cut swiftly through the calm sea. From its stern, two banners floated: the blue, red and gold of the royal household and the three crowns of Tynemouth Priory. Both watchers were cloaked, hooded and visored. One of them, the leader, pushed his horse forward as if he wanted a better view of the cog as well as to more easily stretch down to caress the glossy black hair of the young woman standing beside him.

'So you have been released, girl?' Above his visor the rider's eyes creased into a smile. 'But your comrades, all those who took the blood oath . . .?'

'Condemned,' she spat. 'Condemned by Corbett and his priestly henchmen, fastened on poles to drown.' She gestured towards the beach.

'And Paracelsus?'

'He died. They judged him in the chapter house. He tried to kill Corbett, but the clerk slaughtered him.'

'And you were released?'

'Yes, Corbett said I was to go out as a witness that the Black Chesters were no more.'

'But that is wrong.' The rider moved his horse even closer. 'Paracelsus may be dead, but who is Paracelsus? Not one man, but a being, a spirit.' He edged his horse forward a little more. 'And you, Marissa, you did no wrong? You committed no betrayal? No connivance with the enemy?'

'No, no,' she gasped, stepping back. She moaned as she was pushed further and further towards the edge of the cliff. 'I did no wrong,' she pleaded.

'You betrayed—' The black-garbed rider urged his mount forward, knocking into Marissa. She stumbled back, tottering on the edge of the cliff, screaming, hands flailing, then plunged, turning and twisting, onto the rocks below. The horseman watched her fall, then gently eased his horse back.

'Corbett?' his companion asked.

'In London,' came the reply. 'We shall confront Corbett in London.'

AUTHOR'S NOTE

*D*evil's *Wolf* is a work of fiction, but its many strands are based on historical fact. Edward I launched a most savage war against the Scots and hideous acts of violence were perpetrated by both sides. What we would call war crimes became a staple element of the struggle; the destruction of Berwick and the murder of Red Comyn are only two of the many outrages. The Percys did come from Yorkshire and bought Alnwick and its surrounding estates. They were committed to creating their own small empire in the north and they did so with varying degrees of success over succeeding centuries. The family still own Alnwick and the castle is well worth a visit.

The Scottish coronation regalia were shrouded in legends, with claims that the Stone of Scone, for example, dated back to the time of Moses. Edward I did seize this regalia, including the Lily Crown and other sacred items. Most of these have now disappeared, but until the 1990s, the Stone of Scone rested under the English coronation chair at Westminster. The deepening chaos in England's northern shires at the time is a matter of fact. Gangs like the Middletons even captured a papal legate as well as the Bishop of Durham. Edmund Darel really did exist, and according to the chronicles was 'a most violent neighbour'. Indeed, in 1319 he was suspected of trying to capture and sell the Queen of England to the Scots.

Black magic was rife, but this must be perceived as part of the psychological warfare carried out between the various factions. For example, Hugh Despenser, Edward II's favourite after the execution of Gaveston, complained to Pope John XXII that his arch-enemy Mortimer was using black magic against him. The Pope wrote tartly back saying that if Despenser mended his ways and behaved himself, he would have nothing to fear!

Peter Gaveston, the royal favourite, spent a great deal of his time eluding the great earls and barons of England. He may have well have fled through Tynemouth. He was eventually captured a year later in Scarborough. Tynemouth Priory is also worth a visit; even its ruins are spectacular. Bearing in mind my story, I regard it as rather strange that Edward II and his court became regular visitors to this northern outpost. Finally, it may interest readers to learn that at the beginning of the nineteenth century, excavations were carried out in the medieval cemetery at Tynemouth. Two corpses were found, one decapitated, both bound in cowhide and tied with ropes.

Paul Doherty OBE
October 2016

PAUL DOHERTY

THE MASTER HISTORIAN HAS CAST HIS MAGICAL SPELL OVER ALL PERIODS OF HISTORY IN OVER 100 NOVELS

They are all now available in ebook, from his fabulous series

Hugh Corbett Medieval Mysteries
Sorrowful Mysteries of Brother Athelstan
Sir Roger Shallot Tudor Mysteries
Kathryn Swinbrooke Series
Nicholas Segalla Series
Mysteries of Alexander the Great
The Templar Mysteries
Matthew Jankyn Series
Canterbury Tales of Murder and Mystery
The Egyptian Mysteries
Mahu (The Akhenaten-Trilogy)
Mathilde of Westminster Series
Political Intrigue in Ancient Rome Series

to the standalones and trilogies that have made his name

The Death of a King	The Haunting
Prince Drakulya	The Soul Slayer
The Lord Count Drakulya	The Plague Laws
The Fate of Princes	The Love Knot
Dove Amongst the Hawks	Of Love and War
The Masked Man	The Loving Cup
The Rose Demon	The Last of Days

LIVE HISTORY
VISIT WWW.HEADLINE.CO.UK OR
WWW.PAULCDOHERTY.COM TO FIND OUT MORE

HEADLINE